LILY OF THE SPRINGS

Also by Carole Bellacera

Border Crossings
Spotlight
East of the Sun, West of the Moon
Understudy
Chocolate on a Stick
Tango's Edge

To my loving mother, Lillian Owens Foley
Wynia, my inspiration for Lily.

PROLOGUE

November 1954
New Boston, Texas

I knew my marriage was in trouble the night my husband brought home a streetwalker to teach me how to satisfy him.

It was after midnight, and I was still waiting for Jake to come home. His Army buddies had taken him out for a going-away party–because soon we'd be heading back to a rinky-dink town in central Kentucky called Russell Springs...my hometown, too, but boring as all heck, especially now that I was a woman of the world, having traveled all the way to Texas.

I sighed and dragged a brush through my dark brown curls. Lord, I just didn't know if I could stand it. Once Jake got back with all his tobacco-chewin', moonshine-drinkin', good-for-nothin' friends, he'd return to his old hell-raisin' ways, and these past two years of Army life—where he'd actually started acting like a grown-up—would be as if they'd never happened.

A noise from the living room drew my attention – the jangle of keys followed by the sound of the front door opening. Relief flooded through me. I really hadn't expected him to be home before the wee hours.

I jumped up from the stool. "Oh, honey, I'm glad you weren't out too late," I called out, hurrying into the hallway to meet him. "I really think we need to take Debby Ann to the doctor tomorrow. She's just not…" Stepping into the living room, my voice died away.

Jake stood swaying just inside the front door, a drunken grin on his face, a bottle of Pabst Blue Ribbon in one hand—and a harlot in the other.

The tight, red silk dress with the plunging neckline, the high spiked heels and the blood-red smear of lipstick on her wide, vulgar mouth practically shouted out the word. My throat went dry and my stomach took a sickening dive as I realized the red marks on Jake's jaw and neck perfectly matched the shade of the streetwalker's kiss-swollen lips.

"Well, *there's* my purty little wife," Jake said, his grin widening.

I tried to speak, but the words just wouldn't come. I felt as if an invisible hand had got hold of my throat and was squeezing off the air to my windpipe.

"Lily Rae, this here's Lou Ellen." Jake nudged his bottle at the harlot. "I figgered she could give you a love lesson on how to please your man." He fastened his bleary eyes on the woman and drew her closer to him. "Ain't that right, Lou Ellen?"

The woman, apparently as drunk as Jake, swayed against him, clutching at his shirt with long, spiked red nails. She focused her blood-shot eyes on me. Her lipstick-smeared mouth opened, and in an obscene gesture, she slid her tongue along her bottom lip in a way that made my skin crawl.

"Hi, there, hon. Handsome, here, tells me you need a lesson in giving a good blow-job."

I gasped, not absolutely certain I'd heard right. But before I could decide, Jake released the woman and began to unzip his pants. "That's right, Lily Rae," he slurred. "And all *you* gotta do is watch and take notes." He whipped out his penis and gestured to the harlot. "On your knees, gal. Show her how it's done."

I whirled around and ran out of the room. The blood rushed through my head, roaring like a waterfall. My heart burned like a lump of smoldering coal. I ran into the kitchen, yanked open the drawer near the sink and grabbed the biggest butcher knife I could find.

I knew exactly what I was doing. *Pullin' a Gladys.*

Two years ago, I'd sat at the kitchen table and watched my mother-in-law go after Jake's father with a butcher knife. This time, it was *me* with the knife—and Jake was about to become acquainted with the business end of it.

CHAPTER ONE

May 1952
Opal Springs, Kentucky

$\mathbf{A}$ song played in my head as I trudged down the dusty path toward the highway to catch the school bus—Kay Starr's "Wheel of Fortune." You couldn't turn on the radio these days without hearing it at least once or twice an hour on any halfway decent Top 40 station. It always made me think of Chad, and the sweet kisses we exchanged just about every Friday or Saturday night parked down at Rock House Bottom. Lord, if Mother and Daddy knew about that, they'd set my pants on fire. Good thing they believed I was spending the night with Daisy.

A muted roar broke through my thoughts, and with a start, I realized a car was coming from up the ridge. My heart started pounding—because I knew who it was. I stopped in the middle of the road and began digging in my pocketbook for my compact and lipstick. My hand trembling, I applied a fresh layer of Revlon's "Fire and Ice" to my lips and smiled into the mirror to make sure I hadn't got any on my teeth.

The roar of the approaching car grew louder. I hurriedly ran my fingers through my hair and tweaked the spit-curl in the middle of my forehead with a moistened finger.

Gears shifted into low as the car approached from behind. I knew that meant Jake had seen me. I kept walking, swinging my pocketbook as if I hadn't a care in the world, and gazing off into the brambles at the roadside like it was the most fascinating sight I'd ever seen.

The car pulled up next to me and stopped, a powder-blue Plymouth with suicide doors and fancy chrome hubcaps on white-walled tires. A stranger seeing Jake Tatlow's car would think he had money to burn, but that was far from the truth. Jake had worked full-time at the Gulf station in Russell Springs since he'd dropped out of school at 16, and that Plymouth was the only thing he owned worth a plugged nickel. Rumor had it that the only reason he had *that* much was because his older brother, Tully, had returned from the Korean War, flush with discharge pay from the army, and had helped Jake buy it second-hand. But nice car or not, Jake Tatlow was still trash. No getting around that.

I kept walking, pretending not to notice him, even though his radio was turned up loud enough to wake the dead with Hank Williams singing "Honky Tonk Blues." The music cut off abruptly.

"Hey," he said.

Impossible to ignore that. He'd think I wasn't right in the head or something. I turned and met his gaze, raising my chin a notch to let him know I wasn't at all impressed by him and his fancy car. But beneath my blouse, my heart was racing, and I sensed he knew it.

"Mornin', Jake," I said stiffly, and kept walking. My quick glance at him confirmed it. Jake Tatlow was simply the best looking boy I'd ever seen in all my born days. Yes, even better looking than Chad.

He stared at me now, one brawny, suntanned arm draped over the steering wheel, his cornflower blue eyes scanning me from top to bottom, lips quirked in a way that resembled a smirk more than a smile. It was the only thing about him that reminded me of the boy he used to be, back years ago when the two of us played in a swimming hole on Tucker Creek one summer.

I was a few yards away from the front of his car when he let out the clutch and pulled up next to me again. "Want a ride to the bus stop?" he asked in his slow drawl.

"No, thanks." I kept walking, eyes straight ahead. I could feel his gaze on me as I went on down the road. One more little hill, and the highway would be in sight. I put a little sway into my walk, just the way Marilyn had in "Niagara."

He pulled up next to me again. "Hey, Lily Rae, what time does the bus come?"

"7:40. What's it to you?"

He gave a shrug. "Nothing to me, I reckon." He grinned in a way that never failed to make me weak in the knees. "But you might be interested to know it's…" He turned his wrist so he could glance at his watch. "…seven forty-*five* right now."

"What?" I stopped in my tracks and stared at him. "It *can't* be!"

"Well, it is. And you know as well as I do that old man Thornton ain't never been late a day in his life, so you've done missed that bus."

I knew that was the truth. Even on the snowiest days, if school wasn't canceled—and it rarely was—Wallace Thornton prided himself on being on schedule.

Jake leaned across the passenger seat and opened the door. "Come on, hop in. I'll drive you to school."

I hesitated. I knew I'd catch heck if word got back to my kin about riding in Jake Tatlow's Plymouth. But what was I supposed to do? I couldn't go back home and ask Daddy to drive me in. He was probably already out in the fields with Landry and Edsel.

I knew I'd just *die* if I couldn't go to school and see all my friends one more time. Tomorrow was graduation day, and we'd all be separating soon, some going off to college, others like me, going to the big city to learn a trade. And Chad! Dear Lord, it just killed me to think about it, but in another week, he'd be heading off to England, of all places, where he'd be spending the whole summer with cousins he'd never laid eyes on.

Jake leaned toward me, his eyes admiring, grin cocky. "Well, are you gonna get in or you gonna just stand there looking like the cat's got your tongue?"

I cast a desperate glance up the ridge, then before I could change my mind, scrambled into the passenger seat of the Plymouth. I'd barely got the door closed before Jake shifted into first gear and gave it the gas. We flew down the road at 35 miles an hour—way too fast for a dirt road—with me holding tight to the strap above the door as my bottom bumped up and down on the vinyl seat.

"*Lord*, Jake!" I exploded when he reached the highway and slowed to a stop. "Get me to school, but you don't have to *kill* me doing it!"

Jake glanced down the road heading toward Adair County, and then turned left. "See? Bus is long gone. Good thing you decided not to be so stubborn."

He floored the accelerator, and immediately the rush of wind made a mess of my hair. I quickly rolled up the window.

"I still don't understand how it got to be so dad-blasted late," I muttered, staring out at a pasture of Guernsey cows near a pond covered with kelly-green water lilies.

Jake kept his eyes on the road and didn't respond. He reminded me of somebody I'd seen recently, the way he was dressed in blue jeans and a snug white T-shirt with the sleeves rolled up. Then I remembered. Chad had taken me to the Star Theater on Main Street a few weeks ago, and we'd seen this movie with Dean Martin called "Sailor Beware." Silly movie--forgettable, really, except for this young actor named James Dean who'd appeared in a boxing scene, immediately reminding me of Jake. If Hollywood took a notion to make a movie out of Jake's life, this James boy would be perfect for playing him.

Look at him. Sitting there so cool and cocky, like he thinks he's chocolate on a stick! Jake stared at the road, one elbow resting on the open window frame and his other hand cupping the gearshift with strong, tanned fingers. The way a man would cup...

I blushed at the thought and jerked my gaze away. Lord, what was wrong with me? The things that came into my mind sometimes…well, no decent girl ought to be thinking like that. At the revival meetings last summer, the preacher had ranted and raved about how the devil lay in wait for the weak and sinful of heart, and if I kept thinking about stuff like that, I'd *surely* burn in hell-fire once Judgment Day arrived.

Still, I took some consolation in remembering how I'd pushed Chad's hand away Saturday night when it had briefly grazed my bosom through my blouse. But even as I'd done so, a tiny part of me had thrilled to the caress. I frowned. Maybe I was just born bad.

Jake cleared his throat, and I realized he'd taken his eyes off the road and was staring at me. He grinned when I met his gaze. "Course, there's every possibility that my watch might be running about five minutes fast," he said, then waited for my reaction.

I stared at him. His eyes danced and his grin widened.

"Why, you…" I finally managed to say. "Jake Tatlow, you are so *ornery!*"

He laughed, his straight white teeth gleaming, then looked back at the road.

One thing about Jake--he might be trash, but at least he kept himself cleaned up. Even now, I could smell the spicy scent of homemade lye soap, and maybe even a hint of Pepsodent toothpaste. And he had good teeth—something kind of rare here in Russell County.

"Darlin'…" He threw me a quick glance. "Got news for you. It's *fun* to be ornery." He gave me a slow smile that made me all hot inside like my body was a pot-bellied stove and somebody had tossed a big hunk of coal into its flames. Was this how

Mother felt when she had one of the "hot simmers" she sometimes complained about?

"Tell you what, Lily Rae. Get rid of Nickerson, and go out with me. I'll teach you a thing or two about being bad, and you'll *never* want to be good again."

My face grew hot, and I looked away from him in confusion. "Just drive me to school."

His mocking laughter rang out. Clearly, he was having fun at my expense. Clean or not, Jake Tatlow lived up to his family's reputation of hillbilly trash. From the time I was knee-high to a grasshopper, I'd heard the name Tatlow being talked about in ugly terms around the county. For years, I'd thought *tatlow* was an adjective that meant dirty and filthy and worthless. It wasn't until I'd played with a young boy named Jake down by the creek for an entire summer that I found out Tatlow was his last name.

And that was after Daddy had caught me playing "house" with him on a sultry afternoon in August. I'd been serving "my husband" one of my famous mud pies just after he'd returned from killing a whole tribe of wild Indians when Daddy appeared out of the woods, his eyes burning like two hot coals. In his callused, work-hewn hand, he held a long, vicious-looking switch that I knew had been cut from the hickory tree at the back of the house. I'd learned my lesson that day, and from that time on, I'd done my best to steer clear of any of the Tatlows, especially Jake.

So, what on earth had possessed me to accept a ride with him this morning? I tried to tell myself it was because it was the last day of school, and I'd believed I'd missed the bus. I *had* to get there! We had rehearsal for graduation this afternoon, and I had to know what to do, didn't I?

But my cheeks were still hot, and even though I didn't dare turn my head and look at Jake again, I was so very aware of him, sitting there next to me.

Maybe I am bad. Maybe it was the very fact he was forbidden that made me so fascinated with him. How else could I explain the way I felt when he pulled up in front of Russell Springs High School and waited for me to get out?

Disappointed...and wondering why the trip into town, which usually seemed to take an eternity, seemed this morning to be *way* too short.

Great-Aunt Ona's Chocolate Oatmeal Fudge

1 stick margarine
½ cup milk
1/3 cup cocoa
2 cups sugar
1/3 cup peanut butter
½ teaspoon vanilla
3 cups rolled oats

Melt margarine. Add milk, cocoa and sugar and boil one minute. Remove from heat. Add peanut butter, vanilla and oats. Drop from spoon onto waxed paper.

CHAPTER TWO

I took the starched and ironed red polka-dot dress out of my wardrobe and laid it carefully on the bed where my sister, eight-year-old Norry sprawled, her brown eyes saucer-like. She was curled up on her side, one hand cupping her narrow chin. Dark sausage curls tumbled to her thin shoulders against a lace-edged nightgown.

"Oh, Lily, it's beautiful," Norry said. "You're going to look just like Liz Taylor tonight."

I smiled at my little sister and sat down in a reed-woven chair opposite the vanity dresser, eyeing myself in the mirror. "Oh, yeah. Liz Taylor with brown eyes, right?" I joked.

Yet, I couldn't help but be pleased by Norry's remark. After all, I *did* look like Liz Taylor. That's what a lot of people said, anyhow. I gingerly touched my bobby-pinned curls. Still damp. That was okay. I had hours yet before I had to get ready.

Somehow, I'd managed to get through a simmering-hot graduation this morning in the high school gym. And only Landry and Edsel had been there to watch me receive my diploma. Twelve-year-old Edsel had done his best to try to make me laugh as he crossed his eyes and stuck out his tongue in a grotesque imitation of "Radar Men from the Moon" which he'd seen at the Star Theater a few weeks ago.

Next to him, Landry, at 20, was as sober-faced as a preacher giving the eulogy at the graveside of his beloved mother. There had always been a special

19

bond between me and Landry, forged years ago when it was just the two of us living in the little house in Opal Springs, long before Edsel, Norry and Charles Alton arrived.

I'd been glad my brothers had made it, but I'd sorely missed my parents.

They'd taken my little two-year-old brother, Charles Alton, to old Dr. Scudder in Jamestown this morning because last night had been the worst one yet for the poor little thing. Up all night crying and feverish and vomiting like there was no tomorrow. But even not having my parents there wasn't the worse thing about graduation. Chad and I had had a huge fight last night, parked out at Rock House Bottom—over the same old thing—because I wouldn't go all the way with him. He hadn't even spoken to me at graduation, and the one time I'd caught his eye, he'd looked away. The rat! Well, I'd see him tonight, and he'd be singing a different tune because I was going to look so daggone good, he'd be falling all over me.

I glanced at Norry's reflection in the mirror. "I'd *rather* look like Marilyn."

Her laughter reminded me of Tucker Creek in high summer as the water gurgled over the flat slabs of rock just above the swimming hole. "Lord forbid!" she said, still giggling. "Mother and Daddy wouldn't let you out of the house if you looked like Marilyn!"

I grinned, glancing at her. "Well, it's obvious you're getting back to your ornery self, Miss Smarty-Pants."

I still felt ashamed of myself for thinking she'd been playing possum yesterday. The poor thing had been really sick last night. Thank the Lord she was on the mend; I just wished Charles Alton was, too.

Mother and Daddy hadn't returned from the doctor when we got home from graduation. Here it was, near four o'clock, and we hadn't heard a word from them. What the *dickens* was taking so long?

I got up from the chair. "You hungry, Norry? How about I heat up some of this morning's biscuits? We'll have 'em with butter and molasses."

Just as we reached the threshold of the kitchen, a knock came at the front door. "*Yoo hoo*, Lily *Rae!*" a high-pitched feminine voice called out. "It's me, Sylvie Mae."

I frowned. What, for Pete's sake, was Sylvie Mae Blankenship doing here? I headed for the door. "It's open. Come on in!"

The door opened, and a large woman with salt-and-pepper hair stepped inside, wearing a flowered housedress under an apron soiled with what looked like blood. Killing chickens for Sunday supper, I suspected.

"Excuse my appearance, child." Sylvie Mae rubbed restless, knobby hands down her stained apron. Her gaze darted nervously around the room. And that was when I felt the first stirrings of uneasiness.

Sylvie Mae was our nearest neighbor, living just down the road a piece. She was a widow-woman who kept mostly to herself. Friendly enough, but not the kind of person who made a habit of dropping in on folks to share a cup of coffee and some gossip. And did she always have that pinched look on her face, or was something really wrong?

My stomach muscles tightened. But before I could say a word, Sylvie Mae spoke again, "Your papa just rang and told me to get you a message."

Sylvie Mae was one of the few neighbors here on the ridge that had a telephone. The news that

Daddy had called her made my feeling of doom grow stronger. He hated using "them new-fangled telly-phones" and just didn't, if he could help it, so I knew things must be serious, indeed, to make him call Sylvie Mae.

"Is it Charles Alton?" I asked, holding my breath.

The old woman's face softened. "Yes-um. The baby is real sick, Lily Rae," she said quietly. "They's up in Louieville Hospital. Old Doc Scudder in Jamestown couldn't figger out what was ailing the child, so he sent them up to Columbia this morning. And them doctors up there sent them on to Louieville. Your daddy says it's no telling how long they'll be up there, and for ya'all to come stay with me until they get back."

Oh, Lord, no! Why, I'd up and *die* of boredom if I had to go stay at that widow-woman's dull old house. Nothing to do there at all! Why, she didn't even have any good magazines laying around, like **Photoplay** and **Movieland**, just boring old religious ones, or maybe, once in a blue moon, she'd have **Look** or **Collier's**.

I heard Norry step into the room behind me.

"Hi, there, Sylvie Mae." Norry's dark eyes fixed anxiously upon the old woman's face. "Did I hear you say Charles Alton is in the hospital in Louieville?"

"Yes, hon, he is…and ya'all are gonna come stay with me until your mama and daddy get home."

I swallowed hard and glanced at my sister. She looked curiously vulnerable in her long white cotton nightgown, her shell-like pink toes peeking from beneath its hem. The color had drained from her cheeks, leaving her as pale as she'd been the night before when she'd been so sick.

I understood why. It was fear for our
baby brother. Just a few weeks ago, he'd been a
happy, healthy two-year-old, an angelic, laughing
child, his head covered in bright gold ringlets. When
I'd kissed him goodbye this morning, he'd barely
stirred, poor thing. And his cheek had felt like it was
on fire. But now, at least, he was in the hospital, and
them big city doctors would take good care of him.

One thing was for darn sure, though. There
was *no way* on God's green earth I was going over to
Sylvie Mae Blankenship's. No matter *what* Daddy
said! Tonight was the biggest night of my life, and I
wasn't about to have it ruined. After all, I was a
grown woman now. Not only had I turned 18 back
in March, I now had a bonafide high school
diploma. Didn't Daddy remember that?

"Do they know what's wrong with him?"
Norry asked in a small voice.

Sylvie Mae shook her tightly-curled head.
"They's doing tests. That's all I know." She looked
around the room. "Where's the boys? Y'all need to
get your things together and come on now. I got
soup beans on the stove and cornbread in the skillet.
And later, you can help me fry up a pullet for
Sunday dinner."

"I don't know where the boys are," I said,
trying to sound all grown up. "They're probably
down at the Star Theater watching the matinee.
Anyhow, I really appreciate your offer, Sylvie Mae,
but we're gonna stay right here and wait for Mother
and Daddy and Charles Alton to come home."

The old woman's haggard face darkened like a
thundercloud. That meant she was gearing up for a
fight. "But your daddy tol' me---"

"My daddy is upset about his baby," I cut in,
holding the woman's gaze defiantly. "He's forgotten
he has a grown up daughter here, perfectly able to

23

take care of things while he's gone. So, thank you kindly for your offer, Sylvie Mae, but we're gonna stay put."

Sylvie Mae opened her mouth as if to protest, but I didn't let her get to it. "Thanks for bringing us the message," I added, walking toward the door.

The elderly woman shook her head and *tsked* under her breath, but stepped out onto the front porch when I opened the door for her. "I just don't know," she muttered in a last ditch effort to change my mind. "Your daddy ain't gonna like this one bit."

"It'll be fine," I said firmly, and closed the door in her face, feeling only a little ashamed of myself. But Lord Almighty, I was a grown-up now. When was people going to start treating me like one?

I turned to Norry with a sigh of relief, then stiffened at the stricken look on her face. "Oh, honey…"

She stared back at me, eyes wide with fear. "What do you think is wrong with Charles Alton, Lil? Is he going to be okay?"

I crossed the room and took her into my arms. "He's going to be just fine, honey," I murmured, stroking her dark curls. "You'll see. Them big city doctors are going to fix him right up. Before you know it, he'll be home playing Peek-a-Boo with us, fit as a fiddle."

Norry lifted her head. "You promise?"

I nodded firmly. "Cross my heart and hope to die." Relief settled onto Norry's face, and I hoped desperately I'd spoken the truth.

CHAPTER THREE

"I don't believe it," I moaned to my best friend, Daisy, over the sound of Eddy Howard singing "(It's No) Sin" on Katydid's record player. My eyes scanned the crowd in the Wilkes's large basement recreation room. "Why isn't he here?"

Daisy pursed her ruby-red lips and took a sip of the Coca-Cola her pudgy-faced boyfriend, Lawless, had just brought her. He hulked at her side, watching her every move, trying, I supposed, to anticipate her slightest whim. I'd always thought Daisy could do better than Lawless Russell.

Drinking my cola, I caught a tender glance exchanged between the couple, and it reminded me of what Chad had said last night about our friends going all the way. But *surely* not Daisy and Lawless! Daisy would've told me. *Wouldn't* she have?

The thought of Daisy and Lawless doing it just made my stomach curdle. Trying to erase the image from my mind, I looked away and took a gulp of my Coca-Cola. Where the dickens *was* Chad?

"Well, looky who's here," said a male voice behind me. "Recent graduates from Russell Springs High, acting all high and mighty because they finally got themselves high school diplomas."

I turned to see a tall, lanky boy with his arm wrapped snugly around a petite, auburn-haired girl who barely came to his shoulders. Malcolm and Mardelle, looking, as always, like they were joined at the hip.

I smiled. "Well, look who's talking? I seem to recall you going up on that stage this morning and getting yourself a diploma, too."

"Yes, ma'am," Malcolm said with a wide, easy grin. "And I'm heading off to UK in the fall to play for the Wildcats. Just got the telegram this afternoon."

A chorus of excited congratulations rang out. I studied Mardelle's heart-shaped face as Malcolm accepted handshakes and pats on the back from all the guys. Despite the smile on her face, sadness glimmered deep in her doe-like brown eyes. Oblivious to his girlfriend, Malcolm laughed and joked around with the boys. I felt a wrench in my heart.

Everything was changing. This would be the last summer we'd all be together. These people, most of whom I'd started grade school with 12 years ago, would be going off on their own paths, some to college or trade school, some—the unlucky ones, I thought—going back to the family farm to raise pigs and cows, to plow fields and plant corn and tobacco. But whatever they did, life would forever be different. Never again would we experience these carefree days of high school. That had all ended yesterday. Well, not really. But it *would* end with autumn.

My eyes met Mardelle's, and for a moment, we shared a brief communication. I sensed the petite cheerleader was feeling the same bittersweetness of the moment. "Quite the bash, huh?" boomed a deep voice on my left.

It was Lonnie, who'd been in front of me at graduation this morning. He made his way through the crowd, hand in hand with Jinx who was flashing a 100-watt smile. The couple was even more inseparable than Malcolm and Mardelle, and had been since fourth grade.

Now, *those* two probably *were* doing it, I thought. They just had that look about them. After all, Jinx was known to be a little fast. Right now, she looked like she was about to bust a gut or something. I wondered if she had to use the ladies' room and just couldn't pull herself away from Lonnie's grasp long enough to do it.

But no, it was something else altogether. While the boys were still talking about UK and the never ending subject of basketball, Jinx, apparently unable to hold it in any longer, thrust out a slim, pale hand to us girls, showing off a small diamond on her ring finger.

"We're *engaged*," she trilled, her blond pony-tail bouncing in her excitement. "We're getting hitched next month, and y'all are invited to the wedding!"

Another round of "congratulations" burst around her, and I added my voice to them. But inside, I was feeling a little sorry for Jinx. Why would anyone want to get married to the only boy she'd ever kissed (assuming that was true) just out of high school? Didn't Jinx want to see the world? To do exciting things? It didn't make sense.

Malcolm elbowed Lonnie. "That's some rock, my man. What'd you do? Rob a bank?"

Lonnie laughed. "Cut the gas, Mal. I worked hard for this bread. Anyhow, we got a lot to celebrate tonight." He pulled a silver flask out of his white sports coat. "How about a little Jim Beam in your Coca-Colas?"

Everyone, even the girls, eagerly held out their tumblers, and Lonnie poured a stream of whiskey into each one. I hesitated a moment, then shrugged and held out my own glass. Lord, Daddy would just *die* if he knew I was drinkin' Satan's water.

Lonnie poured a healthy splash of the liquor into my tumbler and I swirled it around, sending the ice cubes clinking against the glass. I took a hesitant sip, then grimaced. It was just downright *awful!*

Watching me, Lonnie threw back his brown flat-top and laughed. "It's an acquired taste, Lily Rae. It'll grow on you."

I wasn't so sure about that, but I took another sip.

"Hey, you better not let Katydid catch you with that stuff," Daisy admonished, even though she hadn't turned down a shot in her own Coca-Cola. "Her daddy will tar and feather all of us."

Everybody knew that Etheridge Wilkes had been a deacon at Poplar Grove Baptist Church for years, and wouldn't take kindly to finding liquor on his property.

But Lonnie just snickered. "Heck, RJ has been spiking his soda pop with Johnnie Walker since he first walked in the door."

I wondered where these boys had got all the liquor. There wasn't a wet county around for at least

60 miles. Bootleggers, I reckoned. I'd heard
tell they not only made moonshine, but drove to the
wet counties to stock up on beer and whiskey for
them that didn't like the stuff from the stills.

I glanced around the room again, narrowing my
eyes to focus my vision. The liquor was already
making my head feel a mite light, but I could see that
more folks had arrived; the place was jam-packed
with bodies.

I turned back to my circle of friends and waited
for a break in the conversation. "Anybody seen
Chad?" I finally asked.

Everyone stared at me, and my cheeks grew
warm. That's when I realized that not one soul had
asked me about Chad, which was really sort of odd,
since everybody knew we were a couple. Could it be
the news about last night's fight was already out?
But I hadn't told a soul this morning at graduation,
except, of course, Daisy. And she wouldn't blab.

"Saw him earlier," Lonnie said, avoiding my
eyes. "Talking to RJ and Katydid. You might ask
them where he went off to."

I glanced across the room and saw Katydid and
RJ dancing to Johnny Ray's "Cry." Her dark head
lay against his shoulder, her eyes closed as they
swayed slowly to the music.

I waited until the song ended, then made my
way through the crowd toward the couple. When
Katydid saw me, her sapphire eyes brightened and a
welcoming smile spread across her face. "Oh, Lily
Rae, that dress is just *scrumptious* on you!" She
reached out a hand toward me. "Why, you're just
the belle of the ball, isn't she, RJ?" She beamed up
at her steady who towered above her by four inches.

RJ Skaggs nodded. Even without his football
uniform, he looked the part of the halfback he'd
played for the past four years on the Lakers' team.

He was big and burly, with a firm, square jaw and a crew-cut. "You sure do look pretty tonight, Lily Rae," he said. "*Especially* pretty."

"Thank you kindly." I gave them my biggest smile. "Lonnie said y'all was talking to Chad awhile back? Do you know where he went off to?"

Katydid's smile dimmed. A brief, awkward pause followed, and then she said, "Well, now, I'm not exactly…" Her gaze darted around the room.

"You might as well tell her, Katy," RJ said quietly. "She's bound to find out anyhow."

"Find out what?" I asked, my stomach tightening in alarm.

Katydid's eyes met mine, her smile gone now. "Oh, hon," she said softly. "I'm so sorry to hear about you and Chad."

I pasted a stiff smile on my lips. "Oh, it was just a little spat. Nothing serious. That's why I want to talk to him…" I looked from Katydid to RJ, and my pulse jumped at the sympathy on their faces. "Well, we'll get it sorted out. We'll both apologize for losing our tempers and we'll kiss and make up. So…do you know where he went?"

The couple exchanged a meaningful glance, and my stomach did another slow somersault. Finally, RJ sighed. "Lily Rae, Chad left about a half-hour ago with Pat-Peaches Huddleston."

I caught my breath. *No! I couldn't* have heard him right. Chad with Pat-Peaches? Why, she was the most notorious girl at Russell Springs High, and she was only a junior.

"That can't be true," I said in a soft, shocked whisper.

RJ and Katydid only stared back at me silently. And with a sick certainty, I knew it *was* true. I turned blindly and elbowed my way through the

throng of teenagers until I reached the
basement stairs.

Pressing a hand to my tummy, I climbed up the
stairs and headed down the hall to the Wilkes's
bathroom. I slammed the door and leaned against it,
my head spinning. Whether it was the result of those
few sips of the whiskey-laced cola or the shocking
news JR had delivered, I didn't know. But one thing
was certain. I felt like I was about to throw up all
over my brand new polka-dot dress. Sinking to the
floor in front of the toilet, my full skirt billowing
around me, I gagged, but nothing came up. Not
even the stupid drink I'd just had. After a couple of
deep breaths, my stomach began to settle.

When the nausea had passed, I closed the lid of
the toilet and sat on it, folding my hands in my lap.
I stared around the bathroom at the gigantic claw-
footed tub, the mirrored wall, and the fluffy white
towels hanging on a brass rack.

This had been the first indoor bathroom I'd
ever seen, and that had been only eight years ago.
The Wilkes's were one of the first families in the
county to get indoor plumbing. Two years after I
first saw Katydid's indoor bathroom, Daddy got the
factory job up in Louieville for the winter, driving up
there every Sunday after church and back home on
Friday night, and as soon as he'd saved up enough
money, he put in our own indoor plumbing. But
ours was about a third of the size of the Wilkes's,
not much bigger than a large closet, and that's the
way it had remained.

I sighed and got to my feet. I'd been comparing
myself to Katherine Ann Wilkes my whole life, and
always came up short. Why would tonight be any
different? After all, Katydid had a boyfriend who
loved her, one who would never, *ever* disappear with
the likes of Pat-Peaches Huddleston.

I stared at myself in the mirror, my brown eyes wounded, bottom lip trembling. *How could Chad do this to me?*

Pat-Peaches was a redhead, really stacked, and she was as loose as a goose lapping up prune juice, as Mother would say. She was, to put it mildly, Russell Springs High's "scarlet woman." Everybody knew Pat-Peaches would crawl in the back seat with anybody who wore britches and had a bit of stubble on his face. Why, that's how she got the "peaches" nickname in the first place, I'd heard. Not that I understood it, exactly, but one boy, long graduated and gone now, had told one of his buddies that Patricia Huddleston was "as tasty as a ripe peach," and from then on, everyone had called her Pat-Peaches. A name that, apparently, she took pride in.

And Chad—*my* Chad—had gone off with her?

My chin lifted. No. I simply wouldn't believe it. Well, he might've gone off with her, but he wouldn't actually *do* anything with her. Why, a couple of years ago, rumors had been flying around the school that Pat-Peaches had cooties! Chad was an all-American, clean-cut boy. Surely, he couldn't stomach touching that trashy girl.

A new thought occurred to me. Maybe Chad was just trying to make me jealous. Yes, that was it! He was trying to teach me a lesson. Boys were immature like that.

I dug into my pocketbook for my lipstick and smoothed another layer of the creamy red color on my lips, then I fiddled with the curls on my head, rearranging them for maximum effect.

I'll just bet you're down there in the basement right now, Chad Nickerson, just wondering where the heck I am, and why your idiotic plan isn't working.

With one last glance in the mirror, I left the bathroom and headed back toward the basement stairs. But just as I got to threshold of the living room, the front door opened, and a feminine giggle floated in, followed by a throaty drawl, "Honey, there's more where that came from. Why don't you let me show you right now?"

I stiffened and hugged against the wall, holding my breath. That was Pat-Peaches! But surely the boy with her wasn't Chad. It better not be!

The male spoke in a soft rumble, but I couldn't make out what he said, and it wasn't enough to know for certain if it was Chad. There was a long silence, followed by a soft sigh.

"There, now," said Pat-Peaches. "I'll bet you don't get kisses like that from Miss Goody-Two-Shoes Lily Rae Foster."

My heart skipped a beat; I could almost feel the blood drain from my face.

"Bet she's never even slipped her tongue in your mouth, has she? Much less massaged your dicky-doo like I just did. Sure you won't change your mind, Chad? Let's go drive down to Rock House Bottom. I know a spot there where nobody goes."

My pulse was racing now, and I knew the color had returned to my face. In fact, my skin felt as hot as a firecracker. I didn't think; I just acted.

"Yeah, Chad," I said smartly, whirling around the corner to confront the couple. "Why don't you take Pat-Peaches up on her offer? Crawl into the backseat of your car with her and do what you have to do. I'm sure it'll be worth risking a case of the crawling cooties."

Chad and Pat-Peaches stared at me in shock. His face and neck were smudged with lipstick—the same hot pink shade the redhead wore on her kewpie-doll lips. She had her arms wound around his neck, her curvy body pushed up against his. Her long red hair streamed around her shoulders in a Veronica Lake style, and as I watched their reaction to my appearance, the totally silly thought that it didn't look dirty or cootie-infested at all went through my mind. The blood had drained from Chad's face, and he finally disengaged the floozy's arms from his neck and stepped away from her.

"You got the wrong idea, Lily Rae," he said, taking a step toward me.

I backed up, glaring. "Oh, yeah. *I* got it wrong. Am I dreaming, Chad? Finding you kissing Pat-Peaches is just a figment of my imagination, I suppose?"

Pat-Peaches' expression of surprise had turned to one of smug satisfaction. But my anger was directed at Chad. *He* knew better.

A flush had spread over his handsome face; he took another tentative step toward me. "Nothing happened, Lily Rae…not much, anyway." He reached out a hand to me. "Look, sweetheart, I had a little to drink. I was upset about our fight, and Pat-Peaches, here, just…" His voice drained away, and his hand dropped to his side.

I gave them a bitter smile. "She felt bad for you, and was just trying to make you feel better, huh?"

Pat-Peaches threw me a mocking smile, and I saw that her two front teeth were starting to decay. The sight made me feel even sicker. How could Chad *kiss* something like that?

"I do what I can to help out," the redhead said in a thin, sarcastic voice.

I wanted to punch her. Instead, I ripped off Chad's class ring. "You can both just go to the devil!" I flung the ring at him, hitting him in the chest. It clattered to the floor. "As far as I'm concerned, you deserve each other!"

With my head high, I swept past them and out the front door. I kept my shoulders straight as I descended the steps of the front porch, grateful that the disgusting twosome couldn't see the tears streaming down my cheeks.

CHAPTER FOUR

The orange oval of the Gulf station sign
glowed in the gathering twilight. I saw it through a
curtain of tears. At first, I didn't know why I felt
drawn to the beckoning light of the gas station. By
the time I reached it, my fashionable spiked heels
felt like torture devises designed by the Gestapo.
Tears had dried on my face, but my eyes still burned
from crying, and I thought they probably looked as
red as the polka-dots on my dress.

And then I saw him, and knew why I'd felt
drawn to the place.

He stood at the pump, dressed in his light blue
Gulf uniform, one tanned hand clamped on the
pump's nozzle as he filled the tank of an older
model black Buick. Under the splash of light from
the bright station, Jake's wind-tossed hair gleamed
with golden streaks. The boss must not be there, I
thought, or Jake would be wearing his Gulf cap. I
had a feeling he liked showing off his hair. He wore
it longer than most boys, which was just another
indication of his rebellious nature, but I'd always
thought its length suited his angular, tanned face.
He hadn't seen me yet; he was too busy talking to
the car's occupant, his teeth flashing white in the
growing darkness.

It had always amazed me, his teeth. They were so straight and white, like a movie star's. Most folks around here had lots of problems with their teeth, mainly because the closest dentists were in Columbia or Somerset, or they just couldn't be bothered.

I stood in the shadows and watched Jake as he worked. Uncertainty swept over me. What was I doing here? What was I supposed to do now? What was I supposed to say to him, this childhood playmate who was now a stranger?

I knew I couldn't go back to Katydid's. My face grew warm as I thought of Chad and Pat-Peaches in each other's arms. How many people had seen them together? The thought of seeing the pity in my friends' eyes would just be too much to bear.

Jake leaned across the hood of the Buick and briskly cleaned the windshield with a cloth, still carrying on a conversation with whoever was in the car. Probably a pretty girl. Jake wasn't so personable with other boys. When he finished cleaning the windshield, he took the money and tipped a forefinger to his head, grinning, as the car moved off.

Heart thumping, I stepped out of the darkness. Our eyes met and for a moment, he looked like the young boy I'd known before my father had ended my visits to the swimming hole. But then a mask seemed to drop over his face. Even though his lips still wore a grin, his eyes took on a look that made it seem like he knew something I didn't. It was the same look I'd seen in his eyes when he'd given me the ride to school yesterday morning. Like he knew some deep, dark secret about me, maybe one that even I didn't know. His eyes scanned me in a way that brought heat to my cheeks.

Lord above, I could almost believe he could see straight through my dress to the lacy push-up bra and garters I'd secretly ordered from the Sears Roebuck catalog with some of the money I'd saved from working at Grider's Drugstore last summer.

Jake took an oil cloth from his back pocket and began to rub at his hands, still watching me. "What brings you here, Lily Rae?"

I took a step closer, breathing in the thick, oddly-pleasant scent of gasoline. "I…just…" My bottom lip quivered. To my horror, fresh tears welled in my eyes, and my throat tightened. The grin disappeared from Jake's face, and even in the dim light, I saw his blue eyes deepen with genuine concern.

That did it. I burst into sobs. With three long strides, Jake crossed the asphalt and took me into his arms. I cried into his shirt as he held me silently, his big, oil-stained hands pressed to my back. It felt good, and I didn't even care if he was messing up my new dress.

But even as I gave myself up to the heartbreak of Chad's betrayal, and sobbed out my pain into the tear-dampened cotton fabric of Jake's shirt, I inhaled the mingled fragrances of motor oil and gasoline, along with the tangy, slightly-animal scent that was purely Jake. And I knew, somehow, that I'd just crossed a line—that I was teetering on a cliff above Lake Cumberland, and if I fell, the path of my life would take a sharp detour.

And even with that knowledge, I knew I was ready to jump.

***

"This'll only take a minute," Jake said, slipping out of the car. The door closed with a soft thud. He stuck his head back in through the window and grinned. "Don't run off, now. I've heard tell there's a bogeyman in these here woods."

I rolled my eyes and tried to act unconcerned, even though I felt a slight chill on the back of my neck. "Oh, go on, Jake! Your bogeyman stories don't scare me anymore."

He winked. "Is that right?" His head disappeared, and a rustling sound marked his progress as he walked off into the underbrush.

I glanced uneasily into the dark woods, and couldn't help but think of those age-old stories where a mad-dog killer would loom up out of the darkness with a deadly hatchet and kill the first pretty girl he saw sitting in a car waiting for her boyfriend. Darn that boy for putting pictures like that in my mind!

I took a deep, calming breath and folded my hands in my lap. That Jake really knew which buttons to push, didn't he? Back in the days when we'd played together, he would entertain me by telling ghost stories that both scared and fascinated me. Judging by his cocky grin, *he* hadn't forgotten that, either.

I looked out the passenger window and wondered where in tarnation he'd brought me to? Somewhere still in Russell County, I reckoned. It hadn't seemed like we'd driven that far out of town.

I'd always known these hills and hollows were thick with bootleggers, but this was the first time I'd actually been with someone who'd gone looking for one. Why hadn't I just insisted he take me home before he went out looking for liquor?

Because, you idiot, you wanted to be with him. Why don't you, for once in your life, Lily Rae Foster, be honest with yourself?

After I'd finally calmed down back at the station, Jake had ushered me into the little office, and brought me an ice-cold bottle of Dr. Pepper. As he attended to the occasional customers, I glanced through an old issue of **Look Magazine** and sipped the soft drink. The spicy cold liquid felt good on my throat, still tender from my crying jag. At ten o'clock, Jake began closing down the station, and I meekly asked him if he might give me a ride home. He threw me a look that made me think my question had been the stupidest thing ever uttered by a human being since the dawn of time.

"Well...I reckon I can," he'd said finally, a trifle mockingly, in my opinion.

But instead of going towards Opal Springs, he'd headed out Jamestown way onto an old, graveled road that had bounced my bottom so hard against the seat cushion, I believed I'd surely be misaligned for the rest of my life. And still, I hadn't uttered a word of protest, not even when he'd flashed a grin and said, "You don't mind if I make a little stop at the 'package store' before I take you home, do you?"

So, here I was, sitting in Jake's blue Plymouth, windows open because it was so darn hot--even at night--crickets chirping, frogs from a nearby pond croaking, and the occasional ghostly call of a hoot owl floating on the breeze. Fireflies flickered in the woods, and I felt joy at the sight, remembering nights of running around the yard, gathering them with Landry and putting them into old canning jars for use as a nightlight. The insects were out early this year, fooled, I supposed, by the unusually warm temperatures.

As the minutes stretched on, I became increasingly uneasy, as one scary thought after another meandered through my head. Maybe Jake was just going to leave me out here in the wild. Just for meanness' sake.

No, he wouldn't do that. He might leave *me*, but he sure as shootin' wouldn't leave his precious car. But what if...

Another thought stopped me cold, and a curl of fear snaked its way through my stomach. What if some wild-eyed old moonshiner took Jake for a revenuer, and decided to pistol-whip him and ask questions later? Lord Almighty, I'd heard stories about them moonshiners and how they protected their stills like a mama wolf protected her pups. Folks had disappeared in these hollers, never heard from again, or so the stories went.

The racket of the crickets and frogs grew deafening, pounding through my head with each beat of my heart. *Durn you, Jake Tatlow, what's taking so dadblamed long?*

I reached out and turned on the radio to help muffle the scary sounds of the night. Bluegrass music blared from the speaker. I grimaced and fiddled with the tuner. Lord! What self-respecting 19-year-old boy listened to that old hillbilly music? That was a Tatlow for you. Hillbilly through and through.

It took a while to find a decent station; there wasn't much to choose from out in the middle of nowhere—not if you wanted to listen to something besides hillbilly or static. But finally, I found a fairly strong station playing Kay Starr's "Wheel of Fortune." Probably Cincinnati or Louieville. I hummed along with Kay, trying to convince my nerves to settle down, but still, I found myself reaching for Chad's class ring which was so

41

conspicuously absent. I frowned and folded my hands together, tucking them into the folds of my dress between my knees.

Drat that boy! Drat all boys! Every last one of them is a low-down, good-for-nothing, no-account...

I stiffened. What was that sound? Some kind of rustling nearby. *Lord help me, what if it's some kind of wild animal or something?* I knew for a fact there were all kinds of wild varmints roaming these woods. The Kentucky Wildcats hadn't just pulled their name out of a hat, had they?

Warily, I looked out my window, then out Jake's, but didn't see a thing except the dark leaves of the trees and bushes swaying gently in the light breeze. The glimmer of a crescent moon cast dancing shadows on the hood of the Plymouth, and even though common sense told me there was nothing supernatural about it, it still gave me a spooky feeling. The Hatchetman loved nights like this when he was on the hunt for a victim. And even if there weren't no such bogeyman lurking around, it was for dad-burn sure that a wildcat didn't much care what kind of night it was, or even if his supper was all decked out in the prettiest red polka dot dress ever seen in Russell County, as long as she tasted sweet.

With trembling fingers, I reached over to the radio dial and turned the volume down. Head cocked toward the window, I listened for a moment, but heard only the rapid thud of my heart. That didn't reassure me a bit, though. My sixth sense—or "the sight," as Granny Foster called it, was working over-time tonight. There was somebody...or some *thing*...out there in the darkness.

Maybe Granny was right, and I *did* have "the sight," because just like that, I saw a picture in my mind of Jake Tatlow gloating over the tom-foolery he'd pulled on me, and relief washed over me like a cool bath on a sticky August evening.

Jaw clenched, I glared out my window. "Jake Tatlow, is that you out there? Doggone it, Jake, why don't you act your age? I ain't scared, you hear me? And I don't think this is one *bit* funny!"

I held my breath and listened to the drone of crickets and frogs, a distant hoot of an owl and the husky rustle of tree branches scraping together in the balmy breeze.

And then, unmistakably, I heard a sound that made my skin crawl—footsteps crackling through the underbrush. A jolt slammed through my heart, and I rolled up the window as fast as I could, and in the same movement, pushed down the lock button.

"*Jake! Help!*" I screamed, suddenly absolutely *sure* it wasn't Jake out there, but a mad-dog killer, eager to slice me into little pieces and feed me to his German Shepherd. I lunged across the car to roll up Jake's window and lock his door. Over the sound of my panicked breathing, I thought I heard a wild laugh somewhere in the underbrush. I gave another shriek.

With the windows up, it was stuffy in the car, and the heat combined with fear made my palms clammy and my armpits ooze sweat. My heart pounded hard against the cotton bodice of my dress; I could feel the fabric growing wet under my arms, and despite my fear, one tiny, vain section of my brain wondered if my brand new dress would be ruined by sweat stains. Better sweat stains than bloodstains, though. Still, the possibility of the most beautiful dress I'd ever owned being ruined added a big dose of anger to my fear, and that had the effect of reining in my troublesome imagination.

A dollar to a doughnut that *was* Jake out there, just messing with me. He was so darn backward; that was probably the only way he knew how to court a girl. The thought brought me up short. Jake *courting* me? Where had that come from? Nevermind. That *had* to be Jake out there, and if he thought scaring the daylights out of me was going to make me sweet on him, he was a doggone jackass.

"I *mean* it, Jake!" I hollered. "This ain't funny! Now you come on out and show yourself, you hear me?" I glared out the window into the dark woods.

Suddenly something thumped against Jake's window, and I jumped, whirling around. The breath left my body and shock iced through me at the sight of a painted face wearing a feathered headdress leering at me through the glass. I screamed at the top of my lungs. The face disappeared.

Heart slamming, I flattened a palm against the car's horn. It blared through the night in an eerie yodel accompanied by my screams. The figure outside the car appeared again, but this time, instead of grinning at me, the creature jumped up and down, waving his arms. I drew in a sharp breath. It looked like he had…oh, Jesus!…a *hatchet* in one hand.

"*Get away*, you *lunatic!*" I shouted, still pressing my hand against the horn. "Somebody *help* me! *There's a madman after me!*"

"Lily Rae, stop your caterwauling! It's *me!*"

My mouth clamped shut. I stared at the lunatic who'd stopped dancing around, and was now peering in through the window at me, the Indian headdress in his hand.

"It's me--*Jake*. I was just funning with you." Seeing that he finally had my attention, he flashed his familiar grin. Familiar, even with the war paint on his face. "Come on, Lily Rae, don't be mad."

My eyes narrowed. My heart was still racing even as relief coursed through my body, immediately followed by red-hot fury. I turned to my door, unlocked it, and threw it open. A second later, I was on my feet and flying around the back of the Plymouth. Jake stood beside his door, grinning his stupid ain't-I-just-the-cutest-thing-you-ever-saw grin. My eyes raked over him. Lord above, he was dressed in nothing but an Injun loincloth, and I'd swear that was a real tomahawk in his hand. But that wasn't as appalling as the fact that he was half-naked.

"Simmer down now, Lily Rae," he said, chuckling as he backed up. "Can't you take a little joke?"

That made me even madder. I stopped a few inches away from him, glaring into his mischief-filled eyes. Tightening my right hand into a fist, I punched him, just the way Landry had taught me, smack-dab into his stomach.

"*Ow!*" The tomahawk thumped to the ground as Jake clutched at his mid-section. Eyes flaring, he stared at me in amazement. "God *damn* it, Lily Rae, that hurt!"

Breathing heavily, I locked gazes with him. "Good," I snapped. "I *meant* it to hurt." And I started to punch him again.

This time he was ready for me. Laughing, he grabbed my flailing fists, one in each hand. His blue eyes danced with amused excitement. "Don't get frosted, Lily Rae. I was just playing a little joke on you. Just like the old days."

His grin infuriated me even more. I struggled to wrench my hands from his grip. "That was just downright *mean*, Jake Tatlow! You scared the dickens out of me!"

His hands tightened on mine. "Aw, come on, Lily, I don't believe that for a minute. You knew it was me all along. Don't you remember them summers? I'd tell you ghost stories, and jump out and scare you as you was walking home."

I narrowed my eyes in a deliberate glare. He was still trying to use his charm on me. It wasn't going to work. "Yeah, I remember, alright. I was eight and you were nine. Your body may have grown up, Jake Tatlow, but your dadblamed *brain* is still nine! Now, I want you to take me home right this minute!"

Again, I tried to wrench my hand free, and was surprised—and a little disappointed—when he released me. I turned to head back to the car, but before I could take a step, Jake grabbed me again and pulled me against his nearly-bare body. Our gazes locked, and suddenly my heart was beating harder than before. He bent his head and kissed me.

My first instinct was to struggle, and I did—for about two seconds. Until I became aware of the heat of his mouth, the silky, hot touch of his tongue darting between my lips, the damp, warm press of his palm against my back where my dress scooped low. Even when his mouth broke away to skim down the side of my neck, and then up my jaw to my earlobe, I could no more utter a syllable of protest than I could stop my heart from beating.

"Oh, Lord, Lily Rae," he whispered into my ear, his lips nibbling at my lobe. "Is this grown up enough for you?"

I couldn't think, couldn't speak, knew it would be impossible to string three words together. Delicious goose bumps prickled my arms, my neck, my back. My legs felt heavy, as if I were wearing Daddy's steel-toed work boots through a mud-slogged field. The blood pulsed through my veins like warm molasses. I felt a yearning to have Jake's mouth on mine again.

He must've read my mind, or maybe it was my body he was reading. I pressed against him, releasing a soft, shuddering moan. His head turned, and again, his mouth found mine, but this time, the kiss was softer, slower, almost teasing. The heat in my lower belly blossomed and arrowed directly to the part of me that was so shameful and dirty—the part that Chad had unsuccessfully tried to stroke just last night.

I was burning down there, wanting...*needing* to be touched. I'd never felt like this with Chad. Never, *ever*.

Then I felt it. A hot, hard nudge against my lower belly. His *thing*! The sword of sin, Mother had called it back when my first monthly curse had arrived, and we'd had "the talk" about boys and how they wanted only one thing from a girl, and how it was the girl's job to make sure he didn't take any liberties, and if she *did* allow him to take liberties, she was nothing but low-down trash like Pat-Peaches.

That's how I was acting right now, I realized. Like Pat-Peaches! I tried to pull my mouth away from Jake's, but he deepened the kiss, sliding both hands down my back, molding me against him so the brick-like object under his flimsy loin cloth felt like it was burning right through my dress. Alarmed and excited at the same time, I moaned what I intended to be a protest, but even to my own ears, it sounded like a cat in heat. He reacted by sliding his hands down until they cradled my bottom, nestling me even closer against him. I gasped sharply into his teasing mouth. He broke the kiss and gazed down at me, blue eyes luminous in the light of the crescent moon.

"Do you remember how we used to kiss down by the creek?" He whispered. Before I could respond, he drew my bottom lip into his mouth and nibbled gently.

My head spun. Over his right shoulder, I saw the big dipper glimmering in the sky like diamonds on black velvet. My heart raced, the fine hairs on my arms tingled, and my knees trembled. I'd never felt more alive in my life.

His teeth released their gentle hold on my bottom lip, and he rocked against me slowly, his gaze holding mine. The subtle pressure of his forbidden maleness sent hot arrows of flame shooting up into my womb. I knew I should push him away and demand he drive me home or, better yet, run as fast as my legs could carry me. But I just couldn't do it.

"You were the first girl I ever kissed," he said, a husky note in his voice. "And you said I was your first, too." One hand moved leisurely from my bottom to my thigh, and with a sense of fascination mixed with something close to horror, I realized he'd taken hold of the skirt of my dress and was gathering the fabric up in his hand.

Another long, sweet kiss. His mouth tasted of Winston cigarettes and peppermint candy. I could feel his heart thumping against mine. His chest was warm and muscular, and that earlier glimpse of him half-naked had revealed a soft-looking carpet of light brown hair veeing down past his belly button. He smelled of gasoline, motor oil, Brylcreem, and something else that was pure male. His fingers skimmed the bare skin above my stockings, and a jolt of electricity jagged through me. I cried out in surprise. His mouth slid along my cheekbone, and slowly, he thrust against me, one hand molded to my left butt cheek, the other stroking my thigh.

His thing is growing, I thought dizzily. *You'd better stop things right now, girl, or it's going to get out of control.* That was the voice of the *good* Lily Rae talking in my brain. The one who went to church every Sunday morning, the one who earnestly cared about fire and brimstone and everlasting hell for bad girls who let boys touch their secret female places. But as Jake pressed his strong body against mine, nibbled at my lips and stroked his fingers closer and closer to that forbidden place between my legs, the *bad* Lily Rae moaned in delight inside my brain, inside every *tissue* of my body.

Oh, my good Lord, this must be what Heaven feels like, the bad Lily Rae thought. *His fingers touching me. His mouth…and oh, my word…his sword of sin pressing against me…no one ever said how good this would feel.* Was that why it was bad? Because it *felt* so good?

And I wanted more, Lord in Heaven, I wanted more, and I couldn't help but press myself against his strong, masculine body, kissing him back as eagerly as he kissed me.

"Remember how we played house?" He whispered, nuzzling a path down my neck to the hollow of my throat. "You told me once you wanted to marry me for real."

His mouth returned to mine for another deep, wet kiss. I moaned, feeling as if I wanted to crawl right into his body and stay there forever. His questing fingers moved to my inner thigh, stroking the soft hollow, damp now with sweat and secretions that were not new to me, that had flowed whenever Chad kissed me, but not like this. It had never been like this.

His moist breath fanned my face. "Let me touch you," he said raggedly. "Let me dip into your honey-pot, sweetheart."

With a soft moan, I thrust my pelvis against his hand and parted my legs to give him easier access, and that's when I knew for sure that the bad Lily Rae had taken over, and now, also for sure, I'd go straight to hell. But even *that* made no difference. Because Jake's fingers had slid under the elastic of my panties, burrowing gently into my aching flesh, where no boy had ever touched me before. I gasped, digging my nails into his muscular arms, and closed my eyes, giving myself up to the pleasurable sensations rivering through me.

Jake kept up a steady rhythm, stroking gently. His breath caressed my face, warm and staggered. I kept my eyes closed, my mouth ajar, as soft, kittenish cries issued from my throat. I felt like a flower opening up to him, a fragrant rose, warm from the sun, wet from the rain, unfurling secret petals.

The pleasure became so unbearable that I thought I was surely dying. My mewling cries turned into impassioned moans, and from somewhere far away, I heard a ragged, feminine voice crying out, "Yes, yes, oh, *yes*. Please don't…oh, please…oh, oh…*Jake!*"

His fingers moved faster, harder, mining my depths with a sure, steady purpose, bringing me higher, closer to a mountain I knew I had to reach, or I would die. He pressed his half-open mouth against my cheek, his gasping breath in rhythm with every sweet plunge of his fingers.

"Yes," he murmured against my skin. "Come for me, baby. Just let yourself go. I want to make you feel good, Lily. Don't it feel good?"

I drew in a sharp breath and stiffened, teetering on the edge of a different kind of cliff than the one I'd stood on at the beginning of this night. Jake's hand stilled, and for a heartbeat of a moment, the world stopped turning. Not a breath of air stirred between us as I stared into his glazed eyes, indigo in the light of the moon.

Finally, his fingers moved again, and the night exploded into a dazzling firework of stars. White-hot flames shot through my core, radiating out from my belly to sizzle along nerve endings from my toes to my fingertips. Clutching him, I gave a sharp cry and shuddered against his hand, still moving, still caressing, still sending ripple upon ripple of glorious pleasure through me. And even when my last gasp had trailed away into silence, and I sagged against him like a limp dishrag, he cupped my female essence, as if reluctant to move away.

He spoke first, his lips soft against my cheek, "Tell me you didn't let Nickerson do this for you," he said huskily. "Tell me you saved this for me."

To my bewilderment, tears burned behind my eyelids as I realized the truth, a truth I'd never admitted to myself. He was right. I *had* saved this for him. That's why it had never felt quite right with Chad. It wasn't because I was a good girl, trying to follow the strict rules of my God-fearing parents. It was because Chad had never been the *right* boy.

A memory came to me then. Of a sun-striped summer afternoon, sitting on an old deadfall, drying off after a splash in the swimming hole. A suntanned boy with sapphire eyes and wheat-colored hair, a little girl with curly, dark hair and wide brown eyes, a first kiss in the dappled sunlight, and words spoken by childish voices.

"When we git big, Jake Tatlow, will you and me git married for real?"

"I reckon so, Lily Rae. Ain't no other gal here in the holler, 'ceptin fer Alma May Mackelroy, and she's as fat as my pa's old sow. I reckon I ain't partial to *her* a-tall."

With this romantic declaration, Jake had fashioned a ring out of a twig from a blackberry bramble and placed it on my hand.

I still had it, wrapped in a bit of cloth and tucked in the cedar jewelry box Uncle Virgil had brought me from England when he'd returned from the war. For years, I'd kept it there along with mementos from high school—a dried, flattened corsage from my first formal, the first Valentine's card Chad had given me, and a picture of Marlon Brando in "A Streetcar Named Desire," cut out of Daisy's mother's **Look Magazine**.

"No," I whispered, my face hot against his warm, bare chest. "I never let Chad do that."

He released a deep sigh and withdrew his hand from my panties. "Good." Still tingling from his touch, I bit my bottom lip to keep from protesting.

He kissed me gently. "Let's get in the car," he said. "You feel how hard I am for you? Let me love you, Lily Rae." He took my hand and placed it firmly against his massive hard-on.

That's what boys called it, I remembered. Once, after a heavy make-out session in Chad's car, he'd complained about having a hard-on and I had had no idea what he was talking about.

Curious, I traced my fingers up and down Jake's rigid member. He drew in a sharp breath and closed his eyes. A thrill of power went through me at his reaction. With a sense of wonder, I grew bolder, molding my hand to his flesh, exploring.

Jake uttered a muffled oath and grabbed my hand. "Stop," he said, his voice hoarse. "Let's get in the car."

I stared at him, my heart racing. Touching him so intimately had rekindled sweet fire between my legs, and now I knew Jake's touch would put it out.

Bad girl. That's what I was. The bad Lily Rae had completely taken over. But I'd crossed that line from good to evil ten minutes ago. There was nothing I could do now but follow this path wherever it led, even if it was the road to Hell and eternal damnation.

Great Aunt Ona's Old Fashioned Chocolate Cake

1 ¾ cup sifted flour (cake flour)
½ cup cocoa
2 ¼ teaspoons baking powder
1 teaspoon salt
½ cup shortening
1 cup plus 2 Tablespoons sugar
2 eggs unbeaten
¾ cup milk
1 teaspoon vanilla

Sift flour, cocoa, baking powder and salt together. Cream shortening thoroughly, add sugar gradually and cream together until light & fluffy. Add eggs one at a time, beating well after each, then add flour alternately with milk, beating after each addition until smooth. Stir in vanilla. Pour batter into 8" pans. Bake in moderate oven at 375 degrees 25-30 minutes.

Chocolate Buttermilk Icing

1 cup sugar
1/3 cup cocoa
¼ cup butter or margarine
½ teaspoon soda
2 cups buttermilk
3 teaspoons corn syrup
1 teaspoon vanilla

While cake is baking, bring icing to low simmer. When cake is done, poke holes in it with fork; pour icing over hot cake.

CHAPTER FIVE

Jake's Plymouth sped down the dark road toward Adair County. From the radio, Eddie Fisher sang "I'm Yours." If Jake had noticed I'd earlier changed the station, he hadn't said anything, nor had he changed it back to his hillbilly music.

Still lost in a pleasant daze, I stared out the window at the dark fields on my right, but fully aware of Jake's hand caressing my left kneecap when it wasn't shifting gears. His touch sent pleasurable shivers rippling through me. We'd barely talked at all since we'd left the weed-choked lane on the moonshiner's property. When I'd asked why he'd dressed up like an Indian just to scare me, he'd admitted that his bootlegger friend had been the one to come up with the idea. I supposed if I had a lick of sense, I'd still be mad about it, because even now, it seemed downright cruel. But how could I be mad at him after what had happened in the backseat of his Plymouth?

It had hurt at first. *Lord*, how it had hurt! I hadn't expected that—not after the delicious feelings his clever fingers had aroused in me. It wasn't that I was ignorant. I lived on a farm. I'd seen roosters rutting with the hens. I'd watched our old workhorse, Solomon, mate with a neighbor's mare. But no one, certainly not Mother, had told me that sex was *pleasurable*...or that it hurt the first time.

It hadn't lasted, though. Jake had waited for it to subside, holding me gently, his lips nuzzling mine. After a moment, the sharp ache was gone, and there was only a satisfying fullness inside me. When he began to move, I forgot there had ever been anything but pure pleasure as an almost unbearable sensation of need and piercing sweetness shimmered through my body.

I was a woman now. A real woman. Everything had changed. I didn't know what would happen tomorrow. I didn't know how this would affect my leaving for secretarial school in August. There was only one thing I *did* know.

I was in love with Jake Tatlow.

"Almost there," he said, down-shifting for the right turn onto Opal Springs Ridge Road.

Glancing at the illuminated clock on the dashboard, I felt a curl of apprehension in my stomach. Almost one in the morning. Oh, dear Lord, I hoped I was doing the right thing.

The car bounced up the rutted road leading to Opal Springs. I'd instructed Jake to let me out just after we passed Sylvie Mae Blankenship's house; I'd hike the rest of the way up the road. Just in case someone should be up, I didn't want them to see me getting out of Jake's car, which they'd surely recognize. If Daddy found out about the two of us, it would make the Hatfield's and the McCoy's feud look downright neighborly.

Jake turned to me, his foot on the brake as the engine idled. He reached out and stroked a finger down my jaw. I quivered under his touch. "Lily Rae, this is just the beginning of the best summer of our lives," he whispered.

I nodded, my heart lifting even higher. "Oh, I know, Jake. I just can't believe…" I shook my head.

"What?"

"I can't believe I ever thought I loved Chad," I said, dropping my gaze shyly. "It's *you* I love, Jake Tatlow. I'll love you forever."

He lifted my chin with a forefinger, his eyes soft, and brushed his mouth over mine in a tender kiss. "Meet me tomorrow after church? In our old spot down by the creek?"

I nodded, already imagining it—the dappled sunlight, the swiftly flowing water over smooth, warm rocks. Jake's naked body sliding over mine. Lord, I *was* bad. There was no saving me now.

He kissed me once more and leaned across me to open my door. I slid out of the car and watched as he drove off down the road, his taillights finally disappearing around the hairpin curve.

***

Something wasn't right. My steps slowed as I neared the house, my heart beginning to pound. All the lights were burning. Even the ones upstairs. Which made absolutely no sense at all. What were the boys doing up at this time of night? Even my own light was on, which meant...

I swallowed, trying to rid my mouth of the sour taste of fear.

Mother and Daddy must've just gotten home from Louieville, and for some reason, they'd got everybody up, including Norry. And I was sure I knew why. Somehow, they'd gotten word that I was missing from the party. They were probably worried sick about me. How could I have been so stupid to leave that party without even telling anybody? Oh, Chad and Pat-Peaches had seen me leave, of course.

But if asked, would they tell anybody the reason I'd stormed off?

Dear Lord, maybe the whole town of Russell Springs had been searching for me during those three hours we had been parked out in moonshine country. Oh, it was for sure I was in big trouble now. And when they saw the state I was in—my dress all rumpled, my curls tangled and damp from the heat of the night and my sweat. Oh, Lord. My cheeks burned, and darned if I didn't smell of motor oil and...my cheeks grew hotter...good loving. How could they *not* know what I'd been doing?

No use trying to sneak into the house. With a sigh of resignation, I climbed the rickety four steps to the porch. Might as well go on in and face the music. What would they do? Graduate or not, I knew I wasn't too big to get a whipping. Not as long as I still lived under Daddy's roof. But would they do worse? Would they kick me out of the house? Would they pin a scarlet "A" on my dress like they did to that poor Hester in Hawthorne's book—the one Mr. Grider had made us read and write a paper on last semester—and make me wear it everywhere I went? Well, then, me and Jake would just have to run off together and get married.

The thought calmed me. I wasn't in this alone. I had Jake now, and if he had to, he would fight for me. I opened the front door and stepped into the house. If the light hadn't been on, I would've thought the room was empty. That's how quiet it was inside. But Mother sat in the rocking chair next to the cold pot-bellied stove with a sleeping Charles Alton in her arms, his blond curls peeping out from his blanket. Mother's head lay back against her chair, her eyes closed. She rocked slowly, back and forth, and with each motion, the floorboards creaked in protest. Her face was pale, and appeared etched with new wrinkles since I'd last seen her.

I felt a pang in her heart. Poor exhausted Mother. She wore the same pale blue dress she'd had on this morning, along with thick, brown support stockings and sturdy black "old lady" shoes that I vowed to never, ever wear.

They must've just gotten home, I figured. Surely Charles Alton was doing better or the doctors would never have sent him home. I glanced around. But where was Daddy? And why was it so quiet if everybody was up?

Mother gave no indication she'd heard me come in. I stood there a moment, hesitating. Should I announce my presence? Or just slip upstairs and pretend I'd been there all along? But that wouldn't work. Surely, they'd already noticed I was gone.

I opened my mouth to speak, but just as I did so, a muffled sob came from the kitchen. Mother showed no reaction to the noise, but just kept rocking.

Like an approaching storm, dread swept through my soul. I didn't worry about being quiet as I headed for the kitchen. The clacking of my high heels on the wood floorboard announced my presence and four pairs of eyes looked up at me as I stopped in the threshold. I stared, my stomach churning.

Norry, Edsel and Landry sat at the oval oak kitchen table, the boys sipping cups of steaming coffee. A full glass of buttermilk rested, apparently ignored, in front of Norry. At her side stood Sylvie Mae Blankenship, dressed in a floor-length nightgown under a girlish pink robe, her graying hair in pin curls and covered with a net. Her liver-spotted hand rested on Norry's slight shoulder.

Tears tracked down my sister's white face. Landry looked like death, his face graver than I'd ever seen. Even happy-go-lucky Edsel looked like a ghost with his freckles glaring from his bloodless face like red ants on a piece of white bread.

My throat was so dry, I could barely move my lips. "What's wrong?" I finally croaked.

Sylvie Mae looked flustered. "Honey, you'd better sit down now. Let me pour you a cup of coffee. I just made it, and it's piping hot."

My gaze flew from the older woman to Norry, then to my brothers. "What's happened?"

Norry's eyes welled with fresh tears. "Charles Alton *passed away*, Lily Rae!" She burst into uncontrolled sobs, burying her face in her trembling hands.

"Now, now," Sylvie Mae said helplessly, patting her shoulder. "Remember what I just told you. He's with Jesus now. Little Charles Alton is in Jesus' loving arms."

I stared at my siblings, feeling as if a wooden beam had been rammed into my belly. Landry met my gaze, then looked away, his jaw trembling. A tear rolled down Edsel's round cheek.

"But that can't *be*," I protested as the full impact of Norry's words hit me. "I just saw him out there with Mother. She's rocking him. He's sleeping."

Norry cried harder. Landry got up and strode into the pantry and out the back door. The screen door slammed behind him, reverberating through the kitchen. Edsel chewed on his thumbnail as another fat tear rolled down his face.

My frantic gaze darted from Norry to Edsel and back to Sylvie Mae. "*Tell* me he's sleeping!"

Sylvie Mae slowly shook her head. Her eyelids were red, I noticed for the first time. "I'm sorry, Lily Rae. Your mama is out there saying her goodbyes to the poor little youngun. It happened up in Louieville, and there wasn't a thing in the world the doctors could do for him, though they tried everything they could. In the end, all they could do was to let your mama and daddy bring home his poor little body for burial. God bless his tiny soul." She bowed her head and wiped a tear from her wrinkled face.

I stood with my mouth ajar, my brain whirling as I tried to digest the old woman's words. "But..." I finally tried to speak. "I don't understand...how...*what* was wrong with him? He wasn't...that sick, was he?"

Slowly, the elderly woman raised her head and looked at me with cloudy blue eyes. Then she said the word that sent chills knifing through my heart.

"Polio, child. Your baby brother had polio."

CHAPTER SIX

I threw back the single cotton sheet that covered me and sat up on the edge of the bed, running a hand through the damp hair clinging to the nape of my neck. Drat these hot August nights! My hair was so wet I might as well have just come out of the old swimming hole on Tucker Creek. In fact, my whole body felt like an old wet washrag. Lord above, would this hot spell ever break?

Light-headedness washed over me as I got out of bed. *Dadblasted heat!* I stood still until my vision cleared, then tip-toed across the plank floors, still warm from the day's heat. Lord, it was going to feel good when autumn got here. Except when that happened, I wouldn't be here.

A stab of fear shot through my stomach, but I forced myself to push it away. Six weeks, I told myself. *It's only for six weeks.* I quietly went down the stairs, being careful not to put my weight on the fourth step from the bottom—the one that creaked. Since I couldn't sleep, I might as well go sit out on the porch for a spell. At least it would be cooler out there.

Maybe I'd even venture down to the pond. Say goodbye to my favorite place in all of Russell

County. The moon was so bright I'd be able to clearly see my way down there. It had been some time since I'd sat out on the wharf, my feet dangling in the cool water, gazing up at the heavens—all the millions and trillions of stars that looked so close, it felt like you could just reach out and grab a whole handful. It would be cool out there, and right peaceful with all the night sounds—an occasional croak of a bullfrog and the musical chirping of the crickets. It was a God-like place, I thought, and I'd always secretly believed that if a soul was looking for God, it was more likely He could be found right there on that lily-covered pond, rather than down the road a-piece at the Baptist Church. But I'd never say that out loud, of course. Some folks would probably think that was blasphemous.

Then again, what did I know? My cheeks grew hot as I thought about what me and Jake had been doing all summer. No two ways about it, I was one of the worst kinds of sinners. Because I knew what I was doing was wrong, and I went right ahead and did it anyway. And after every time I let Jake have his way with me, I vowed it would be the last time until we were married. But no matter how strong I tried to be, every time he touched me, my voice became paralyzed and my body melted like cotton candy on a tongue.

Oh, dear Lord, how could I leave him? What if he found another girl while I was gone? If that happened, how would I go on living without him?

Stop it! Jake loves you. It's only six weeks, not six months.

I cautiously pushed open the screen door, being careful so it wouldn't squeak. I surely didn't want to wake the whole household. We had to be on the road bright and early tomorrow morning.

The slightest of breezes fanned my hot cheeks as I stepped out onto the porch. I sniffed the air, wondering if rain was maybe on the way. Lord knew we could sure use it. I stood motionless on the porch and gazed up at the full moon, hanging there in the velvet sky like the background in one of them pictures from the Russell County Fair. I had one of me and Chad from last summer, and after I'd started going out with Jake, I'd tried to make myself burn it, but in the end, I just couldn't do it.

I frowned, pushing away thoughts of Chad. He was history now, and I was in love with Jake. I turned to step off the porch and head down to the pond, but hesitated when I heard the squeak of the swing to my right.

"What you doin' up this time of night, Lily Rae?" said a weary voice from the shadowed end of the porch.

I whipped around, pressing a hand against the lace neckline of my nightgown, trying to steady my bumping heart. "Why, Mother! You gave me a start." What on earth was she doing up at this hour?

The swing creaked again, resuming its motion. "You can't sleep, I reckon," she said, answering her own question. "To be expected. Headin' off to Louieville and all. I reckon you can't hardly close your eyes, much less sleep."

"Yes'um." I nodded. "Seems like I've been waiting for this day all my life, and now it's here I'm feeling..." My voice trailed off. How could I tell my mother how I was really feeling? That now I'd found the love of my life, I wasn't all that excited to get away?

Well, I just *couldn't* tell her that. Because then she'd want to know who *was* the love of my life, and of course, I couldn't tell her it was Jake.

"I don't know," I went on. "I just feel all mixed up inside. I want to go, but then I think about leaving ya'all, and...it just saddens me."

"Well, now...that's just part of life," Mother said. "Younguns grow up, leave home and start their own lives. Would be peculiar if they didn't, I reckon."

I opened my mouth to agree, but before I could draw a breath, she went on, "It ain't easy for a body to give up their children, but I reckon they's nothing we can do but obey the Lord's plan. It ain't gonna seem the same around here without you, though."

My throat tightened at the undercurrent of emotion in her voice. Why, I'd had no idea Mother was pining about me going off to Louieville. She'd never given a sign all summer long it was bothering her at all.

"Well..." I began, trying to think of a way to tell her how much I loved her and how I was going to miss everybody, without getting all sappy on her. Lord knows, ours wasn't a family that got all dewy-eyed and sob-storied around each other.

"'Course," Mother went on, "I'd druther have you all growed up and gone than not growed up a' tall."

I felt a pang in my heart. Oh, poor Mother. I chewed on my bottom lip, wishing I could find words to comfort her. It had only been three months since the death of little Charles Alton, and of course, Mother was still mourning, just as we all were.

After a moment of silence, Mother said quietly, "I remember last summer on a night just like this one." Her voice sounded faraway and dreamy—not at all like her usual no-nonsense tone. "I was sittin' out here with Charles Alton layin' up against my chest, just a-swingin' to and fro. Poor little'un. He'd got a-hold of a crab apple while I was takin' down the wash that afternoon, and by the time I saw what he was up to and got it away from him, he'd et half of it. Law, that boy was sicker than an old hound dog that night. I reckon his belly was achin' something fierce. So, I rocked him in that swing and he finally fell asleep. Just tired to the bone, he was." She fell silent.

I waited a moment before responding. Mother and Daddy were like most older folks around these parts. They only spoke when they had something to say, and when they had something to say, they took their time saying it. So I waited, even though what I wanted to do most was walk over to that swing, sit down and wrap my arms around my mother and tell her how much I loved her. But that kind of emotion just wasn't something folks did around here. Why, they'd probably think I was dying or something.

"I remember sittin' there holding him, not thinkin' about anything in particular, jus' enjoyin' his warm little body against me, listenin' to his breathin.' He still smelled like a baby, not a little boy. I remember thinkin' how peaceful it was out here now that he'd fallen off to sleep. And then, somethin' queer happened. I got this shivery feelin'…the kind that loosens up your bowels and makes you feel like somebody is walkin' over your grave. I wonder now if it was the second sight, warnin' me about what was gonna happen…warnin' me to enjoy the time I had left with him."

Moments ticked by in silence. I searched for a reply that would give Mother comfort but came up empty. I glanced up at the moon, shining like a big silver dollar in the sky, then looked out toward the pond, glimmering in its light.

And suddenly I knew what to say. "Mother, come down to the pond with me. Let's sit on the wharf and put our feet in the water."

When there was no response, I felt a flicker of disappointment. What an idiot I was for even suggesting such a thing. Why, Mother probably thought I was as crazy as a Junebug!

But then the swing stopped creaking and I glanced over to see the slight silhouette of her approaching. The light from the moon crossed her face as she paused at my side, softening the fine lines etching her mouth and forehead and revealing a twinkle in her eyes. "I think that's a right fine idea, Lily Rae." She started down the rickety steps of the front porch.

Minutes later, the two of us sat on the end of the wharf, our bare feet splashing in the cool water. I grinned, imagining the bullfrogs glaring at us from the shadowed edges of the pond, probably madder than wet hens because humans had invaded their space. I leaned back on the palms of my hands, feeling the rough boards of the wharf still warm from the day's sun, and gazed up at the moon. Then I looked around at our land, feeling my heart brimming with love for this place, my home.

"I'm scared, Mother," I said suddenly. "About leaving. Maybe it's all wrong. Maybe I should stay right here in Russell County where I belong."

Mother didn't speak for a long moment, but just stared up at the moon, a placid look on her face.

Just as I was beginning to think she was lost in her own thoughts and hadn't even heard me, she said softly, "How do you know where home is, child, if you never left it?"

My brows furrowed. "I don't
understand." I wanted to go on to say that that
didn't make one bit of sense, but I respected my
mother too much to sass her.

Art Credit: Jim Miller

She turned and looked at me. "You know how
old I was when I married your daddy? 13. One day
I was wearing pig-tails and playing Cowboys-and-
Injuns with my brothers, and the next day, I was
wearin' a weddin' dress and going home with a man
I barely knew. I never had no chance to go out and
see the world. I was born right here in Russell
County, and this is where they'll bury me when my
time comes.

I ain't complainin'...I'm just statin' the truth.
But you, Lily Rae..." To my surprise, Mother
reached out and placed a hand on my knee, giving it
a gentle squeeze. "You have a chance to get out
there and make somethin' of yourself. Why, you can
learn to drive a car." She shook her head wistfully.
"I always thought I'd enjoy drivin' a car," she added
softly.

Well, why don't you learn, I started to say. But I didn't get the chance as Mother went on, "You can go to a job every day and bring home your very own pay check. Imagine that! Why, wouldn't that be a sight? A check made out to Lillian Rae Foster? And who knows? If you get yourself a nice secretarial job up there in Louieville, you might even get to go on a business trip someday to some fancy place like New York City. You might get to ride on one of them airplanes, wouldn't that be somethin'?"

I stared at my mother, amazed. Maybe it was a trick of the moonlight but she looked almost like a teenager sitting there with her feet in the water and her eyes dancing with what could only be excitement. Why, I'd never imagined in a million years that Mother thought about such things! She'd always seemed like she was perfectly happy with her life here in Opal Springs.

"Maybe you *do* have the second sight," I finally said. "I had a dream tonight about the Empire State Building." I looked down into the pond, sending the water rippling with my feet. "But I just don't know about going up to Louieville, Mother. I've never been away from ya'all before...not more than a night, and...well, I'm just gonna miss everybody."

"Of *course* you're gonna miss us," Mother snapped. Then she added in a softer tone, "I reckon we'll miss you, too, child. But that's no reason not to spread your wings and fly." She looked up and fastened her gaze on the moon. "You see that there moon? That's what my great-grandmother called a shepherd moon. You see how that dark shadow looks like a shepherd? See the hook he carries to grab his lost sheep? There's some folks that believe the scriptures got it wrong when they said the wise men were led to the baby Jesus by a star. In my family, story was that it wasn't a star a'tall, but a big old yeller moon like that'un. And that shepherd moon led them home to Jesus."

Mother fell silent again, and I didn't know if that meant she was done with her story, or just thinking about what she wanted to say next. An owl hooted in the night, its lonesome call echoing down from the ridge. It brought tears to my eyes.

Lord, I was going to miss this place.

"Trust in the shepherd moon, Lily Rae," Mother said. "Nobody gets out of this life without pain, but if you trust in the shepherd moon, it'll always lead you home. Maybe not to *this* home where we're sittin' right now, but your real home. The one that's inside your heart."

I still didn't understand what Mother was trying to tell me, but I felt comforted, anyway. How odd, I thought, that although she'd always been kind and patient and even loving in her reserved way, we'd never had a good conversation like this before. One that seemed so...woman-to-woman. It made my heart ache with love, but with sadness, too, because we'd waited until my last night at home to have such a talk.

"So...you really think I'm doing the right thing in leaving?" I asked.

Mother stared out over the pond. "I reckon if you don't get out there and try something new, you might just regret it the rest of your life."

But what about Jake, I thought. *What if I lose Jake?*

Suddenly I wanted desperately to tell Mother about Jake, about how much I loved him. I almost believed she'd understand. If she'd felt the same about Daddy, if she'd grown to love him like I loved Jake--which, surely she had, because, after all, she'd had five children with him—surely, she'd

71

understand. Would she remember what young love felt like? That beautiful, giddy feeling that made your head spin, your heart race and that, sometimes brought you to tears for no reason at all?

I took a deep breath, trying to figure out how to begin. At that moment, a ghostlike cloud slipped in front of the moon, darkening the summer night.

Mother heaved a sigh and drew her feet out of the water. "It's late. I reckon you and me better hit the hay. Got to get up with the sun tomorrow."

And the moment was gone.

CHAPTER SEVEN

**September 1952
Louisville, Kentucky**

The clacking of typewriters sounded like a bunch of lovesick cicadas ratcheting up for a long night of courting. I kept my eyes on the hand-out clipped to the stand at the side of my Royal typewriter, and cautiously pecked on the keys.

"Now is the time for all good men to…"

Around me, the other typewriters sounded like they were going a thousand times faster than mine. All the other girls were experts already, I thought, chewing on my bottom lip. My typewriter dinged as it approached the margin, and I slammed the carriage to the left, then continued to type. I reached the end of the paragraph and rolled up the paper so I could read what I'd typed.

Now os rhe rme gor a;gii ,et t'k;

I slumped in my chair. Darn! I'd done it again. Why couldn't I keep my dratted fingers on the right dadburned keys? Oh, this was impossible!

I clenched my teeth, trying to hold back a frustrated groan. Dadgummit, I was just *awful* at this! Whatever had made me think I could be a secretary, anyhow? It wasn't turning out at all the way I'd imagined.

I furtively glanced around at the other girls. They all seemed to be doing just fine. Their long, slender fingers were tapping on the keys, so elegantly, so *effortlessly*, like they were already professional secretaries instead of students.

I sighed, and my thoughts drifted to home. What was Mother doing right now? It was almost ten o'clock on a Thursday morning. Maybe she'd be putting up apple butter for the winter, which meant she'd probably be frying up some of her scrumptious apple turnover pies. My mouth watered, and I swallowed hard, wincing at the scratchiness in my throat that had been with me since I'd got up this morning. I sure hoped I wasn't coming down with a cold. That would be just perfect! Trying to type, and having to stop every few minutes to blow my dratted nose.

My mind strayed back to Mother's fried apple pies. Oh, what I wouldn't give to have a bite of one of them right now. Aunt Jenny was a good cook, but she didn't make down home recipes like Mother did.

Home.

To my horror, tears blurred my vision as the ache of homesickness surged through my chest, as it had almost every day since I'd left Russell County. I might as well just face it; I didn't belong up here in the city. And I'd known it from the very beginning.

Oh, the first few days had been exciting, with Aunt Jenny driving me all around Louieville, going to lunch in restaurants as fancy as the ones in the movies, and shopping at big department stores like JC Penney's and Grant's. It had been an adventure at first. But as soon as school started, everything changed.

The other girls were so different from me. They were mostly city girls and they wore nice clothes and perfect hairdos and seemed so worldly and...*sophisticated!*

From the very beginning, I'd felt like an outsider, and that hadn't changed now that we were in our second week of training. During the breaks, the other girls clustered together as if they'd been friends forever, chatting about the same kind of things my friends in high school had talked about—boyfriends, movie idols, nail color shades. But not one of them had approached me. And I, who'd always been so popular and outgoing back at Russell County High School, had found myself too shy to make the first move. So, I'd spent the breaks alone, sipping stale coffee from a paper cup and pretending to be interested in the latest copy of **Life Magazine** in the break room.

I inserted a new sheet of paper into the typewriter, and placing my fingers carefully on the correct keys, began to type slowly. Once I fell into a rhythm, my mind began to wander again. This time, to Jake.

My heart twinged. Was he working at the gas station this morning? Or was he still home in bed after a night of drinking with his buddies? My fingers froze on the keys. Maybe drinking wasn't *all* he was doing at night. Had he found some other girl to take my place? Look how quickly Chad had replaced me with Pat-Peaches. Mightn't Jake do the same thing?

The thought filled me with despair, and for a moment, I wanted to shove the typewriter to the floor, jump up and run out of this place as fast as my feet could carry me. This secretarial training wasn't worth losing Jake for, that was for sure.

But it's only for a few weeks, the logical part of my brain reminded me. *And you're going to need a good job if you and Jake end up getting married, with him working at the gas station and all.*

Not that Jake had ever said anything about marriage. It was only a matter of time before that happened, of course. All summer long we'd been doing the things married couples do, and Jake knew I'd only do that with the man I'd marry someday. So, it would happen, and once we were married, we'd both have to work if we wanted to live in a place of our own. Why, I'd just die if me and Jake had to live with my parents...or even worse, *his* parents.

With that horrible thought spurring me on, I began to type a little faster, casting a glance down to make sure my fingers were still on the right keys. A sudden rapping of a ruler against a desk drew my gaze to the black-haired woman in the front of the class.

"Okay, Ladies," called out Miss Lenora Fines, the typing instructor, a tall, sharp-boned woman with Joan Crawford eyebrows and a slash of crimson lipstick on her too-wide mouth. "Let's take a ten-minute break."

The ultimate Old Maid, I thought, every time I looked at her. I'd bet a dime to a donut the poor old thing was still a virgin.

The other girls were all getting up from their desks, smoothing manicured hands down fashionable pleated wool skirts and chattering to each other as they filed out of the room on stiletto heels. I moved slower, wishing I had the self-confidence the other girls had. Why couldn't I be the Lily I'd been in high school—the vivacious, fun-loving girl that everyone adored? Why did these girls make me feel so inadequate?

When I walked into the break room, all the other girls had formed into their own little groups and were already engrossed in conversations. I wandered over to the big stainless steel urn of coffee, not really wanting any, but feeling like I needed to find something to do with my hands so I wouldn't look like a total idiot. Besides, maybe the hot liquid would feel good on my increasingly sore throat.

Someone had brought in doughnuts, I noticed, as the dispenser gurgled black, military-strength coffee into my paper cup. They were big and greasy-looking, but I decided to try one, anyway. Maybe a doughnut would get the taste of Mother's fried apple pies out of my brain. I grabbed one in a napkin and headed over to my favorite spot by the window that looked out over the Ohio River. Munching on the doughnut, I stared at the river, half-listening to the conversation of the nearest group of girls discussing the movies they'd seen the past weekend.

"You've got to go see 'Monkey Business,' Susie. Marilyn's hairstyle is just *crazy*! I've already made an appointment with my beautician, and I'm taking in her picture from the latest **Photoplay**. Do you think I should go blonder?"

I took a sip of bitter coffee. Now, *here* was the perfect opportunity to go over to those girls and get to know them. Aunt Jenny had taken me to the matinee on Saturday, and we'd seen that very movie. I hadn't particularly thought Marilyn's shorter hairstyle was all that attractive, but I could pretend I'd liked it. Making friends here would be worth one little white lie.

I swallowed the bite of doughnut I'd just taken, resolving to do just that. But just as I took a step toward the girls--all of them beautiful, three of them blonde, one, a redhead--the room began to tilt and shrink in size. My blood pounded in my ears and an unnatural heat ignited deep within my body like a wood stove fired up for a cold winter's night. My Peter Pan collar suddenly felt like it was shrinking around my neck, making it difficult to breathe; my vision swam.

It's like a dream, I thought, like I was looking through one of those telescopes in astronomy class back in high school. I saw the four girls turn as if in slow motion to look at me. I opened my mouth and tried to say something but couldn't quite form the words. The room was spinning now, like the colorful top Santa Claus had brought me one Christmas when I was little. I felt like I was riding on it. Through the shrinking hole of my vision, I saw the pretty redhead's ruby lips move, murmuring something I couldn't hear. Her brown eyes were full of concern.

I stumbled toward her, reaching out for help. That was the last thing I remembered before everything went black.

CHAPTER EIGHT

I awoke to a blissful coolness on my forehead and gentle fingers brushing damp hair away from my hot face. For a moment, I lay still, my eyes closed, giving myself up to the comfort of familiar, loving hands, so glad to be back home where I belonged, where I was loved, where I was special. I smiled and whispered, "Oh, Mother, I've missed you so much."

The cool, motherly hand adjusted the wet cloth on my forehead, and then gently stroked my cheek. "It's Jenny, hon. How are you feeling?"

I opened my eyes and saw my aunt's pretty, oval face. Her blue eyes—the most beautiful color of blue I'd ever seen—were filled with worry. As I realized I wasn't home at all, but still here in Louieville with my aunt and uncle, I had to bite my lip to hold back tears.

"Oh, sweetie, don't cry," said Aunt Jenny, fussing with the blanket, tucking it up around my shoulders. "You've just got an old flu bug, Dr. Sullivan says. A little bed rest and lots of liquids, you'll be up and about before you know it."

So, that explained the sore throat. I moistened my dry lips with my tongue then rasped, "If it's just the flu, then why do you look so worried?"

Two splashes of color appeared on my aunt's English porcelain cheeks, and she averted her gaze, giving my arm a pat. "We'll talk later. Right now I'm going to go make you some chicken soup. It'll help you get your strength back."

She bustled out of the room.

I looked around, still half-dazed. When had we come back to Aunt Jenny's house? I vaguely remembered lying on a sofa in the office of the Simpson School. And then Aunt Jenny had arrived. We'd driven somewhere in her car...not back to her house. Not at first. I remembered a kind-eyed old man with white hair and a white coat. Of course! Aunt Jenny had said we'd been to the doctor.

I closed my eyes and gave a relieved sigh. Well, that was it, then. If I was down with the flu, I'd never be able to make up the lost time at the Simpson's. There was nothing to do now but go on back home. Right back to where I belonged.

I smiled, thinking of Mother's story of the shepherd moon. Well, I'd followed her advice. I'd gone out into the world and tried it out. Given it a chance. But that old shepherd moon was leading me right back home.

Right back to Jake—just where I wanted to be.

***

Aunt Jenny had been acting strange all week. It wasn't anything I could put my finger on exactly. Like a few minutes ago when she'd brought in a steaming bowl of Campbell's tomato soup and placed it on the TV tray where I'd been having my lunch since I'd felt well enough to move from the bedroom to the living room sofa. Aunt Jenny's face had looked a million miles away. I'd had to ask her twice for an RC Cola before she'd even responded with a distracted "I'll get it directly," and then hurried out of the room, gnawing on her bottom lip.

It was a dark, rainy Tuesday afternoon, five days after I'd come down with the flu. I was feeling much better, thanks to my aunt's gentle pampering. Glancing out at the rain pelting against the window, I shivered, glad to be snuggled up in a warm blanket on the sofa, and not out in the dank weather like Uncle Virgil, who worked at an insurance agency downtown, but spent a lot of his time driving to appointments around town.

I looked back at the television screen where a box of laundry detergent with legs and high heels danced across the screen. Lordy, I was going to miss TV when I got back home. Not even Katydid's rich parents had one of these new-fangled boxes that broadcasted entertainment right into the living room. In a few minutes, "Search for Tomorrow," would be on. It was a serial I'd got caught up in during my recuperation, and Lord, it was a good show. Just full of twists and turns and handsome doctors and nurses, and best of all, *forbidden love.* They sure knew how to tell a good story! Wouldn't it be just the greatest thing in the world to be able to write stories like that? And to think, people got *paid* for doing it. Now, *that* would be a fine way to make money, a million times better than being a secretary.

The idea flickered across my mind, and I paused with my soup spoon halfway to my mouth. I could *do* it! Why, I'd been writing stories since I was in primary school. Not many of late, of course. Life had been too busy these past four years, what with high school being so much fun and all. But that's what I could do now that I was laid up with this flu. I'd write a book—my own soap opera, but unlike "Search for Tomorrow," mine would have an ending—a happy ending. I grinned and began to eat my soup faster. Aunt Jenny stepped into the room, a bright gold-metallic aluminum tumbler in her hand. I looked up and smiled. "Guess what, Aunt Jenny?"

My aunt placed the tumbler on my TV tray. "Here's your RC, hon."

"Thanks. Aunt Jenny, I just had the best idea…" My voice trailed away as I registered the grave look on her face. "What's wrong?"

Aunt Jenny stood in the middle of the living room, staring at me.

Strange, her face was without its usual warm smile. In fact, it looked a little pale. I hoped she wasn't catching the flu from me.

"Are you feeling sick, Aunt Jenny?" I asked fearfully. "I've been trying hard not to cough in your direction."

Aunt Jenny shook her head, and then glanced at the TV where the opening credits of "Search for Tomorrow" were in progress. "Can I turn off the television for a few minutes, hon? We need to talk."

"But 'Search for…'" I began to protest, but then I saw the tightening of her jaw, and my stomach dipped. Never in my life had I ever seen such a stern look on Aunt Jenny's face. What on earth was wrong with her?

"This is more important than a TV show," she said. She walked to the television set and turned the knob. Like water circling down a drain, the screen blackened, leaving only a white spot in the center, accompanied by a magnetic hum before disappearing altogether. My aunt turned back to me, her lips set in a thin, grim line.

Oh, Lord, I thought. *What have I done wrong?* And then it hit me. Maybe I'd worn out my welcome here. Maybe Aunt Jenny was just sick and tired of having to wait on me since I'd been down with the flu. The poor woman had been fetching and cleaning and dosing me with aspirin and fixing me treats for three or four days now. No wonder she was sick to death of it.

Aunt Jenny sat down in an armchair across from the sofa and nervously smoothed out the folds in her full skirt. Her gaze darted around the room, looking everywhere, it seemed, except at me. The color in her cheeks was high as if she'd dipped too heavily into the rouge pot. I opened my mouth to make it easy for her and volunteer to leave, but before I could utter a word, she spoke, "Lily Rae, you know I love you with all my heart. You've been like a daughter to me, and if I could have a daughter, I'd want her to be just like you, you know that."

I nodded, drawing the blanket closer around me as the rain pounded on the tin roof. It was something that nobody ever talked about, the fact that my aunt and uncle couldn't have any children of their own. Lord knows that Aunt Jenny would've made a wonderful mother, but for some reason, they hadn't been blessed that way.

Aunt Jenny sighed and looked out the window at the dreary weather. "Oh, dear. I just don't know how to say this."

"It's okay, Aunt Jenny," I said. "I think it's time I should go home, too. We could call Sylvie Mae Blankenship, and have her get a message to Daddy to come get me this weekend."

"What?" Her surprised eyes connected with mine. Then understanding dawned. "Oh, *no*, honey! That's not it at *all!* I love having you here. I get lonely during the day when Virgil is at work. No, it's just..." She closed her eyes, took a deep breath then met my gaze. "Lily, the doctor told me you're...expecting."

I stared at her blankly. "Expecting what?"

The color in her cheeks deepened. She took a deep breath and said, "A baby, Lily. You didn't realize?"

I blinked. My aunt's words lingered in the silence, pounding through my head like a heartbeat. *A baby...a baby...a baby.*

No. Jenny had to be mistaken. It couldn't be true. After that first time, Jake had used a rubber. Every time. Well, *almost* every time. There had been that one stormy afternoon in his daddy's hay-loft. Could I have been so unlucky?

I shook my head and murmured, "No, it's not possible."

But my mind raced as I tried to remember when I'd last had a visit from my monthly course. It hadn't been since I'd arrived in Louieville, and I'd been here just over three weeks. Then I remembered, and an icy coldness swept over me. I'd been on my period over the fourth of July. I knew that because a bunch of kids from school had planned a day of swimming and picnicking at Lake Cumberland, and I'd been disappointed because I couldn't go in the water, and had ended up skipping the whole thing.

But in August, my period hadn't come. I hadn't really been concerned because when I'd mentioned my lateness to Daisy, she'd told me she'd read somewhere that major life changes and stress could interfere with the female workings of the body. And for sure, I'd been under a lot of stress in August, preparing to leave home.

But it hadn't come again this month...

I swallowed the acrid taste of fear in my mouth and began to tremble. Aunt Jenny was staring at me, her face the color of the elaborately-dressed porcelain dolls encased in a curio cabinet in the corner of the living room.

"Honey," she said gently. "You know I'm not going to judge you. I want to help you if I can."

At her sympathetic tone, I burst into ragged sobs, covering my face with shaking hands. "Oh, my God! *No*! It can't be true! It just *can't*!"

In an instant, Aunt Jenny was beside me on the sofa, drawing me into her arms. I clung to her in desperation as the horror of the situation sank in. I imagined the stunned, disbelieving faces of my parents. The shame and condemnation in their eyes. Then I thought of Landry and what his reaction would be. I cried harder, burying my face in my aunt's floral-scented shoulder. Somewhere in my consciousness, I heard her murmuring words meant to comfort. But there were no words that could change the facts. That could make it all go away.

I was a girl in trouble. I was a *bad* girl who'd done bad *things*…and got caught.

I wanted to die. I might as well *be* dead, I thought frantically, a new wave of grief shuddering through my body. I *would* be dead to my family. They'd disown me. Especially once they found out it was Jake who'd got me into trouble.

"Lily Rae, hush, now. It's not the end of the world, and you're not alone." Aunt Jenny rubbed my back. "Sweetie, listen to me. I'm here for you, and you're going to get through this. I promise you."

I drew away and looked at her through my tears. "They're going to hate me, Aunt Jenny. Oh, my God! *Mother*! What will she say? What will she think about me? How will she ever be able to go to town again with her head high after what I've done?"

Jenny brushed damp hair away from my face. "Your mother doesn't have a mean bone in her body. I've never known her to judge a soul. And there's nothing you could *ever* do, Lily Rae, that would make her stop loving you."

I shook my head as fresh tears welled in my eyes. *Landry!* Oh, how ashamed he was going to be of me. His sheer goodness made my wickedness even worse. How would he ever be able to look at me again? And Daddy. As religious as he was, he'd probably call me the spawn of Satan. And what would Norry think? Norry, who idolized me. Who thought I could do nothing wrong. I began to cry harder, burying my face against Aunt Jenny's motherly shoulder.

"You're not the first girl to get in the family way," she murmured, stroking my hair.

I pulled away to meet her gaze. "Yeah, we all know what kind of girls get in the family way, don't we? Bad girls. *Evil* girls."

Jenny gazed at me steadily. "It happened to me. Do you think *I* was an evil girl?"

My mouth fell open.

She nodded. "Yes. I was pregnant when Virgil and I got married. And just like you, when I found out, I was scared and didn't know where to turn."

"What did you do?" I whispered, still reeling from her admission. How was it possible? Aunt Jenny was so good. So sweet and…well, it was just hard to believe that she and Uncle Virgil had…done stuff like that before they were married.

"When I missed my period, I went to my older sister, Carla. She took me to her doctor, and when we got the news, she went with me to tell my parents."

"And it was awful, wasn't it?"

Aunt Jenny nodded. "It wasn't fun. But I knew it wouldn't stop them from loving me, and it didn't. But that's why Virgil and I ended up at the justice of the peace before he shipped off to the Pacific."

"But then..." I began. My voice trailed off.

Aunt Jenny nodded, her blue eyes misting over. "I miscarried. It happened four times before they told me I'd never be able to carry a baby to term."

I bit my bottom lip. It wasn't fair. Jenny, who'd be the most perfect mother imaginable, was denied a baby, while I...*oh, God.* I was too *young* to be a mother! Life was just starting for me. How could God be so *cruel?*

Well, don't you deserve it? This is what you get for sinning. You should've known you wouldn't get away with it.

"But let's get back to you," Aunt Jenny said, drawing an embroidered handkerchief from her pocket and daintily dabbing at her eyes. "I heard you were dating a boy in your class. Is he the father?"

I shook my head, still hearing the harsh voice of my conscience snarling at me. "We broke up last spring. It's somebody else." My jaw tightened as I forced myself to meet my aunt's gaze. "I love him, Aunt Jenny."

She nodded, and some of the tension seemed to leave her eyes. "Well, that's good. That'll make it easier on everybody."

I wished I could believe her. But when my family found out I was going to have a baby, and worse, that Jake Tatlow was the father...well, it was going to be hell on earth.

Then an even worse thought occurred to me. When Daddy found out what Jake had done to me, he might just grab a shotgun and go after him. Look what had happened when he'd caught me playing house with him in the woods.

My stomach spasmed at the thought. If only there was a way I could talk to Jake. Warn him. If I could tell him first...

In my mind, I saw the two of us standing in front of Scoot Clyde, Russell Spring's Justice of the Peace. Jake would be wearing his Sunday best, and I'd be in a white suit, holding a bouquet of lilies. They were my namesake flowers, and I didn't care if some people thought they were flowers meant for a funeral, not a wedding.

Jenny gave my arm a reassuring pat. "I'll talk to Virgil tonight, and if you're feeling up to it on Saturday, we'll take you home, and I'll stay with you while you tell your folks...if you want me to."

"*No!*" My protest sounded abnormally loud, even with the drumming of rain on the roof.

Aunt Jenny stared at me in shock. "Well, if you don't want me to..."

"Not that." I shook my head emphatically. "I *can't* tell my folks. Not until I've had a chance to talk to Jake first. Aunt Jenny, do you know how old you have to be to get married without your parents' permission?"

"I think 18 is still the legal age in Kentucky," she said slowly. "Do you think the father...this Jake...will marry you?"

I didn't hesitate. "Of course. He loves me. We've loved each other ever since we used to play together out near Tucker Creek when we were younguns. Otherwise, I would never have..." My cheeks grew hot, and I looked down, tracing a finger over a blue velvet patch of the crazy-quilt Aunt Jenny's mother had made. "...let Jake take liberties with me."

Take liberties. What an odd way to describe the delicious way he'd made me feel with his touch. Even now, knowing the trouble I was in because of those forbidden pleasures, I couldn't wish it hadn't happened.

"Lillian?"

My head shot up at the odd tone of Aunt Jenny's voice. And she never called me Lillian! My aunt was staring at me, her face white. "Are you telling me *Jake Tatlow* is the father of your baby?" The shocked whisper hung in the air between us.

Anger swept through me. I'd always thought Aunt Jenny was an angel on earth, but apparently, she was just as shallow as everybody else, judging Jake because of his name. Tatlow. It might as well have been Low-down Trash.

Defiantly, I met her gaze. "Jake is my baby's father. And I'm not a bit ashamed of loving him. Maybe it was wrong to do things with him without being married. I might be ashamed of that, but I'm not ashamed of loving him. He might be a Tatlow, but he's not trash. And if you knew him like I do, you'd know that."

Aunt Jenny's expression softened. "Oh, honey. I didn't mean that to come out like it did. I was just...surprised." She reached out and gave my hand an absent-minded squeeze, her dark brows furrowed in thought. "Maybe you're right," she said finally. "Talk to Jake first. If he'll marry you, it'll make it easier to break the news to your folks."

"He will," I said confidently, feeling a sudden calm settled over me. "He loves me."

He loves me as much as I love him. And because of that, he'll love the baby we created. And everything will be just fine.

CHAPTER NINE

Jake was wearing his Gulf cap, which meant only one thing. His boss, Slim Jessup, was inside the station. I chewed on my bottom lip and watched from across the street as he leaned over the hood of a blue Packard and cleaned the windshield, his bare forearms gleaming golden in the afternoon sun against the rolled-up cornflower-blue sleeves of his uniform shirt.

My heart pounded beneath my sleeveless cotton blouse. It was still hot in central Kentucky this third week of September, and my underarms were slick with perspiration. But maybe that wasn't because of the heat. It was nervousness. Now that the moment was at hand, and I was about to tell Jake he was going to be a father, a niggling doubt had crept into my mind. Maybe his reaction wouldn't be what I hoped for, what I'd imagined.

I watched as Jake finished cleaning the windshield of the Packard and pocketed the bills handed to him. As the car pulled away, he saluted the driver with a forefinger to the brim of his cap, grinning in the way that always made my heart beat faster.

I took a deep breath. It was time to bite the bullet. To take the bull by the horns. To get the show on the road...there must be a million clichés to choose from, but they all boiled down to one thing. It was time to act. If I didn't do it now, Aunt Jenny would be back to get me before me and Jake had a chance to decide what to do. Ten minutes ago she'd dropped me off down the street once we'd driven past to see if Jake was working.

Steeling myself, I looked both ways, and then crossed the street. Jake was already halfway to the station office. I knew I had to catch him before he went inside. Slim Jessup knew everybody in Russell County, and was a worse gossip than any old busybody. His shaggy white eyebrows would shoot sky-high if he heard me talking to Jake. And then it would be all over town before the sun came up that Lily Rae Foster was canoodling with Jake Tatlow.

"Hey, Jake, wait up!" I called out, hurrying to catch up with him.

He turned, and my heart lifted at the way his eyes lit up when he caught sight of me. A smile of pure delight crossed his face. "Hot *damn*! Is it really you, Lily Rae, or am I dreaming?"

Suddenly it didn't matter if the whole world saw us. Euphoria swept through me. I ran up and threw my arms around him, burrowing my face into his sweat-dampened shirt, breathing in the heady scents of gasoline, motor oil and healthy male. "Oh, Jake! I've missed you so much!"

His big, oil-stained hands had automatically tightened on me, but now, as if he'd suddenly remembered we were standing out in the middle of the Gulf station parking lot in Russell Springs on a busy Saturday afternoon, he pushed me away and stepped back. "*Lord*, Lily! Ain't you always the one to say we have to be careful not to be seen together?"

I grinned at him, blinking back tears. "I know. But it's just so good to see you. It feels like it's been years since I went away."

He glanced uneasily at the door to the office. "I thought you weren't coming back until the middle of

October." He took off his cap and ran a tanned hand through his rumpled, damp hair.

My pulse quickened. Oh, how I loved Jake's hands, so slender, yet strong. But when I realized he was waiting for an answer to his question, my smile faltered. "Well…that's why I'm here. To tell you that I quit school. And the reason why…" My voice trailed off. I looked down at the grease-stained asphalt, my cheeks flaming. *How did you go about breaking news like this? Just come right out and say it?*

"Yeah? I'm listening."

I let out a tremulous breath and lifted my head. "Jake, I found out something while I was in Louieville." My cheeks were on fire, and the way he was looking at me told me he'd noticed.

A lazy grin crossed his face; his blue eyes began to glow like they did when he was touching me in secret places. "What was that, Lily Rae? You found out you missed me?" His voice lowered to a seductive rasp, "You found out you missed having a man lovin' on you, didn't you?"

The heat intensified on my face. "Jake, this is *serious!*"

He sobered. "Okay, so what is it you found out?"

The door to the station office opened, and a fat man in a Gulf uniform identical to Jake's lumbered out, his pudgy fist wrapped around a bottle of Dr. Pepper. His eyes, like blue marbles stuffed into a rising batch of biscuit dough, shot from me to Jake, then back again.

"Why, Lily Rae Foster! What brings you around these here parts?" Slim Jessup bellowed. "Heard tell you was up in Louieville going to sec-a-tery school."

I stared at the gas station owner, and couldn't think of one intelligent thing to say.

Jake came to my rescue. "She was just tellin' me her daddy is stalled up the road a-piece in that old Chevy of his. I told her I'd go take a look, and see if I can get it runnin' again."

Slim took a long swig from his Dr. Pepper, then scratched his protruding belly and let out a deep, rumbling belch. "Well, I reckon you better get to it then. Take the wrecker jus' in case you can't git it goin'. I told him last week, 'Edson,' I said, 'you need to trade that old junker in and git yerself one of them purty new Buick Skylarks.'"

Jake was already striding toward the wrecker parked at the side of the station. I didn't want to be impolite and walk away while Slim was still talking, but catching my eye, Jake jerked his head in the direction of the wrecker.

"I'll be sure and tell him that, Mr. Jessup," I said hastily, cutting Slim off in mid-sentence as he described all the new colors of the 1953 Skylark. *Jiminy Cricket, you'd think he owned stock in Buick.* "But I'd better be on my way now. Daddy will be fit to be tied if I keep him waiting much longer in this heat." Feeling guilty for the lie, I gave him a wide grin and started after Jake.

"Hey, Miss Lily!" He called after me. "You never did tell me how's come you're here and not in sec-a-tery school up in Louieville!"

I waved and called over my shoulder, "I'll tell you all about it later, Mr. Jessup."

Jake already had the motor running when I climbed into the passenger seat of the wrecker. I barely had the door closed before he put the vehicle in gear, and with a jerk, it began to move.

"Fat bastard," Jake muttered, glancing over his right shoulder before pulling out onto the street.

"He's probably heading down to the **Times Journal** right now to file a report about you being back, and you know, don't you, that he'll tell anybody who'll listen that your pa's car broke down."

I'd already thought of that, but it was out of my hands. Soon, none of that would matter. As we approached the flashing yellow light at the junction of Highway 80 and 127, I saw Aunt Jenny's red Packard convertible heading toward us from downtown. Darn! She was on her way back to the gas station to pick me up!

"Jake, that's my aunt! Stop for a minute; I need to tell her something."

Apparently Aunt Jenny had recognized the Gulf wrecker because she was already slowing down.

"Hey, Aunt Jenny!" I leaned forward to look past Jake.

"Hi, there!" Aunt Jenny flashed a warm smile, but there was an appraising look in her eyes as they swept over Jake.

I knew she was wondering if I'd told him yet, and I gave a slight shake of my head. "Can you pick me up at Grider's in…say, fifteen, twenty minutes?" I silently begged my aunt to understand I needed more time.

Aunt Jenny didn't disappoint me. "Mom needs a few things at the grocery store. I'll come by and get you on the way back." With a friendly wave, she drove off.

Jake let out the clutch and shifted to first. "So, that's your aunt," he said as the truck rumbled down the road. "Good looking woman. Well-preserved for her age. What is she? Thirty?"

"Thirty-two, I think. Did you know she was Miss Russell County at the 1938 county fair?"

"You don't say." Jake released a low wolf whistle as he made the left turn onto Main Street. "I'd sure like to see how *she* looks in a bathing suit."

I gave him a dark look, unable to hide my irritation at the remark. "Uh...that's my aunt you're talking about. Not a calendar pin-up girl."

Jake chuckled, swinging the wrecker into the drug store parking lot. "Hey, you and me might be messing around, but that don't mean I'm dead. You ain't the only pretty gal in the world, you know."

No, but I'm the only one carrying your baby. <u>Better</u> be the only one, anyway.

Jake parked the truck, turned off the ignition and turned to me. "Come here." He pulled me into his arms, his mouth claiming mine.

My bones melted at the hot, sweet thrust of his tongue. I eagerly responded to his kiss, momentarily forgetting we were sitting here in an open truck in a busy parking lot, visible to anyone who happened to look our way. But when his hand cupped my tender right breast over my thin cotton blouse, I wrenched away from him as if I'd been burned.

"*Stop*, Jake! It's because of this that we're in trouble!"

His eyes smoldering, he gave a bemused smile. "Sorry, Lily Rae. It's just that you look good enough to eat in that pretty white blouse. And it's been almost a month since we..." His gaze held mine. "...had some time alone together." His voice vibrated through my body like a quivering guitar string, raising goose bumps on my forearms.

With an effort, I drew my mind back to the reason I was here.

"Jake." I grabbed his hand, the one that was busy tracing up and down my bare arm. "You got to listen to me now. I've got some news that may take a little getting used to."

"Okay. I'm waiting."

I swallowed hard, conscious of the minutes ticking by. How much time had passed since we'd seen Aunt Jenny at the junction? For a moment, I allowed myself to imagine the perfect outcome. In a few minutes, Aunt Jenny would pull into the parking lot next to the wrecker. I'd be nestled in Jake's arms as he tenderly kissed the top of my head. He would be holding me so tightly he wouldn't want to let me go—even for the short drive to the courthouse.

I smiled, watching a dust mote drifting in the air above the dashboard.

Jake snapped his fingers. "*Hey*! Dreamy Eyes!"

I jerked my gaze back to him. "Oh, sorry."

"So, what's the news I'm going to have to get used to? You ain't breaking up with me, are you? You tryin' to tell me you found some city boy up in Louieville?" His cocky grin told me he didn't believe that was the case at all.

The boy is way too sure of me, I thought. And if it weren't for the situation I found myself in, I'd be inclined to take his ego down a notch, and maybe let him think there *was* another boy in the picture. But there was no time for that now.

"I'm going to have a baby," I said.

Jake stared at me, still wearing his cocky grin. His eyes gleamed with the adorable mischief that reminded me of the boy he'd been back in the Tucker Creek days. Later, I'd wonder just how much time had passed before I saw the change come over him.

His grin froze. His ocean blue eyes turned wintry and his hand slackened in mine. I tightened my grip on it, sensing he was going to withdraw it.

"Did I hear you right?" he said quietly. "You said you're going to have a baby?"

I nodded, and the words that had been so difficult to say tumbled out like Cumberland Falls spilling over the boulders. "At first, I thought it was the flu. Well, it *was* the flu, but the doctor did some tests, I guess, and that's when I found out. I don't understand how it happened myself. We used...I mean you used them...what do you call 'em...rubbers, so..." My cheeks burned with embarrassment.

Jake was still staring at me, his grin absent now. Under his tan, his face was the color of dirty bed sheets. I began talking faster, trying to make him understand. "I know the timing is bad, and everybody will talk, and our parents will raise Cain, but Jake, think what it'll mean! No more sneaking around and hiding our love anymore. Aunt Jenny and Uncle Virgil have already said they'll be our witnesses. We can get married Monday morning as soon as the courthouse opens."

I realized Jake was trying to disengage his hand from mine. Tightening my grip, my voice rose with urgency, "I'm sure Aunt Jenny's father will give me my old job back here at the drug store..."

My heart cringed as he wrenched his hand out of mine and turned to face the steering wheel, his jaw clenched, arms folded across his chest. "Jake, don't be like this. It's not the end of the world! We'll save our money until we can afford to rent a little house. I'll ask Mother if we can let Norry sleep in the parlor so you and me can have my room, at least until we get on our feet..."

Tears welled in my eyes. I twisted my hands in my lap to stop myself from clutching at him, pleading with him to...what? Marry me and make an honorable woman out of me? "*Say* something, Jake! Don't just sit there like you're made of stone."

Slowly, he turned and looked at me. Coldness invaded my belly at the expression on his face. Like he was looking at something he'd found on the bottom of his shoe after a stroll through the cow pasture. He stared at me for a long moment while I held my breath, waiting for the words that would kill fantasies of heading over to the courthouse to become Mrs. Jake Tatlow.

Because that's all they were, I realized. Girlish fantasies of love and happy-ever-after. But when the words finally came, I still wasn't prepared for their cruelty.

"How do I know it's mine?"

There was no trace of irony in his tone. Or any feeling at all. But the words sliced through my heart as surely as if he'd used a butcher knife. He waited for my response, his eyes as impersonal as a stranger's.

"How can you ask me that?" I finally managed to whisper. "You were my first. You know that."

"Yeah, well…" He gave an offhand shrug and glanced out his window as a gray Ford pulled up next to us. A lanky boy with a buzz-cut and a cigarette dangling from his mouth got out, his eyes sweeping over us with mild curiosity. He nodded curtly.

Jake responded with a jerk of his chin. He watched the youth saunter into the drugstore. My heartbeat pounded in my ears.

"How do I know," Jake said, still in that terrifyingly calm voice he'd used before, "you weren't out ruttin' in the woods with good old Chad? Maybe once I broke you in, you figured one man wasn't enough for you."

The sound that escaped my throat was one of a wounded animal. I slapped him hard across the face. The red imprint of my hand on his skin sent a surge of satisfaction through me.

It didn't last. Rage flared in his eyes. His right hand closed on my face like a vise. He squeezed, sending shockwaves of pain vibrating through my jaw. He brought his face close to mine and spoke through clenched teeth, "The last time somebody hit me like that, he was picking his teeth up off the ground. You'd better not ever do it again, you hear?"

I nodded frantically through burning tears. Jake's eyes were as hard as concrete. His hand tightened on my jaw. I whimpered, feeling as if my cheeks were going to explode. There would be bruises later, and how would I explain that?

He released me abruptly, a look of disgust on his face. I rubbed my tender jaw, tears running down my cheeks. I was afraid to say anything more, even though every nerve inside me was screaming in outrage that Jake believed I was capable of bedding Chad—or any other man—after I'd pledged my love to him. Instead, I huddled against my door, watching as he took off his cap and tunneled his fingers through his hair.

"Jesus H. Christ," he muttered, staring blankly out the windshield. "How could this have happened?"

I didn't say anything, but a tiny flare of hope ignited in my heart. If he would at least acknowledge he was the father, that would be a step in the right direction.

He looked at me, and the little ray of hope flickered out. There was no love in his eyes—only scorn. "Who knows? Besides your aunt and uncle?"

I shook my head. "No one. I wanted to tell you first. I thought if we went ahead and got married…"

"Aw...*fuck*!" He exploded, digging his fingertips into his temples.

I flinched.

Jake stared grimly out the windshield. "God *damn* it!" He banged his hands on the steering wheel, causing the truck to tremble. "I'm only 19 fuckin' years old!" His gaze skewered me. "And you expect me to tie myself down to a wife and a squalling brat?"

His words were like a physical blow. I placed my palms on my still flat belly as if to protect the fetus inside me and licked my dry lips, knowing I risked reviving his wrath if I spoke, but I had to know. "I thought you wanted to marry me," I whispered, trying desperately to keep my voice neutral. "You said...that first time...you'd been waiting for me to grow up. You talked about when you gave me the ring made out of a twig. You said we'd pledged ourselves to each other way back then..."

His eyes blazed. "*We were fuckin' kids back then!* We didn't have a rat's ass clue about nothing!"

"I'm not talking about Tucker Creek," I said, knowing I was risking his anger, but unable to stay quiet. "I'm talking about the night you took my virginity. Do you think I would've let you do that if I hadn't believed you loved me?"

He remained silent, but his fingers tightened on the steering wheel.

A group of bobby-soxed teenage girls in poodle skirts climbed out of a Chrysler and headed, giggling, into the drug store. I recognized them as juniors from RSHS...no, they'd be seniors now. School had started two weeks ago. I stared after them, feeling like I was a million years older. A year ago, I'd been just as carefree. When had life gotten so serious?

"There's been nobody else, Jake. I love *you*. I could never love anybody but you."

He just stared straight ahead.

My heart sank when I saw Aunt Jenny's car pull into the parking lot. Time had run out. I watched her pull into a space far enough away from the wrecker so she wouldn't invade our privacy, but close enough to make sure I knew she was here.

I looked at Jake. "I've got to go. Do you have anything to say?" I studied his profile, silently begging him to say the words I needed to hear. But he sat rigidly, avoiding my gaze. A muscle twitched in his jaw, the only visible sign of his turmoil.

My hand fastened on the door handle. My heart felt like lead. "I made an agreement with my aunt. She'd let me talk to you before we told my parents. If we was to go to them, man and wife, it would make things easier." My cheeks burned with embarrassment. Oh, how humiliating to have to say words like this; it was tantamount to begging. It should be *him* asking *me* to marry him.

No response.

A tear ran down my cheek. Angrily, I brushed it away and opened the door of the truck. "Okay, then…I guess that's my answer." I gingerly jumped out of the wrecker and slammed the door. Even as I walked away, I kept waiting for his voice, calling me back. But it didn't happen. As I came around to the passenger side of Aunt Jenny's car, I heard the rumble of a motor and glanced back just in time to see Jake pull out of the parking space and onto the road heading toward the junction.

Numb with shock, I slid into Aunt Jenny's car, keeping my eyes averted from her expectant gaze. "Well, what happened?"

I stared glassily out the window, my hands tightening on the rayon material of my circle skirt.

"Let's go home," I said in a flat monotone. "It's time to tell Mother and Daddy."

CHAPTER TEN

"It's okay, Lily Rae, please stop crying."

Norry's plea, meant to be comforting, only made me sob harder.

Nothing was ever going to be okay again.

"Can't you tell me what's wrong? Maybe I can help."

I buried my face in my pillow, trying to smother the bitter, hysterical laugh choking my throat. *Can you turn back time, Norry Jean? That's the only way you can help me.*

She gave my shoulder an awkward pat, momentarily running out of words of comfort. Even though I couldn't see her, I could feel the warmth of her body, curled up on the bed next to me. I could also feel her love and concern. But once Norry knew the awful truth, would she be like everyone else, and treat me like the fallen woman I was?

It had gone much, much worse than I'd ever expected. On the drive back to Opal Springs just as we neared Webb's Cross Roads, terror had engulfed me. I'd pleaded with Aunt Jenny to give Jake some time—at least through the weekend—to do the right thing, but for the first time ever, Jenny had revealed a side of herself that I'd never glimpsed, and it was made of steel. Eyes straight ahead, hands locked on the steering wheel, she'd listened to my pleas without interruption.

When I'd finally run out of words, she turned gentle blue eyes on me and said quietly, "Lily Rae, I promised you I'd be with you while you broke the news. Virgil has to be at work on Monday, so we have to leave first thing tomorrow morning. Now, unless you want to face your mama and daddy alone, you'd best get it over with."

So that's what I'd done. Got it over with.

I shuddered at the memory of those awful moments following my confession, and a new shock wave of grief burst from my aching lungs. Oh, God! I *hurt*. I'd thought my heart was shattered when Chad broke up with me. But that was nothing compared to what I felt now.

Oh, *God*! The looks on their faces would be imprinted on my memory for as long as I lived. There had been no easy way to tell them.

My family had been in the kitchen, just sitting down to supper. Mother was standing behind Daddy, a basket of cornbread in one hand, the black enamel coffee pot in the other. Landry, Edsel, and Norry were busy helping themselves to the food on the table—pork chops, mashed potatoes and creamed corn, I saw. Only Norry looked up when we entered.

"Lily Rae!" she exclaimed, delight crossing her face.

At Norry's excited announcement, Mother's gaze fastened on me and her blue eyes twinkled. "Well, looky who's here." Without missing a beat, she filled Daddy's coffee cup, placed the pot on the stove, and reached into the cabinet for more plates. "Sit yourselves down and have a bite of supper. We got plenty."

"Hey, Lily Rae," Landry said with a grin. "What you doin' back down here?"

"Homesick, ain't you?" Edsel snickered. His freckles looked darker than ever. "I knew you wouldn't stay gone for long."

I tried to speak, but my throat suddenly felt paralyzed.

"Hi, ya'all," Aunt Jenny said. "Lily Rae has something important to talk to ya'all about. But…" Her gaze swept over Norry and the boys. "I think it might be best if we had a few minutes alone with you and Edson, Alpina."

Edsel's mouth opened—to object, I was sure, but a look from Daddy quelled him. Chairs scraped on the pine floor as the boys got up and shuffled out of the kitchen. Norry's saucer-sized brown eyes darted from me to Jenny to our parents as she reluctantly vacated her chair and headed for the door.

Their footsteps thudded up the stairs, Edsel's plaintive grumble trailing behind them, "Doggone it! I'm so hungry my backbone is scraping my belly!"

Two doors closed, the boys with a slam, and Norry's with a milder thud.

"Well, girl?" Daddy spoke gruffly. "What's so important that the younguns couldn't hear?"

I threw Aunt Jenny a panicked look. *I can't do this! I'd rather die!*

As if reading my mind, she grabbed my hand and gave it a reassuring squeeze. She fastened her eyes on Mother and said, "Alpina…Edson…Lily Rae has some…disturbing news. I promised I'd stay with her because this isn't going to be easy for…any of us."

I felt two pairs of eyes turn my way—one dark, the other light. I tried to swallow, but my saliva had run dry. My hands were clenched into fists, nails digging into my palms. I couldn't look directly at Daddy. He sat at the table, a big bear of a man with deep-set brown eyes and sun-weathered skin like tanned leather.

Bowing my head, I stared at the tips of the pretty black pumps Jenny had bought me at JC Penney's just before I'd started school. "I'm in trouble," I said softly.

Moments ticked by in an unearthly silence.

"What sort of trouble, Lily Rae?" Mother's voice sounded unnaturally loud in the kitchen.

I kept my eyes on my shoes. "I'm going to have a baby." The words came out in a soft gush. And then I burst into tears.

Aunt Jenny was right there, holding me, just like she'd said she'd be. I sobbed into her shoulder, terrified of looking at my parents. But in the end, I couldn't not look. I dragged myself away from my aunt, and turned. "Please don't hate me! I'm not a bad person. I just…" I shook my head, tears streaming down my face. "I love him."

Daddy's face was like stone. Only his eyes revealed his emotions—anger, dismay and yes, there it was…shame. And Mother. Her face was white, eyes horrified. She sat stiffly, hands in her lap. And right before my eyes, she seemed to age ten years.

"Who is the boy?" Daddy asked. His voice was emotionless as if he'd just asked if it was raining outside.

I'd thought that once I'd got the words out about my pregnancy, the worst would be over. But now I knew it wasn't. The worst was right now. When I had to tell them who'd got me in this situation.

"Tell them, Lily Rae," Aunt Jenny said, giving my shoulder an encouraging squeeze.

Through a curtain of tears, I looked at my parents as they waited for my answer. Both of them so stoic on the outside, but crumbling on the inside, I knew. So disappointed, so ashamed of me. Panic welled inside me.

How can I break their hearts any more than I already have by telling them Jake is the father?

With one wild, pleading glance at Aunt Jenny, I broke away from her grasp. "I can't do it, Aunt Jenny! I just *can't!*"

And I'd run out of the kitchen and up the stairs to my old room. Sobbing, I'd thrown myself onto the bed next to an astonished Norry. That had been some time ago. I didn't know, or much care, how much time had passed. It didn't matter. Nothing mattered now.

A soft tap came at the door, and I felt Norry scuttle off the bed. I kept my face buried in the pillow, finally spent of tears, but unable to muster the energy to move. I heard the soft murmuring of voices followed by the door closing. There was a rustle of cloth as someone approached. I stiffened. If it was Mother, how could I bear to see the shame and disappointment in her eyes?

"Lily Rae?"

It wasn't Mother, but Aunt Jenny. Bitter disappointment raged through me. I'd wanted it to be Mother. I needed to know that despite everything, she still loved me. That she could forgive me.

The bed shifted as Aunt Jenny sat on the edge of it. "Hon, the worst is over now. Once they get used to the news, they'll come around. They love you, baby. That hasn't changed." My aunt's fingers caressed my hair lovingly. "That will never change."

I summoned the strength to roll over and face her. Her blue eyes were pink-tinged as if she'd been crying, too. "Even after you told them who the father is?" I whispered. "You *did* tell them, didn't you?"

She nodded, pulling one of her lace-edged handkerchiefs out of her pocket and dabbing at my eyes. "I did."

My stomach plunged. So, they knew. "And what did they say?"

Aunt Jenny met my gaze steadily. "Not much. Nothing at all, really." She brushed a curl, damp from my tears, away from my face. "Alpina just got up and started to clear the dishes. I guess she'd forgotten nobody had eaten yet. And your father...well, he went upstairs and came down a minute later with Landry. They got in his car and drove off toward town."

I sat up. "Where do you think they're going?"

"My guess is...to pick up the justice of the peace...and maybe the sheriff." Aunt Jenny gave my hand a pat. "So, if I were you, I'd fix my face, brush my hair, and put on my prettiest dress. This might well be your wedding day."

I stared at my aunt in shock. "No!" I shook my head. "I don't want it to be like this! It *can't* happen like this!"

Aunt Jenny just looked at me sadly. "Honey, I don't think you have a choice."

CHAPTER ELEVEN

I heard the crunch of wheels on gravel outside my opened window, and my heart gave a lurch. My eyes met Aunt Jenny's. For a long moment, neither one of us moved. Then my aunt turned to the door. "I'll go down and find out..." Her voice trailed off as she slipped out of the room.

But I knew what she meant. Had Daddy and the boys come back with Jake? It had been more than an hour since they'd left. Aunt Jenny had gone down to my car and brought up my suitcase, packed with the few outfits I'd taken with me to secretarial school, along with the few she'd bought for me. One of them, I supposed, would serve as a wedding dress.

Tears had rolled down my face as I donned a simply-cut gray linen suit. I'd always imagined wearing a beautiful white gown and a veil of lace on my wedding day. I'd imagined gliding down the aisle of Poplar Grove Baptist Church, carrying a bouquet of white roses and lilies-of-the-valley, perhaps with a tear or two in my eyes as I smiled radiantly at the people I loved. Not so long ago, I'd imagined Jake waiting at the end of the aisle beside the preacher, Brother Joe Bob Riddle, his eyes shining with adoration as I marched to Lettie Sue Cunningham's rendition of "Here Comes the Bride" on the piano.

But then, I reminded myself that dreams like that only came true for good girls. Car doors slammed outside, and I moved to the window to peer out. In the feeble light of a crescent moon, I could just make out four figures walking toward the porch. I caught my breath. That was Jake's devil-may-care gait; I'd recognize it anywhere. He made his way up the porch steps behind my father and another man, followed closely by Landry. I expelled a long, relieved breath. At least they weren't *dragging* Jake into the house.

A flash of headlights at the end of the driveway caught my attention. Now who the blazes was that? The car pulled up behind Daddy's old Chevy, and it was then that I saw the bubble light on the top. My stomach took a dip. It was Burps Dewey, the county sheriff.

My heart began to pound. I turned away from the window and moved woodenly toward my bed. A part of me wanted to rush downstairs and put myself between Jake and our mutual enemies—my family and the law—just in case things should spin out of control. Like every other able-bodied man in these hollows, Daddy had a shotgun, and knew how to use it. But the other part of me—the cowardly part—wanted to crawl into bed and sleep for a hundred years like Rip Van Winkle...or was it Sleeping Beauty?

Downstairs, I heard the deep rumble of male voices. Deciding my future, I supposed. It didn't

seem right. Shouldn't I be down there to have
a say? But then, what *would* I say?

*Marry me, Jake? I don't care whether you love me or
not, just marry me and make an honest woman of me.*

A soft tap came at the door, and I looked up.
The door opened and Aunt Jenny stuck her dark
head into the room. "They're ready for you, Lily
Rae," she said with a gentle smile. But I didn't miss
the worry in her blue eyes.

I ran my hands down my skirt, trying to smooth
out the wrinkles. "Do I look all right?" I asked
Jenny, glancing sideways in the mirror at the dressing
table. The bruises caused by Jake's cruel grasp on
my chin were barely visible after an application of
pancake make-up. I pressed a hand over my flat
tummy. Impossible to believe there was a growing
baby in there. Even now, it seemed unreal.

Aunt Jenny stepped into the room and came
over to me. She grasped my hand, giving it a
squeeze. "Honey, you look beautiful."

I thought I saw a tear glistening in her eye, but
she released me and turned away too quickly for me
to be sure. My heart thudded as I followed her trim
figure down the narrow stairs and into the front
parlor where a crowd awaited us.

With the exception of Norry, they were all
there—Jake, Mother and Daddy, my brothers and
two others—the sheriff and the preacher, Brother
Joe Bob. And all of them—except for
Edsel—looked as if they were at a funeral.

Mother stood near the doorway leading into the
kitchen, poised for flight, it seemed to me. Her
hands were clasped tightly in front of her, her face as
grim as the preacher man's who stood between me
and Jake, holding a well-worn Bible in his tobacco-
stained hands. Brother Joe Bob had been preaching
at Poplar Grove since I was in diapers. My cheeks

grew hot. What he must think of me! Because of course, he *knew*. How could he not?

My gaze darted to Jake. He stood between the preacher and my father, his arms stiff at his sides, his gaze fastened on the tips of his oil-splotched work boots. He still wore his Gulf uniform. Lord, if Daddy had gone down to the station to collect him, it would be all over town by morning.

In the back of the room stood my brothers. Landry kept his gaze averted from me, his body unnaturally stiff. Edsel looked like he was having trouble holding back a smirk. The ornery little scamp was enjoying my misery.

I shifted my gaze to Daddy who stood on Jake's left side like a big, implacable bear, his hound dog-like face glowing mahogany in the lamplight. His dark eyes skewered me, and I saw a multitude of emotion in them. Anger, disgust, disappointment and...yes...heartbreak.

I had to look away. In desperation, my gaze fastened on Jake again. He was still staring at his boots.

Look at me, I willed him. *The only way I can get through this is if I know you're with me. That we're in it together. If we love each other, Jake, we can get through anything.*

And just like that, he lifted his head and looked at me. I swallowed hard. Just as I'd deciphered the range of emotion in Daddy's eyes, I was now able to do the same with Jake. In the depths of his gaze, in those few seconds before he looked away, I saw a combination of fear and shame--and something else I couldn't put a name to.

My father broke the tense silence in the room by clearing the phlegm from his throat. "No sense in puttin' it off, Brother Joe Bob. You can get started now." He gestured to me. "Git on over here, girl, and stand next to your man."

Eyes on the floor, I obeyed. I took a position on Jake's left side, and only then did I find the nerve to look up. My gaze met Aunt Jenny's across the room. She nodded and gave me an encouraging smile.

I knew what she was trying to communicate to me. *This is your wedding day, Lily Rae. Don't let anybody ruin it for you.*

I gave her a tremulous smile. *Thank you.* Out of the corner of my eye, I glanced at Jake, silently urging him to look at me, but he kept his gaze fixed on the floor. Preacher Joe Bob opened the Bible and turned to face us. "Dearly Beloved…" he began.

I began to tremble. Despite Aunt Jenny's heartfelt nod of encouragement, despite my love for Jake, despite the baby growing in my womb, I knew with a sudden clarity that this was all wrong. As the preacher's monotonous words droned through my brain like an annoying bee, I chewed on my bottom lip while hot, liquid panic bubbled up inside me.

"If there's anyone here who objects to this union between Lillian Rae Foster and Jacob Royce Tatlow, let them speak now or forever hold their peace."

Seconds ticked by and there was nothing but cold, unnerving silence in the room. I looked across the room at Aunt Jenny. She stared back solemnly, her upper teeth gnawing at her bottom lip.

A memory flashed across my mind. Another wedding, ten years ago. I'd been only eight, but I remembered it well. Most of all, I remembered the look on Uncle Virgil's face as he slipped the ring on Aunt Jenny's slender finger—adoring, almost worshiping. Like a man in love. Through my eyelashes, I stole a glance at Jake. He was staring at the Bible as if it were a coiled snake.

"Ya'all have rings?" Preacher Joe Bob asked.

Jake looked at me. I stared back at him. I knew intuitively he was thinking about the ring made out of twig he'd placed on my finger when we were children. My heart lifted.

He does love me. Maybe he's not all that excited about getting married so young, but he loves me, and that's what's important.

But then I saw his eyes go dead, and that was when I could finally put a name to the emotion I'd seen earlier. Resignation. My throat tightened, and I had to look away from him or risk bursting into tears and humiliating myself further on this, the most mortifying day of my life.

Daddy spoke up, "Alpina, give me your wedding ring."

Mother hesitated only a moment, and then twisted off the simple gold band she'd worn as long as I could remember. She handed it over to Daddy who gave it to the preacher. He passed it to Jake.

"Do you, Jacob Royce Tatlow, take Lillian Rae Foster as your wedded wife, to have and to hold, for better or for worse; in sickness and in health until death do you part?" As he spoke, Preacher Joe Bob gestured for Jake to put the ring on my finger.

I held out my shaking hand. Keeping his head down, Jake slipped the ring on my finger, and it seemed to me that he was trying his best not to touch me as he did so.

An awkward silence filled the room.

"Son," Preacher Joe Bob said gruffly. "We need an answer."

Jake's head shot up, and a tide of crimson washed over his face. "I do," he mumbled, looking back down.

Where was the cocky boy who'd tricked me into his car on that spring morning—a hundred years ago, it seemed now. This boy standing in front of me certainly bore no resemblance to him at all.

"Do you, Lillian Rae Foster, take Jacob as your lawfully wedded husband…?"

I chewed on my bottom lip and waited through the preacher's monologue, remembering when I used to "play bride" with Daisy when we were just little girls. I'd known this whole speech by heart.

"I do," I whispered when it was time.

The preacher took our joined hands in his. "I now pronounce you Man and Wife." His voice rose in a tone of defiance. "Those whom God hath joined together, let not man put asunder." He dropped our hands, and immediately, Jake released mine.

My body went cold. I felt like I'd been stabbed through the heart.

"You can go ahead and kiss your bride, Jake," said Brother Joe Bob.

I looked at Jake, wondering if he'd humiliate me further by refusing to kiss me. His face seemed redder than before. With his gaze fixed on a point above my hairline, he placed his hands on my shoulders and leaned forward just close enough to brush his mouth against mine. His lips felt like cold marble, not at all like the same lips that had delivered hot, sweet kisses to me throughout the summer.

As he released me, a youthful voice broke the uneasy silence, "Well, if that ain't the most pansy-ass kiss I ever did see! *Ouch!*" Edsel glared at his older brother. "Why'dja hit me for? I was just sayin' what everbody else is thinking!"

Daddy turned to Edsel, his shaggy brows lowered in a menacing scowl. "One more remark like that, and I'll be seeing you in the woodshed, boy. Landry, get him out of here."

But my little brother wasn't one to go without putting up a fight. As Landry grabbed his arm and tugged him toward the front door, the freckle-faced youngster twisted in his grip and shouted, "Ain't nobody gonna tell Lily Rae how we found Jake Tatlow gassin' up his car at the Texaco out Liberty way? He was *skaddaddlin, Lily* Rae*! Ouch!* Dad*burn* it, Landry, quit yer hittin' me!" Edsel probed the back of his head where Landry's wallop had landed. "She's got a right to know, ain't she?" he managed to yell before Landry pushed him out on the front porch.

The door slammed behind them. I looked at Jake, feeling the room tilting around me. He stared down at the floor.

"Is that true?" I whispered.

When he didn't answer, my gaze swept over the others in the room—my mother, my daddy...Aunt Jenny...the preacher...the sheriff, who hadn't spoken a word but whose very presence seemed ominous. No one spoke. But they were all staring at me—Aunt Jenny and Mother with pity in their eyes. Daddy's expression was stone-like, as was Burps Dewey's. Preacher Joe Bob made an attempt to look pious, but I saw the gleam of satisfaction in his beady little eyes. The saintly man of the cloth was enjoying my fall from grace.

Surprisingly, I took strength from his hypocrisy. My jaw lifted. I fixed my eyes on Jake's bowed head.

I might be a sinner and a tramp, but I wasn't a hypocrite.

"The least you can do, Jake Tatlow," I said in a firm, clear voice, "is give me a truthful answer."

Slowly Jake lifted his head. His blue eyes connected with mine, as brilliant as glittering sapphire, and just as hard. "What's done is done," he said finally, and then he turned his head, and looked toward the door with a deliberate stare.

I followed his gaze, and my heart lurched. There, on the floor, rested an old army-green duffle bag stamped with a rank and a name: *Private T.L. Tatlow.* At one time, apparently, it had belonged to Jake's older brother, Tully. But now, there was only one reason it was laying there on the floor of our front parlor.

It had been Jake's getaway bag.

***

After the ceremony, I returned to my room to pack my meager belongings. I hadn't been in there two minutes when a knock came at the door. My heart leapt. What now?

Landry stood there.

The composure I'd regained crumbled again. "Oh, Landry!" Shame settled over me, and I couldn't look him in the eye. What he must think of me! "I'm so sorry," I whispered, gazing miserably down at the floor.

"Hey..." His finger nudged my chin up so I was forced to look at him. "You got it all wrong, Lily Rae. I'm not judging you. I know what it's like to get caught up in..." He flushed and looked away. "...in tender feelings with somebody. It's just that..." Hesitating, he brought his gaze back to mine.

I saw sadness and something like fear in the depths of his soft brown eyes.

His hand tightened on my shoulder. "I don't trust Jake, Lily. His pa is the meanest man in the county. I'll bet he's been whipping that boy since he was knee-high to a grasshopper. What comes around goes around, know what I mean? And it's plain he wasn't exactly jumping up and down to get hitched. I don't want him taking out his anger on you."

"He won't," I said firmly. "You don't know him like I do, Landry. He loves me. It may not look like it, but he does. This all just took him by surprise. Once he gets used to the idea of being married, he'll settle down. I know it."

He nodded slowly, but he couldn't hide the doubt on his face. "I sure hope you're right. Just know, Lily Rae, if you ever need me…for anything. I'm here for you. And that's a promise, little sister."

His words brought grateful tears to my eyes. I should've known Landry wouldn't stop loving me because of the mistakes I'd made. He was way too kind-hearted. I hugged him quickly and then hurried down the stairs, my suitcase in hand.

My new life with Jake had begun.

Glady's Kentucky Soup Beans and Cornbread

2 cups Great White Northern Beans, Soaked
Overnight
4 cups water
1 bay leaf
1 ham hock or other pork
½ teaspoon pepper
1 Tablespoon salt (to be added later)

About 3 hours before supper, bring beans and
other ingredients **except salt** to a boil in a heavy
iron pot. Reduce to Low and simmer for 2 to 3
hours until beans are soft and tender. Add salt and
using a wooden spoon, smash some beans against
side of pot to thicken. Serve hot with cornbread.

Cornbread

1 cup yellow corn meal
1 cup flour
1 teaspoon salt
4 ½ teaspoon baking powder
1/3 cup hot bacon grease or shortening, melted
1 egg
2/3 cup milk

Mix together dry ingredients. In separate bowl,
mix egg and milk. Add bacon grease or melted
shortening. Mix liquid ingredients into dry
ingredients. Stir only until moistened. Drop batter
into generously greased corn pone pan or muffin
tins. Bake at 425 degrees for 25-30 minutes.

CHAPTER TWELVE

"**P**ass the cornbread, Inis," Royce Tatlow ordered through a mouthful of string beans, his dark, mean eyes fixed on the rapidly disappearing food on his plate.

Please, I added silently as a familiar wave of dislike swept over me. I'd never met a ruder man in my life than Jake's father. Or a more ill-tempered one.

Twelve-year-old Inis passed the plate of cornbread pones to her mother then cast her eyes back on her plate and resumed eating. Like Jake, the girl had somehow inherited a natural beauty that was missing in both her parents and her older sister, Meg. She had long, naturally-curly dark brown hair and big, brown doe-eyes. But she was one of the most backward girls I'd ever met, barely speaking a word to anybody, and always keeping her eyes downcast. There would be no ally in her.

Nor in anyone in this house.

I took a bite of Gladys's fried potatoes; they were delicious—crunchy on the top, tender underneath. That was the one good thing about living here with the Tatlows—my mother-in-law could cook like a dream. Not better than Mother, of course, but pretty darn close.

The food was the only thing about suppertime here that reminded me of home, though. Here, the only sounds at the table was of food being chewed—noisily by Royce—the scrape of Gladys's chair against the worn linoleum as she got up to get something Royce wanted but didn't see on the table. No one asked how anybody's day had went or talked about what was going on in the world or even mused about the **Farmer's Almanac's** prediction of a cold winter, and how surely that must be true because the wooly worm's black coat was the thickest I'd ever seen it. No, it wasn't like supper at my home at all.

But the unnatural silence was better than the alternative—the fights. There had been two of them since my arrival almost a month ago—three, if you counted the one that concerned me on the evening of the wedding when Royce had raged at Jake, and Gladys had wailed and sobbed through the night. The next one had been between Royce and Meg when she'd shown up at the supper table with her drab dark brown hair cut in a new short style, which I thought actually suited her, opening up her narrow, cat-like face and making her dark eyes large and luminous. But Royce Tatlow had a conniption fit about it.

The worst fight, though, I'd witnessed here in this nutty home had been between Royce and Gladys, and it had shocked me to the core. Mainly because I'd been under the assumption that Gladys Tatlow was a typical Kentucky wife under the thumb of her husband, the lord and master. But that night last week had changed my opinion of my mother-in-law forever.

Gladys Tatlow was a stout, stern-faced woman with gray-streaked dark hair pulled back in a severe bun. I figured she was around the same age as my own mother, maybe a year or two older. But unlike Mother, who wore a simple dress every day of her life, except for Sundays, Gladys frequently wore cuffed blue jeans teamed with a button-down work shirt, only wearing a dress when she went into town. That mere fact should've told me that Gladys wasn't typical at all.

The fight started innocently enough with Royce taking a slurping mouthful of soup beans and proclaiming them "too damn salty." Gladys had stared at him for a long moment and then quietly got up from her chair, went over to him and snatched his bowl away. He protested, but she ignored it, and as the rest of the family stared, dumbfounded, she marched over to the back door and slung the bowl's contents across the yard, scattering squawking chickens in all directions.

"I reckon it ain't too salty for the chickens," she said mildly, sitting back down in her chair to finish her supper.

Royce stared at her, eyes bulging like he couldn't believe what he'd just seen. He blinked and his hands clenched down on the arms of his chair. It was as if he'd just then realized what his wife had done. "*Good God, woman!*" he roared, his forehead wrinkling up like a dried prune. "What in tarnation did you do *that* fer? I said it was too damn salty, but that don't mean I won't eat it, you *stupid bitch!*"

Seemingly unconcerned, Gladys slid a piece of cornbread into her mouth and chewed, not even looking his way. I could almost feel the tension coming from Jake's body in the chair next to me. The two girls sat with bowed heads, almost supernaturally still. When Gladys still didn't acknowledge her husband, Royce's face darkened like a summer thundercloud and his fists crashed down on the table, rattling dishes and utensils.

"God *blast* it, Gladys! Git your fat ass over to that there *goddamn* stove and git me some more beans and cornbread *lickety-split!*"

I stifled a gasp. Never in my life had I ever heard a man utter such foul language in front of women and children! But amazingly, Gladys didn't appear to hear. She just kept eating—neat little spoonfuls of soup beans broken by occasional sips of thick, creamy buttermilk, fresh from their own cows.

"Did you hear me, woman?" Royce shouted, a thick tide of crimson streaking up his neck to flood his face.

Still, Gladys didn't budge. Instead, she took another long sip of buttermilk and daintily wiped the cream from her upper lip with the sleeve of her shirt. It was as if Royce wasn't even at the table, much less screaming at her at the top of his lungs. Furious now, he scraped his chair back so hard it toppled over with a crash. Everyone flinched, especially me, but Gladys seemed completely oblivious as she calmly popped another piece of cornbread into her mouth.

Cursing violently, Royce stomped toward the stove, and that was when Gladys went into action. She jumped up from her chair and moving with a grace that seemed impossible, maneuvered past her husband to reach the stove before he did. He stopped, watching her. Afterwards, I would realize he was thinking just what everybody else was thinking—that Gladys's brief uprising was over, that she was back in her role as wife, servant and caretaker, and she was going to get her man his supper after all. But what happened next astonished everyone. Royce waited as Gladys grabbed two potholders and headed for the cast-iron pot on the stove.

"Sit yourself down, Royce Tatlow," she said shortly.

With a grunt of disgust mixed with satisfaction, Royce righted his overturned chair and plopped his skinny hind-end into it. And everyone at the table watched as Gladys picked up the kettle, marched to the back door, and flung the whole thing—pot and all—out into the yard.

She turned, placed her hands on her generous hips and stared at her husband. "I reckon," she said slowly, "that if you *want* it, you'll have to go out and lap it up with the chickens."

All hell broke loose. Royce jumped up from the chair and hurled himself at his wife. She whirled around and ran into the kitchen with him right behind her, cursing like a madman. Jake jumped up and headed for the fracas. Meg and Inis sat frozen in their seats, eyes wide with fear. I watched the whole scene, stunned.

Just as Royce grabbed the back of Gladys's bun, she wrenched open the utensil drawer and pulled out a lethal-looking butcher knife. Quick as a snake, she had the tip of it poised at the bottom of Royce's bobbing Adam's apple. Jake froze between the table and the kitchen. Royce froze, too, his eyes bulging in shock. All the color had drained from Gladys's face, and her eyes gleamed like blue diamonds.

Her mouth curled in a completely mirthless smile. "Let go of me, Royce Tatlow, or I swear to Lord, my God, I'll *gut* you like a barnyard chicken. And there won't be *a soul* in Russell County who'll see me hanged for it."

For a long, tense moment, the couple eye-balled each other, and then, apparently using the lick of sense God gave him, Royce decided to back down. The fury left his eyes, and abruptly, he released her hair and began to grin. It wasn't a likeable grin, because I suspected he couldn't produce a likeable grin if his life depended on it. It was sort of sickly and pathetic, but apparently, it was enough for Gladys.

"Now," she said softly, looking into his eyes. "If you're ready to act like a decent human being, you can go scrounge up something for your supper. *I'm* going to bed early." Slowly, she withdrew the butcher knife from the vicinity of his neck. But she took it with her as she ambled out of the room.

Silence followed her departure. Finally, Royce uttered a curse word so foul I couldn't help but gasp. Then he stomped out the back door, slamming it behind him. A moment later, the rumble of his old pick-up truck broke the quiet of the autumn evening.

Once the sound of the truck disappeared down the road, I looked around at Jake and his sisters who'd gone back to eating as if nothing had happened. I shook my head in astonishment. "I can't believe your mama just did that."

Jake shrugged and reached for another pone of cornbread. "Aw, it ain't nothing to worry about. She gets like that once a month, and we all just learn to stay out of her way." He crumbled his cornbread into his soup bowl, and then added matter-of-factly, "But sometimes, Pa forgets."

Gladys's Apple Dumplings

2 cups peeled, pared and sliced tart apples (or 1-
16 oz. can apple slices)
Pie crust for two pies
1 cup sugar
1/2 t cloves
1 t cinnamon
1/2 t nutmeg
1 cup milk
1/4 c flour

Prepare pie crust. Roll out into 8 equal squares.
Place two T apple slices on each and fold up each
corner. Place in greased baking pan and dot with
butter. Bake at 425 degrees for 30 minutes. (For
fresh apples, bake at 350 for 45-50 minutes). While
cooling, prepare cinnamon sauce. Mix sugar, spices
and flour together and gradually stir in milk. Cook
over low heat, stirring constantly until thickened.
Spoon warm sauce over dumplings and top with
vanilla ice cream or fresh whipped cream.

CHAPTER THIRTEEN

The knock came at the door just after seven the next morning. I was helping Gladys and my sisters-in-law with the breakfast dishes. My eyes were puffy from all the tears I'd cried that morning when I'd awakened to find that Jake hadn't come home at all. This was the first time he'd stayed out all night. His absence hadn't gone unnoticed by Gladys, either. Not that she'd said a word. But the excessive banging of pots and pans as she'd made the sausage gravy and biscuits had revealed her irritation.

From the kitchen, I heard Royce answer the front door, followed by the rumble of another male voice. And suddenly my heart began to gallop. It had something to do with Jake. I knew it!

I threw down the drying rag and hurried down the hallway toward the front door. Through the gap between Royce's body and the door frame, I saw a blue uniform. It was the Sheriff, Burps Dewey.

"We got him in lock-up, Royce," he drawled. "Drunk and resistin' arrest. Chased him with the siren goin' all the way into Columbia, and that sum-bitch drove around that circle with me on his damn tail three or four times before he finally pulled over. And then that smart-alec son of yourn put up a fight when I tried to cuff him." The sheriff turned his head and spat a stream of blood-brown tobacco juice onto Gladys's half-dead rosebush at the side of the porch. "He goes before the judge at ten this morning, and once bail is set, ya'all can come on down and get him out."

I pressed my fingers against my mouth. *Oh, Lord God. Jake, you've done it now.*

Royce's response was amazingly calm. For Royce. "*Son-of-a-bitch!* I reckon I'll be to town directly, Burps. Mighty good of you to come out here to let me know."

With a nod, the sheriff turned and made his way down the porch steps. Royce closed the door and turned.

"I'll get my coat," I said.

Royce frowned. "You git that round little butt of yours back into the kitchen and help out my missus. I'll take care of that no-account, lazy ass husband of yourn. And when I'm through with him, he's gonna wish he was never born."

I caught my breath. "You're not going to hurt him."

He gave me one of his evil grins. "He's too big to hurt anymore, missy. But what I got in store for him, is gonna make him *beg* for the lickin' of his life."

He gave a braying laugh, grabbed his weather-beaten hat on a rack beside the door and walked out.

***

"It ain't gonna happen agin because you ain't gonna *be* here for it to happen agin!" Royce glowered at his son.

Jake sat on a straight-back chair in the parlor, his eyes blood-shot, hair tangled. A greenish-yellow pallor tinged his face, and his jaw was slack and stuporous. Like something the cat drug in, I thought. Drunker than a skunk. Well…maybe not now, but he *had* been. I was almost as angry with him as Royce was.

Gladys, too, could barely contain her disgust. She sat in her usual chair by the stove, her fingers nimbly shelling peas. Her blue eyes—the only thing about her similar to Jake—were furious, but she'd stayed as silent as a clam during Royce's tirade.

It had started more than ten minutes ago with their arrival back home after Royce had scraped together fifty bucks to bail Jake out of jail. He whirled around, his dark eyes shooting venom at his son. "And you're gonna pay back ever penny of it, you hear me? My money don't grow on trees! If I had an extry fifty dollars layin' around, I'd damn well put it to better use than to bail *your* sorry ass out of jail! Only reason I did it is because of *this 'un*." He jerked his chin toward me, a look of loathing on his rabbit-like face.

My stomach dipped.

"I'll pay it back," Jake muttered, head bowed as if it was too heavy to lift. His fingers restlessly massaged his forehead.

My jaw tightened. *Got yourself a headache, huh? Well, good! You get what you deserve.*

"Damn *right* you'll pay it back!" Royce roared. "But I ain't waitin' for you to nickel and dime me at that fat-ass Slim Jessup's gas station! You're gonna git yourself a *real* job, boy!"

That got Jake's attention. His head lifted and his red-rimmed eyes peered blearily at his father. "There ain't no real jobs in Russell Springs."

Royce gave a smile so big and smug, I could see his false teeth gleaming from across the room. "You got that right, boy. That's why tomorrow mornin', bright and early, you and I are gonna head up to Louieville. Because I happen to know the perfect job for the likes of you."

The sneering tone of Royce's voice made Gladys sit up straighter. Her hands paused on the pea pod she held as her gaze fixed upon her husband. Jake, too, seemed to sense that something was in the air. His face had taken on a wary look.

Royce's nasty grin widened. "Private Jacob Tatlow," he said slowly. "Has a nice ring to it, don't it?"

Gladys dropped the pod into the bowl in her lap, her face whitening. Jake stared at his father. As Royce's meaning became clear, my body went ice cold. *No! He couldn't be serious!*

No one spoke. In the corner of the parlor, an ancient grandfather clock pealed out the hour with eleven chimes as three pairs of eyes stared at Royce. He still wore a self-satisfied smirk, but kept his gaze reserved for his son. As the last peal of the chime echoed away, Jake shook his head. "No. I ain't gonna join no army."

Royce gave an ugly laugh. "You ain't got no choice!"

"*Pa!*" Jake's eyes flashed fire. "Soldiers are gettin' *killed* over in Korea! I ain't gonna be one of 'em!"

My heart gave a lurch. Oh, God! I'd forgotten all about Korea. My first thought had been about myself—how awful it would be to be separated from Jake. But if they sent him to war, he could die!

"Royce." Gladys stood and put the bowl on her chair. "Jake has a point. There's lots of boys dying over there in that heathen country. I'm not gonna sacrifice my youngest boy for them funny looking little slant-eyes over there."

"You ain't got no choice neither, Gladys," Royce said, not even sparing her a glance. "Stay out of it. It's like this, son. You're the one who knocked up this here little gal and brought her into the family, and for all I know, she might've spread her legs for every Tom, Dick and Harry in the county, but you're the one who got caught."

I gasped in outrage and started to protest, but Gladys threw me a look of warning that all but screamed at me to keep quiet. My mouth clamped shut, but my fingers itched to claw at Royce's skinny throat.

"But if you think I'm gonna keep supporting Little Miss Princess and that brat she's carrying in her belly, you got another think comin'. Now, I don't want to hear another word about it. Tomorrow mornin, sun-up, we're headin' to the Army recruiter's office. And if I was you, I'd pack me a bag, because you're gonna tell the U.S. Army you're ready to go right now."

Hitching up his overalls, Royce strode out of the parlor, leaving the three of us stunned. I looked from Gladys to Jake, my heart racing. "They won't do that, will they?" I stuttered. "Take you away tomorrow? Not that fast, right?"

Jake just stared bleakly at the floor. In desperation, I turned to my mother-in-law. "Gladys, they'll give him some time, right? I mean, they can't just take him away like that, can they? Won't he have to take some tests? A physical? Surely that takes time!"

An inscrutable look appeared on Gladys's face and she turned away. She bent and scooped up the bowl of peas, then padded out of the room. I looked back at Jake.

"You can't let him do this to you, Jake." I gnawed on my bottom lip, trying to control the panic boiling inside me. "We don't have to stay here. We can leave, just you and me. You can go find a job up in Louieville or Lexington. Jake, I don't think I can bear it if you get sent to war. What if something awful happens? What if..." My voice died away. I couldn't even say it.

Slowly Jake got to his feet, moving gingerly. "I can't think. I gotta go get some sleep."

And he, too, left the room.

Mother's Chocolate Gravy
2 heaping T cocoa
½ cup sugar
Pinch of salt
¼ cup flour or 2 T cornstarch
1 T butter
2 cups milk

In small bowl, mix cocoa, sugar, salt and flour. Add a few drops of water until it's a thick paste. Taste. If it isn't sweet enough, add more sugar. Pour into heavy cast iron skillet and gradually add milk. Cook over medium heat, stirring constantly until thick. Add butter. Serve over hot biscuits.

CHAPTER FOURTEEN

One more storm like last night, and all the leaves would be stripped clean off, I thought as my rubbers sank into the spongy ground of the path that wound through the woods—the short cut to the place I used to call home.

Indian summer had given way to a wet and cold November. It had been raining for the past three days, culminating in gusty winds and heavy downpours through the night. This morning wasn't much better. The rain had stopped, but it was still overcast, and much colder. I sniffed. Snow was in the air; I'd bet my life on it. Early for snow, though. It rarely snowed in Kentucky before Christmas.

My heart gave a pang. Christmas. Surely, I wouldn't make it to Christmas. My heart would break before that. Jake had been gone five days. The Army had taken him just like Royce had said they would. He'd taken the pledge that very day up in Louieville, and the next morning, they'd put him on a bus to boot camp in Aberdeen, Maryland.

135

Oh, God. How was I going to get through the next eight weeks without him? I stepped out of the woods onto the hill that looked down on the south side of my family home. Without the protection of the trees, an icy wind from the north hit me straight on, and I shivered, wrapping my old wool coat more tightly around my expanding belly. A wisp of smoke spiraled from the stone chimney down below, and the scent of burning wood drifted on the wind.

My heart ached with homesickness. Mother would be in there alone, busy with one of her daily tasks—maybe baking bread or putting up some apple butter from the autumn harvest. Norry and Edsel would be in school, and Landry would be working at the feed plant in Columbia. Since it was the farm's off-season, Daddy would be up living in Louieville where he worked at the GE Plant, only making it home to Kentucky on weekends.

Head down to shield my face from the wind, and with tears burning my eyes, I made my way down the hill and up the steps of the front porch. I hesitated at the door, wondering whether I should knock or just go on in like I used to. The decision was made for me when the door suddenly opened, and there stood Mother, a rolling pin in her hand, flour smudged on her forehead where she'd brushed away an errant lock of graying hair.

"I heard ye comin' up the steps," she said with a pleased smile. "Come on in. I've just put on a pot of coffee."

Stepping into my old home and being greeted by the strong, rich aroma of Mother's coffee mixed with the lingering scent of fried bacon felt like heaven. I blinked back my tears, determined not to let Mother see how close to falling apart I was. If the plan I'd formulated as I made my way through

the woods had a chance of succeeding, I
would have to appear strong and mature. I'd have
to act like an adult.

"I'm making a couple of pies for a potluck after
meetin' tonight," Mother said, bustling back into the
kitchen. "Come and sit yourself down."

I shrugged out of my coat and hung it on the
rack near the door, then made my way into the
kitchen. It looked just the same as it always had
with its burnished pine cabinets and gleaming wood
floor. Mother's handmade red and white-gingham
curtains over the sink looked freshly washed and
starched. Scraps of pie dough and flour covered the
big oak table. One unbaked pie rested on top of the
stove, and another one on the table, filled high with
sliced apples, waited for its top crust. Coffee perked
in the black enamel pot on the stove. I felt an
overwhelming impulse to plop myself into one of
the chairs and just breathe in the atmosphere of the
warm, apple-scented room…maybe just stay here
forever.

Mother deftly picked up the rolled out circle of
dough and arranged it on top of the pie. Quickly,
she trimmed, then pinched the edges of the crust
and cut four slits in the top. "That'un's cherry, and
this un is apple." She glanced at me. "You had any
breakfast? I could make you something soon as I
get these in the oven."

I shook my head. "I was feeling sort of sick
this morning."

"Coffee's done. Pour yourself a cup. I'll have
one with you while you think about what you want."
Mother slid the two pies into the oven and turned,
wiping her work-worn hands on her apron.

I took two cups from the cabinet and poured
our coffee as Mother brought a small blue-flowered
porcelain pitcher of cream out of the icebox and

placed it on the table. "You still take cream, I reckon?"

I smiled, placing the two cups of coffee on the table. "Yes, Mother. I still take cream." I sat down and reached for the creamer.

"Well, expectin' mothers get peculiar notions." She settled into a chair and reached for her coffee. "How you feeling, Lily Rae?"

"Okay, I guess. Except for feeling sick to my stomach some mornings." I stirred cream into my coffee. "Reckon you heard about Jake?"

"Yes, I did. Ran into Louisa Ledbetter at Johnny's Market on Saturday. She told me." She paused a moment, then added, "I expect you're pinin' for him."

Something about the way she said it, perhaps the gentle tone in her voice weakened my resolve to be brave and mature. My chin trembled and hot tears blurred my vision. I placed my coffee cup back on the table with an unsteady hand. "Oh, Mother! I feel like I'm dying, I miss him so much." And just like that, I was sobbing.

She let me cry for a minute, then got to her feet, came around the table and placed a gentle hand on my shoulder. "Alright, now, Lily Rae. It's not the end of the world."

I turned a tear-streaked face to her. "But Mother, it's so awful! You just don't know what it's like living there with Jake's family. Gladys is so bossy and I can just tell she hates me. And the girls aren't friendly and Royce is just…well, he's just as mean as a bag of rattlesnakes! I *hate* it there! And now, with Jake gone…" I buried my face in my hands and sobbed.

Mother seemed at a loss for words as she stood there awkwardly patting my shoulder. Finally, she

said, "I know what you need. Sit right there
and I'll make you some chocolate gravy to go with
the biscuits I made this mornin'."

I cried harder. It was so like Mother to think
that her chocolate gravy would heal all the problems
in the world. True, when I was a child, the velvety-
rich chocolate sauce, served hot over feather-light
biscuits had been a treat that could cure all ills. But
now…

Slowly, I lifted my head and wiped away my
tears. "Chocolate gravy sounds like heaven," I said.
"Can I help?"

She shook her head, moving toward the stove.
"You just sit tight and drink your coffee. This won't
take more than a minute." She pulled out a cast-iron
skillet from the bottom of the stove, and then
moved to the pantry and reached for a tin of cocoa.

A few minutes later, the seductive aroma of
chocolate wafted through the kitchen, and my
mouth began to water. "You've got to teach me
how to make chocolate gravy, Mother," I said, my
palm pressing against the small mound of my
tummy. "This little one will love it."

"Ain't nothing to it," she grunted, stirring the
gravy with a wooden spoon. "Just mix some cocoa
and sugar with a little flour, and add a cup or two of
milk. Then cook it until it thickens. That's how
your grandma taught me, and how her mama taught
her. I reckon it's about ready." A moment later, she
slid a plate in front of me, and then picked up my
coffee cup. "I'll get ye a refill."

Suddenly ravenous, I ate every bite, and then
asked for a second helping. Mother smiled and
refilled my plate. As I ate, she filled the sink with
soapy water and began to wash the dishes.

"I reckon you heard about them bombs they're testing out in the middle of the ocean somewheres," she said.

I nodded. "Yes, it was on the news. The Marshall Islands. I think that's out in the Pacific."

Mother shook her head and stared out the window over the sink. "I can't help but think all this bomb-making will lead to no good. It'll likely lead to more war."

I nodded soberly. "And more of our boys going *off* to war." I put down my fork. My appetite had disappeared at the reminder of Jake and the possibility of him going to Korea.

Mother, apparently sensing my mood, changed the subject. "Oh, I ran into Shirley Nickerson at Johnny's Market...la, I think everbody I know was shoppin' there on Saturday. Anyhow, she told me that that boy of hers up and married Patty Huddleston last week. Did you know about that?"

I pushed my plate away, absorbing the news. So Chad had married Pat-Peaches. What had happened to his college plans, I wondered?

"Shirley didn't say anything, but I heard tell from Sadie Wilson that Patty might be in the family way. 'Course, that old woman is such a gossip; she likely made the whole thing up out of sheer orneriness."

I was glad Mother had her back to me. My whole body had gone numb with shock. Pat-Peaches, pregnant with Chad's child? That would explain what had happened to his college plans. But everyone in Russell County knew how Pat-Peaches slept around. How could Chad be sure it was his baby?

I no longer felt hurt and betrayal when I thought of Chad. But now, despite the fact that he had nothing to blame but his own foolishness, I couldn't help but feel pity for my old boyfriend. He'd had so many dreams of a better life, and now, here he was, trapped in a loveless marriage with a woman he probably didn't even like.

Of course...some would say that Jake was in the same situation.

I got up from the table and carried my plate and coffee cup over to the sink. "Here, Mother, I'll wash these."

"You sit back down. It'll only take me a minute." She took the dishes from me and slid them into the soapy water.

I remained standing, staring out the window that overlooked the pond. I squinted. Something was coming down out there, and it wasn't rain.

As if reading my mind, Mother glanced out the window. "It's flurryin.' I reckon we might be gettin' our first snow before too long."

An overwhelming longing swept over me as I gazed out into the gray morning. I loved winter, especially when it snowed. There was nothing better in the world than to curl up next to the woodstove on a cold, snowy afternoon, sipping hot cocoa and reading a good book. "I want to come home, Mother."

Her hand paused on the plate she was washing.

I went on, trying to fill the sudden silence, "It makes sense, don't you see? They don't want me there. I'm nothing but a burden. I can move back into my old room. You know Norry would love to have me home. I'll just be here for a little while. Until Jake gets out of boot camp. I've been praying and praying to the Lord not to send him to Korea, and I know He is not gonna let that happen. We're gonna go somewhere together...maybe some place like Hiwalya. So...what do you say? I'll go right back to the Tatlow's and pack my things. I can be back here in time to help you with supper."

Mother didn't speak. She moved methodically, rinsing the plate and placing it on a dish cloth next to the sink. Slowly, she turned to grab a clean dishtowel and began to dry her work-worn hands. Only then did she meet my expectant gaze. Her face was as sober as it had been that evening when me and Jake had been joined in matrimony. Sadness glimmered in her blue eyes.

"No, Lily Rae," she said softly. "You can't come home. Your place is with your husband's family now. You can come home and visit any time you want, but you can't come back to stay. I'm sorry, but you're a young woman now. I reckon it's time you start acting like one."

I swallowed hard to hold back my tears. Finally, I nodded. Whatever had made me think she'd ever, in a million years, agree to me coming back home?

The snow flurries had stopped when I left my childhood home a little while later. As I trudged through the woods back toward the Tatlow property, a steady freezing rain began to fall.

CHAPTER FIFTEEN

Grider's Drugstore was all gussied up for Christmas with artificial greenery framing the windows and sprayed-on "snow" depicting snowmen, candles, Santa Clauses and what-not, so thick it was impossible to look outside and see who was passing by on Main Street. This was especially frustrating for me because it was the last Saturday before Christmas, and just about everybody was out and about, doing last-minute shopping.

I bent my head and sucked at the paper straw nestled deep into one of Grider's delicious strawberry sodas. The ice cream drink was so cold, it gave me a headache, but it was well worth it, and I hadn't had one since summer.

Twisting back and forth on my stool, I looked over at Inis next to me. "So, who all do you have left to buy for?"

"Just Meg." Inis dabbed a French fry into a pool of ketchup and slipped it into her mouth as she flipped through the latest copy of **Photoplay Magazine** on the counter in front of her.

I couldn't believe how much our relationship had changed in the past couple of months. And all because I'd rescued a litter of kittens that Royce had threatened to drown. Inis and I had trudged them over to the barn on our property, and given them into the care of Norry.

Inis flipped a page of the magazine and gazed down at Doris Day in awe. "La, ain't she the purtiest thing you ever saw?"

I'd bought it for her when I'd seen her wistfully glancing through it at the magazine stand. I'd bought her lunch, too—or rather *Jake* had. Two days before, a check had arrived in the mail with a note from him.

Dear Lily Rae, here's thirty dollars for you to buy my folks some Christmas presents. See you soon. Jake.

And that's what I'd done after getting Daddy to drive me and Inis to town this morning. We'd been to every shop in Russell Springs, and I felt like I'd spent my money wisely; I'd even had enough left over to treat the both of us to lunch. Surprisingly, upon hearing of our plans, Gladys had slipped Inis a ten-dollar bill so she could buy Christmas presents, forcing me to reassess my opinion of the woman. Maybe she wasn't as heartless as she let on.

"Yes, she's pretty, but don't forget, all them movie stars have make-up artists and beauticians to make them look that gorgeous. So, what are you going to get Meg? Maybe you can find something for her here," I glanced around the drugstore. "I saw a pretty compact over there at the Toni display."

"Meg don't wear make-up," Inis said, flipping another page of the magazine.

"Well, maybe if you buy a compact for her, she'll start wearing make-up. I think she could really be pretty if she tried." I took a bite of my cheeseburger.

Inis shook her head. "Pa would tan her hide if she showed up with make-up on." She reached for her chocolate milkshake and took a long draw from the straw. "This is *so* yummy, Lily Rae. Thank you so *much* for lunch!"

I smiled, feeling a tug at my heart. "You're welcome, sweetie."

Poor thing, I thought. Inis had lived here in Russell Springs all her life, and I'd bet a dime to a doughnut that this was the first time she'd ever eaten at Grider's soda fountain. And to think, I'd always felt that *I* had been underprivileged because I couldn't come here for lunch every school day like some of the other popular kids had.

Beneath my feet, tucked between the bottom of the stool and the counter, rested the several packages I'd collected this morning—the Christmas gifts for Jake's family...except for Royce.

"What on earth should I get for your father?" I asked.

Inis shrugged, her eyes on her magazine.

"What did *you* get him?"

"Nothing," Inis mumbled, slurping on her milkshake.

"Well, what are you *going* to get him?" I prodded.

"I ain't gettin' him nothing," Inis said, staring balefully at a Revlon ad for "Fire and Ice" lipstick. "I *hate* him! I wish he'd die!" Her face whitened as if she'd just realized what she'd said. She abruptly closed the magazine and looked up at me, her eyes turbulent. "I know that's wrong of me, but it's true. I *do* hate him."

I gazed at the girl, and summoned the courage to ask the question that had been hovering in my mind since we'd grown close. "Inis, does he ever hit you?" Now that I knew Royce first hand, I'd come to believe all the rumors I'd heard about him beating up on Jake and his older brother, Tully. And I wouldn't put it past him to do the same to his girls.

But Inis shook my head. "Not me or Meg. He hollers at us, but never lays a hand on us. Ma would probably kill him if he did. She won't truck with him beatin' up on girls. But he like to beat Jake to an inch of his life one time."

I chewed on my lower lip. *That can't be the time he'd got into trouble for playing with me in the woods.* Inis would've been only two, and surely wouldn't remember it even if she *had* witnessed it. But then, a horrible thing like that might leave its mark on a poor child's mind.

"He always beat up on Tully, too," Inis went on. "That's why he left home and never comes back. We haven't seen him in almost five years. Ma got a letter once from Cincinnati, and that's it. Pa got even meaner after Tully left, and he mostly took it out on Jake."

I shook my head. Poor Jake. No wonder it was so hard for him to show love and affection. He'd grown up deprived of both, so how could he show it to someone else? Well, that was going to change when he came home.

My heart gave a jolt. That would be in exactly four days. His bus would be arriving in Somerset on Christmas Eve, and I'd already arranged for Slim Jessup to drive me there to meet him. I could hardly wait.

And when we were together again, I vowed to do everything in my power to make up for Jake's

146

horrible childhood. I would give him all the
love he'd never got at home, and we'd both shower
our baby with love and attention, and it would grow
up to be secure and confident and...

A gust of cold air swept into the drugstore as
the front door opened and an obviously pregnant
redheaded woman entered. It took a moment
before I recognized Pat-Peaches. She looked nothing
like the girl I'd last seen on graduation night nestled
in Chad's arms. Her freckled face was devoid of
make-up and oddly bloated, and she looked like
she'd gained fifty pounds—and not just because of
her protruding belly. Even her legs, visible beneath
a shapeless wool coat, looked like gnarled tree
trunks.

I cupped my hands over my own rounded belly,
wondering if it was possible I looked as bad, and just
didn't know it. I certainly hadn't *thought* I looked
bad at all when I'd glanced into the mirror this
morning. In fact, I'd thought I looked especially
pretty. My eyes had sparkled and my skin had
glowed with good health. I'd gained only twelve
pounds—right at average, the doctor had said. The
only parts of my body that had expanded had been
my belly and my titties, which, I was pretty sure, Jake
was going to be pleased about.

Pat-Peaches glanced around, her gaze skating
over me and Inis to fasten on the candy aisle beyond
us. She lumbered toward it like a thirsty horse
heading for water.

I looked back at the door, wondering if Chad
was with her. I hadn't seen him since this summer
when I'd run into him at the library. The moment
had been awkward with a brief exchange of
pleasantries before he'd hurried out with the books
he'd come in with.

What would he say when he saw I was pregnant? What would *I* say to him?

The door opened, and a handsome man in uniform stepped into the drugstore. He carried a duffle bag slung over one shoulder and wore his cap at a rakish angle. For a moment, he stood just inside the door, scanning the interior.

I caught my breath as his blue eyes connected with mine. "Oh, my Lord," I whispered.

"What's wrong?" Inis asked, looking around.

The soldier's face broke into a big grin, and my heart began to race.

"*Jake!*" I jumped off the stool as gracefully as my condition would allow and ran toward him. He dropped his duffle bag and reached for me.

I burst into tears as he wrapped me in his arms, holding me so tight I could barely breathe. I inhaled the scent of him—starched cotton, Winston cigarettes and Brill hair crème—still not quite believing I wasn't dreaming.

He kissed me, deep and hard. And I knew it couldn't be a dream. He was really here!

When he finally released me, I clung to him, and gasped, "But you're not...your letter said..."

He shook his head, grinning. "They let us out early for the holidays. I hitch-hiked from Somerset. You happy to see me, Lily Rae?"

"What do *you* think?" I giggled, and took a step away from him. "Look at me, Jake. You see how big I've gotten? Oh, and Jake, the baby is moving all the time now. Doesn't it, Inis?" I looked around at Inis who was still sitting on her stool, staring at her brother like she'd never seen him before. "Inis! It's your brother! Don't you recognize him?"

Inis nodded and gave a little smile. "Hey, there, Jake. You look different."

He took off his cap and gave his head a scratch. "I reckon I do," he said wryly. "Lord, I'm glad to be home. I ran into Burps Dewey at the junction where my ride dropped me off, and he told me Twila Foley had mentioned just seeing you two at the drugstore, so I decided to walk on down here before heading home. And here you are!"

I smiled up at him, still feeling the urge to pinch myself. I couldn't get over how different he seemed, and it wasn't just the uniform. No, he seemed older and more easy-going. The Army, apparently, had had a good effect upon him. Maybe my man had finally grown up.

"Oh, Jake, I'm so glad you're home," I whispered, wanting nothing more than to get him back to our room at his parents' house and strip that uniform clean off him.

He grinned down at me. "Not for long, baby," he said, giving my shoulders a squeeze. "Come January 1st, you and me...we're going to Texas."

Mother's Kentucky Oatmeal Cake

1-1/4 c boiling water
1 c oats
1/2 c butter, softened
1 c sugar
1 c brown sugar
1 t vanilla
2 eggs
1-1/2 c flour
1 t soda
1/2 t salt
3/4 t cinnamon
1/4 t nutmeg

Pour boiling water over oats, cover and let stand 20 minutes. Beat butter until creamy. Add sugars gradually. Beat until fluffy. Blend in vanilla and eggs. Stir in oats. Sift flour, soda, salt and spices together and add to mixture. Pour into greased and floured 9 x 12 pan. Bake at 350 degrees for 30-35 min.

Topping

1/2 c butter, melted
1 c brown sugar
6 T milk
1/2 c chopped pecans
1-1/2 c coconut

Mix all together and spoon on cake the last 5 minutes of baking.

January 1953
New Boston, Texas

CHAPTER SIXTEEN

I stood at the sink, my hands thrust in hot, sudsy water. On the counter nearby, a decade-old radio played Mario Lanza's "Because You're Mine," and I hummed along with it through the occasional static. It was better than nothing, and it was ours. Jake had bought it secondhand with his first paycheck after we'd moved to New Boston. And he'd promised me we'd buy a TV set if he had enough left over from his next paycheck—after paying for rent and groceries, of course.

The rustle of a starched uniform behind me caught my attention. I glanced over my shoulder as Jake stepped into the kitchen, looking gorgeous in his Army fatigues. He grinned at me, and I caught my breath as a wash of pure love rushed over me. As if in response to his appearance, the baby gave a hard kick inside my rounded belly.

"How's my handsome husband this morning?" I asked, flashing a smile his way.

He'd been fine and dandy an hour earlier—and randier than an alley-cat in spring. Back in my days of innocence, I would've figured that a husband wouldn't be hankering for sex when his woman was near eight months gone with pregnancy, but now I knew that didn't make a bit of difference. Jake wanted it all the same, big belly or not, and...as a matter-of-fact, so did I. In fact, I couldn't seem to keep my hands off the man these days. Partly, I supposed, because for the first time in our relationship, we could have sex just about any time we wanted it. And...well...we wanted it a lot.

As if reading my mind, he gave me a wink and came over, pressing his hands against my belly, and rubbing up against me from behind. "I feel like staying home with you instead of going to work," he muttered, nuzzling my neck.

I giggled as a delicious shiver rippled up my back. "Well, you got to. We got to eat, right? Oh! And speaking of eating, remember...I invited the neighbors over for supper tonight. Betty and me have been talking about this for ages, and she wants you to meet her husband."

Jake sighed and drew away from me. "Lord, Lily! I don't know why you have to go and invite strangers over here. I have to deal with folks all day at the post, and I just want some peace and quiet when I get home."

I rinsed a plate and put it into the rack on the drain board. "Come on, Jake! I get lonely here when you're working. And I miss my folks. I *gotta* make some friends. And Betty is just a barrel of fun! She and her husband have been looking for another couple to play cards with, and...oh, Jake, *please* do this for me. We'll have them over just this once, and if you don't like them, I'll never ask again. Please, honey? I'm making your mama's fried chicken recipe and…" I smiled hopefully at him. "Mother's oatmeal cake."

His face softened. "Well…I guess I can put up with company for a little while tonight. But I'll tell you right now, Lily Rae, if I don't like them folks, they ain't coming over any more."

"You'll like them!" I grinned. "I know you will."

How could he *not* like Betty? She was simply the most fascinating person I'd ever met.

***

"Soon as you pop that bun out of your oven, hon, I'm going to teach you how to drive," said Betty, lifting her coffee cup to her lips. "It's a *goddamn* shame that a woman your age doesn't know how to drive a car."

I drew a box of Bisquick from the grocery bag and gave it a skeptical look. I still wasn't sure Betty knew what she was talking about when she'd urged me to add it to my grocery cart, swearing it made biscuits just as good—better, maybe—than ones from scratch. But since I'd calculated that the cost of the items in my cart would be well below the fifteen dollars Jake had budgeted for weekly groceries, I'd gone ahead and bought it.

"I don't know," I said, placing the box in the cabinet next to a tin of Chase & Sanborn coffee. "I can hear Jake right now. He'll say…" I placed a hand on my hip and lowered my voice to imitate him, "'what's the goddurn sense in teaching you how to drive when you don't have a car, and why do you *need* a car, anyway, when you should be staying home and taking care of the baby?'"

Betty rolled her eyes. "Oh, to *hell* with Jake and his old-fashioned opinions!"

"*Betty!*" Half-laughing, but shocked all the same, I closed the cabinet door and moved to the coffee pot to pour myself a cup. I glanced over at my friend. "You want a warm-up?"

"No, thanks. Carrying Davy around for almost ten months shot the hell out of my bladder. I'll be running to the little girl's room every ten minutes if I have another cup." The wavy-haired titian-blonde took a long draw from her cigarette and allowed the smoke to curl out of her nostrils in a long gray ribbon. How on earth did she do that, I wondered. It was just one of the many marvels of Betty Kelly.

Hard to believe it had only been three weeks since Betty had breezed into my life and become my very best friend here in this military town in northeast Texas. Make that my *only* friend here. I hadn't met anybody else.

On the first day Jake reported for duty at the Red River Arsenal west of Texarkana, I'd been in the middle of unpacking our sparse household goods in the small one-bedroom apartment we'd rented, feeling a little sorry for myself, and more than a little homesick for Kentucky. Everything changed when a knock came at the front door, followed by a female voice on the other side, trilling, "Knock-knock!"

When I opened the door, Betty Kelly stepped inside, talking a mile a minute before even introducing herself, bringing with her the sunshine of her home state of California and instant friendship. I couldn't resist her, and didn't want to. Since that day, we'd visited each other every afternoon for coffee or a Coke, sometimes here, and sometimes at Betty's more spacious two-bedroom apartment down the hall.

Twenty minutes ago, we'd returned from grocery shopping at the post commissary. When Betty had first learned (with a rapt expression of horror on her face) that I not only didn't have a car, but didn't know how to *drive*, she'd insisted on taking me grocery shopping every week—and other places, as well. One day we'd gone shopping in downtown Texarkana and Betty had practically bought out Briley's department store while I'd just looked around in awe.

"Oh! *Turn that up!*" Betty squeaked, stubbing out her cigarette in the ashtray on the table and jumping up from her chair. "I *love* that song!"

I reached for the volume knob on the radio and turned it up. Georgia Gibb's "Kiss of Fire" filled the small kitchen. Betty closed her eyes and began to sway her curvy hips to the music, singing along with the song. I watched her with a bemused smile.

Lord, that girl had a good figure! Hard to believe the six-month-old baby boy sleeping on the couch in the living room had come out of her trim body. Dressed in form-fitting gray trousers cinched with a wide double-buckled leather belt and a clinging red turtleneck sweater with three black penguins marching across her generous breasts (that's what she called them, saying that only horny men and little girls said "titties"), Betty looked like the beauty queen she'd been in high school when she'd reigned as the Napa Valley Chardonnay Queen at the 1948 California State Fair.

Everything about Betty fascinated me. First, she was an older woman—almost 24--and coming from California, land of movie stars and glitter, she was worldly and sophisticated. She was also bright and pretty and opinionated and bubbly—and…I wanted to be just like her.

She whirled around to face me, still swaying to the music as Georgia sang about the fire consuming her. Betty beckoned me with a slender crimson-nailed hand. "Come on, dance with me." She grabbed my hand, moving her hips to the Spanish-inspired melody.

"I feel silly," I protested, but Betty's contagious enthusiasm was impossible to resist. Grinning self-consciously, I imitated my friend's dance moves.

Her smile widened. "'*don't pity me…*'" She sang along with Georgia, her mascara-rimmed eyes shining.

I grinned back, putting more sway into my hips the way Betty was doing. I needed to get started on the oatmeal cake for tonight, but…oh, it could wait. I still had hours before Jake got home from the post.

The song on the radio built to its dramatic close, and still holding hands, Betty and I stopped dancing and sang out with gusto, "'*Your kiss of fire!*'" We burst into laughter, hugging each other.

"We should be onstage," Betty giggled. "Hell with this military life! We can be *stars!*"

Still smiling, I disengaged myself from her arms. "Well, maybe later. Right now, I have to get started on my dessert."

Betty sat back down at the kitchen table and picked up her pack of Winston's. She gave it a tap on the table top, drew out a cigarette, and slipped it between her crimson-glazed lips. Her blue eyes gazed thoughtfully at me as she ran her thumb down the ridged wheel of her cigarette lighter. "How long will it take to get it into the oven?"

I shrugged. "Half-hour or so. Why?"

"Perfect." Betty grinned. "As soon as I finish my cigarette, I'm going to go home and get my make-up kit. Honey, you're a gorgeous girl. No doubt about that. But I'm going to make you *glamorous* for tonight. Jake won't know what hit him."

CHAPTER SEVENTEEN

The mouth-watering aroma of Southern fried chicken filled the apartment. The plates and utensils were laid out on the small dinette table where Betty had sat, smoking, several hours earlier. The food—Gladys's fried chicken, creamy mashed potatoes and gravy, green beans simmered in bacon fat, skillet-fried corn just like Mother used to make and a big basket of Bisquick biscuits—was covered with dish towels to keep warm, and the oatmeal cake glazed with its crunchy coconut-pecan topping cooled on the counter.

Everything was ready for our visitors. Betty had asked for a traditional Southern-style supper, and that was exactly what she was going to get. Now, if only Jake would get home!

I untied my apron and slipped it off my head, glancing up at the clock on the stove. Ten minutes to six. Dagnabbit, why did he have to be late tonight, of all nights? Usually he walked in the door at five-thirty sharp. Betty and Eddie would be here any minute!

With nothing else to do, I went into the bedroom to take another look at myself in the dresser mirror-- the new me. Betty had loaned me one of her maternity dresses—a navy poplin with a white sailor collar and a bright red scarf. But the dress wasn't what had made me "new." It was my hair and make-up. Betty had pulled my hair back in a sleek French roll, and made up my eyes, cheeks and lips with her stash of cosmetics.

I stared at myself in the mirror. *Who __was__ that beautiful stranger?* My eyes were rimmed with liquid brown eyeliner—something I'd never dared try to apply—and my lashes were coated with midnight black mascara. My high cheekbones were defined further with pink rouge and my lips lined with a scarlet lip pencil, then filled in with Coty's "Rhapsody in Red."

I smiled at myself to check if any of the vivid lipstick had traveled to my teeth as it was wont to do, and that's when I heard the key in the lock. I whirled around and hurried into the living room, as fast as my baby-bulk would allow.

"Jake! Thank goodness you're home," I called out as he stepped through the front door. "I thought sure Betty and Eddie would get here before you did."

He frowned and swept off his cap, tossing it on the end table. "What's that crap on your face? You look like a two-bit hooker."

My smile froze. "Well, that's not a very nice thing to say."

He strode past me, heading into the kitchen. "I call 'em like I see 'em. Christ! It's been a long day. I need a beer."

I followed him, trying to swallow my disappointment at his reaction to my transformation. Lately, I'd been feeling less than pretty and more than awkward with the added weight of pregnancy. And darn it--Betty had done a good job on my new look, even if Jake couldn't appreciate it.

When I stepped into the kitchen, I found him peering into the refrigerator. "Son-of-a-bitch!" he growled. "Only one beer left." He grabbed the lone can of Falstaff and slammed the refrigerator door. "What the hell are we supposed to drink tonight if we're playing *goddamn* cards with the *goddamn* neighbors? Goddamn *lemonade*?" He scowled at me and pulled the utensil drawer open, peering inside. "Where the hell is the goddamn can opener?"

My lips tightened. Even if I wasn't the most religious person in the world, all those "goddamns" really offended me. "Gee, I'm glad you're in a good mood tonight. Seeing as how Betty and Eddie will be here any minute."

He found the can opener and plunged the sharp tip into the beer can with an efficient, well-practiced hand. Tilting back his head, he took a long, thirsty draw on it.

"I'm sorry I didn't think about the beer," I said, trying to placate him before our guests arrived. "I should've mentioned you were getting low."

Bowie County, Texas, was dry just like back home in Russell County. Whenever Jake needed to restock his alcohol, he had to drive the twelve or so miles over to the Arkansas side of Texarkana. We hadn't been here long enough for him to acquaint himself with the local bootleggers. I had no doubt that would change soon enough.

Jake didn't acknowledge my apology. Taking another swig of beer, he moved past me toward the door. "I'm going to go change. What time are they supposed to get here?"

I opened my mouth to tell him, but before I could speak, a loud rap sounded on the front door.

A pained look crossed his face. "Shit," he muttered, and left the room.

Patting at my French roll, I hurried to the door.

"We're not late, are we?" Betty was talking before I had the door fully open. She breezed in with a wide smile, giving me an affectionate hug. "I know you've seen Eddie in the mailroom, but I guess you've never officially met. Yes, can you believe it? I'm married to the handsomest man in the building. Eddie, this is Lily."

I smiled up at a tall blond man with crystal blue eyes and deep, attractive grooves bracketing his smile. He was fashionably attired in brown dress trousers, a beige sweater over a shirt and tie, and a brown and white herringbone jacket. To me, he looked like a movie star—a combination of Gregory Peck and Gary Cooper. Somehow, I wasn't at all surprised about that; after all, Betty looked like she'd just stepped down from the silver screen tonight in a clinging red-orange dress of rayon adorned with an oval gold pin at the shoulder that matched the clunky gold bracelet on her wrist.

She scanned the room. "So, where's that good-looking husband of yours? The *second* handsomest man in the building."

"Oh, he's changing out of his uniform," I said. "He got home from the post late tonight, naturally. It figures, don't it? With y'all coming over."

Betty giggled and nudged her husband. "Didn't I tell you she was the cutest thing you ever saw? Don't you just *love* that accent?"

Eddie Kelly grinned down at me. "It's so good to finally meet you, Lily. Betty just can't say enough about you. You've really captured her heart. Oh, this is for you." He handed me an "Evening in Paris"-blue bottle tied with a red satin ribbon. "It's Pinot Grigio from a vineyard close to our hometown. Every time we go home, we always bring back a couple of cases."

I took the bottle. "Thank you kindly, Eddie."

I'd never tasted wine before—and couldn't imagine how it would go with fried chicken. But at least now, Jake would have something to drink besides his one beer. He might not be able to pronounce the name of the wine, but he'd surely have no trouble drinking it.

"Well, why don't we go ahead and open it while we wait for Jake?" Betty said, moving toward the kitchen. "Where's your cork screw?"

I frowned. "I don't have one. Wouldn't even know what one looked like."

Betty wheeled around and headed for the front door. "Not to worry. I'll get ours. I need to talk to the sitter, anyway. I forgot to tell her about Davy's pah-pah." And she was gone, leaving Eddie and me in the room alone.

At my look of puzzlement, Eddie shrugged. "Pacifier," he explained with an impish grin.

An awkward silence fell. I suddenly felt shy standing there with a man I'd just met. "Well, I'd better go check on supper," I said, knowing full well there wasn't a thing to be done in the kitchen.

Before I could move, though, Eddie's blue eyes shifted from me to the doorway leading into the hall. I turned to see what he was looking at.

Jake stood there, dressed in faded Levi's, a plaid short-sleeved shirt and a worn pair of Converse sneakers. Clutching the Falstaff can, he stared at Eddie, an odd look on his face.

What on earth was wrong with him, I wondered. Darned if he didn't look as pale as a ghost.

Suddenly Jake straightened and brought his free hand to his forehead with a sharp snap. "Captain Kelly, sir!" he barked, his body rigid.

Eddie Kelly saluted him back. "At ease, Private."

I stared as Jake dropped his hand to his side, but remained at attention.

"I've got it," Betty's voice floated in from the hallway. "Let's get that damn bottle of wine opened."

She burst into the room, waving the corkscrew, and came to an abrupt halt, apparently feeling the tension in the room. Her gaze darted from her husband to Jake, and she let out a disgusted sigh. "Oh, come on, you all. We're not on the goddamn post, and even if we were, you two are off-duty. There's not going to be any of that bull-shit kow-towing between us." She flashed Jake a brilliant smile and moved toward him, her hand extended. "Jake, I'm Betty, and it's so good to finally meet you."

Jake nodded and took her hand. "Ma'am," he said, staring at a point beyond her head.

"Oh, hell!" Betty dropped his hand and gave him a quick hug. "That's better. Look, Jake, I want you to forget Eddie is an officer as long as we're off-post. We're from California, and we don't believe in that non-fraternization rule. I'm Betty and this is Eddie, and don't you forget it."

"That's right, Jake," Eddie said, crossing the room and extending his hand. "We don't stand on ceremony off-post."

I was still reeling with shock. Not once had Betty ever mentioned Eddie was an officer. Why, if she had, I would *never* have had the nerve to say two words to her.

"Now, how about that wine?" Betty said, turning to me. "And good Christ, what smells so delectable? Eddie, I'm telling you, this girl can cook like you wouldn't believe. Well, you couldn't stop raving about her raisin cookies last week."

As we moved toward the kitchen, Jake caught my eye. I swallowed hard and looked away. For an eerie moment, he'd looked just like his father.

There would be hell to pay later.

***

"We'll get together at our place next time," Betty said, giving me a brief hug. "Thanks, hon. We had a ball. Didn't we, Eddie?"

Eddie Kelly smiled down at me. "We sure did. And dinner was great—the best fried chicken I've ever tasted."

I suspected he was just being polite, even though the chicken had turned out pretty good, if I said so myself. But Eddie was such a nice guy, he, no doubt, would've complimented me even if it had tasted like an old shoe. Jake, on the other hand, had scarfed down his food without a word of thanks, barely saying a thing to anybody during the whole meal.

With one last goodbye and "see you tomorrow," I closed the door and glanced up at the sunburst "atom" clock on the living room wall—ten-forty-five. Early for a Friday night. I'd expected the Kelly's to stay at least until midnight. But it was no wonder they'd left. Jake hadn't been exactly hospitable, answering any questions in as few words as possible, and never initiating conversation, even while we were playing Hearts.

With a sigh, I headed for the kitchen to wash up the dishes that had been soaking in the sink since supper. Just as I was wondering if Jake had gone to bed already, I heard the toilet flush. He appeared in the kitchen doorway a moment later, a half-empty wine bottle in his hand.

That was one thing, I thought. Eddie Kelly probably hadn't been impressed with Jake's conversation skills, but he'd surely been amazed by his capacity to drink. After the first bottle of wine had disappeared at supper, Eddie had gone back to their apartment and brought back another three bottles—the last of which Jake was finishing off now.

Feeling his gaze upon me, I reached for the hot water faucet and turned it on full-blast. My earlier dread of what would happen once the Kelly's left had turned to cold anger. Jake had promised me he'd make an effort to be friendly tonight. Was it *my* fault that Betty had never told me she was an officer's wife? How could I have possibly suspected that? From the very beginning, she'd treated me like an equal. Of course, their two-bedroom apartment and the careless way she spent money should've been a clue.

"Well, I hope you're satisfied with yourself," Jake said finally, slurring his words. "Embarrassing me like that."

The baby gave a hard kick inside my womb, and I drew in a sharp breath. I turned off the tap, thrust my hands into the sudsy water and began to furiously scrub the dishes.

"I don't know what the big deal is," I said. "Betty and Eddie both said we didn't stand on ceremony off the post."

"You don't know what the big deal is?" Jake slammed the wine bottle down on the table so hard I thought sure it must've cracked. "I'll tell you what! It's a goddamn *rule*! No frater...frataner...*shit*! No *socializing* between officers and enlisted. And if somebody found out about it, you know who'd get in trouble for it, right? *Me*! Not smooth-talking Mr. High and Mighty Captain Edward Kelly. I'd probably get booted right out of the Army, and it would be *your* fault. *God*! You're as dumb as a bag of rocks!"

I stood stiffly, staring down into the dishwater. The suds from the cheap dish detergent I'd bought at the commissary were already dissipating. Hot tears blinded me, but I was determined not to let Jake see them. I wasn't about to give him the satisfaction of knowing how much his cruel words had hurt me.

Suddenly he laughed. "Yep, *dummmm* as a bag o' rocks."

Maybe it was the sneering tone of his voice or maybe it was his cruel laughter that did it. Something snapped inside me and I stiffened, my hand tightening on the dishrag. Behind me, I heard a slurping sound and knew Jake had grabbed the wine bottle again. I reached for the dish towel and turned. Drying my hands, I stared at him.

"The only one who embarrassed you tonight was yourself, Jake. You and your disgusting drinking."

Jake lowered the wine bottle and wiped his mouth with the back of his hand. He was grinning, his blue eyes sparkling with meanness. "Dumb as a bag of rocks," he said.

I threw the dishtowel at him. "Oh, *go to hell!*" Never in my life had I ever said such a thing to another living soul, but this time, Jake had gone too far. I headed for the door.

He moved like a flash of lightning, his hand curling around my upper arm, nails digging into my tender flesh. He wrenched me toward him so that his face was inches from mine. I flinched at the sour smell of wine on his breath. The grin had disappeared from his face. His eyes blazed. "It's a damn good thing you're pregnant," he said. "Or I'd have to teach you a lesson about sassing me."

I stared back at him defiantly, but my heart was hammering. "Let go of me, Jake."

For a moment, our gazes remained locked. Jake's grip on my arm didn't loosen. My free hand cradled my bulging belly protectively. I didn't really think he'd hurt me or the baby, but his drinking changed his personality. Anything could happen when he was drunk.

But then I saw the flexed muscle in his jaw relax. He released me. "I'll let it go this time, Lily Rae. I reckon all them raging hormones you got these days make you say stupid things. Just watch your mouth next time, okay?"

I couldn't trust myself to speak. Instead, I gave him a withering look and turned toward the kitchen door. But before I could step out into the hall, Jake spoke again, "Hey, if you want to play the part of a little handmaiden, you just keep on being friendly with Miss Shit Don't Stink Betty Kelly. But don't be invitin' them over here anymore, you hear? I have to kiss them officer's asses at work. I sure as shit don't intend to do it at home."

CHAPTER EIGHTEEN

I had no intention of breaking off my friendship with Betty. The girl had been nothing but kind to me, and it didn't matter a bit to me if she was an officer's wife. Who cared about stupid Army rules, anyway? After all, *I* wasn't in the Army; Jake was. So I'd be darned if I let the Army tell me who I could or couldn't be friends with.

The Monday after the Friday night the Kelly's had come over, Betty knocked on the door a few minutes after Jake left for the post. With the baby in her arms and a bottle of formula stuck in his mouth, she settled herself down at the kitchen table just as she usually did, talking a mile a minute while waiting for me to pour her a cup of coffee. With Jake's sharp words ringing in my mind, I couldn't help but feel awkward with my friend. And Betty picked up on it right away.

There was a soft pop from Davy's mouth as she withdrew the bottle, and with a practiced movement, she positioned the baby on her left shoulder and began to pat his back, eyeing me from across the table. "What's up with you, kid? You've been acting like the cat's got your tongue since I walked in. What's wrong?"

And I blurted it all out—everything Jake had said about Army rules and how we weren't supposed to socialize with officers and their wives.

"Well," Betty said when I finished. "That's about the biggest load of crap I've ever heard in my life."

And as if to second that motion, Davy let out an explosive burp and looked around the room with his bird-bright eyes as if to ask, "Who did that?" Betty and I stared at each other, and then burst out laughing. That's when I knew she'd be my friend for life, despite Jake's feelings.

Almost a month had passed since that morning, and Betty had become a mentor of sorts, teaching me to become more grown up and independent and to learn to think of myself as Jake's partner in life, not his doormat. There was one more thing Betty had taught me, and that was how to drive a car.

She'd taken me down to the DMV where I'd applied for a learner's permit, and that very afternoon, I'd found myself behind the wheel of the Kelly's '51 Packard convertible in a deserted church parking lot with Betty sitting next to me and teaching me the basics.

And today…

I stepped into the DMV waiting room and triumphantly waved a sheet of paper at Betty who was pacing the floor with an irritable Davy.

"I passed," I called out.

A delighted grin crossed her face and she gave me a thumbs up. "Good for you, hon," She raised her voice over the baby's whimpering. "I knew you would."

"I just have to go get my picture taken. Shouldn't be much longer."

When the man behind the counter gave me the license, I saw that my picture wasn't half-bad. In fact, I looked healthier and prettier than a ripe peach in a Georgia orchard.

Pregnancy agreed with me, I realized. Once the morning sickness had gone away, I'd started to enjoy being pregnant. And Jake was beginning to enjoy it, too. Well, maybe not *enjoy* it, but he'd certainly been lavishing attention on me lately. Since the baby had become so active, he'd started taking an uncharacteristic interest in my growing belly. The first time he felt the baby kick, a grin had spread across his face as wide as the Red River that flowed north of Texarkana. And one evening last week, he'd sat in the bathroom with me as I reclined in the tub and watched my belly go up and down like the baby was riding a bicycle in there, and the whole time, he seemed as fascinated as a boy with his first train set. He hadn't been drinking as much lately either. I didn't know why, and honestly, I didn't *care* why. I was just glad because he was a lot easier to get along with when he wasn't drinking. Maybe he was finally realizing it was time to settle down and take some responsibilities as a grown-up.

Heading back to the waiting room, I thought about the evening ahead. It was pay-day, and Jake had promised to take me into Texarkana to see "Titanic" which had just opened at The Paramount on Main Street. I'd been dying to see it since I'd first heard it was coming out.

Across the waiting room, Betty smiled when I walked in, waving my license. She rushed over and gave me a hug, squashing a disgruntled Davy between us. "I'm so proud of you, hon."

My happiness dimmed a bit as I wished fervently that I could invite Betty and Eddie to join us at the movies tonight. But that's one thing Jake would never change his mind about. He wanted nothing to do with the Kelly's. So I'd learned to keep my mouth shut about Betty and our friendship.

If that was what it took to keep the peace, then that's what I'd do.

***

We stepped out of the movie theater into the chill of a rainy March night, along with the rest of the crowd who'd just watched "Titanic" in a packed auditorium. As the cold rain pounded against me, I caught my breath and tried to pull my short wool car coat closer around me, even though I knew it would be a futile attempt. My tummy had grown so big I couldn't get the darn coat buttoned.

"Stay here," Jake said, dropping my hand. "I'll go get the car."

"*No!*" I grabbed his coat sleeve. "I'll get just as wet standing here than if we go together." I didn't want to admit it to him, but I couldn't quite shake the country girl fear of being alone in a big city at night.

Jake shrugged. "Alright, let's go."

The car was parked just down the street, not even half a block away. We'd be there in no time. But still, I couldn't wait until we got in the car to talk about the movie. Why, it had been the best picture show I'd ever seen!

"Oh, Jake, it was just so sad," I wailed as we scurried down the sidewalk, heads bent against the rain.

If Jake made a response to my comment about the movie, I didn't hear it because I was distracted by something happening inside my body. It was a queer feeling down there in my nether regions—a warm wetness between my legs, like I'd sprung a leak or something. I kept walking, though, a step or two behind Jake's long stride. But when he opened the car door for me, (something he'd only started to do lately) the fluid seeping into the crotch of my panties turned into a hot gush.

"Oh, *Lord!*" I clutched at my belly. "*Jake!*"

"What?" He stared at me, the rain pelting his face, flattening his Brille-Cremed hair against his skull.

I felt a half-hysterical urge to giggle as the river of liquid ran down my nylon-clad legs. "*I think my water broke!*"

***

"Oh, *dear God! Jake, I can't take it anymore! I gotta push. I gotta!*"

With one hand flattened on the dashboard, I tried to maintain my balance as Jake took a curve on two wheels, or so it seemed. Beneath my saturated skirt, I felt the baby's head bulging against my vaginal wall as if it was bound and determined to escape its womb.

"*No!*" Jake yelled. "Hold on another minute! I see the lights of Hot Springs just down the hill."

"I *can't* hold on!" I moaned as another excruciating pain tightened its vice-like grip around my mid-section. "It's *comin*, I tell you!"

"We're here, Lily Rae! Hush, now! There's the sign for the hospital. Just another minute, okay?" Jake hunched over the steering wheel, trying to see through the rain.

Through half-slitted eyes, I saw the illuminated red letters—*Emergency*! The words shimmered and danced in front of my eyes as yet another pain sank its vengeful teeth into my womb on the heels of the one that had just eased. I dug my nails into the arm rest and lifted my bottom from the seat, searching for some kind of relief.

And then I was alone in the car. Leaving the motor running, Jake had run into the emergency room entrance—to get a doctor or nurse, I hoped.

I squeezed my eyes shut, moaning. A moment...an hour later—I didn't know how much time had passed—I heard a kind, feminine voice. "Okay, honey. It's going to be just fine. I need you to help me get you into this wheelchair."

Another pain was gearing up, and I knew it was now or never. If I didn't get in that wheelchair, this baby was going to be born right here in the front seat.

Drawing strength from somewhere, I eased out of the car, and with the help of the kind-faced brunette nurse, I dropped into the seat of the wheelchair, and just like that, I was being whisked into the ER. That's when I realized Jake wasn't with me.

Wild-eyed, I looked back. He was getting into the driver's side of the car.

"I'll go park the car," he shouted over the sound of the drilling rain. "And then come looking for you."

By the time I saw my husband again, Debra Ann Tatlow was almost ten hours old.

"Ah, she sure is a pretty one, that babe is. Look at all that golden hair."

I looked up at the coffee-skinned army nurse and gave her a shy smile. "Thank you kindly. She's the spittin' image of my baby brother, Charles Alton. He died when he was only two."

The smile disappeared from the nurse's face. She folded her arms across her generous bosom, her chocolate eyes glimmering with sympathy. "Well, now...that's a real tragedy, honey."

"I know." My gaze returned to my baby. Debby Ann's eyes were closed as she sucked rhythmically on her bottle of formula. Her delicate eyelids looked as fragile as a butterfly's wings. My heart welled with love. "I always thought I understood how awful it was for my mother—losing Charles Alton like she did," I murmured. "But now I know I had no idea how much she must've been hurting."

The nurse didn't speak for a moment, but just gazed down at us, a compassionate look on her pretty brown face. She heaved a sigh and said, "The Lord works in mysterious ways, and sometimes that means folks have to suffer."

I looked at her. Something in the tone of her voice told me she'd done her share of suffering. I wanted to ask her to tell her story, but I just couldn't make myself do it. Captain Johnson, RN, was the first Negro woman I'd ever actually met. Oh, I'd seen a few dark-skinned people during the few weeks I'd spent in Louieville; there had even been a Negro girl in my secretarial school. But this was my first opportunity to actually talk with one. And Captain Johnson had been just as sweet as shoofly pie, but still, I felt a little awkward with her.

This morning right before shift change, Captain Waldman, the nurse who'd delivered Debby Ann—because the doctor didn't get there in time-- had brought Captain Johnson into the maternity ward, saying she was going to be taking over for her, and if I needed anything, just give her a holler. I'd still been drowsy from the sleeping pill they'd given me, and all I'd remembered from the encounter was a pretty dark face smiling down at me, and a gentle touch on the top of my head.

An hour later, the captain had come in again, delivering breakfast trays to me and another woman who'd been brought in sometime after I'd fallen asleep in the early hours of the morning. The tousle-haired blond refused her tray, but I discovered I was ravenous. I hadn't eaten anything since the popcorn at the movie show last night. We'd been planning to stop at White Castle for a couple of hamburgers on our way home, but Debby Ann had vetoed that idea.

With barely contained amusement, Captain Johnson had watched me scarf down two scrambled eggs, two slices of toast, a mound of hash browns and four slices of crisp bacon, and then wash it all down with a tall glass of chilled orange juice. It was almost the best breakfast I'd ever tasted—except for the hundred or so Mother had made every morning from the earliest I could remember.

"Well, that's a first," Captain Johnson said as she removed my tray. "I've finally met a girl who has an appetite to rival my teenage son's."

I let out an unladylike belch, and daintily dabbed at my mouth with a napkin. "I reckon birthing babies works up a mighty hefty appetite."

The nurse chuckled. "Well, I reckon it does."

Ten minutes ago, Captain Johnson had brought in Debby Ann for her first feeding, showing me how to hold her and how to give her the bottle. I'd seen my mother breastfeeding Norry and the two younger boys; not one of us had been raised without the breast. For a while, I'd considered breastfeeding. But after talking to Betty, and reading articles in different magazines, I'd decided to be a modern mother and give my baby the best. All those vitamins and minerals they put in baby formula had to be better than what came out of me, I reckoned. Besides, according to Betty, it was just so much easier to use a bottle—except for the sterilizing, of course.

The baby felt so warm against my hospital gown, and she smelled of Ivory soap and sweet, milky formula. My heart rose, feeling as if it were climbing up through my chest to lodge somewhere between my chin and my throat. I'd never felt emotion like this. Such love, such tenderness. *So...this is what if feels like to be a mom.* I felt special, as if I'd accomplished a great feat—like climbing Mount Everest--even though I knew I'd only done what billions of women had done since the dawn of time.

I felt the nurse watching me and gave a tremulous smile. "I still can't believe it," I whispered.

"It's a true miracle, isn't it?" Captain Johnson returned my smile. "I see it happen every day, and I'm still filled with wonder when a new life comes into the world."

A soft sound came from the baby—a teeny, tiny burp—nothing at all like the shots heard around the world that Davy could expel, and I brushed my lips over her downy, golden head. I repositioned Debby Ann into the crook of my arm and looked up at the nurse.

"Should I try and feed her more?"

Captain Johnson shook her head. "She looks mighty content to me. You still have some time before we take her back to the nursery, though. Why don't you just love on her a while?" She turned to go. "You call if you need me. I'll be back in a little while to pick her up."

"Oh, Captain Johnson!" I called out as the nurse headed for the door. "Still no word from my husband?"

A guarded look crossed the captain's face. "We're still trying to locate him, hon."

My gaze dropped back to the baby. I lovingly ran a hand over her soft down. "That's okay," I said. "I know what happened. He'll be here directly, I reckon."

***

Jake arrived just as Captain Johnson took the sleeping baby from my arms to transport her back to the nursery.

"Is that my youngun?"

At the sound of his raspy voice, both me and the captain looked over at him.

He was hung-over, I saw immediately. I could tell by the bloodshot eyes and pasty skin. Not that I was surprised. When he hadn't shown up at the hospital last night, I'd known he was getting himself liquored up—and here in Arkansas, he could do it without breaking the law.

Captain Johnson eyed him up and down, her jaw tight, and then turned to me. "Does this boy have the right room, sweetheart? He your husband?"

"Yes, ma'am," I said tightly.

"Well, then..." Captain Johnson walked over to Jake, cradling Debby Ann in her arms. She stopped a few inches away from him and stared him in the eye. "Private Tatlow, is it?"

He straightened as if someone had stuck a cattle prod up his hind end. I guessed that meant he'd suddenly remembered he was in the military and was being addressed by an officer.

"Yes, Ma'am," he said smartly.

A slow smile spread across the nurse's face, but her eyes remained frosty. "Well, now, Private Tatlow, it took you quite a while to park the car, didn't it, soldier?"

A tide of red crept up Jake's neck and over his cheekbones. "Yes, Ma'am," he said again, his eyes fixed straight ahead.

The captain nodded as if she understood. "Let's see...your baby girl here, was born at 12:55 this morning; that makes her just over ten hours old. Why, you must've parked plumb over the Texas state-line and walked back. What else would take a young man so long to get back to the wife he left in hard labor at the ER doors?"

A muscle flexed in Jake's jaw and his flush deepened. He swallowed hard. "Ma'am, I..."

I could see his brain spinning, trying to think of a plausible explanation. But obviously the liquor had pickled it inactive.

"*Quiet, Private!*" The smile had disappeared from the captain's face. Her dark eyes bored into Jake's.

I could hardly believe this was the same sweet-faced nurse who'd been instructing me on how to feed the baby. It was as if she'd had a complete personality change. On one hand, I felt some satisfaction in the captain's dressing down of Jake—he deserved it for being such a selfish

fool—but I also felt a little scared. Jake didn't take
no guff from anybody, and now, here was this
colored woman ripping him a new asshole, as Betty
would put it. What if he talked back to her
or—Heaven forbid!—hauled off and hit her? I
knew that look in his eyes. He was madder than a
wet hen. His jaw was rigid, his eyes sparkling with
fury. He was seconds away from exploding.

"Captain Johnson!" I called out. "It's not
Jake's fault. I told him to stay away…" I thought
quickly. "He was dog-tired, poor guy, making that
drive from Texas. I told him to go get some sleep in
the car." Even as the lie came out my lips, I knew
how ridiculous it sounded—and I also knew that the
Army nurse wouldn't buy it. "See, he'd just got off a
double shift, and hadn't had no sleep in twelve
hours. And I always heard that first babies took a
while to be born, so I thought he'd be back with me
in plenty of time…" My voice trailed off.

Captain Johnson stared at me with something
like pity in her eyes. Then she shook her head
slowly, snuggling Debby Ann closer in her arms.
"Honey," she said softly. "I've been where you are,
and I know what it's like to make excuses for a man.
I did it for twenty years before I wised up and kicked
his sorry ass out. And I'm telling you right now, I
wish I could have those twenty years back. I
wouldn't have put up with him for a New York
minute." She turned back to Jake, giving him a look
that would've frozen hot cocoa. "I can't stop you
from visiting your wife if she wants you here, but if
you want to hold your daughter, Private Tatlow, you
come back at two o'clock. That's the next feeding
time. But before you do, you find yourself
somewhere to take a sponge bath because you reek
of beer, and I don't want this sweet little girl to have

that be the smell she associates with her daddy. You understand me, soldier?"

"Yes, Ma'am," Jake barked.

Captain Johnson turned on her heel and strode out of the room. As the swish of her starched uniform faded down the hall, Jake's posture settled back to normal, but his eyes remained furious. He moved toward my bed, and was still a few steps away when I smelled the stale beer. I wrinkled my nose in distaste.

"Uppity nigger, ain't she?"

A hot bolt of fury ripped through me. "*Jake!* That's just downright *mean!*"

It wasn't as if I hadn't heard the word before. Living in Kentucky all my life, I'd heard it bandied about, usually by old men in overalls sitting out on the porch of Red's General Store, chewing tobacco. But I'd never heard my Jake say it, and it sounded particularly ugly on his lips.

"She's been nothing but nice to me, Jake Tatlow, and if you say one more bad word about her, you can leave right now. We just brought a new soul into this world, and I'm going to protect her from the ugliness just as long as I can. And if that means I have to protect her from you, so be it."

I glared at him and waited for his infuriated response, determined not to back down this time, not just for my sake, but for Debby Ann's.

To my astonishment, Jake's blue eyes swam with tears. I gaped at him as shock radiated through me. "Jake!" I finally gasped. "What is it?" My stomach clenched in fear. Was something wrong with Debby Ann, and they'd told him so he could break the news to me?

Jake shook his head and reached blindly for a chair to draw over to the bed. He sat down, reached for my hand and grasped it like it was a rope saving him from a tumbling death. His red-rimmed eyes stared into mine as tears tracked down his handsome face.

"Jesus save me, Lily Rae. They're sending me to Korea."

Lily's Oatmeal Raisin Cookies

1 c brown sugar
1 c sugar
1 c margarine, softened
2 c flour
1 egg
1 cup raisins
1 c cornflakes, crushed
3/4 c oatmeal
1 t soda
1 t baking powder
1 t vanilla

Cream margarine and sugars. beat in eggs & vanilla. Sift soda and baking powder with flour. Stir in flour mixture. Add raisins, cornflakes & oatmeal. Drop by teaspoon onto ungreased cookie sheets. Bake at 375 degrees for 8-10 minutes.

CHAPTER NINETEEN

Jake had been gone exactly a week, and I could barely function. If it weren't for Debby Ann, I probably wouldn't have been able to drag myself out of bed.

During the day, I found myself crying at the drop of a hat, and nights were no better. I was either awake and pacing the floor with a cranky baby, both of us bawling, or I was tossing and turning in bed, missing the warmth and musky scent of Jake's body, and tensing at every little creak in the apartment, sure it was a mad-dog killer breaking in to rape and strangle me. Most of the time, I hadn't bothered to get dressed in the mornings, wearing my baby-doll pajamas throughout the sweltering Texas days. What was the point? I wasn't going anywhere.

I barely had the energy to run a brush through my hair, much less put on any make-up. Dirty baby bottles and a few stray dishes were piled up in the sink, waiting to be washed. Since there was no one to cook for, and because I had little or no appetite, I'd been surviving on Trix Cereal, Ritz crackers and Cheez Whiz, and an occasional tuna fish sandwich.

Thank God for Betty! Like clockwork, she'd come over every single afternoon, plopping Davy down on an old quilt on the living room floor. Then she'd spend the next couple of hours trying to *keep* him on the quilt—he was just starting to crawl—while making a gallant attempt to cheer me up. Both tasks seemed just as impossible, I thought. Davy was a strong-willed boy who'd suddenly realized that knees and hands came in quite handy when you wanted to see a different view of the world.

And I, on the other hand, missed Jake so much, it felt like a wild raccoon had made itself at home inside me and was gnawing away on my heart. I'd thought it was awful the first time Jake had left me, back when he went off to boot camp. But at least then I'd had my family close by. This time, within hours of seeing him off at the train station, it had hit me that I was all alone here in this big, unfamiliar state of Texas—just me and a helpless little baby. But at least there was Betty—a lifesaver.

A wail came from the bedroom. Lying on the couch in the living room, I glanced up at the atom clock on the wall. Right on time. Debby Ann might have her days and nights mixed up, but she sure knew when it was feeding time—every three hours on the dot. Not every *four* hours, like the nurses at the hospital told me it would be. I sighed and swung my legs over the side of the couch. My head swam dizzily as I sat up.

That's what you get for laying around all the time and not eating, I told myself. I sat there a moment, rubbing my aching forehead with my fingertips as the cries from the bedroom grew louder.

When Debby Ann had first arrived home from the hospital, I'd really tried to follow the nurses' advice to feed her every four hours. That meant listening to the baby's steady fussing for an hour before each feeding time. Finally, in desperation I'd turned to Betty for advice.

"For God's sake, feed the kid every three hours, Lily," she'd advised. "The world isn't going to stop turning because you're feeding her on *her* schedule rather than the hospital's."

So, that's what I'd been doing. Every three hours, day in and day out, around the clock. Only trouble was, Debby Ann would feed greedily for the first five minutes, and then fall asleep with the nipple still in her mouth. Which was fine, really, in daytime. But at night—*every* night, it seemed—as soon as I put the baby down into her bassinet, she'd wake up and start crying. Not just crying, but shrieking as if some evil person was poking her with a hot stick. The first time it had happened, I'd checked to make sure her diaper pin hadn't opened; I'd been *that* sure something was causing the baby unimaginable pain. But when it kept happening, night after night, I'd called the hospital in a panic, only to be told that the baby was suffering from something called "colic," and there was nothing to do but "let her grow out of it."

But I was worried all the same. It didn't seem like Debby Ann was getting enough to eat. Well, how could she? She always fell asleep before she'd taken in a couple of ounces. But even though she seemed hungry, when she was in the middle of one of these colic attacks, she wouldn't feed. At first, she'd act like she wanted the bottle; she'd start sucking away like she was starving. But a minute later, she'd rear her head back, scrunch up those little dark eyes and let out a banshee wail. And I'd be up, walking the floor with her for the rest of the night.

The shrieks coming from the bedroom had grown more piercing. I stood up on wobbly legs, and began to make my way to the kitchen. "Just hold on, baby doll," I called out. "I got to heat up your formula."

I took out a baby bottle from the Norge, noticing with dismay there were only two bottles left. Time to mix up more formula and sterilize it. One *more* thing to do.

I grabbed a saucepan from the cabinet, filled it with water and put the bottle into it. Then I placed it on the coiled burner and turned the electric stove on medium.

Lord, I'd had no idea how much work it was to have a baby in the house. I'd never been so dog-tired in my life. Then again, I couldn't remember the last time I'd had a good night's sleep. God knows Jake hadn't been any help in that department before he left. He'd made it clear that taking care of the baby was *my* job.

Three hard raps came at the apartment door. "Knock, knock!"

Debby Ann's cries were beginning to reach the screeching level. I felt like screaming, too, as I headed for the door. I wondered if it would help.

I opened the door to let Betty in. Watching "Love of Life" together had become a ritual even before Debby Ann was born, first in Betty's apartment on her nice RCA, lately on the second-hand Airline Jake had bought at a yard sale. But today, I knew right away something was different about this visit. Betty breezed into the apartment dressed in a coral summer dress with a white Peter Pan collar cinched at the waist with a white patent leather belt and matching heels. On her head, she wore a jaunty white wide-brimmed hat.

"You go jump in the shower," she said before I had a chance to open my mouth. "I'm taking Debby Ann over to my place. You know Merline, don't you? That teenager down in 2-B? She's agreed to sit for us."

Betty was already on her way down the hall toward the bedroom, her shapely behind swaying, ala Marilyn, beneath the snug cut of her linen dress.

"But…" I sputtered. "It's feeding time. And…" I followed Betty into the bedroom. "Why do you have a sitter? Where are we going?"

Betty smiled down at the wailing baby. "What's wrong, sweetheart?" she cooed, scooping Debby Ann up in her arms and cradling her. "Yes, that's it. Auntie Betty has you now."

Amazingly, the baby had stopped crying. I shook my head. If that didn't just beat all. Betty grinned over at me. "Methinks this one is on her way to being spoiled already."

"Or maybe she just doesn't like *me*," I said bitterly.

Betty laughed. "Oh, don't be silly." Her gaze sharpened. "What are you doing just standing there? Get in the shower. It's a beautiful summer-like day outside, and I'll be damned if you're going to spend one more afternoon in this tomb of an apartment feeling sorry for yourself. And don't you worry about this little one. I'll feed her while you're getting ready."

"Ready for *what*?" I cried out, exasperated.

Betty rocked the baby in her arms and smiled from across the room. "You need cheering up, don't you? Well, I've got the perfect idea. We're going to Texarkana, and we're going to have a late lunch at The Savoy, and then, honey, we're going to shop until we *drop*."

***

I stretched out my legs and gazed up into a sapphire sky meringued with white marshmallow clouds towering into the heavens. That one there looked like the mast of an Old World sailing ship like the one Christopher Columbus sailed to America, I mused. But even as this thought meandered through my mind, it changed, and now it looked like a giant Mickey Mouse.

A soft, cooing sound drew my glance down to the patchwork quilt on which I sprawled—Mother's handiwork--and I smiled and turned on my side to gaze down at Debby Ann. The baby wore only a diaper and a thin summer T-shirt that snapped down the front. It was still spring in Texas, but hotter than blazes, even here under the shade of a Spanish Oak.

Debby Ann cooed again, then blew a spit bubble, her tiny feet, clad in pink knit booties, pumping the air like an Olympic bicyclist. Her pebble-brown eyes gazed up at the sky with rapt attention as if she were studying it for a pop quiz that would be given to her at any minute. I grinned. She sure was a pretty little thing—and for once, she seemed to be content. I brushed a tender hand over her soft down of golden hair, and then frowned. She still wasn't eating good, though. And she didn't have that plump, healthy look that Betty's baby boy had.

189

I glanced over at the playpen where Betty had left Davy a few minutes ago while she went in to make lunch. He was standing up, holding onto a slat with one chubby hand and gumming on a Gerber's biscuit with the other. Every couple of minutes, though, he'd stop long enough to babble a few words of baby talk and then go back to his biscuit. I hoped Betty would remember to bring a wet washcloth with her when she came back out. He was a sight for sore eyes!

Turning on my stomach, I heard paper crackling beneath my shorts, reminding me of the two letters that had come in the mail yesterday. I'd brought them outside with the latest issue of **Radio Mirror**, intending to read them again, even though I'd already read Jake's so many times, the cheap, Army-issue paper was smudged and worn.

I smiled, thinking about the romantic things he'd written—well, romantic for *him*. Poor guy. He was really missing me. Korea was a hell-hole, he'd written. It was cold and rainy and muddy. The food was awful and—he was lonely. He couldn't wait to come home to me and his little girl. That was pretty much all he said, but for Jake, that was more romantic than I'd ever expected.

The other letter I'd received yesterday had been from Inis, and it had contained a bombshell. Meg had up and joined the WACs. Didn't that just beat all? According to Inis, Meg hadn't told a soul what she was up to; one Monday morning last month, she'd got up, packed a bag and hitch-hiked into Russell Springs where she'd caught the morning Greyhound to Campbellsville. These details, the family had only found out about a week later when her letter arrived from Maryland.

Good for her, I thought with a wry smile.
I never would've thought she'd have the gumption.
But what on earth would Jake think about it?
According to him, any woman who joined the
military was nothing but a slut and a whore.

"Oh, please, no! Don't move. I don't need a *bit*
of help!"

I looked up to see a barefoot Betty picking her
way across the grass, balancing a tray of two icy-cold
bottles of Coke, two sandwiches and a plate of my
oatmeal raisin cookies. She looked pretty as a
picture in blue short-shorts and a white peasant
blouse that revealed perfectly-molded shoulders
tanned golden from days of lying out in the sun.

I scurried up from the quilt to grab the two
bottles of Coke to help lighten her load.

"Hope you like grilled cheese," Betty said,
placing the tray on the quilt. "You'd better. It was
hotter than Hades in that kitchen." She settled
down on the quilt next to me.

"Yum! Thank you." I took a sandwich from
the tray and began to nibble on it. "Well...this isn't
exactly how I imagined my first Mother's Day to be,
but I suppose it's not too bad. It's a beautiful
day...hot, of course, but look how pretty the sky is.
And I have Debby Ann and..." I blushed, casting
my eyes down to a bright yellow patch of quilt.
"...you," I added, still embarrassed to look at my
friend. "Thank the good Lord I have you."

"Hey," Betty reached out and gave my hand a
squeeze. "I'm glad I have you, too, hon." She
glanced up at the clouds. "Don't have a conniption
fit or anything, but while I was fixing lunch, I heard
on the radio they've issued a tornado watch for parts
of north-central Texas."

I felt that familiar gut spasm I always
experienced at the mention of a twister, but I tried

191

with all my might to hide the reaction from Betty. "But not for here, right?" I asked, forcing an unconcerned lightness into my voice.

Betty shook her head. "No. Just the Waco area."

I felt a little better. "Waco? But that's on the river. Indian legend says that twisters don't strike close to rivers. That's what the landlord told me, and he's lived here all his life."

Betty lifted a slim shoulder in a shrug. "I'm just telling you what I heard on the radio." She took a long draw from her Coke bottle, and then grinned. "I heard something else while I was fixing lunch. How would you like to do something special tonight? We can call it a Mother's Day present."

"What?"

"Well, there's this new honky-tonk opening up on the Arkansas side of Texarkana tonight. Let's see if we can get Merline to baby-sit, and you and I will go have a little fun."

I stared at my friend. "You mean a bar? And it's open on Sunday night?"

"On the hush-hush," Betty said. "The owner is a friend of a friend, and tonight's opening is by special invitation only. And you and I are invited."

"Oh, I don't know, Betty." At my side, Debby Ann screwed up her face and began to fuss, her bootied feet cycling the air. I placed my hand on her belly and began to pat her. "Jake wouldn't like it."

Betty frowned. "Jake doesn't have to know about it. Come on, Lily! We've been cooped up in this place for weeks. Don't we deserve a little fun? For God's sake, are we supposed to just shrivel up and die because we're married and have babies? We're not over the hill; we're in our twenties!"

"I'm still nineteen," I said.

Betty scowled. "Bitch." Then she grinned and gave me an affectionate shove on the shoulder. "You make me feel like an old lady at 23! But seriously, Lil, what's wrong with us going out and having a couple of drinks and maybe doing a little dancing?"

Debby Ann began to fuss in earnest now. I sighed and picked her up, snuggling her against my shoulder. I peered down the stretch of lawn that separated the two apartment buildings. Someone's laundry hung limply on a clothesline that paralleled the side of one building. In this heat, it had probably been dry ten minutes after it had been hung out.

"Please, Lily." Betty's blue eyes implored me. "If I don't get out for a little while, I swear, I'm going to just die! And you know I can't go alone."

"Well..." It *would* be nice to dress up and go out.

"*Pretty* please, Lily? We don't have to stay long. Just for a little while."

I sighed and gave Debby Ann's back a rub. "I reckon we could go out for an hour or so. But..." I stared at Betty. "Lord, Betty! What do I wear? My nice dresses are too tight for me now! And I thought it would take me no time at all to get back to the weight I was before I got pregnant."

Betty rolled her eyes. "Dream on, sister." She scrambled up from the quilt. "But don't you worry. I have a dress that's too tight on me—thanks very much to Master David over there in that playpen. I'm betting it will look perfect on you. Let's go inside and see if Merline can sit for us. If she can't, I swear, I'm going have one of your famous conniption fits."

Luckily for Betty, Merline was available. And although I was happy about that, I couldn't help but

wonder what my friend would look like having a
conniption fit.

CHAPTER TWENTY

August 1953

"**O**h, Lord, Betty! Here comes another bus. *Surely* they'll be in this one!" I practically jumped up and down, and probably *would* have if I hadn't had a squirming, unhappy baby in my arms.

Beside me, Betty grinned and crossed her fingers. "Let's hope so. I don't know about you, hon, but I'm horny as hell."

My cheeks warmed at Betty's off-color remark. "Oh, you!" I said. "Is that *all* you think about?"

Betty snickered. "What *else* is there?"

I shook my head and smiled. Lord, Betty said the most outrageous things! True, though…she only said out loud the things I'd been thinking. I hadn't been able to sleep a wink last night; all I could do was think about Jake's arrival, and how my body was yearning for him.

Over Debby Ann's fuzzy blond head, I watched the green Army bus lumber to a stop in front of the

Post Ops building. It was the third one we'd seen on this stifling August morning at the Red River Arsenal, spilling out dozens of uniformed soldiers arriving home from Korea.

Two weeks ago, Betty had received a telegram from Eddie announcing that the war was over, and all the troops would be coming home. Since the moment she'd burst into my apartment, telegram in hand, I'd been counting down the hours until this moment.

Through the windows of the bus, I saw soldiers standing up and grabbing their gear from the overhead racks, but I couldn't make out any faces. Jake and Eddie better be on this one. If I had to wait for another bus, my heart would give out. I just knew it.

The door of the bus opened and the soldiers, clad in their khaki uniforms, began to file out, duffle bags in hand. I watched, my heart in my throat.

In the stroller at Betty's feet, Davy suddenly let out an ear-piercing squeal—a new trick he'd learned in the past few days, having discovered how much fun it was to see his mother wince every time he did it. Debby Ann, on the other hand, had been fussing all morning, as if she knew something in her world was about to change. Every time I tried to put her in her carriage, she'd have a hissy-fit. The only place she wanted to be was in Mommy's arms.

A tall, handsome blond soldier appeared in the doorway of the bus. Sun glinted off the double silver bars on his Garrison cap as he climbed down the steps.

Betty caught her breath. "Ding dong damn," she said softly. "He looks good enough to eat."

Shrieking his name, she flew across the lawn toward him. My heart bumped. *Jake, you better be on this blame bus.* Debby Ann, as if feeling my tension, squirmed and let out a peevish whimper.

"Shhhh." I rocked back and forth on my heels, patting the baby's back. "Be good now, sweetie. Your daddy will be here soon."

I hoped. Over by the bus, Betty was locked in a passionate embrace with Eddie. She'd knocked off his cap and had her long, slim fingers laced in his blond locks and they were kissing the daylights out of each other.

I looked back at the soldiers still piling off the bus. It was almost empty. Only three dark forms moved down the aisle toward the door. Jake *had* to be one of them.

My heart caught in my throat as a horrible thought occurred to me. What if Jake had become a casualty in the last hours of the war? That happened sometimes. The boys fighting on the battlefields were often the last to know the war was over. And with all the red tape the Army had to put up with, wasn't it possible the bad news hadn't reached me yet? Could the fates be so cruel?

I swallowed hard, clutching Debby Ann so tightly that she let out a frustrated cry. And then, there he was! I drew in a sharp breath. Looking trim and handsome in his Army khakis, Jake stepped down from the bus and looked around.

Oh, Lord, he's grown a moustache. And darned if he doesn't look like a young Clark Gable.

My limbs felt paralyzed. I could only stand there, holding onto Debby Ann, and drink him in. My man. He was *my man.* My heart swelled with pride. He was a hero, and he was home.

His eyes swept over me and moved on without recognition. It was the new clothes and hairdo, I knew. When we'd found out our husbands were coming home, Betty had made appointments for us at "Clip & Curl" on Main Street, where we'd both got shampooed and styled in the latest starlet "dos"—Betty chose the sophisticated "bubble" style of Sophia Loren while I, not so adventurous, went with more of a Doris Day "down home" style, short with a little flip in the back. The new hairstyles had inspired Betty to go through her closet and pull out all her "pre-pregnancy" summer clothes, and give them to me, which, as luck would have it, fit me perfectly.

Today, I wore a grass green capped-sleeved linen sheath, belted at the waist, along with dyed-to-match high heels Betty had loaned me (which were, incidentally, a half-size too small and *killing* me.) Betty had also loaned me a single strand of pearls and clip-on earrings to finish my new look.

No wonder Jake didn't recognize me, all dolled up as I was. When he looked away from me, my paralysis disappeared.

"*Jake!*" Startled by my shout, Debby Ann began to scream. I waved and took a step toward him, and that's when his eyes found me, the vivid blue of them piercing through my skin and raising goose bumps on my bare arms.

He's lost weight, I thought. His cheekbones seemed sharper than I remembered. He looked older, too. But after all, he'd been fighting in a war. I supposed killing folks would make anybody grow up.

For a long moment, Jake simply stared at me, and the look on his face reminded me of the young boy I'd known down by Foster Creek. He looked lost, unsure of himself. And somehow, vulnerable. My heart swelled with tenderness.

And then he smiled. His eyes crinkled at the corners in that endearing way that had always turned my limbs to jelly. Debby Ann screamed louder, her little face turning as red as a cherry. I barely noticed. Because Jake had dropped his duffle bag on the sidewalk and was coming toward me.

I rushed forward, almost tripping on my wobbly spiked heels. Debby Ann kept screaming. And then Jake's arms closed around me, pocketing the crying baby in between our bodies. I clutched him, breathing in his Old Spice aftershave, feeling the warmth and substance of his body against mine, the thud of his heart, the comforting, measured breathing that assured me that, yes, he was here, alive and well, in my arms.

"Lord, Lily Rae. I missed you." His gaze swept over my face as if he was trying to convince himself it was really me.

My eyes blurred with tears. "Oh, Jake. You don't know how bad I missed you. Them fourteen weeks seemed like forever."

Lowering his head, he kissed me long and deep, with an urgency I never remembered experiencing before, not even in those early days of stolen passion in the backseat of his car. His moustache felt exotic as his mouth moved against mine, tasting leisurely as if we had all the time in the world. I sighed into his kiss. From somewhere in the back of my consciousness, I heard Debby Ann still squalling, in full tantrum-mode now.

Jake finally broke the kiss and gazed down at me.

I giggled, looking up at him with adoration. "Your moustache tickles."

He grinned, and shot a glance at Debby Ann. "What's she all riled up about?"

I turned my attention to the baby, drawing away from Jake's embrace and patting Debby Ann on the back. "Oh, she's been fussin' all morning."

"Let me have her."

To my astonishment, Jake took her out of my arms and cradled her. It was the first time I could remember him holding Debby Ann by choice. My man *had* grown up.

Jake rocked the baby in his arms and gazed down at her, grinning. I didn't think I'd ever seen a happier look on his face.

"You listen here, little lady. Your poppa's home from the war, and you're gonna have to settle down now. I'll just bet your momma has spoiled you rotten." He looked up and gave me a grin. "Well, the boss is home now, and things are gonna get back to normal."

***

I lay naked on my side and traced the broad expanse of Jake's shoulders as he slept next to me. Lord, I felt loved all the way through to my bones.

The first time, it had been over way too quickly, but the second time, Jake had made up for it, loving me so sweetly and thoroughly that I'd climaxed three times—something that had never happened to me before. And afterwards, instead of rolling over and falling asleep as he usually did, he held me in his arms, his head propped up on a pillow as he smoked a Camel, and began to talk.

"At first, the boredom almost kills you. Sittin' in that cold hootchie...that's a earth bunker built into a hillside on the frontlines. It was still cold in early April and quiet for the most part...the Chinese were hunkered up for the winter, but we were on alert because of some action on Old Baldy where we overran a UN force to take the hill. So by the time my company got there, nothing much was happening. The weather had turned cold again, and I reckon a man don't feel much like fightin' when we're chilled to the bone."

He took a drag on his cigarette and stared into space. Even though I could feel the heat of his body next to me, it felt as if he'd left me...had gone somewhere far away. I lay with my head against his shoulder, barely breathing, my fingers playing with the silky hair on his chest.

"We sat in that stinkin' hootchie, smokin' cigarettes, playing cards, bull-shitting each other. There was seven of us...from all over the country. Most of them farm boys like me. And then there was this fella from New York City called Salvatore Bertocelli...Sal, we called him, because it was easier. At first, I didn't much care for him. He was a smartass Italian fella, and he liked to kid me about being a hillbilly from Kentucky. But hell! He kidded everbody about everything. You just couldn't help but like the sonuvabitch. He was always grinnin' and makin' us laugh. And in a place like that…*shit!* You either had to laugh, or you'd be bawlin' like a baby if you gave into how scared you were.

Sal's daddy owned a pizza pie place in…Brooklyn, I think it was. And Sal was always talkin' about how he couldn't wait to get back there and eat one of his daddy's pizza pies. Lord, he made it sound so good, it had *my* mouth waterin' and I ain't never tasted a pizza pie, and don't know if I care to. But that Sal…he was the one that kept us all going. No matter how down we got…how homesick we was…Sal would up and say something that would make us bust a gut laughing."

He paused and took another drag of his Camel, slowly releasing a stream of smoke. It wafted through the sultry air of the bedroom and disappeared. Jake was silent so long I wondered if he'd fallen asleep. But then he spoke again, "Sal took three bullets in the chest on July 13th on the banks of the Kumsong River. I was with him when he died."

I drew in a sharp breath, whispering, "Oh, no, Jake."

His voice roughened with emotion. "I was holdin' onto him, telling him it wasn't so bad…he was going to be okay. Bald-faced lyin' to him. I could see the light in his eyes going out. Blood was bubbling out of his mouth. He looked at me, and he said, 'Hey, Hillbilly. This thing's almost over. You keep your head down, pal, and go on home to your pretty wife and baby.' I told him to hang on, that help was on the way. He just shook his head, grinned and said, 'You ever get to Brooklyn, go order a pie at Salvatore's on Rockaway Avenue. It's the best in town.' That's all he said…and then, just like that, he died."

After a long moment of silence, I turned my head and planted a kiss on his chest. "I'm so sorry, honey. I can't imagine how awful that was for you."

Jake didn't respond. He drew away from me to stub out his cigarette in the ashtray on the bedside table, and then turned on his side with his back facing me. I snuggled up against him, my hand caressing his arm.

"It's good to be home," he said quietly.

After a few moments of silence, I realized he'd fallen asleep. I cautiously crawled out of bed, tugged on a robe and went down the stairs to check on Debby Ann. She was still sleeping like a log—a real danger sign that I'd be up all night—but I left her there and returned to Jake.

Now I traced a fingernail across the tattoo of an eagle on the back of Jake's neck—something that hadn't been there when he'd left for Korea. Something else he'd brought back from that foreign country along with a new maturity.

He *does* love me, I thought, my heart swelling with joy. There had been lots of doubt in our nine months of marriage. That memory of our wedding day—the moment when I'd seen his getaway bag on the floor—always intruded even during the good times. But now, for the first time, I felt like I could stop thinking of myself as the girl who'd trapped a husband, forcing him into an unwanted marriage. He loved me. This afternoon's tenderness was proof of that. So was his sharing of what had happened to him in Korea.

"Are you trying to tickle me?"

I gasped as he rolled over to face me, blue eyes twinkling. I hadn't realized he was awake. "I was just admiring your tattoo. Did it hurt to get it done?"

"Nah." Jake yawned and stretched his arms over his head. "And even if it did, I wouldn't admit to you," he added with a grin. "Hey, I brought you something from Korea. You want it now?"

I gave him a playful swat on the arm. "Well, of *course* I do! Go get it!"

He scrambled off the bed, and naked as a jaybird, stalked out of the bedroom. I giggled. "Did anybody ever tell you what a cute behind you have, soldier?" I called after him.

His voice came from the living room. "At least once or twice a week!"

He returned with his duffle bag and placed it on the foot of the rumpled bed. I sat, my knees drawn up and my back resting against the headboard, a sheet drawn modestly around me. I watched as Jake drew a cardboard box from the duffle bag and handed it to me. Then he settled himself on the side of the bed next to me, his eyes sparkling like a young boy on Christmas morning.

I smiled and began to open the box. "This is so sweet! You know how much I love presents...*oh, Jake!*" I looked up at him, amazed. "Oh, she's *so beautiful!*"

It was a Korean doll wearing a traditional silk gown of red, gold and blue. Her porcelain face was oval-shaped and flawless; her slanted dark eyes exotic. In one hand, she coyly held a brightly colored traditional fan etched with Korean letters.

"Oh, Jake! Thank you! I *love* her!" I threw my arms around him, smothering his face with kisses.

Jake laughed and finally drew away from me. "Wait! What do you think of her necklace?"

I looked down at the doll again, and for the first time, noticed a narrow gold circlet around her neck. "Hmmm...interesting looking necklace. In fact..."

I examined it closer. "It don't look like a necklace at all. It looks like a..." My voice faded away. I looked up at Jake, and suddenly realized why he had that goofy grin on his face. "Oh, Jake!" I touched the band of gold around the doll's neck, my finger trembling. "Is it what I think it is?"

He nodded and took the doll out of my hands. With a twist of the wrist, he popped the doll's head off and slipped the ring off the stem of her neck, cupping it in his hand.

He gazed into my eyes, and although he was still smiling, I could see the earnest look in his. "Lily Rae, I always felt guilty about you getting married with your mama's ring, and having to give it back. When I thought I might die in Korea, my biggest regret was that I never got you a ring. So just before we shipped back home, I found this for you in a little shop in Pusan. I'd already bought the doll in a village near the front, and when I saw how slender her neck was...well, it seemed like a good way to surprise you." He took my left hand and slipped the ring on my finger.

My eyes blurred with tears. I was so overcome with emotion, I couldn't say a thing except, "Oh, Jake..."

He lifted my chin so to meet my gaze. "I love you, Lily Rae," he whispered.

"Oh, I love you, too, Jake. I always have." Tears streamed down my face. "And I swear to you, I'll *never* stop loving you. Not as long as I live."

***

Later that afternoon, I brought the body of the Korean doll and its head to Jake so he could put it back together again. I'd tried, but it wouldn't stay on. After several unsuccessful attempts, Jake finally

resorted to carpenter's glue to reattach the head. It
stayed on for almost a year. But one day in June of
1954, I walked into the bedroom and saw the
decapitated doll on the dresser, her beautiful black
head lying at her dainty feet. And from that time on,
no matter how many times it was re-glued, the doll's
head refused to stay on.

Mother's Kentucky Butterscotch Pie

Flaky Pie Crust:

1 cup flour
½ cup shortening
1 teaspoon sugar
½ teaspoon salt
¼ teaspoon vinegar
1 egg
2 T water

With fork, mix together flour, shortening, sugar and salt. Mix egg with vinegar and water. Add to flour mixture, adding more water if needed, one teaspoon at a time. Form into a ball and chill fifteen minutes. Roll out and place into pie pan. For baked crust, prick dough with fork tines and bake at 400 degrees for 8-10 minutes. Cool before filling.

Filling:

1 c brown sugar
3 T butter
4 T cream or evaporated milk
1 c milk
6 level T flour
3 egg yolks
3 egg whites

Cook the first three ingredients until thick and brown. Mix milk into flour and add beaten egg yolks. Stir into first mixture, stirring constantly on

207

low heat until thickened. Pour into baked shell. Beat egg whites until stiff. Cover top of butterscotch mixture and bake in 400 degree oven for 3-5 minutes.

CHAPTER TWENTY-ONE

June 1954
New Boston, Texas

"**H**ere, Debby Ann, chew on this for awhile." I pulled a Gerber's teething biscuit from the box and handed it to the baby. "Maybe it'll make your gums feel better." Poor thing. She'd been especially cranky for the past few days, and her constant slobbering told me she was probably cutting some new teeth, which meant...*oh, joy!*...she was going to be more of a pill than usual. And today, of all days, that was not good.

"Come on, sweetie. I'd better put you in your high chair or you'll get that sticky mess all over my nice clean coffee table." I swept Debby Ann up from the floor and took a few steps into the kitchen. "I'll put you here in the doorway so you can still see Mommy while she cleans, okay?" With my free hand, I dragged the high chair over the linoleum and settled her into it, latching the silver tray in front of her.

Of course, this wasn't to her liking. As soon as I walked away, she began to fret. I sighed and turned around. "Debby Ann! What am I going to do with you? I've *got* to finish cleaning for the Tupperware party tonight. You don't want my friends to come into a dirty house, do you?"

Debby Ann's cries intensified. She began to pound at the tray with the flat of her hands, kicking and squirming as if she could propel herself out of the high chair by sheer will. With a frustrated cry, I dropped the dust rag and stomped over to her.

"Lord Almighty, Debby Ann! You're gonna be the death of me." Thank the good Lord I'd managed to prepare the refreshments for the party this morning while she napped. Because once she was up, she'd become a holy terror.

"Maybe I should take you down to Betty's. Let you play with Davy for a while until I can get my work done."

Not that Debby Ann and Davy actually played together. More like fought together. Neither one of them had mastered the idea of sharing. As soon as Debby Ann went for one of his toys—one that he'd barely spared a glance at—he suddenly decided it was the one toy he absolutely couldn't live without. Which always prompted a screaming fit on Debby Ann's part.

On second thought…maybe taking her over to Davy's right now wasn't the best idea in the world.

As I pondered what to do, I heard the apartment door down the hall open, followed by a male voice sounding as clear as if he was in the room with me. "Don't forget, hon, I'm going to the NCO Club to listen to the fight after work."

I frowned. Darn walls in this apartment building were so thin, you could probably hear your neighbors let go of a stinky one. Which must make us real popular, I thought. Lord, with Debby Ann's racket, the new neighbors probably thought me and Jake tortured the poor kid day and night.

A feminine voice responded to the man, but I couldn't make out what she was saying. His footsteps faded as he reached the stairwell at the end of the corridor. And suddenly, I had an idea. I'd been meaning to stop in at the new neighbor's and introduce myself, but I'd wanted to wait until they were settled in a bit first. They'd only moved in two days ago, and I suspected they were still unpacking boxes. But if he was going to the club to listen to the fight—like every other male in Texas, apparently, including Jake—that meant the Missus might like to come to the Tupperware party.

"Come on, Debby Ann. Now seems like a good time to go meet our new neighbor." I anchored the baby on my hip and stepped out into the hallway. Seconds later, I was knocking on the door of Apartment 27.

"Just a minute!" a musical voice called from inside.

I kissed Debby Ann's moist forehead as I waited. "You're pretty happy now, aren't you, baby girl?" I whispered. *As long as you're in Mommy's arms, you're fine.*

The door opened, and I plastered a big smile on my face.

"Yes?"

I stared, my speech momentarily deserting me.

"Can I help you?" the woman said, her dark eyes questioning.

"Uh…yeah, hi. I'm Lily Tatlow, your next door neighbor, and this here is my little girl, Debby Ann. I…uh…was wondering…I'm having a little Tupperware party this evening…seven o'clock.

And…uh…would you like to come?" I knew I was blushing; my cheeks were hot as fire. The woman probably thought I was a durn fool.

But if she did, she was polite enough not to show it. Instead, she gave me a sweet smile. "Well, thank you, Lily. That sounds really nice. We just moved here from Chicago, and I haven't met anyone yet. And Merle just told me he's staying at the club after work to listen to that prize fight he's been talking about all week."

I nodded and hoped I wasn't staring. "Yeah, my husband has been going on about it, too. The silliest durn thing I've ever heard of—gettin' all riled up over a couple of fellas beatin' the stuffin' out of each other."

The woman gave a soft laugh that reminded me of the sound of water running over smooth rocks. "Seven o'clock, right?" she asked. "Would you like me to bring anything?"

I shook my head. "Not a thing. I spent all weekend looking through **Ladies Home Journal** for recipes, and I think I've come up with some humdingers. Well…gotta go. Still have lots of things to do before seven. It's really nice to meet you…" I stopped, realizing I still didn't know the woman's name.

As if reading my mind, she stuck out a slim brown hand, her smile widening. "Barbara. Barbara Kinway."

I shook her hand. "And I'm Lily Rae Tatlow. Oh, I already told you that, though, didn't I? Well…I'll see you tonight. I live right down the hall—Apartment 25."

Back in my own apartment, I closed the door and slowly walked to the couch. Cuddling Debby Ann to me, I sank down onto it, my mind jumbled.

Well, what's done is done. I just hoped Barbara wouldn't feel too uncomfortable here tonight with all the other ladies.

She sure was nice as pie, but…she'd be the only colored woman in the bunch.

***

"Betty, could you help me in the kitchen with the refreshments?" I asked, heading toward the kitchen door.

The other women in the living room didn't even look up. They were too busy exclaiming over the various pastel plastic containers displayed on a table and trying to decide which ones they could absolutely not live without. The Tupperware lady had finished with her sales program, having introduced each piece, suggesting different ways it could be used.

I'd asked Betty to help in the kitchen, not so much because I needed help, but because I wanted to get her alone and thank her for saving the party.

"What would I do without you?" I said, turning to her once inside the kitchen. "I just wanted the floor to open up and swallow me whole when I saw the looks on them girls' faces after I brought Barbara into the room. And I swear, if you hadn't been the first one to say hello to her, I don't think they *ever* would've found their tongues."

Betty shrugged. "That's what happens when you live in a place with a lot of hicks who've never met people of a different race. They act like morons."

I went to the icebox and took out a tray of individual tomato aspic molds resting on beds of lettuce. I'd made them this morning with lemon Jell-O and tomato sauce, one of the recipes I'd

found in **Ladies Home Journal**. "Well, it was just
so nice of you to talk to Barbara and make her feel
welcome."

"No thanks necessary." Betty glanced around
the kitchen. "What can I do to help?"

"You can start slicing that butterscotch pie
there on the counter, and dish it out."

Betty opened a drawer and pulled out a knife.
"Well, I'm just impressed you invited her to the
party. I'll bet there's not another woman in that
room who would've had the guts to do it...even if
they *wanted* to."

I bit my bottom lip as I placed a dollop of
mayonnaise on each gelatin mold, glad that my back
was to Betty. My flushed cheeks would give me
away, and I'd have to admit to her I hadn't known
Barbara was colored when I'd invited her. Truth
was, if I *had* known, I wouldn't have considered,
even for a moment, to ask her to the party. Not
because I was mean or prejudiced, but
because...well, it just wasn't done. White folks
didn't mix with colored folks. Not where I came
from, anyway.

But why, I couldn't help but wonder. That
Barbara Kinway was just the nicest woman. Polite
and well-spoken. And Lord, she was just as
pretty—maybe prettier—as any of the women in the
room. She was dressed elegantly in a belted dress of
butter-colored jersey, with white gloves and heels. A
single strand of pearls encircled her graceful neck
under a sleek, ebony chignon. If it weren't for the
rich, chocolate tone of her skin, Barbara would've fit
right in with the other ladies, most of them
acquaintances of Betty's from the Officers Wife's
Club.

I turned with the tray. "I think these are ready to go."

Betty placed the last slice of butterscotch pie on a plate. "It's just a matter of time before things change," she said. "The way we whites...especially down here in the South...treat the Negroes is shameful. Sooner or later, they're going to rise up against it, you wait and see." Betty looked up, her blue eyes more serious than I'd ever seen them. "And when it happens, if I have the chance, I'm going to be right there with them."

I was still thinking about Betty's passionate words as I followed her back to the living room. Not much had changed since we'd left. The Tupperware Lady was still taking orders. Several of the women were bunched together, sipping from coffee cups; others were examining the merchandise. Barbara Kinway was sitting primly in a chrome-back kitchen chair, legs crossed at the ankles, her gloves in her lap as she daintily sipped from her cup, virtually ignored by the women around her. Her dark eyes were watchful as she glanced around the room, her pretty face composed. If she was at all bothered by the other ladies' cool treatment, she certainly hid it well.

Or was used to it...

I could've kissed Betty when she walked directly over to Barbara with a plate of pie in each hand. "Barbara, you absolutely *have* to try some of Lily's butterscotch pie. It's her mother's recipe, and let me tell you, this little Kentuckian knows how to cook. I guarantee it's the best thing you've ever put in your mouth."

A hush fell about the room as all eyes went to Betty and Barbara. I saw raised eyebrows, especially from the older NCO wives. One of them, a haughty blonde from Charleston, looked absolutely outraged that Betty had offered the pie to Barbara first.

Barbara hesitated as if she wasn't quite sure what to do—take the offered plate or avert the situation by refusing.

Betty grinned. "Come on, Barbara. It's only fair that the newest tenant in the building should get first taste."

I felt like cheering. It was clear to her—and everyone else—what Betty was doing. She was making a statement–prejudice would not be tolerated here. Barbara was my guest, and she'd be treated as such.

Following Betty's lead, I moved over to stand beside her. "But before you have something sweet, you should try this tomato aspic. Fancy, huh? Didn't I tell you I scrounged up some highfalutin' recipes out of **Ladies' Home Journal**?"

Barbara's gaze moved from Betty to me, and then down to the tray of molded red Jell-O. She smiled. "I'd love to try both," she said. "What a lovely job you've done, Lily. These are almost too pretty to eat."

I beamed. "But eat them, we will. Tell you what, Barbara, you set down that coffee cup and I'll refill it for you in a jiffy."

Conversation began again, and the awkward moment passed. I was sure, though, that Betty would catch heck for it as soon as that Charleston gal got her alone. But I wasn't a bit worried about her going up against that scrawny little Dixie-gal. Likely, Mrs. Charlene Steadman, wife of Sergeant-Major Steadman, would come out of that exchange with a new exit for her bodily functions.

It was almost nine o'clock when the party started breaking up. To my surprise, a few of the other women had followed our lead and had made an effort to include Barbara in our conversations. No doubt, it had been the first time they'd ever talked to a colored girl in a social situation. It was a start, and I was glad I'd acted on my impulse to go over and invite my new neighbor to the party.

But most of all, I was glad I hadn't known beforehand that Barbara was of a different race. Because I'd learned a valuable lesson tonight. Listening to her talk about her husband whom she'd married just recently, their former lives in Chicago, her hope to have children some day, to see them grow up in a country of prosperity and freedom, I'd come to a startling conclusion. Beneath the color of her skin, Barbara was pretty much just like me and Betty.

Everyone had left by nine-fifteen, except for Betty, Barbara and Karen Graham, a plump redhead from Vermont who'd been one of the first women to chat with Barbara after Betty's dessert moment. The two women had found they shared a passion for sewing and were discussing the latest Butterick patterns while me and Betty started clearing up.

I heard the front door open as I carried a tray toward the kitchen.

"*Lily Rae!*"

The swish of my taffeta circle skirt was audible in the room as I spun around. Barbara and Karen stopped in mid-sentence, obviously shocked by the apparent fury in Jake's voice. Betty was already in the kitchen, washing the dishes.

"*Goddammit*, Lily Rae!" Jake shouted from the hallway. "Why is it that hallway light is on every time I come home? It wasn't more than two days ago I showed you that goddamn electric bill and told you to stop leaving lights on all over the damn place!"

I cast an apologetic glance at the two women on the sofa, placed the tray down on the coffee table and hurried out of the room.

He was coming toward me down the short hallway, weaving like a drunken circus clown. My heart sank to my toes. He'd been doing so good lately. Since his return from Korea, he'd been the kind of husband I'd always dreamed he'd be—attentive, sweet and fun-loving…with just a few slips here and there. But not once had he come home like this.

He stopped when he saw me, still swaying. His brows lowered in a scowl.

"What're you so dressed up for, girl? Going out on the town with your boyfriend?" His voice was unnaturally loud, and I just knew the women in the living room—and probably Betty—were hearing every word of it.

I marched over to him and grabbed his arm. "Lower your voice, Jake Tatlow," I said, not even making an effort to contain my fury. "Did you forget that tonight was my Tupperware party? Yes, I suppose you did, seeing as how your brain is all pickled from liquor. Oh, Jake! How *could* you?"

He shook his arm free from my grip. "Who the *hell* do you think you are, talking to me like that, woman?" he shouted.

I'd forgotten the cardinal rule. *Don't ever tell Jake what to do when he's been drinking.*

"Jake, please!" I pleaded. "Some of the women are still here. Please don't embarrass me like this."

"Well, it's my *goddamn* house, and I'll be *damned* if I'm gonna be bossed around by a *damn woman!* Just because I'm married to you don't mean I'm going to let you cut my balls off whenever you feel like it." He pushed past me. "I've got to piss like a racehorse. You get them women out of my house, you here? When I'm done in the bathroom, I'm going to bed, and I want you there beside me." He glanced back and gave me a leer. "Naked and wet for me."

Rage coursed through my bloodstream. How *dare* he be so vulgar? "I'd rather sleep with a nest of rattlesnakes," I said quietly, staring him directly in the eyes.

He blinked, and the blood drained from his face. His blues eyes turned icy, and I knew I'd gone too far. But I didn't regret it.

"Is everything okay, Lily?"

It was Betty's voice from the living room. I turned, and there she was, standing at the other end of the hallway, eyes watchful. In one hand, she held a cast-iron skillet. Behind her stood Karen and Barbara, looking scared but resolute. I knew, without a doubt, they'd protect me from Jake if need be.

Jake knew it, too. "You can put that skillet away, Betty." He lurched toward her. She backed up, but kept a good grip on the skillet. "I ain't gonna hurt her. Even if she *should* know better than to sass me like that. Well, what the hell do we have here?"

I followed him into the living room, knowing he'd caught his first glimpse of Barbara. *Oh, please, God, don't let him say anything mean to her.*

But when Jake was drunk, there was no telling what he'd do. I knew I had to get Barbara and Karen out of the apartment. Betty had seen Jake at his worst before…or if she hadn't seen it, she'd heard about it from me.

"Jake, Barbara and Karen were just leaving…"
I cast a desperate glance at the two women, hoping
they understood.

Jake was staring at Barbara, a stunned look on
his face. And then, to my amazement, he began to
laugh. Over his shoulder, I met Betty's confused
gaze. I could almost read her mind.

The man has gone off his rocker.

Still chuckling, Jake looked at me. His eyes
were in direct contrast to his grin. In fact, they
looked a lot like what I imagined the eyes of them
rattlesnakes I'd rather sleep with would look.

"Well, now. You've really done it this time,
haven't you, Lily Rae? Here I am hollerin' at you
because of the electric bill, and you've gone ahead
and hired yourself a Aunt Jemima maid behind my
back! Now, how do you think we're gonna pay for
that?"

I heard an audible gasp. I wasn't sure whose it
was, maybe my own.

"Jake! How dare you…" I managed to stutter.

Poor Barbara's face had gone ashen, and
redheaded Karen had two red spots on her
cheekbones as if a cosmetic fairy had materialized
out of thin air and waved a rouge wand in her
direction. The blood had drained from Betty's face,
too, but her eyes were blazing with contempt.

"Jake Tatlow, there is no call for that kind of
ugliness," Betty said, her voice trembling with anger.

He ignored her, keeping his eyes on Barbara.
"I'll say this once, whoever you are. Get the fuck
out of my house. Niggers ain't welcome here."

"*Jake!*" I shouted. I turned to Barbara. "I'm *so*
sorry, Barbara. He's drunk. He doesn't know what
he's saying."

But my new neighbor wasn't listening. All
the life had disappeared from her beautiful face. It
had become as if it were carved in stone. She turned
stiffly to grab her pocketbook from the couch, and
then with her head held high, she walked past Jake
and then me, her eyes straight ahead, as lifeless as
Kentucky coal. Her high heels tapped with furious
intensity on the wood floor as she headed for the
front door.

And then she was gone, leaving the room
stunned and silent.

Betty was the first to speak. "I'm sorry, Lily. I
know he's your husband and you love him, but I
hope he rots in Hell for that."

It was as if Jake didn't hear her. He turned and
lurched unsteadily toward the hallway that led to the
bathroom. Without meeting my eyes, Karen
scooped up her pocketbook, mumbled a "thank
you," and left without a backward glance. I had a
strong feeling I'd never see the woman again.

I met Betty's stunned gaze. It was so quiet in
the apartment we could both hear the sound of
Jake's urine streaming into the toilet bowl.

Finally, Betty spoke, "Get your things, Lily.
You're not staying here tonight."

"But…Betty, I can't just leave him…" My
voice faded away as I recognized the steely look in
her eyes and the rigidity of her jaw.

She spoke slowly and precisely. "I'm not
leaving you here alone with him tonight, Lily.
Debby Ann is already over at my apartment, and
she's probably sleeping by now. There's no reason
on earth for you to stay here tonight. Are you going
to get your things, or do you want to sleep in that
taffeta skirt? Your choice. But get this through that
pretty little head of yours—I'm not leaving here
without you."

CHAPTER TWENTY-TWO

I stood at Betty's living room window and watched Jake's blue Plymouth pull out of the parking lot and head toward the post. I could tell just by watching him walk to his car that he was suffering from a humdinger of a hangover.

Well, good. After the horrible way he'd acted with Barbara last night, he deserved to feel rotten. I still felt mortified by what had happened. I'd wanted to go right over to Barbara's apartment to apologize for him, but Betty had convinced me to wait until today to give her some time to calm down. No doubt she was right. Probably the last person in the world Barbara wanted to see last night was anyone connected with Jake.

A movement behind me drew my attention, and I turned to see Betty standing in the threshold. "Is he gone?"

I nodded. "I reckon it's safe for us to go back now." I slanted a glance at my friend. "But I still don't think I was in any danger last night. Jake yells a lot, but he'd never hurt me."

Even as I spoke, my brain flashed on that one time in the pick-up truck when I'd first told him I was pregnant. I could still remember his pinching grip on my chin after I'd slapped him for his ugly words insinuating I'd been sleeping around. His eyes had burned with rage, and yes, I'd been afraid of what he might do to me in that moment.

I blinked the thought away. "Anyhow, he cools down just as soon as the drink wears off."

Betty tightened the belt of her satin robe, eyeing me thoughtfully. "How can you live with someone like that? Having to tiptoe around him, thinking about everything you say, hoping you won't somehow set him off?"

My jaw dropped. "Betty, don't you hear what I'm saying? He only gets like that when he's been drinking!"

Betty didn't speak for a long moment, then released a frustrated sigh. "How do you know which one is the *real* Jake? The sober man...or the ugly thug who comes out when he's lubricated with booze?"

My hackles rose at Betty's frank question. There hadn't been many times in our friendship that I'd spoken up against her dominant personality, but this remark, I couldn't let go. "You don't know Jake like I do," I said tightly. "He may say some ugly things and he may act ugly at times, but beneath all that, he's a beautiful soul, and I see that in him. If you only knew what kind of horrible childhood he had, growing up with an ornery snake like his father, you might not be so quick to judge him."

223

Betty stared at me, obviously stunned at my outburst.

I took a deep breath and gentled my tone, "Why do I put up with him when he gets like that? It's simple, Betty. I love the man. Have ever since we were younguns…and that won't *ever* change."

***

After putting Debby Ann down for her afternoon nap, I curled up on the couch with **Ladies' Home Journal,** and within moments, I'd become engrossed in a novel excerpt by Anya Seton. It was just the sort of novel I loved—the sort I'd *write* if I had the talent to do it—one full of romance set in an exotic foreign country, and by the time I'd finished the first page, I'd already decided I was going to pick up the *real* book next time I was at the drugstore.

It was just after three when I heard Jake's key in the front door. My body tensed, and for a split second, I wondered if it was fear I was feeling. But no, of course it wasn't. Apprehension, maybe, as I wondered what kind of mood he'd be in after last night's ruckus…but not fear.

I laid the magazine face-down on the couch and composed my face into a smile as his combat boots clumped down the hallway. He appeared in the doorway of the living room, dressed in his fatigue uniform. Exercises must be going on at the post today, I thought, searching his face for a sign of his mood.

"You're home early," I said lightly, hoping against hope that all was well.

He seemed to be having trouble meeting my eyes. And wasn't his face a little flushed? Finally, he cleared his throat. "I was afraid you wouldn't be here."

I looked down, my fingers playing with the fringe of my cut-off jeans. "Why not? It's my home, ain't it?"

When he didn't speak, I looked up at him and caught the tormented expression on his face. "Sorry about last night," he said softly. "Guess I had too much to drink."

"Yes, I reckon you did." I didn't want to forgive him too easily. He had to know that what he'd done was dead wrong. "And I reckon you've got some apologizing to do...and not just to me."

I'd stopped by Barbara's apartment on my way back from Betty's, but no one had answered the door. Maybe she'd gone out. Or maybe she just hadn't wanted to answer, knowing who it was outside. But I couldn't let more time go by without an apology, so I'd gone home and scribbled a note on the stationery pad I used to write Mother every week.

Dear Barbara: I am so very sorry for the horrible things my husband said to you last night. I know it's not much of an excuse, but he was very drunk, and he just gets ornery sometimes with the drinking. I just want you to know that I was pleased as punch that you came to my party, and I hope we can be friends in the future. Yours Very Truly, Lillian Rae Tatlow.

I'd slipped the folded note under Barbara's door, and hoped for the best. But Jake really needed to be the one to apologize. Surely he knew that.

I opened my mouth to say exactly that, but he beat me to it, giving me that soulful look he knew I couldn't resist. "Don't you worry, I'll take care of the apologies. But you're the only one that really matters to me, Lily Rae. I just got to know you're not mad any more."

As always, my resistance melted against his boyish charm, even knowing deep down inside that his apology to the others...*if* he ever got around to doing it...might not be all that sincere. But how could I stay mad at him when he looked at me like that? All contrite and adorable like a mischievous little boy who'd got caught with his hand in the cookie jar?

I sighed. "'Course I'm not still mad. Come here, you."

He gave me his trademark lop-sided grin—the one that always sent flutters through my heart, and then strode purposely toward me. I met him halfway. He took me into his arms and kissed me thoroughly.

Within seconds, my body was on fire, as if he were the kindling and me, the log of wood. His hand found its way under my cotton blouse, and with unerring ease, he unfastened the hooks of my bra. Then, still kissing me, he slipped both hands under my blouse and loosened bra, cupping my breasts tenderly in his palms. I moaned into his open mouth, my brain spinning.

He broke the kiss and skimmed a wet trail up my cheek to my ear, murmuring, "Is the baby sleeping?"

"Yes," I gasped, clutching his muscular arms, breathing in the healthy male scent of him.

"Good. Come on."

He led me into the bedroom, and still holding onto me, drew the shades down. Moments later, both of us were stripped naked. We tumbled onto the bed, and in the sleepy heat of the summer afternoon, he made love to me. As I writhed under him, I told myself I'd blown it all out of proportion. Jake had his faults, but he wasn't a bad guy. He didn't mean half the stuff he said. And he *had* said he'd apologize to Barbara, hadn't he? I was sure of it.

And then I stopped thinking.

***

"I've got a surprise for you," Jake said.

Zipping up my cut-offs, I looked over at him. He lay on the bed, propped up against a pillow, naked as a jaybird and smoking a cigarette. A light sheen of sweat glistened on his arms and chest in the afternoon light that crept beneath the edges of the drawn shades.

Despite the open windows beneath us and an electric fan on the top of the dresser that ineffectively stirred the hot air around, it felt like it was over a hundred degrees in the little room. The curls at the back of my neck clung damply to my skin and the discarded cotton blouse I scooped up from the floor felt as soggy as if it had been forgotten in the bottom of a laundry basket on the way to being hung on the line.

"A surprise, huh?" I asked, buttoning my blouse. I moved over to the window to let the blind up some. Maybe get a little outside air in. Even if it was hot as blazes outside, it might help a little.

Jake released a stream of smoke and gave me an enigmatic grin. "Grab my fatigue pants over there. Got something in the pocket for you."

I arched an eyebrow at him. "Lord, Jake Tatlow, don't you look like the cat that swallowed the canary! What you got up your sleeve?"

His grin widened. "Nothing up my sleeve," he said. "But check the pockets of my fatigues."

I giggled. Now, *this* was the Jake Tatlow I'd fallen in love with. Why couldn't he be this playful and sweet all the time?

He watched as I grabbed his pants off the floor and rummaged through one pocket, finding nothing but a matchbook from a diner near the post.

"It's in the other one," he said, still wearing a self-satisfied grin.

My fingers found a small envelope. I drew it out and stared at it. "What's this?"

"Open it up and see."

I drew two tickets out of the envelope. "Oh..." I tried not to show my disappointment when I read what they were for. Slim Whitman—one of Jake's favorite country music singers who had a thing about yodeling—a sound I found about as pleasant as nails clawing down a blackboard. But...I reminded myself...it *was* a night out, so I pasted on a bright smile. "Hey, that's super, Jake! Where's this Overton Park Shell, anyway?"

Jake's grin grew bigger. "Memphis."

I gasped. "You're taking me all the way to *Memphis* to see a singer?"

He nodded. "I reckon it's about time we got away from here for a spell. It's on a Friday, so the Sarge will probably let me out early. We'll get there in plenty of time. And if it don't cost an arm and a leg, maybe we can get a room in one of them motels and come back the next mornin'."

I stared at him, trying to wrap my brain around this amazing turn of events. "But what about Debby Ann? We'll have to get Merline to baby-sit, and you know that costs money. She just upped her charge to fifty cents an hour."

For a split-second, he looked outraged. "That's highway robbery! But..." He gave me a wink.

"Friday's pay-day. Anyhow, you let *me* worry about the money. Just hire the baby-sitter."

I gave him a happy grin. "You betcha." I peered down at the tickets again. "Never heard of these other fellas. The Blue Moon Boys. Have you?"

Jake shrugged. "Nah. Must be the warm-up act. Probably some no-talent cusses we have to suffer through before Slim takes the stage. We can always arrive late. Seats are paid for." He gave me a wink and crooked a finger at me. "Hey, come here. Don't this deserve a kiss?"

I grinned and walked over to him. "I suppose it does." I bent down to kiss him.

With a whoop, he wrestled me down on the bed and rolled on top of me, nuzzling my neck. When I felt his penis hardening against my thigh, I wished I hadn't gone to all that trouble putting my clothes on again.

***

"Oh, my Lord, he's just *too much!*" I shrieked.

Clinging to Betty, I jumped up and down, screaming at the top of my lungs along with all the other young women at the open-air shell in Overton Park. Betty grinned, and in her excitement, dug her nails into my bare arm. I'd mentioned to Betty about our tickets to Slim Whitman, and she'd up and bought two for her and Eddie, and I hadn't dared tell Jake about it, figuring it was best if we just "ran into them there. And that's exactly what had happened. No sooner had we got to the gates when Betty had shouted out my name, waving frantically like she hadn't seen me in years, instead of just that morning.

Jake had been put out, of course. I could tell that by the ugly glint in his eyes. But maybe our last fight was too fresh in his mind, and he'd remembered how he'd promised to do better. When Betty and Eddie made their way toward us, Jake shook Eddie's hand and gave Betty a curt greeting.

"*Shake* it, baby!" Betty yelled, waving wildly at the bandstand with her free hand. "Oh, honey boy, you've got the right moves!"

Up on the stage in front of a giant rainbow background, the Blue Moon Boys, consisting of two guitarists and their front man, a brown-haired boy with electric blue eyes and full, molded lips, began another song. The girls in the audience shrieked even louder, especially as the lead singer began to do his leg-shaking thing again. Betty and I were no exception.

I felt light-headed from screaming, and I swore Betty was about to faint, the way her eyes were rolling back in her head as she shouted out the singer's name. "*Ellis*! Oh, my God, *Ellis*! Where have you been all my life?"

I knew without looking that both Jake and Eddie were fuming in their seats behind us. Like all the other men in the audience, I reckoned. They just couldn't understand why us girls were on our feet in excitement for the gorgeous, mellow-voiced Ellis Presley up on stage.

I knew why, though. He was like nothing I'd ever heard before as he sang a rollicking tune called "That's Alright Mama," gyrating on the stage like an old man with palsy—except that he wasn't old. According to the newspaper we'd picked up at the drugstore, he wasn't even 20. What the newspaper *didn't* say was that he was as pretty as a man could be with those blue bedroom eyes and sweet-looking lips. And he was a southern boy, too—from right here in Memphis.

As far as I was concerned—and Betty and all the other girls in the audience—Slim Whitman could just *stay* backstage the whole blessed night. Ellis, there, was *more* than worth the price of the ticket.

The end of the song was nearly drowned out by the shrill screams of the girls. Ellis threw up a hand, beamed a grin out at the audience and spoke into the mike with a heart-melting southern accent, "Thank ya very much. Goodnight and God bless."

And the Blue Moon Boys left the stage to groans of dismay from the females in the crowd. The night's MC came out with a grin as big as Texas stretched across his fleshy face. "Put your hands together for the Blue Moon Boys, folks. We're proud to say that y'all just witnessed their first live show, right here at the Overton Park Shell, and I got me a feeling we ain't heard the last of them boys. Oh, and folks...the newspaper got Mr. Presley's name wrong. It's *Elvis* Presley, not Ellis. What's more, we've got a special treat for y'all. Elvis just cut his first record at Sun Studio about three weeks ago, and every one of you, just for being here tonight, is gonna get a *free copy*!"

The crowd roared. Betty and I hugged each other, just as delighted as all the other women around us. We were going to get to take *Elvis*...*not* Ellis...*home!*

I caught Jake's sulky expression as I twirled around. Well, it was clear *he* was no fan. Especially when he cupped his hands around his mouth and shouted, *"Get on with the damn show! Where's Slim?"*

CAROLE BELLACERA

Betty and I looked at each other, and then Betty rolled her eyes. I grinned back. And we continued to dance up and down in excitement.

CHAPTER TWENTY-THREE

I clutched the 45-LPM of Elvis's single in my right hand as Jake and me followed Eddie and Betty up the stairs to the second floor of our apartment building. So much for staying in Memphis tonight, I thought. I should've known that as soon as Jake got some liquor into him, he'd change his mind about the motel.

Right after the concert, he and Eddie had gone to the closest liquor store for a couple of six-packs, and the four of us had ended up on the banks of the Mississippi, drinking Pabst Blue Ribbon until they were all gone. Well, Betty and the boys drank the beer; I stuck to Coca Cola because I hated the bitter taste of beer.

Funny how the men's mutual dislike for Elvis Presley had brought the two of them together. Why, Jake had actually seemed to almost be hitting it off with Eddie by the end of the night. Still, I figured I was probably going to catch hell later for not telling Jake the couple was planning to be at the concert.

By the time the men drank the last beer, they were laughing and messing around like they'd been best pals forever. Eddie, though, didn't seem able to hold his liquor as well as Jake did. Betty had insisted on driving him back to New Boston, and he'd readily accepted. Jake, though, wouldn't hear of me driving him. When I'd tentatively suggested he might be too drunk to drive, he hadn't even bothered to reply, so silly, apparently, was the idea, but thank the Lord, he'd done a perfectly capable job of driving the four-hour trip home.

Up in front of us, Betty, her arm around her stumbling husband, reached the top of the stairs and fumbled in her handbag for the keys to their apartment.

"Hold him for me, will you?" she said to me, propping Eddie up against the wall.

"I got him," Jake said, grabbing onto Eddie so he wouldn't slip to the floor.

His blond head lolled to his shoulder, and through slitted blue eyes, he gazed at Jake. A slow, goofy grin crossed his handsome face. "What'd ya know," he garbled. "You're not such a bad guy after all, Jake the Snake." He giggled. "Thass what Bets calls you anyway."

Betty shot her husband a glare as she turned the key in the lock. "Eddie! Don't be crude!" The door opened. "Merline, we're home!"

I noticed the heightened color on Betty's cheeks. Jake the Snake, huh? Well, that was no surprise. Betty had never pretended to like him. Avoiding his gaze, she turned to her husband to help him inside.

Jake stopped her. "I'll take care of him. You go pay the babysitter. Lily Rae, you got some money?" He grabbed hold of Eddie and walked him into the apartment.

Yeah, Laundromat money, I thought. *Famous last words about you worrying about the money.*

"You know what?" Eddie said, grinning. "I think you're...A-okay, Jake. A little hard to...get to know, maybe...but a helluva guy! And to think...I thought you didn't like me..."

"Now, whatever gave you that idea?" Jake said dryly, depositing him on the living room sofa.

Merline, sleepy-eyed and rumpled from the long night, accepted the cash Betty and I gave her, and slipped out of the apartment to go home. The black and white sunrise clock on the wall showed two-fifty a.m.

"Guess I'd better put on some coffee for him," said Betty, heading for the kitchen.

"I'll get Debby Ann." I turned toward the hallway leading to Davy's room. "Jake, you want to go ahead and unlock our apartment? I'll be right there."

Debby was sound asleep in the upper half of Davy's crib; Davy sprawled out at the other end. When I picked her up, the baby mewed a soft protest but didn't wake.

My lips quirked. *You little rascal. You'll sleep for the whole world, won't you? For everyone except me.* Sure as anything, she'd be up and squalling the minute I got into bed. Nestling her against my shoulder, I went back out to the living room. It was empty, so I figured Jake had gone on home. I'd just slip into the kitchen to say a quick goodbye to Betty before joining him.

But Betty wasn't alone in the kitchen. I stopped short when I saw Jake standing with her. I knew instinctively that I'd interrupted something…a fight maybe. From the look on Betty's face, whatever had passed between them hadn't been pretty. She was glaring at him as if he were a piece of dog shit smeared on her shoe. Jake was staring right back, but his blue eyes were gleaming, and he wore a smirk on his face. They hadn't noticed me yet.

"You lowdown son-of-a-bitch," Betty said clearly. "Get the hell out of my house!"

Jake just kept grinning.

"What's going on?" I said.

They both looked at me, and an awkward silence fell. A slight flush crept up from Jake's shirt collar, pooling onto his carved cheekbones. Betty glanced at me, and then turned her gaze back to Jake, her eyes frigid. "Do you want to tell your wife about your suggestion or shall I?"

Jake ran his fingers through his Brill-Crèmed hair, his eyes avoiding mine. "Ah, hell. It was just a joke," he muttered.

"Really?" Betty said coolly. "Sounded pretty serious to me."

"What's going on?" I asked again.

Betty waited for Jake to speak, but when he didn't, she gave him a look of disgust. "He suggested that we have a little wife-swapping party. He said he and I could get started right now over in your apartment, and once Eddie woke up, you and he could have your own little party right here."

I felt as if someone had just punched me in the gut. I stared at my husband. "Is that true?"

For the briefest of moments, I saw shame in his eyes, and I had my answer.

But he recovered quickly. "Son-of-a-bitch! Can't a guy crack a goddamn joke without you women gettin' your panties in a wad?" He strode out of the kitchen. A few seconds later, we heard the apartment door slam shut. Betty and I stared at each other.

"I'm sorry," Betty said. "I don't mean to cause trouble between you two. I should've just kept my mouth shut."

"No," I said slowly. "I don't want to be in the dark about such things. But Betty...I just can't believe Jake was serious. Surely he was just fooling around with you."

She turned to the counter and began to fill the percolator basket with coffee grounds. "I'm sure you're right," she said finally. "But joke or no joke...I didn't find it a bit funny."

    ***

I didn't find it funny either. After putting Debby Ann down in her crib, I found Jake in the kitchen, mixing himself a drink—Johnny Walker and Coke. I watched him a moment, debating whether to rip into him about the wife-swapping joke or to chide him for drinking more when he was already lit to the gills. Or...a third option—leave him alone, go to bed and let him drink himself silly.

That seemed like the best idea.

He pinned his glittering blue eyes on me. "What the hell are you looking at?"

I couldn't help herself. Even as I opened my mouth and said it, I knew I was making a huge mistake, but I could no more stop myself than I could stand at the bottom of Niagara Falls and stop the water from raining down upon me.

"A damn idiot, I reckon."

My stomach did a slow flip-flop as my words hung in the air between us. I held my breath, waiting for Jake to turn into the same ugly man he'd been the other night at the sight of a colored woman in his house.

But to my astonishment, he laughed. And it wasn't an ugly, mean-spirited laugh, but a genuine one. He placed his glass of whiskey down on the chrome-edged dinette table and grinning, came toward me.

"You're quite a little spitfire tonight, ain't you, darlin'?" His gaze swept down my body, lingering on my breasts under my cropped blue-striped top. "Did I tell you how pretty you look tonight, Lily Rae? I swear, it was all I could do all night to keep myself from slipping my hand inside them skimpy little short-shorts you're wearing." He gave me a wink and moved closer.

Mesmerized, I watched his approach. And felt myself falling under his spell. Why, he looks a little like *Elvis*, I thought. That sexy grin...something between a sneer and a smile. Warmth flooded through my lower regions, pooling in my womanly parts.

His hands closed around my buttocks. He pulled me against him so I could feel the hot brick of his erection beneath his Chinos. His mouth clamped down on mine, his tongue seeking entry. I sighed into his kiss, wrapping my arms around his waist. Deep in the recesses of my brain, I knew I should still be angry with him, whether he'd been serious or not about the wife-swapping thing, but somehow, it seemed unimportant now. Still kissing me, his hand moved from my butt cheek to my belly, slipping down inside the narrow waistband of my navy linen shorts. Gasping with excitement, I dutifully parted my legs, allowing him access to my most secret place. He began to caress me.

Suddenly he stiffened. "What the hell is this?"

I became aware of a tugging sensation in my vagina, and drew back in horror. "Oh, God, Jake! I forgot. I started my period a couple days ago."

His face twisted with revulsion. He pulled his hand out of my shorts as if it had been burned. "Well, *shit.*" He looked like a little boy who'd been told he couldn't have a cookie before dinner. "What the hell is that string-thing, anyway?"

My cheeks grew hot with embarrassment. "It's a tampon. Betty told me how to…"

He turned away from me. "I don't want to know the details! Goddammit, Lily Rae, I'm so horny, I could hump a mattress. And you have to be on the damn rag!" He grabbed his drink off the table and took a healthy slug.

"Oh, that's nice," I said, my blood still thrumming from his caresses. "Is that all I am to you, just someone to…hump?"

He stared at me without responding and lifted his glass to his lips again. In disgust, I turned to leave the room, but he called me back.

"Wait a minute." His eyes glittered with a speculative, barely suppressed excitement. It made me nervous. "There *is* something you can do for me…if you want to please your man."

"What?" I asked, my voice ringing with suspicion. What about me, my brain shrieked. *You get me all hot and bothered and then leave me aching just because you get queasy at the thought of blood.*

But I could never, *ever*, in a million years say such a thing aloud.

Jake put down his glass, unzipped his trousers and withdrew his erect penis from the opening in his boxer shorts. He began to stroke himself.

I thought I understood. He called it a "hand job."

"Shouldn't we go into the bedroom?" I asked.

He shook his head, his eyes heavy-lidded as he continued to touch himself. "Let's do it right here, baby. Right now."

I shrugged and came toward him. If he was as horny as he claimed to be, it shouldn't take long. But then...would he do the same thing for me? Just because I was on my period didn't mean my desires had disappeared.

I stopped a few inches away and reached out to touch him.

"On your knees, baby," he said, his voice husky, eyes slitted.

I looked at him in confusion.

His free hand settled on my right shoulder and nudged me downward. "Just a little blow-job, Lily Rae," he urged, his voice ragged with arousal.

I wrenched away from him in horror. "*No*! I can't do *that*!"

Only recently had I'd found out what a blow-job was. And when Betty had told me, I could hardly believe people actually did stuff like that. It was so nasty! Lord, he *peed* out of that thing!

And I remembered being so thankful that Jake had never expected me to do anything like that.

Until now.

I backed away, shaking my head. "No, Jake. Please...I just can't do that."

His eyes became as hard as diamond chips. I kept my gaze on his face, knowing if I allowed myself to look down at his erection and think about where he wanted to put it, I'd surely vomit right here on the kitchen floor.

"What do you mean, you can't?" he snarled.

I shook my head helplessly. "It's just that...oh, Lord, Jake! I just can't bring myself to...you know...put my mouth there. I'll gag..."

For a long moment, he stared at me in disgust, then stuffed his penis back into his boxers and zipped up. "Well, *get the fuck out of here then*! What the *fuck* are you good for?" He grabbed his whiskey glass and drained the contents.

My eyes swam with tears. "Please, Jake, try to understand..."

He looked at me as if I were a stranger. "Did you hear what I said? *Get the fuck out of here*! It makes me sick to look at you!"

I whirled around and ran out of the kitchen. In the bedroom, I threw myself on the bed, sobbing. Why did he have to be so mean? Every time I started to believe he was making an effort to be the sort of man I knew he could be, he went and did something like this! And in the process, always seemed to make me feel like *I* was the one in the wrong.

Like now. Had I overreacted to his request? After all, Betty had said that husbands and wives did it all the time. That even though most women didn't particularly *like* to do it, they did it to keep their men happy. And that's when I'd been so smugly thankful that Jake didn't need to be kept happy like that.

I cried harder, wetting the pillow with my tears. Why hadn't I just squeezed my eyes shut and let him do what he wanted to do? What was there for me to do anyway besides let him put it in and...well...I'd have to lick it a little.

My stomach spasmed at the thought and for a moment, I thought I truly was going to be sick right there on the bed.

What the fuck are you good for?

Jake's sneering words rang through my brain.

Apparently, nothing. I'd failed him as a wife. As a lover. By refusing to do what Betty said was a pretty standard sexual practice in a normal marriage these days.

Had Daddy and Mother...?

"*Aggggghhhh*...." I buried my face in the pillow, trying to scrub my brain free of that thought. It was just too revolting.

But then another one, almost equally as disgusting came to me. Betty's voice. *If a man can't get it at home, then believe me, honey, he'll go looking for it elsewhere.*

I sat up on the bed and blinked into the darkness, my last sob dying in my throat. What if Betty was right? I slid my legs over the edge of the bed. I'd go to him right now, beg his forgiveness, tell him I'd do anything he wanted me to, anything! Even that, if it was what it took to be a good wife.

A crash came from the kitchen, then another one. I stood and headed for the door. Lord above, was he breaking my dishes? Not that they were good dishes, but they were all we had. The crashing continued. My heart pounding, I ran down the hallway and burst into the kitchen.

Jake stood at the kitchen table, a hammer in his right hand. He looked up and gave me a grin that could only be described as malicious, and then he brought the hammer down again on the table. Bits of black vinyl flew, skittering across the table and onto the linoleum floor.

"What are you *doing*?" I shouted.

And then I saw it—the brown paper wrapper with the circular hole in it. The one that had contained Elvis's record.

"*No!*" I screamed, instinctively reaching for the hammer, even though I knew it was way too late.

Jake pushed me away. "Bet you'd suck *his* dick, wouldn't you?"

"Jake! Don't be an idiot! Give me that hammer!" I reached for it again as he aimed for another blow.

This time he pushed me hard. Off-balance, I fell against the corner of a cabinet, and stars exploded behind my eyes. Something warm trickled down the left side of my face. I brought my hand up. Touched it to my face and looked at it. Blood. Stunned, I looked at Jake.

His face had paled, and the anger had drained from his eyes. "Oh, Lily Rae, I'm sorry," he whispered. "You know I didn't do it on purpose."

I stared at him. "You never do," I said softly.

He lifted his hand to wipe the blood away from my cheek, but before he could touch me, I turned away.

"Lily, please...you've got to believe me. I didn't mean for you to get hurt."

"I know, Jake," I said wearily. "Let me go and clean this cut."

Just as I moved, a pounding came at the front door followed by Betty's anxious voice. "What's going on in there? Lily, are you okay?"

We locked gazes. Jake's face was ashen and vulnerable-looking. His fingers entwined in one of my curls.

"Please, baby," he murmured. "Let me send her away. She don't need to know about this. You know how much she hates me. That's why she keeps trying to poison you against me, can't you see that?"

"Lily!" The pounding came again, harder this time. "You want me to call the police?"

My heart jolted. "I'm okay, Betty!" I called out. Cupping my hand to the cut on my forehead, I hurried into the living room and over to the front door. "I was just making Jake a…BLT, and cut my finger slicing a tomato," I lied. "It's not deep, though. I'm fine."

For a long moment, there was nothing but silence on the other side of the door. Then Betty's voice came again, heavy with suspicion. "Why don't you open up the door, Lily? So I can see you."

I thought quickly, and gave a little laugh. Another lie rolled off my tongue. "Well…uh…it's like this, Betty. I ain't got a stitch on. Jake and I were sort of…fooling around."

"While you were making a BLT for him?" she asked smoothly. It was clear she didn't believe a word of it.

"Well, now, Betty," I said slyly. "Do I pry into the what and wherefores of you and Eddie's bedroom secrets?"

Another brief silence, then, "Touché."

"But thanks for checking up on me, Bets." I had to get to the bathroom and clean this cut. It was bleeding profusely, creating a red stream down my jaw onto the blue and white-striped scoop neck of my top. "Goodnight!"

"Wait!" Betty called out. "What was all that banging?"

I bit my bottom lip, thinking. "Oh! That was Jake…finally putting in them shelves in the kitchen I've been nagging him about." I heard a movement behind me and turned to see Jake standing in the threshold of the living room, listening.

"Goodnight, Betty," I said again.

This time Betty must've believed me. There was only a moment's hesitation before her response. "Okay. Goodnight. See you tomorrow."

Without glancing at Jake, I went into the bathroom to grab a towel, pressing it against the bleeding cut.

"How bad is it?" Jake said, hovering in the doorway, his face anxious.

"I'll live, I reckon." I peered at him out of the eye not covered by the towel. "You *do* know you're gonna have to put up them shelves tomorrow, don't you?"

CHAPER TWENTY-FOUR

I slept on the couch that night, even though Jake tried several times to cajole me into bed. I was just furious at him—not so much about the cut on my forehead, because I knew he hadn't meant for me to get hurt when he pushed me. No, I was spit-fire mad at him for destroying my Elvis record. That was just out and out meanness, and as far as I was concerned, it took the cake.

Last night as I'd laid there on that couch, staring grimly into the darkness, it was all I could do to keep myself from gathering up a stack of Jake's Hank Williams albums and take that hammer of his and smash them to smithereens. But then that would make me just as bad as him, wouldn't it?

Sometime before daylight, I'd finally fallen asleep, only to be awakened just after seven by Debby Ann's listless wails. Stumbling to the baby's room, still half-asleep, I cast an evil glare at the closed bedroom door, and murmured a curse under my breath. What magic power made a man able to sleep through the racket of a crying child?

I tried to force a few spoonfuls of oatmeal into Debby Ann who managed to be even more stubborn than usual, defiantly turning her wispy blonde head to avoid the spoon coming at her. And when I *did* get a spoonful of cereal in that sweet rosebud of a mouth, the kid would stare me right in the eye and spit it out. The third time it happened, I gave up, washing her face with a wet cloth, none too gently and without a smidgen of guilt, and took her out of the high chair. Placing her on her feet on the floor, I plugged her mouth with what she'd wanted all along—her *ba-ba*—which the baby doctor had sternly advised me to start weaning her from at the last check-up.

"Fine with me if you're still sucking on that thing when you get to high school," I muttered, watching grimly as Debby Ann parked her butt on the floor, and began to suck enthusiastically, her tiny hands clamped on the bottle.

I sighed. "You're just as strong-willed and stubborn as your daddy, aren't you?"

Debby Ann's big brown eyes watched me as she drank from the bottle. She sure was a pale little thing, her fine hair so light it practically blended into her porcelain face. Her dark eyes looked like a couple of raisins embedded in an unbaked cream puff.

"You sit right there and drink your bottle," I told her. "I'm going to get your daddy up. If *I* can't sleep, I don't see why he should."

Besides, he had shelves to get up. I'd be darned if I let him make a liar out of me. Them shelves better be up by the afternoon, or I'd know the reason why.

I opened the door to the bedroom. "Jake? You need to get up now."

No response. I stepped into the room. The blinds were drawn, but there was enough sunlight filtering through the slats so I could see that the bed was empty.

"Well, I'll be!" Hands propped on my hips, I stared at the rumpled sheets.

Where the dickens had that man gone off to? And why hadn't I heard him leave? He would've had to go through the living room to get out of the apartment.

He'd better not have gone out to drink more and carouse. That would really be the last straw! I blinked at the thought, wondering where it had come from. What did that mean, the last straw? And what would I do if it *was* the last straw?

Turning my attention to the bed, I smoothed out the top sheet and pulled up the gold-and-green chenille bedspread, tucking it over the fluffed pillows so it looked as pretty as a catalog picture.

"There, now."

The truth was, there *would* be no last straw. As Mother would say, I'd made my bed, and now I had to lay in it. Come hell or high water. So, I might as well make the best of it. Make it nice and smooth and pretty as a catalog picture...just like that bed. I wasn't a bit sure how I could do it, but what choice did I have but to try?

So just after eleven, the apartment was sparkling clean, Debby Ann was napping, and I sat at the kitchen table in a sunshine-bright yellow sundress and white sandals, my hair still damp from the shower, licking green stamps and placing them into a booklet.

On the radio, Frank Sinatra sang "Three Coins in a Fountain," and I hummed along as I placed the last stamp in the book. It was more than half-filled. Maybe it wouldn't be too long before I could use it to get that new steam iron in the catalog.

When Jake appeared in the doorway of the kitchen, I pretended not to notice him; instead, I turned my attention to the grocery list. For a moment, he just stood there and watched me. Finally, he came into the room, and I began to scribble on my pad of paper…anything that came into my head, whether we actually needed it or not.

Instant pudding. Nescafe. Wesson Oil. Campbell's Soup.

Jake pulled out a chair and sat down. Even though I could feel him watching me, I pretended to be absorbed in my grocery list.

Bisquick. Kleenex. Soap.

"Lily Rae?" he said softly.

Pretending to be surprised, I jumped a little, clutching at the bodice of my sundress. "Oh! You startled me."

His gaze swept my face, and then stopped on the Band-Aid I'd applied to the cut on my temple. "How's your head?"

I refused to meet his eyes. "I'll live."

Wish I could say the same for my Elvis record.

I almost said it aloud. Had to bite my tongue to stop myself. To cover, I made a move as if to get up from the table, but Jake reached out and grabbed my hand. "Hon, I'm really sorry for last night. I couldn't sleep a wink over it."

I finally looked at him, and as soon as I saw the vulnerability in his eyes, my anger drained away. And God help me, all I wanted to do was take him in my arms, cover his unshaven face with kisses and tell him I forgave him. But following on the heels of that impulse, was the image of him slamming that hammer down on my Elvis record.

"Jake, apologies are fine and good, but…"

He touched his index finger to my lips. "I know. It's the drinkin'. I know that. And I'm gonna stop, Lily Rae. I mean it. I'm stopping today." He squeezed my hand. "Babe, I've already been to the hardware store. I was the first customer there this morning. I've got the boards to build them shelves you've been wanting. And I'm going to get started on it directly, but first…" He gave me his lop-sided grin and took a slim paper bag from his lap, sliding it across the table toward me. "Got something for you."

I looked down at it.

"Go ahead. Open it," he said, his grin widening. "I had to go to three different stores to find it."

Before my fingers even touched the sack, I knew what was in it. "Oh, Jake…" I whispered, as I drew the 45-LPM record out, and stared down at the yellow Sun Records label.

I looked up at him. "You really *are* sorry, ain't you? *Aren't* you?" I corrected. Lately, I'd been trying hard to talk more like Betty, but I still slipped into "country-talk" more often than not.

Jake's grin had disappeared, and he was watching me, a hopeful expression on his face. He nodded. "I am sorry, hon." His fingertips brushed the Band-Aid covering my cut. His voice roughened with emotion. "I hate myself for hurting you."

My throat tightened. I reached up to grasp his hand. "It wasn't your fault. You didn't mean it."

"It *was* my fault. If I hadn't been drinking, and if I hadn't ruined your record..."

I reached toward him and cupped his bristled jaw in my hand. "It's over now. You've apologized, and I forgive you. Let's just forget it, okay, Jake?"

He reached out and took my hand. "I just don't want to be like my old man, you know? Sometimes, even as it's happening, I see him in myself, and yet, I can't do a thing to stop it."

I shook my head. "You're not like him, Jake. You're *not*. If you were, how could I love you like I do?"

He stared at me a long moment, and then nodded. I leaned closer and kissed his lips softly. He drew me into his lap, and wrapping his arms around my waist, deepened the kiss. After a long moment, he drew away. His index finger traced the outline of my lips. "How many more days will you have your period?" he whispered.

I sighed. "This is only the fourth day. I still have one more day at least."

He groaned, and then gave me a little peck on the lips. "Okay. Why don't you go put that Ellis-guy's record on the hi-fi? I reckon I ought a give him another chance."

I grinned and jumped up from his lap, grabbing the record. "It's *Elvis*, Jake. Elvis Presley...and don't you forget it. I predict one day we'll have quite a story to tell our grandkids about seeing him in person."

But I'll never tell them the <u>real</u> story.

CHAPTER TWENTY-FIVE

November 1954

I stood at the stove, stirring a spoon through a skillet of half-cooked scrambled eggs. From the radio on top of the refrigerator, Rosemary Clooney sang "Mambo Italiano." The record had just been released the week before, but KOSY had been playing it so much, I already knew the lyrics; I sang along with her now as I made Jake's breakfast. Debby Ann, a frail 20-month-old, stood nearby in her footed Bugs Bunny pajamas, tugging at my pajama leg and whining for her "ba-ba."

I shook my head. "I told you, Debby Ann, doctor says no more *ba-ba*. Go get your sippy cup. It's on the table."

"Noooooo," Debby whined, rubbing her fist into a tear-filled eye.

Ignoring her, I turned to the **Ladies' Home Journal** on the counter next to the stove. I'd found this new recipe on how to dress up ordinary scrambled eggs with deviled ham, and today, that's what Jake was going to get, like it or not.

I heard him come into the kitchen and turned to flash him a smile. "Good morning, sleepy-head!"

Clad only in a pair of plaid pajama bottoms, he growled something unintelligible and headed for the percolator to pour himself a cup of coffee. Smiling, I turned back to the eggs and added the Underwood deviled ham. "Got a special surprise for you this morning, hon."

Jake took a sip of coffee, placed the cup back on the table and ran his hands through his greasy hair so it stood up in comical spikes. "God help me...especially if you got it from one of them fancy magazines of yours."

He wasn't exactly grinning, but I could tell by the quirk of his lips that he was just kidding around. He wouldn't admit it, but he actually *liked* some of the fancy stuff I made for him out of my magazines.

"Here you go." I took the skillet from the stove and moved away from Debby Ann, forcing her to release her grip on my pajama leg. The toddler gave an indignant squeal. I winced but ignored her. The ear-piercing squeal was one of Debby Ann's latest tricks in her attempt to maintain Mama's attention at all costs.

"Mama! *Ba-ba!*" she demanded, her heart-shaped face screwing up in a familiar pout.

I scraped the eggs onto Jake's plate. "First of all, you're old enough to say it right. *Bottle.* And second of all, you heard me...you can't have it."

"I don't know why you're always trying to reason with her," Jake said, shoveling the eggs into

253

his mouth. "Just tell her no, and leave it be." He swallowed and looked up at her. "Hmmmm...not bad. What's in it?"

"Deviled ham." I scooped the whimpering toddler into my arms and sat down across from Jake. "Surprised?"

He shrugged and shook his head. "One thing about you, Lily Rae, you're not a bad cook."

I smiled and reached for Debby Ann's sippy cup. For Jake, that was a real compliment. Things had been really good between us ever since that last big fight about the Elvis record in June. And it was because Jake had made a real effort to change. As far as I knew, not a drop of alcohol had passed between his lips since then, and it sure made a difference in our home life.

"Here." I put the sippy cup into Debby Ann's hands. "Drink this."

"*No!*" In a fit of temper, she threw the cup, and it went spinning across the table, spilling milk all over the scratched Formica.

Jake, who'd just picked up his coffee cup, gently placed it back down. He got to his feet, came over to me, and took Debby Ann from my arms.

"*Bad girl!*" He gave her a right smart swat on the behind, and for a moment, Debby Ann looked startled, then she released a howl that sounded like a squalling ambulance on the way to the hospital with a critical patient. "If you can't behave yourself, you can go right back to bed, young lady."

He carried Debby Ann out of the room, and her cries diminished the farther away he got. A moment passed, and I heard a door slam followed by Jake's footsteps heading back to the kitchen--and in the background, Debby Ann's piercing cries.

"That little gal is spoiled rotten," Jake said, stepping back into the kitchen. "And I don't want you running in there and picking her up. She's got you wrapped around her little finger."

The screams grew louder. Apparently, Debby had just realized that her daddy really *was* leaving her in her crib. I shook my head. "She's on her way to having a major conniption fit."

"She'll simmer down...once she realizes you aren't going to give in to her." Jake sat back down at the table and resumed eating.

I got up to pour myself a cup of coffee, hoping the caffeine would distract me from the baby's crying. I supposed Jake was right, but it was all I could do not to run in there and scoop her out of the crib just to shut her up.

"Get me a refill, will you, hon?" Jake said through a mouthful of eggs. "Any more biscuits?"

"In the oven. I'll get you a couple." I grabbed a potholder and removed the tray from the oven, scooping up two golden biscuits with a turner and depositing them onto Jake's plate. He sliced one open and began to slather it with butter.

With my coffee cup in hand, I started to sit down.

"We got apple butter?" Jake asked.

"I'll get it." I put the cup down on the table and turned to the refrigerator, glancing up at the Coca Cola Neon clock on the wall I'd bought at the PX last pay day. I rubbed my temple and grabbed the jar of apple butter, trying to ignore Debby's screaming. Honestly, it was way too early for her nap. She'd never go down at eleven o'clock in the morning.

"I don't think she's simmering down," I said, placing the jar on the table.

"She will." Jake spread a thick layer of apple butter on top of the butter and took a bite. He glanced at me. "Sit down. Got some news."

"What?" I took my seat and reached for my coffee. Was it my imagination or were Debby Ann's cries petering out? Could Jake actually be right?

He popped the last of the biscuit into his mouth and reached for the second one. "Any more of them eggs?"

"No, but it'll only take a minute to make you some more." I started to get up.

"Nevermind. That can wait." He pressed the top half of the biscuit on the one topped with butter and apple butter, eating half of it in one bite. "Talked with Sarge this week about reenlistment."

My heart skipped a beat. Had he received orders for his transfer? Much as I was excited about seeing other parts of the country—and maybe even the world—I didn't look forward to moving away from Betty. But then, Eddie was due to get transfer orders soon, too, so it was inevitable we'd eventually be separated. After all, that was military life.

"So, what did he say?" I asked eagerly, one ear still listening to the sounds from down the hall. Darned if she *wasn't* winding down! Her cries had gone from ear-piercing shrieks to muffled sobs. "Did he think you might be able to get orders to Hiwalya? Oh, Jake, it would be so wonderful if we could go there! Oh, *darn*! Betty told me it's not pronounced like that. Let's see…how did she say it? Ha…*wah*…eeee." I grinned at him. "So, what did he say? Please don't tell me we have to go somewhere awful like North Dakota!"

Jake frowned. "Don't it bother you that Miss Know-It-All is always correcting you on everything? Must make you feel like an ignorant hillbilly."

I bristled. "She's not like that at all, Jake. She's trying to teach me how to speak correctly so I don't come off *sounding* like an ignorant hillbilly!"

He rolled his eyes and pushed away his plate. "Anyhow..." He took a sip of coffee, then cocked his head toward the doorway. "Hear that? Didn't I tell you? She's dropped off to sleep. Just goes to prove...coddling ain't the way to raise kids."

"Okay, you're right. Anyway, so what did your sarge say?"

"Just what I expected him to say. No guarantees we'll be sent to *Hi...wal...ya*, or any other place interestin'. Hell, I might end up in Timbuktu or Southeast Asia somewhere. I hear things are startin' to heat up over there again." He took another slurp of coffee and set down the cup. "I just can't take that chance, Lily, so I told him I'm not going to re-up."

I stared at him, shock radiating through my body. There was no mistaking what he'd said. It was clear as daylight. But I still couldn't quite believe it. "But Jake," I said finally. "We *talked* about this. We *agreed* that the money was too good to give up, especially since you got that promotion to buck-sergeant. Remember how we talked about all the places we'd like to go to? Germany and California...Colorado. Why, there's a whole world out there we've never seen, and the Army will pay for it all! How can you turn down an opportunity like that?"

"Well..." Jake drew a pack of Winston's from the arm of his rolled up T-shirt, tapped one out and stuck it between his lips. "I just don't like the odds." He struck a match and lit the cigarette, taking a long draw of it before releasing a stream of smoke. "Like as not, they'll end up sending me over to some hellhole in Southeast Asia, and I just ain't gonna go through that shit again. I did my part in Korea, and that's enough."

I just stared at him, my brain spinning. He *couldn't* be serious! I'd always assumed Jake would be a "lifer." With a wife and kid to support, a steady pay check wasn't something to take lightly. How could he give up the security of the military for...*what?*

I suddenly realized how quiet it was in the apartment. When had Debby Ann stopped crying? On the radio, Kitty Kallen sang "Little Things Mean a Lot." Jake sat leaning back in his chair, smoking his cigarette as if he didn't have a care in the world. But I saw the wary look in his eyes. He'd been prepared for a fight about this. I took a deep breath and consciously tried to calm down. The only way I could make him see sense about this was to simmer down.

"So, what's your plan?"

He took another draw on his cigarette and blew out a smoke ring. "Go back home. Get a job. Settle down."

It took all my strength to hold back a shriek of dismay. I reached for my coffee cup, thinking carefully before speaking. I took a sip, then said, "Last I heard, there weren't many jobs in Russell County...unless you want to shovel manure."

Or work for pennies at the gas station. I practically had to bite my tongue to stop myself from saying that out loud.

Jake shrugged. "I can always get my old job back at the gas station."

I tried not to laugh in his face. "Pumping gas for Slim Jessup wouldn't pay for Debby Ann's baby food. And where are we gonna live? Have you even thought about that?"

"My house. Where do you think?"

"You mean your mama and daddy's house, right? Or are you trying to tell me you've up and bought us a place, sight unseen?"

Jake chuckled, making me want to slap him silly. "Now, Lily Rae, you know me better than that."

That just made me madder. And all thought of remaining calm disappeared. I slammed my coffee cup down on the table. "Well, if you think I'm gonna move back in with your mama and daddy, and put up with all the shenanigans I did two years ago, you've got another think coming, Jake Tatlow. Because I *ain't* gonna *do* it!" I stared him down, my jaw set.

His lips tightened; anger sparked in his eyes. "You ain't got no choice, Lily Rae," he said quietly. "I'm the head of the household, and you're my wife. What I say goes. And I say, come December 1st, we're gonna be right back in Russell County where we belong. And if that means we gotta spend a few months living with my folks, then that's the way it has to be and I don't want to hear another word about it."

I stared at him, blinking back tears of fury. I knew better than to continue the argument. For now, anyway. But somehow, I had to reason with him, make him see that staying in the military was the only way we'd ever be able to make a decent life for ourselves. Later…when he was in a better mood, I'd try to convince him of that.

"Ba-ba?"

The childish voice came from the doorway of the kitchen. I looked beyond Jake's shoulder to see Debby Ann peeping into the room, her thumb in her mouth, her face flushed and eyes swollen from crying. Jake's head whipped around; he scowled at her.

259

I jumped up and headed for the toddler. "How did you get out of your crib?"

"Why, you little son-of-a-gun!" Jake shoved back his chair. "So help me, I'm going to blister your little behind."

I reached her first and swept her into my arms. Debby Ann, seeing the anger on her father's face, began shrieking. I turned and glared at him. "No, you're not! You're not gonna lay a hand on her!" I placed a kiss on the baby's forehead. "Come on, sweetie. Mama will go lay down with you."

My heart pounding, I turned and headed down the hallway, half-expecting Jake to follow me. But there was only silence behind me. It wasn't until I reached the bedroom door that his voice rang out in disgust.

"No wonder the brat is so goddamn spoiled!"

That was followed by the slam of the apartment door and footsteps as he stomped his way down to the 1st floor. I collapsed on the bed with Debby Ann in my arms. Hugging the whimpering toddler against me, I burst into sobs of my own.

Mother's Fried Apple Pies

6 oz. dried apples
½ cup water
½ cup sugar
Pastry (see below)

Put apples and water in medium-sized saucepan and let stand for 1 hour or overnight. Cook, covered, over low heat until thick enough to cling to a spoon, about 45 minutes. Stir in sugar.

Pastry:

2 cups self-rising flour
¼ cup shortening
¾ c milk

Cut shortening into flour, using pastry cutter or fork until mixture is well combined. Stir in milk to make soft, but not sticky dough. Add more flour if necessary. Heat shortening in heavy skillet to 1/8" depth to medium hot. While skillet is heating, prepare dough. Pinch off piece of pastry the size of a small egg. Place on well-floured surface and roll into 5" circle. Place 2 T of apple mixture on bottom half of circle, leaving 1/2" uncovered. Fold top of pastry over apples, forming a half-circle. Press sealed edges together with tines of fork. Prick top of pastry with fork in several places. Place in heated skillet and fry on both sides until golden brown. Serve hot.

CHAPTER TWENTY-SIX

"Jesus Christ, Lily. How on earth do you find time to cook when you're in the middle of moving?" Betty asked.

After flipping the fried apple pie, I glanced back at Betty who sat at the kitchen table, smoking her ever-present cigarette and sipping a cup of coffee. As usual, she looked gorgeous in a trim, royal blue pantsuit, one that reminded me of pictures I'd seen of an airline stewardess's uniform. For the past year, Betty had been letting her reddish-blond hair grow out, and now it was down past her shoulders, pulled up on the sides and fastened with tortoise-shelled combs, leaving the back flowing sleekly. It was a style that suited her, but then, I doubted Betty could look bad no matter how she wore her hair.

I wiped my hands on my apron. "I'm trying to make something Debby Ann will eat," I said. "By the time she's up from her nap, these'll be cool. And Mother's fried apple pies is one of the few things she don't throw her nose up at." I slid the turner under one and lifted it a bit to see if it was browned. "If she don't eat these, then I know something's bad wrong with her."

"Well, if you ask me, you just worry too much. *No*, Davy! *Don't throw!*"

From the linoleum floor near the refrigerator, the little boy looked up at his mother, an innocent expression on his round face. The block he'd just thrown with a pudgy hand had landed a few inches from Betty's suede slip-on. She reached down to get it and handed it back to the little boy. "Now, play nice, or you'll have to take a nap like little Debby."

Davy grinned at his mother and threw the block again. Betty shook her head and rolled her eyes. "It's like talking to a concrete wall." She looked back at me. "So, what's the problem, hon?"

I slid the steaming apple pies onto a plate, sprinkled them with powdered sugar, then took off the apron protecting my jeans and draped it over a chair. Sitting down at the table across from Betty, I reached for my cup of coffee.

"She just don't look right to me. Haven't you noticed how pale she always is? And lately it seems like all she wants to do is sleep. Yesterday afternoon, she slept for four solid hours. I had to wake her up for supper, and then she'd barely eat at all."

"When was her last check-up?"

"In August. She's due, I reckon." I shook my head. "I keep meaning to make an appointment, but with trying to get all packed up for the move, and all...I just haven't got around to it."

"Well, you *better* get to it. Once those discharge papers are signed...no more free medical care."

I sighed. "Don't I know it? I'll make the appointment first thing tomorrow morning."

"Good." Betty glanced over at the boxes stacked against one wall. "It looks like you're getting a lot done. What I don't understand, though, why are *you* doing the packing? Didn't Jake tell you the Army will do that for you?"

"Yeah, I know…but he wants me to get a head start on it. Lord, that boy is so anxious to get back to Russell County, he's got me as busy as a stump-tailed cow in fly time!"

Betty almost choked on her cigarette, and then burst out laughing. "God, I'm going to miss you, girl! No one can turn a phrase quite like you do." Her grin faded, and a sad look came into her blue eyes. "I still can't believe you can't make him see reason."

I frowned. "I know. But that's Jake. He gets his mind set on something, and God Himself won't get him to budge. I'm just *sick* about going back to Kentucky."

Betty's lips quirked. "Hard to believe this is the same girl talking that was so homesick when she first got here."

"Well, it's not like I don't want to go home and see everybody. I just don't want to go back to the kind of life we had before Jake enlisted. Besides…" I nibbled on a hangnail on my thumb. "I like being out in the real world, you know. And I want to see more of it."

"Too bad Jake can't change assignments with Eddie." Betty's gaze fastened on the plate of cooling apple pies on the counter. "Those look scrumptious. Are they cool enough to eat yet?"

I grinned and got up to get her one. "Probably not, but I'll let you decide." I transferred one of the pies to another plate and put it down in front of her. "Lord A-mighty, Betty Kelly, how can you *not* want to go to Germany?"

She raised a slim, arched eyebrow. "Because it's goddamn cold there, that's why. I'm a Californian, remember? I've got thin blood. And here we are, being transferred to Heidelberg in the middle of *December*, for God's sake! When does it start getting warm in Germany? July?" She cut into the apple pie and gingerly slid a bite into her mouth. "Oooooh! Too hot...too hot..." She fanned her mouth with a hand, then swallowed. "But *delicious*! Have I told you how much I'm going to miss your cooking?"

Her compliment brought tears to my eyes. I got up from the table again, this time on the pretense of refilling our coffee cups, even though we'd already had two cups each. But I didn't want Betty to see how her words had moved me. I knew it was more than my cooking that Betty would miss. In the almost two years we'd been next-door neighbors, we'd become as close as I'd been with my girlfriends in high school. It just killed me to think we'd be going our separate ways this time next week.

As I reached for the coffee pot, the phone rang from the living room. "I'll be right back," I said, heading toward the door. It was on the third ring when I picked up the phone. "Hello?"

"Lily Rae, it's me." Jake's voice sounded rushed. "Hey, the boys are takin' me out tonight...sort of a going-away party. So, don't wait up for me, okay?"

My hand tightened on the receiver. "But Jake...I was gonna fry up a chicken. It's already thawed out and everything."

"You can fry it tomorrow night," he replied, sounding irritated. "The boys already planned this, and I ain't gonna disappoint them. Anyhow, it'll be a late night. Gotta go." Before I could say a word, the phone went dead. I sighed and placed the receiver in its cradle on the end table.

"What's wrong?" Betty asked when I stepped back into the kitchen. "You look like...how did you put it last week? A mule eating briars?"

I released an exasperated breath and plopped back into my chair. "Jake! He's going out with the boys' tonight. Told me not to wait up."

Betty licked her index finger, pressed it onto a bit of powdered sugar on her empty plate and slid it into her mouth. "Well, you'll just have to come over and have dinner with us, then. If you don't mind having Vienna sausages and Kraft Macaroni and Cheese, anyway."

"Why don't ya'all come on over here? I can fry up the chicken I've got thawed out."

Betty grinned and sat up straight. "Hey, I have a better idea. Let's get Merline to come over and watch the kids, and I'll get Eddie to take us *out* for dinner. It's about time both of us had a night out, don't you think? We'll have our own going-away party."

"But the chicken," I protested. "I already..."

"Yeah, I know. Thawed it out. The *devil* take the damn chicken, Lily. We're going out tonight, and that's final!"

***

I wasn't at all surprised to find the apartment empty when I stepped inside with a whining Debby Ann just after midnight. When Jake said he'd be late, he meant *late*. Still, I couldn't help but be disappointed—and a little put out—that he was still out honky-tonking.

Debby Ann was already in her Bugs Bunny pajamas so all I had to do was put her into the crib. By the time I tucked the soft pink blanket around her small body, she was asleep, her thumb plugged into her mouth. Alarmed, I stared down at her. Something was definitely wrong here.

She'd been sleeping when I'd taken her over to the Kelly's this evening; she'd been sleeping when we returned from dinner. On Betty's insistence, I'd stayed for several hours, listening to records on their brand new hi-fi while Eddie and Betty taught me how to play Pinochle. And Debby Ann had slept through it all.

Gazing down at her, I touched a finger to her petal-soft, white cheek-- so pale it could've belonged to a china doll. "What's wrong with you, baby girl?" I whispered, my stomach twisting with anxiety.

Forget making an appointment! I'd take her into the emergency room first thing in the morning. If I had the car, I'd do it right now. But then...

I brushed a hand through her golden curls—so like little Charles Alton's—and felt her forehead. Cool. This made me feel a little better. If the baby was really sick, like Charles Alton had been, wouldn't she be feverish?

Assuring myself this was so, I turned away from the crib and began to unbutton my knit dress, another Betty hand-me-down. I slipped out of it and carefully hung it on a hanger, sliding a hand down its soft, ribbed bodice. Such a pretty color of turquoise. Betty must've spent a fortune on it, if the fancy California department store label was any indication.

Would there ever be a day when I could walk into an I Magnin and buy a dress like this? My lips curled at the thought as I perched on the stool in front of the dressing table and reached for my brush.

Yeah, *that* would happen. With Jake getting out
of the service and us moving back to Kentucky, I'd
be lucky to be able to walk into Grider's Drugstore
and buy a bottle of Evening in Paris.

I sighed and began to brush out my hair. This
time next week, I'd probably be back sitting in
Gladys Tatlow's living room, watching a snowy TV
and listening to old man Royce snoring in his chair
by the woodstove.

Tears blurred my vision at the thought. It just
wasn't *fair* that I had to go back to Russell County
and live under Gladys's roof...no, it was worse than
that. I'd be living under her blame *thumb*! No
cooking my own meals anymore, no taking pride in
cleaning my own house...and what would it be like
with Debby Ann there? Just those few days we'd
spent at the Tatlows' over Christmas last year had
demonstrated that my mother-in-law had some
strong opinions on child-rearing and not a bit of
compunction in expressing every one of them. I'd
just gritted my teeth and smiled politely, knowing I'd
soon be back in Texas and doing exactly what I saw
fit. But there would be no grinning and bearing it
once I had to do it on a daily basis. I'd up and die
first.

I gently placed my brush on the dressing table
and gazed into the mirror, seeing an attractive, dark-
haired woman wearing a full-length white slip, her
brown eyes watery and mournful, her still girlishly
round cheeks wet with tears. I was only 20 years
old...had my whole life ahead of me.

And I was going back to Russell County,
Kentucky, where I'd live with my in-laws, probably
spit out a baby every year like clockwork, and grow
old before my time just like Mother and Gladys
Tatlow had...like just about every woman did down

there in the sticks. It was my destiny, I supposed. What had made me think I'd escape it?

I dropped my face into my hands and burst into sobs.

Lord, I'd rather die than live a life like that. Even as I sobbed my heart out, I knew that wasn't true. In fact, in a secret place in my heart, I had to admit a tiny part of me was looking forward to going home.

I'd grown up so much since that cold January day I'd left Kentucky, pregnant with Debby Ann, and clinging to Jake as if he were a life-buoy keeping me afloat as I drifted out to sea. I would return home a different person—a sophisticated and worldly lady, thanks to Betty's influence. Why, everybody in Russell Springs would sit up and take notice. I could just imagine the faces of Katydid and Daisy. They'd be so impressed at the change in me.

And Chad. I caught my breath in mid-sob and slowly lifted my head. Lord, if Pat-Peaches looked half as bad as she had in the drugstore the Christmas of '52, Chad would take one look at me and wish he could turn back time.

Sniffling, I grabbed a tissue out of the Kleenex box on the dressing table and dabbed at the smudged mascara under my eyes. Going home wouldn't be all bad, I reckoned. One thing was for sure. If Royce Tatlow gave me any grief—about anything!—I'd tell him to stick it where the sun don't shine! Gladys, too. Them two was going to find out that the scared little wallflower they'd bossed around two years ago had grown into a tiger-lily with claws that could draw blood if need be.

And of course, it *would* be nice to be back home with Mother and Papa and Norry and Edsel and Landry. I'd never heard much from the boys but every week, a letter had arrived from Norry, so regular you could set your clock by it. Lord, that girl had probably grown like a weed since I left. After all, she'd turned ten back in July.

A noise from the living room drew my attention. It was the jangle of keys followed by the sound of the front door opening. Relief flooded through me. I grabbed the brush, ran it through my hair once more and got up from the stool. I really hadn't expected Jake to be home before the wee hours, but I was glad he was.

"Oh, honey, I'm glad you weren't out too late," I called out, hurrying into the hallway to meet him. "I really think we need to take Debby Ann to the doctor tomorrow. She's just not..." My voice died away as I stepped into the living room.

Jake stood swaying just inside the front door, a drunken grin on his face, a bottle of Pabst Blue Ribbon in one hand--and a harlot in the other.

"Well, *there's* my purty little wife," Jake said, his grin widening. "Lily Rae, this here's Lou Ellen." He nudged his bottle at the harlot. "I figgered she could give you a love lesson on how to please your man."

***

When I stepped back into the living room with the butcher knife in my trembling hand, I saw what was happening in a blur—the harlot on her knees in front of Jake...my husband cradling her head, his eyes rolling back with passion.

"You lowdown good-for-nothin' bastard," I said with icy calm. I marched over to them and grabbed a handful of the woman's hairspray-stiff bottle-blonde hair and yanked with all my might. "*Get your filthy mouth off my husband, woman!*"

"*Ouch!*" The woman shrieked, tumbling onto the floor at Jake's feet. "*Son of a bitch! That hurt!*"

I glared at her. "It was *meant* to hurt. Now, get the hell out of my home before I use this here knife to scalp you bald as an Injun!" I didn't wait to see if the woman would take me at my word, but turned my attention to my low-life husband who was gaping at me like I was an escapee from the loony bin. "And *you*, you disgusting piece of dog-shit, get yourself and your filthy little ding-dong out of my house or I swear to God Almighty, I'll cut it off at the root and *feed it to the pigs out on Rt. 82!*" To emphasize my words, I thrust the butcher knife at his exposed penis. He flinched and quickly pushed it back into his pants and zipped up.

"Now, Lily," he said, a wary look on his lean, handsome face. "Don't go all batty on me. I was just kiddin' around."

I took a step closer, moving the knife in threatening little circles, and stared him in the eye. "You *dare* to tell me you're just *kiddin' around*? That whore had your goddamn *penis* in her mouth! Now, I mean what I say, Jake. Get the *hell* out of my house! And don't come back, you hear me? It's *over*!"

Even though he was still drunk, my words apparently penetrated into his beer-pickled brain. His slack face took on an expression of fear and remorse. "Come on, I…"

"*No!*" I cut him off. "I *mean* it this time, Jake. I've had enough! You don't love me. I don't think you ever did! A man who loves his wife don't bring a tramp home to give her 'love lessons.'" I flicked a glance toward the harlot, and saw that she was gone. Apparently, she'd realized I meant business. "Now, get on out of here. Go find your little whore and finish what she started. I don't *care* anymore!"

He extended a placating hand. "Lily Rae, you don't mean that…"

The nausea I'd felt earlier threatened to engulf me. With as much strength as I could muster, I stepped closer to my husband and positioned the knife just beneath his jaw.

"You care to make a wager on that?" I whispered, my gaze holding his. "I've never in my life been as mad as I am right now, Jake Tatlow. A little slip of this here knife and you'll be pumping blood all over the floor. And you know what? Even a Texas court won't put me away when they find out what happened here tonight."

For a long moment, we stared at each other. Seconds ticked by. Finally, Jake swallowed hard and backed away. Relief swept through me. Despite everything, I hadn't wanted to kill him, but if he'd touched me…I knew I would've done it. I'd never felt rage like this. Never thought it was *possible* to feel rage like this.

He waited until he stepped out into corridor before summoning his courage. Straightening his shoulders—as well as he could with being dead dog-drunk, he pasted a half-assed sneer on his face. "Well, *fine*, Miss Goody-Two-Shoes! If that's the way you want it, *fine*! You go on and file for divorce. You just go right ahead." His eyes blazed. "I'll find me a wife who knows how to please her man! Who's not so damn persnickety that she can't perform oral sex on her own blame husband. Well, fuck you, Lily Rae. *Fuck you!*"

I slammed the door in his face and locked it. I heard him shuffle off down the hall, still screaming "fuck you" at the top of his lungs.

I crumpled to the floor, my hands covering my ears to block out his shouting. Rocking back and forth, I released the sobs that had been held tight in my chest since the moment he'd walked into the apartment with that tramp in his arms.

A pounding came at the door, and I stiffened, thinking he'd returned, and this time, I'd really *have* to kill him.

"Lily! It's Betty. Open up!"

I tried to get to my feet, but my legs were trembling so badly, they refused to work. "Betty, I..." My voice came out ragged and weak.

"Lily!" Betty's voice rose in alarm. "Are you okay?"

"Yes," I whispered, and tried again to stand. This time I was successful, but it took me a moment as I fumbled at the lock.

"Lily, goddamn it! *Answer me*!" Panic rang in Betty's voice. "What the hell did he do to you?"

The lock gave, and I opened the door, leaning against the jamb to support myself. I looked at my friend and said softly, "I almost killed him, Betty."

She stepped inside. She wore a plain white cotton nightgown and had her hair up in rollers. Moving quickly, she wrapped an arm around me, helping me over to the sofa. I hugged my bare arms, realizing how drafty it was in the apartment, and here I was, wearing only a thin nylon slip.

"I'm cold," I murmured.

"Hold on." Betty disappeared down the hall and came back with a blanket she'd pulled off the bed. She draped me in it and sat down beside me, pulling me close. "Tell me what happened."

In halting words, I told her everything. She remained quiet, but I felt the tension in her body. The heat of her growing anger was so intense it almost burned my skin.

"I *could've* killed him," I said, after finishing the story. "If he hadn't left when he did..." I looked down.

"I wouldn't have blamed you a bit," Betty said. Her hand fastened on my chin. "Look at me, hon."

Lifting my head, I gazed into her livid blue eyes.

"You know what this means, don't you?" Her grip tightened on my chin. "It's *over*, Lily. No woman has to put up with this kind of treatment. You're a young, beautiful woman. You deserve so much more than Jake Tatlow. You *do* know that, don't you?"

Tears welled in my eyes. I nodded, and Betty released my chin. "Well, then," she said matter-of-factly. "Tomorrow I'm going to find a good divorce lawyer for you. And don't you worry a bit about money. If it's the last thing I do, I'm going to help you get that man out of your life."

Shock was settling in now. My thoughts spun. How could everything change so quickly? A half-hour ago, my life had been normal; now, it had turned upside down.

Betty stood, running her hands down her cotton nightgown. "Okay, you're coming over to my place tonight, just in case that piece of slime decides to come back. I'll pack you some overnight things while you go get Debby Ann, okay?"

Moving as if I were in a fog, I glided down the hallway to the bedroom. The thud of my heart seemed to keep time with the shuffle of each foot. I went over to the crib and gazed down at Debby Ann. For a long moment, I just stared at the tiny form lying motionless. Finally, I reached out to wake her. And a chill crept up my spine. The baby's skin felt odd—cool and clammy. Turning, I flicked on the light. "Debby Ann?" I scooped the little girl into my arms and cradled her.

No response. Her legs dangled listlessly like the rag-doll Mother had made for her last summer. Her face looked like yellowed cottage cheese.

Fear bubbled up inside me. Clutching my daughter to my chest, I threw my head back and screamed, "*Betty! Debby Ann ain't breathing!*"

CHAPTER TWENTY-SEVEN

A young military doctor stepped into the
waiting room. "Which one of you is Mrs. Tatlow?"

I jumped up from the uncomfortable plastic
chair I'd been sitting on for what seemed like weeks.
"I am, doctor. Is she okay? My little girl…is she…"
I stopped, anxiously chewing on my bottom lip,
unable to add the dreaded word. *Dead.*

The doctor wore a grim look on his face, and it
sent a spear of terror through me. "Please have a
seat, Mrs. Tatlow. I'm Captain Austin."

Eddie Kelly got up from his chair next to me
and moved down so the doctor could take his seat.
I stared at the doctor's brown eyes, trying to read
what he was going to say. My hands tightened into
fists as I struggled to hold onto my composure.

It had been two hours since Eddie had driven
us to the emergency room on the post—an hour and

five minutes since they'd whisked Debby Ann out of my arms and disappeared with her into a cubicle where I couldn't follow.

Since then, I'd been sitting in a desolate waiting room with Betty on one side and Eddie on the other, alternating between crying helplessly and chewing on my fingernails. Everything that had happened with Jake hours before had paled in comparison to what was going on behind those closed doors. My baby was fighting for her life back there. And it was all *my* fault! Why hadn't I taken Debby Ann to the doctor months ago when, deep in my heart, I'd known something wasn't right?

Now, I finally found my voice. "She's dead, ain't she? My little girl is dead."

A look of puzzlement appeared on Captain Austin's face. "No, ma'am. She's a sick little girl, but she's far from dying."

I slumped with relief. Next to me, Betty gave me a pat on the arm. "See? I told you she'd be okay."

I barely noticed. My eyes were fixed on the doctor. "What's wrong with her, then? I swear she wasn't breathing when I picked her up."

"Debby is suffering from severe anemia, Mrs. Tatlow. And it looks as if it's been going on for some time. She's dangerously dehydrated, and from the jaundiced skin, it's a certainty her liver is enlarged." A stern look appeared in his eyes, reminding me that he *was* an officer. "Mrs. Tatlow...I can't help but wonder why this little girl hasn't been seen by a doctor until now. Surely you've noticed the symptoms...the pallor, the pale nail beds, and if not that, surely the irritability and fatigue. What about her easy bruising? What has her appetite been like? Does she eat red meat...or any other iron-rich foods like chicken liver, lentils…blackstrap molasses?"

His questions came at me like machine gun clatter. I shook my head, focusing on the one about how she'd been eating. "She's not much of an eater. It's hard to get anything much down her."

"Well, we've got to change that. We've got to find some source of iron-rich nourishment for her. Meanwhile, I've ordered a transfusion. Blood from St. Michaels is on its way. Good thing your daughter's blood type is A-positive. If she'd been one of the rare types…" He shook his head. "Her condition would be much grimmer." He got to his feet and I stood, too. "I'm going to admit her overnight and start her on an iron supplement, and then we'll see what happens." He turned to go.

"Captain Austin!" I couldn't keep the anxiety from my voice. He paused. "Is she really going to be okay?"

Some of the hardness melted from his eyes. "We're going to put the roses back in her cheeks, ma'am. And working together, we'll keep them there." With a slight twist of the lips—his version of a smile, I reckoned—he was gone.

For a moment, I stood stiffly, looking at the empty doorway. Betty got up from her chair and slipped an arm around me, giving me an affectionate squeeze.

"You see? I told you everything would be alright. You just wait and see, Lily. When Debby Ann gets out of the hospital, she'll be a whole new little girl."

Her words were all it took to make the dam burst. I began to sob.

"Oh, come here, honey," Betty murmured, taking me into her arms.

And I cried out my relief, allowing it to sweep through me like a gentle balm.

***

After a scant four hours of sleep at Betty's apartment, she drove me back to the hospital the next morning just after eight o'clock in time to meet Captain Austin leaving the children's ward. He looked as if he hadn't slept for days. Or maybe that was because of all the screaming coming from the room. It was as if he couldn't escape fast enough.

Casting me a disgruntled look, he said, "You can take your little brat home, Mrs. Tatlow. If you can recognize her. She's had her transfusion, and…well, let's just say she's not the same little girl you brought in here. Just follow the screams."

That's when I realized the loudest scream coming from the ward—the one that sounded like someone was being attacked by a swarm of enraged hornets--*had* to be Debby Ann. But no…on second thought, that wasn't a scream of fear. It was pure, unadulterated *fury*.

"Be sure and stop by the nurse's desk to pick up your prescriptions and a list of foods to try to get down her," Dr. Austin said, striding off down the hall. "I don't want to see that child in here again."

I hurried into the room and saw my daughter standing up in a crib, dressed in an over-sized hospital gown, clutching the bars with her tiny fists and screaming her head off. Her wispy blond hair was damp and matted, her eyes blazing with anger and streaming tears. Her face was scarlet, like an over-ripe garden tomato. Plenty of good, red blood in her now, I reckoned.

Debby wasn't the only child crying. The ward held six cribs, and three others were occupied. Two

children, a boy and a girl, howled in chorus with
Debby Ann, but were nowhere near her decibel.
The third child, a boy of about four, just stared at
the others, a perplexed look on his round little face
as if he were wondering what on earth was wrong
with them. A psychiatrist in the making, I
suspected.

"Aw, sweetheart..." I headed for Debby's crib.
At the sight of me approaching, her screams
intensified to an even higher pitch. She began to
stamp her bare little feet on the crib mattress,
holding out her arms in such a piteous gesture that it
made my heart pang. "It's okay, baby." I swept her
up in my arms and rocked her back and forth.
"You've really been put through the wringer, haven't
you, sweetie? But it's okay, now. You're all better,
and Mommy's gonna take you right home."

Debby clung to me as if she were certain her
mama was going to up and disappear again. Guilt
swept through me as I comforted her. Betty had
insisted I leave the hospital and get at least a few
hours of sleep before returning. I hadn't wanted to
go, but I'd had to admit I was exhausted from
packing all day, not to mention *emotionally* exhausted
from the scene with Jake, and so I'd given in.

When we'd pulled into the apartment complex
just after four in the morning, I'd noticed that Jake's
car wasn't in its usual spot. And despite all that had
happened, and knowing I shouldn't care, I felt an
ache deep in my chest. No doubt he was still with
his whore. But I'd immediately shaken the thought
away, concentrating on the fact that Debby Ann was
going to be okay. *That* was what was really
important.

Now as I kissed the top of my daughter's
sweaty blonde head, I wondered what on earth was

going to happen to the two of us. If I kept the appointment Betty had made for me at the divorce lawyer's this afternoon...

Almost as if my thoughts had conjured her up, Betty appeared in the doorway of the ward, looking like a catalog model in a full-skirted white dress with scarlet polka dots and matching high heels. A perky ruby-red cap nestled on her sleek auburn head.

That's Betty for you, I thought. *Tell her a redhead can't wear red, and she'll prove you wrong in a heartbeat.*

Her blue eyes zeroed in on us. "Well, would you look at that little stinker? She's full of piss & vinegar now, isn't she?"

Debby Ann, who'd turned her head at the sound of Betty's voice, plugged a thumb into her mouth and buried her face in my bosom. Thankfully, her crying had turned to a whimper.

"Enough that the doctor is kicking her out," I said. "He told me to take 'my brat' home."

Betty laughed. "I love a man who speaks his mind. Okay, then. Let's go. Why don't we stop at The Coffee Cup on the way home and get some breakfast?" she suggested. "You were so keen to get to the hospital, I barely got a chance to drink my cup of coffee. And we don't have to be at the lawyer's office until two. Plenty of time for you to get home and get ready."

I felt the muscles on my face tighten at the mention of the lawyer. Lord, was I really going to *do* this? Throw my whole marriage away just like that? Go back to Kentucky a divorced woman? Why, that would really be something, wouldn't it? Bad enough I'd embarrassed my family by getting pregnant out of wedlock, and now, here I was, ready to shame them again—worse, maybe, this time. Everybody in Russell County thought a divorced woman was just a step up from a harlot.

Well, I didn't have to make a decision this very minute. It was time to get Debby Ann dressed and get her out of here. Later, I'd think about my options. I grimaced. Options. Like I *had* any. Talk about being between a rock and a hard place.

At The Coffee Cup, I sipped on my cup of joe and nibbled a slice of toast spread with strawberry jelly while Betty devoured a breakfast hearty enough for a lumberjack. And miracle of miracles, Debby Ann was actually *eating* the scrambled eggs and bacon I'd ordered for her. It was as if she'd woken up from a winter's hibernation with the appetite of a hungry bear. The candy-apple red of outraged fury had disappeared from her face, leaving it with a rosy glow. And instead of whining and being her usual pain in the behind, she was actually sitting in a high chair, picking her food up with delicate fingers and managing to get most of it into her mouth. Thank God for this, I thought. *My baby girl is on her way to a normal childhood.*

If only our lives weren't crumbling down around us. What would become of us if I divorced Jake? I wanted to talk to Betty about my doubts...about the second thoughts crowding my brain. But I knew what her answer would be. She'd made it perfectly clear she thought Jake was a lowdown son-of-a-bitch. And he *was*. I knew that. But he was *my* lowdown son-of-a-bitch. For better or for worse. Isn't that what we'd said when we stood up in front of Brother Joe Bob and pledged ourselves to each other 'til death did us part?

No, I couldn't talk to Betty about my doubts. She didn't know what it was like in Kentucky. She didn't understand the way folks thought down there.

My stomach was churning by the time Betty pulled into the parking lot of the apartment complex. It was almost 11 o'clock—three hours before I was supposed to be at the lawyer's office.

Betty saw the car the same time I did.

"Well, *shit*," she said.

I couldn't summon the energy to speak. I could only stare at Jake's blue Plymouth, and wonder what awaited me inside.

***

It was quiet when I opened the door of my apartment. Jake was sleeping it off, I supposed. As if nothing had happened.

"Lily, let me come in with you," Betty pleaded, hovering anxiously in the hallway. "I really think…"

"I need to do this alone, Betty," I said, a firm resolve in my voice. I met my friend's concerned gaze. "I owe this to him….and to myself."

Betty's jaw tightened. "You don't owe that man *anything*!" Then she gave a resigned sigh. "Okay, have it your way. I'm leaving my door open just in case you need me. If you so much as *breathe* a sigh of distress, I'll be on his ass like spit on shine."

Even though my stomach was twisting with apprehension, I couldn't help but give Betty a wry grin at her attempt to sound "country." "Okay, but if I know Jake, he'll be nothing but apologetic."

Betty frowned. "That's what I'm afraid of, kiddo. Don't let him talk you into staying, Lily. You need to get that man out of your life."

"Don't worry." I gently closed the apartment door. Adjusting Debby Ann on my hip, I walked into the living room, fully expecting it to be empty. But to my astonishment, I saw Jake slumped on the couch, staring blankly into space. His jaw was stubbled, his eyes bloodshot, his face the color of gray putty. When he heard me step into the room, he turned his head and focused upon me.

"I thought you were gone for good," he said in a toneless voice.

His face was expressionless, but in the depths of his blue eyes, I saw a wounded look I'd never seen before. I tried to harden my heart to it, forcing myself to focus on the memory of the tramp he'd brought into our home, the ugliness of his voice when he'd instructed me to watch the woman perform oral sex on him.

I stared at him a long moment, trying to keep my face as cold as my heart had felt last night. Before I could summon my voice, Debby Ann squirmed in my arms, wanting to be let down.

"*Daddy!*" As soon as I put her on the floor, Debby Ann toddled over to Jake and crawled up into his arms.

My heart panged. What would a divorce do to my daughter? She adored her father, even though he spent so little time with her. Still…I had to remember what he'd done. *He'd brought a whore into our house and instructed me to watch them have sex.*

"Hey, baby girl." Jake cuddled Debby Ann, kissing the top of her wispy blonde head. "You're looking mighty chipper this mornin'."

I finally found my voice. "She should. She had a blood transfusion last night. That's where I was all night. At the hospital in Texarkana."

Jake's head shot up. "What happened?"

Do you really care, I wanted to snarl. Instead, I forced an even note to my voice. "Apparently, she's been suffering for some time from anemia. She isn't getting enough iron in her blood. The doctor couldn't believe we'd let it go on as long as it has. I guess he thinks we're piss-poor parents."

"But she's okay now?" Jake asked.

I shrugged. "For now, I reckon. We've got to make sure she eats right from now on, and you know that's not going to be easy." I grimaced. *I should've said I, not we.* "He's put her on iron supplements," I added. "So maybe that'll help."

Jake looked relieved. He kissed the top of Debby Ann's head again. "Poor little girl."

I watched him. He lowered his head to the baby's and sat motionless for a long moment. When he finally spoke, his words came out in a rough, husky tone, "So, what are you going to do?"

Silence hung between us.

"I don't know," I said finally.

He lifted his head to look at me, and shock radiated through me. His eyes were awash with tears, his face ravaged with pain. "I'm not going to beg you to stay," he said quietly. "Let's face it, Lily Rae, you deserve more than I can give you. You deserve a man who'll worship the ground beneath your feet. Not an asshole like me. Don't you see, Lily, I love you, but I *can't* show it. I don't know *how* to show it. That's why I do these awful things to you. I guess your family is right. I come from bad seed. And that's what I am. A bad seed."

Debby Ann, who'd been watching her father with wide eyes, reached up and touched his bristled face where a tear had left a moisture trail. "Don't cry, Daddy," she said, concern in her sing-song voice. "You got boo-boo hurt, Daddy?"

Jake swallowed hard and gazed down at his daughter. "I reckon I do, Debby Ann. Inside…where you can't see it."

My throat had tightened. And I felt my heart thawing. I tried to stop it by summoning Betty's voice to my mind. *Don't let him talk you into staying, Lily. You need to get that man out of your life.*

285

"Debby Ann got boo-boo hurt, too. See?" She stuck out her tiny arm and pointed to the tape-covered cotton ball on the inside of her elbow where the I.V. needle had been inserted. Then she looked up at her father with solemn brown eyes. "It feel better, Daddy. Boo-boo hurt go away."

Jake swallowed hard, his Adam's apple bobbing with emotion. Then he nodded. "Yeah, your boo-boo hurt will go away. But I'm not so sure about mine." He turned his gaze back to me. "I reckon we can file for divorce here or...if you want to move back home, we can do it there. Up to you."

The word shook me to my core. *Divorce.* It wasn't as if this was the first time it had been said out loud. That's all Betty had been talking about this morning. And it had been reverberating in my mind since I'd started considering it. But to hear Jake say it out loud made it so...final.

I studied him. After a moment, I walked over to the couch and sat down on the other end of it, leaving a large gap of space between us.

"Jake, do you love me?" I said quietly. "Because sometimes...*most* of the time...it don't...*doesn't* feel like you do."

Jake closed his eyes and shook his head. I'd never seen him so vulnerable-looking. "I've always loved you," he whispered.

I sat quietly, unable to find an adequate response.

He opened his eyes and looked at me. There it was again—that wounded look. "I know that's not enough. You deserve a man who can give you more than that. And I know if I let you go, it won't take you long to find one. You got so much to offer, Lily Rae."

My heart skipped a beat and my throat went dry. "Is that what *you* want, Jake? A divorce?"

He stared at me a long moment, then nodded. "I want that for *you*. Because I know I can't make you happy. But for me?" He shook his head slowly. "The selfish bastard that I am wants you to stay. Because the selfish bastard that I am knows if you walk out, Lily Rae, I'll lose the best thing that ever happened to me." His voice choked, and he turned away, blinking back fresh tears.

Despite everything, my heart ached for him. Silence fell between us. Even Debby Ann seemed to sense the tension in the air. She looked up at her father and then turned her wide brown eyes to me.

It seemed she, too, was waiting for my answer.

Gladys's Blue Ribbon Peach Cobbler

6 ripe peaches, poached and sliced
1 - ½ cup sugar, divided
½ cup butter (do not substitute margarine)
1 cup self-rising flour
½ cup milk

Combine sliced peaches with ½ cup sugar and ¼ cup water. Bring to boil, and simmer for 20 minutes. Melt butter in 13x9" pan in oven at 350. Mix together remaining sugar, flour and milk. Pour batter over melted butter. (Do not spread.) Spoon peaches and juice over batter. Bake 30-45 minutes until golden brown. Serve warm with vanilla ice cream.

CHAPTER TWENTY-EIGHT

December 1954

"**C**ome on, Mommy! Debby Ann hungee!"

Running as fast as her little legs could carry her, Debby darted through the woods in front of me, stumbling twice over fallen tree branches blocking the path.

"Debby Ann, you'd better slow down, girl, or you're gonna land flat on your face," I warned, picking my way carefully through rotting leaves and other decades of debris from trees felled by lightning and wind. It was clear in the two years I'd been away that no one had used the trail that connected the Tatlow's to my family home.

Debby Ann stopped in the middle of the path, turned around, placed her hands firmly on her tiny hips and glared at me. "Mommy! I *hungee*, I *said*!"

"Don't you sass me, you little pipsqueak." I gave her a stern look even as I tried to hide an amused smile. That blood they'd given her back in Texarkana must've been full of orneriness; Debby Ann was like a different little girl these days, and it wasn't just her uncommonly big appetite that had changed. She'd become a bossy little squirt since we'd come back to Kentucky—probably the result of having two sets of grandparents waiting on her hand and foot and giving in to her every whim like she was Queen of Sheba or something.

"I don't know how in the world you could be hungry again. Didn't you have two bowls of soup beans and cornbread *and* butterscotch pie at Mother's house?"

Debby didn't bother to answer. She was already off and running through the woods again, the fluffy white ball on her red-striped knit cap bobbing behind her. *Two bowls of soup beans!* Lordy, that gal was probably tootin' all the way home.

I hoped to heaven she was all done by bed-time; when we'd first arrived at the Tatlow's, we'd figured Debby Ann could sleep in Meg's old bed across from Inis, but the little brat would have none of it. She'd screamed her head off until a disgruntled Gladys had moved an old army cot into our room for her, and that's where she'd been sleeping ever since, the little tyrant! It had been weeks since me and Jake had had any…privacy. No wonder he'd been going to the pool hall in town after supper two or three nights a week. I couldn't really blame him for that, could I?

I shook my head and followed after Debby Ann. My tennis shoe sank into a soft spot in the ground, muddying a quarter-inch of the white canvas, and I muttered one of Betty's favorite curse words. Last night's rain had been a drencher.

It had been a mild winter so far in Kentucky; at least that was what everybody was saying. Here it was, mid-December, and folks said there'd been only one good frost back in late October. Since we'd arrived back in Russell County three weeks ago, the weather had been pleasant with just a few soaking rainfalls like last night's. But on the walk over to Mother's this morning, I'd seen a black woolyworm with a half-inch thick coat—a sure sign of a bad winter to come. And according to Daddy, the Farmer's Almanac said the same thing. *Lord help me!* If I had to stay cooped up in the Tatlow's little house with Gladys and Royce all winter, I just might murder somebody.

Up ahead, Debby Ann reached the clearing that marked the boundary of the Tatlow's property. I could hear her high-pitched cry of delight as she caught sight of Hero, a scrawny black mutt that had replaced Bandit, the old three-legged dog that had finally died after years of mistreatment from his owners. It had been mutual love at first sight for Debby Ann and Hero from the beginning. And hate at first sight for me and that blasted dog.

The thick, homey fragrance of wood smoke carried on the afternoon breeze, a scent that would always and forever remind me of Kentucky, no matter where I ended up living. I reached the clearing and saw the mongrel sitting on his haunches, staring longingly at the back door of the house. So...Debby Ann had already gone inside. I quickened my pace. I knew exactly what was going to happen if I didn't get in there lickety-split.

Hearing my approach, the dog turned, saw me and began to bark like he thought I was a mad-dog killer intent on slaughtering the family. I sighed. It was clear he, like Gladys and Royce, still considered me an outsider.

"Aw, shut your yapping," I growled as the mutt ran up to me, barking his fool head off. "So help me, sometimes I'd like to knock you to Kingdom-come."

I wouldn't, of course. Poor dog probably had enough abuse from his new family. I was usually fond of any animal, but God's truth, this one sure annoyed the heck out of me.

I skirted the barking dog and climbed the rickety steps of the back porch. Slamming the screen door in Hero's face, I stepped through the pantry area lined with shelves holding jars of Gladys's summer canning frenzy, neatly arranged in groups of tomatoes, string beans and limas. There were also three rows of peaches, six deep, because peach cobbler was Gladys Tatlow's claim to fame in Russell County.

Gladys's voice came from the kitchen. "What do you say, Miss Debby?"

"Thank you, Grandma Gladys," piped Debby just as I stepped into the room.

"Oh, no, you *don't*!" I swooped down and grabbed the chocolate moon-pie from Debby's hand. "What did I tell you about eating junk like this right before supper?"

Debby Ann began to howl, stamping her red rubber boots against the linoleum like she was auditioning for **The Ed Sullivan Show**. Gladys folded her arms over her chest and glared at me, her mouth fixed in a disapproving straight line.

I ignored her, focusing a matching glare on Debby Ann. "Hush yourself this instant, young lady!"

Gladys made a sound that reminded me of one of the hens out in the yard—something between a "cluck" and a hiss, and it always meant the same thing--that I didn't have a brain *one* in my head.

"Now, Lily," Gladys said. "You need to simmer down. A little moon-pie ain't gonna hurt that youngun's appetite. Why, Jake and the rest of my younguns like to eat themselves silly during the day, and they still put away enough supper to feed a half-dozen farmhands."

Debby, smart little minx that she was, took her grandmother's words as a sign of encouragement, thinking perhaps I'd give in. She stopped in mid-scream and looked from me to her grandmother, her tearful brown eyes gleaming with new hope.

Purposely avoiding Gladys's gaze, I focused on my daughter. "Debby Ann, I want you to go to your room and lay down for a while before supper."

As my words sank in, Debby's heart-shaped face grew dark as a thundercloud. Her lower lip poofed out and her blonde brows furrowed. "Debby Ann want moon-pie," she said in a deep, growly voice that at one time had amused me enough that I'd dubbed it her "demon-child" voice.

But I wasn't amused now. "You are *not* getting a moon-pie before supper, young lady!"

With an outraged shriek, Debby Ann threw herself on the floor and began to thrash back and forth, kicking and screaming to raise the devil. I stared at her a moment and then turned to my mother-in-law. "Well, I hope you're happy, Gladys." I had to raise my voice to be heard over Debby's tantrum.

Gladys gave me an outraged look. "Don't you go blaming this on me. I'm not the one who has spoiled that youngun rotten. Why, I've never seen such behavior! If my younguns ever threw a fit like that, well, I'd just have to whop the daylights out of them. 'Spare the rod and spoil the child.' That's what the Bible says."

That did it; I'd had enough of Gladys and her endless insults. I released a groan of disgust and narrowed my eyes at her. "Well, it's pretty clear you and Royce are the holiest of the holy, then. You sure didn't spare any rods when you raised your hellion boys, did you? Maybe that's why you never see hide nor hair of Tully! Or why Jake is always off at the pool hall getting drunk with the old gang, and doesn't know an *iota* about how to be a decent husband and father! Maybe that's why you have a daughter half-way around the world in a military uniform who won't even drop a line to anybody in this family except her little sister. And speaking of that little sister, *Lord help her* living in a family like this! It's amazing to me she's as normal as she is when she's lived her whole life surrounded by *lunatics* like you *Tatlows*!"

Gladys sucked in a shocked breath and took a step backward. I realized that Debby Ann had stopped screaming, but my gaze remained focused on my mother-in-law.

"And now that I've got your attention, let me tell you again why it's so important not to give Debby Ann snacks before supper. I know I've said it before, and I guess I'll have to say it 'til I'm blue in the face, but Debby Ann *needs...to be...hungry...when she comes to the supper-table.* So she doesn't...get...anemic...again. Now, is that *clear enough* English for you, Gladys? That means *no* moon-pies, no *brown sugar toast*, no *Fig Newton bars*, no *Jell-O pudding*, no *Oreos*, no *shoofly pie*, *no* apple dumplings, no *peppermint sticks*, no *Sugar Babies*...Gladys, I don't even want you to give a *sugary smile* to that child if it's within *two hours of suppertime*. Do I make myself *crystal clear?*"

Locking gazes with my mother-in-law, I thought, Lord Almighty, I can't believe I heard them words come out of my mouth. *I'm actually standing up to the old biddy, and now she's gonna haul off and knock my block off.*

Instead, the oddest thing in the world happened. Gladys smiled. Well, if a stranger saw that stiff twist of the lips, they'd think she was having a spot of indigestion, but I knew it for a smile. I'd seen it once or twice before when Gladys had claimed victory in a battle with Royce. This time, though, I saw something else—a flare of respect in the woman's ice-cold blue eyes.

And as if that wasn't enough, she went a step further and gave a throaty laugh. "Well, I'll *be!* It appears Texas and the army life grew you some backbone."

I was so taken aback by Gladys's reversal that I couldn't find a word to say in response.

Just then, Debby Ann let out a mournful howl from the floor. "Debbbeee Annnnnnnnnn waaaaannnnts mooonnn-*piiiiiiie!*"

It was all I could do to stop myself from wrenching the brat off the floor and slapping her silly. And lord, I knew that was flat-out wrong, but that child surely could annoy the dickens out of a saint.

But before I could move a muscle, Gladys turned her piercing gaze on Debby Ann and spoke in a voice that even an almost-Terrible Two couldn't ignore. "Pick yourself up off that floor, young lady, and get along to your room like your mama says. I'm not gonna put up with that temper tantrum nonsense. No grandchild of mine is gonna get away with that as long as I'm around."

Debby's eyes had widened to the size of half-dollars. Her mouth slammed shut so hard, I thought I heard the crack of her jaw hinges. The little girl looked up at her grandmother, a wounded expression on her face that plainly said, "You talkin' to me?"

"You heard me," Gladys said briskly. "Haul yourself up off that floor and get on out of here. I don't want to see you again until you can act like a little lady, not a heathen."

Debby obeyed her, but not without a final show of rebellion. She puffed out her bottom lip as far as it would go, lowered her brows to thunderstorm-level and got to her feet. Then she stomped out of the room as loudly as she possibly could in her rubber boots.

Staring after her, Gladys shook her head grimly. "Mark my words. *That* one is going to be a pill when she's a teenager. "

And I just couldn't resist. If I'd been lined up against a stone wall opposite a firing squad, I wouldn't have been able to hold my tongue after that statement. "Well, she *is* a Tatlow, isn't she, Gladys?"

And again, Jake's mother surprised me by giving another dour smile.

"Yes, I reckon she is," she said. "I can see that ornery streak in her a mile away."

I couldn't help but smile back.

"It's all from *his* side of the family, I reckon." Gladys gave a disgusted nod towards the garage where Royce was doing an oil change on his truck, then looked away from me as if suddenly embarrassed by the moment of kinship. She wiped her knobby hands on her apron and turned to the cook stove where something simmered in a blue-speckled pot, giving off a savory aroma that suddenly had my stomach growling. "I reckon the beef stew will be ready directly. You want to go out to the garage and tell Royce and Jake to clean up for supper while I make the cornbread?"

"I can do that," I said. I was still smiling as I stepped out the back door and headed across the yard to get the men.

CHAPTER TWENTY-NINE

I didn't even try to pretend to myself that Jake hadn't gone back on his word and started drinking again. True, he wasn't out to all hours when he went off to the pool hall in town. He hadn't come in a minute past 11:00, and although I clearly smelled beer on his breath, he'd never been so drunk that he couldn't walk a straight line. So, he was *trying* to live up to the no-drinking, no carousing bargain he'd made back in Texas.

Trouble was, I knew it couldn't last forever. It was just a matter of time before he tied one on, and that was why it was so important to get him out of Russell County where he was under the influence of all his old cronies, the sorry lazy-ass good-for-nothing high school drop-outs who had nothing better to do than hang around the pool hall all day and drink themselves cross-eyed all night. But how in the world was I going to get him out of this county where he was born and raised?

The answer came on the Saturday a week before Christmas, the first frigid day since we'd arrived back home. Temperatures had plummeted the night before, and gathering gray clouds had the old-timers predicting snow by nightfall. I'd planned to go into Russell Springs for a little Christmas shopping that day (it could only be a *little* shopping because Jake's last paycheck from the military had dwindled from grocery shopping we'd done to help out Gladys.) After talking Jake into letting me borrow the car, I'd tucked Debby Ann into the back seat and headed off to town.

I hadn't been in Gracie's Drygoods more than ten minutes when the door opened and Jenny Lynn Cook—also known as "Jinx" in high school—sashayed in…as well as someone *could* sashay with a belly that exceeded her by a good foot.

When Jinx caught sight of me, her blue eyes widened and a big grin crossed her face. "*Lily Rae Foster!*" she shrieked. "*I haven't seen you in ages!*"

It was true. The last time I remembered running into Jinx had been at the Russell County Fair just before I'd left for my ill-fated job in Louisville. Jinx and Lonnie hadn't even gotten married yet, although she'd sported that gleaming diamond ring on her finger like it was as big and fancy as the one Eddie Fisher gave to Debbie Reynolds.

I finally found my voice. "Oh, my *Lord!* Jinx Cook, would you look at *you!*"

Jinx laughed and headed toward me. "It's Jinx Foley now! You stinker, you didn't even make it back to Russell County for our wedding! Your mama had some sorry excuse…you were off gallivanting around Texas. Having babies and stuff. Come here and give me a hug."

Laughing, I threw my arms around my old friend, sandwiching the unborn baby between us. Then I drew back and scanned her. Jinx was just as pretty and sassy as she'd looked in high school, if not prettier, thanks to the glow of expectant motherhood. *Lord, either she has triplets in there or that's one humongous baby!* And it looked like she could drop it at any moment.

Me and Jinx were still shrieking over each other when Debby Ann reached up and tugged on the hem of my black wool car coat.

"Mommy, who is that fat girl?"

My cheeks burned. I pulled away from Jinx and frowned down at my daughter. The little imp stood with her hands propped on her tiny hips, gazing up at us like a stern librarian scolding a couple of rambunctious kids. "Debby Ann, that was a very *rude* thing to say!"

But Jinx was laughing. "She's right! I *am* a fat girl!" She bent over so she could look Debby Ann in the eyes. "You must be Lily Rae's little girl. I'm your mommy's old girlfriend from high school. We were like two peas in a pod back in the good old days."

Well, that was an exaggeration, I thought. We'd run in the same circle but hadn't been particularly close. Jinx had been so besotted with Lonnie, she'd barely given any of the other girls the time of day.

Debby, having decided she didn't particularly care for being addressed by a "fat girl," stuck her thumb in her mouth and tried to hide behind my leg.

"Yes, this is my little Debby Ann. Spoiled as the day is long, she is." I stood back and gave Jinx another once-over. "It looks like you're ready to give birth any minute now. Is this your first?"

Jinx brushed a lock of wavy blond hair away from her forehead. "Lord help me, yes. My first, and it was due four days ago. I told Lonnie if it didn't come soon, I aim to go back to Bowling Green and check myself into City Hospital and have them yank this baby out, surgically, if necessary. I don't aim to be in a hospital bed when his company throws the big Christmas shindig. It's the only chance I have to doll up in sparkly clothes. And you ought to see the dress I ordered from the Montgomery Wards catalog, thinking I'd be trim and slim again by the 21st." She shook her head. "But this ornery child is determined to mess things up for me."

I laughed. "Get used to it. Everything changes when the kids come along. Like sleep. I haven't had a good night's sleep since March 9, 1953, the last night before I went into labor."

Jinx rolled her blue eyes. "Thanks for sharing that, Lil." Her face brightened. "But I do declare, we've got a lot of catching up to do, hon. What say we head over to Grider's for a milkshake? I've been craving chocolate milkshakes 'til the cows come home."

***

Debby Ann twirled on the soda fountain stool between me and Jinx, stopping every once in a while to take a messy slurp of her strawberry milkshake. On the counter in front of Jinx rested a frosted glass containing what was left of the chocolate milkshake she'd been craving so desperately. I'd ordered a Coke and French fries, more by habit than because I was hungry.

When Wallie, the soda jerk, placed the red and white checkered cardboard box of hot golden fries in front of me, I said, "You two are going to have to help me eat these. I don't know what it is about Grider's, but every time I come in here, I crave these things."

Jinx smiled, eyeing me speculatively. "Hmmmm...maybe I'm not the only one who's expectin' here."

I shook my head vehemently. "Bite your tongue! Lord, that's all I need. Jake out of a job and us living with his folks. And expecting on top of that? Huh! Why, I'd sooner take a swan dive, naked as a jaybird, off Cumberland Falls."

Jinx picked up her milkshake and took a long draw from the straw. Afterward, she dabbed at her lips with a napkin and said matter-of-factly, "Lonnie could get Jake a job if you're willing to move to Bowling Green."

I almost choked on a french fry. "Are you serious?"

Jinx nodded, finishing off the last of her milkshake. "He just made foreman at the iron factory outside of town, and he's looking to hire a few more men to work the second and third shifts. You think Jake would be interested?"

I caught my breath and tried to remain calm. For a moment, I was at a loss for words as hope swelled up inside me. Finally, I found my voice. "Oh, he'll be interested," I said, my jaw tight with determination. "God help him if he's not...because this is my ticket out of this podunk town, and I aim to use it."

***

Amazingly enough, Jake didn't put up a fight about the job, and he promised to get in touch with Lonnie after the holidays. As it happened, Lonnie got in touch with him first.

Two days before Christmas, he showed up on the Tatlow's front porch with news that Jinx had delivered twin boys the day before, and she'd made him promise to come by and tell me—and to set up an interview for Jake after the new year.

I began counting down the days. I'd listened as Lonnie discussed the job with Jake. He'd start out on day shift doing training, and after a few weeks, would be moved to the 2nd shift, 4:00-midnight. The starting pay was even better than he'd made in the Army, and best of all, it included a health insurance plan and a housing allowance if we chose to live in a rent-to-own subdivision close to the factory. We'd actually have our own little house! When I heard that, I was so excited I had to jump up and run into the kitchen on the pretense of getting them more coffee just to expend some energy. A flour-dusted Gladys stood at the table, rolling out pie dough.

"We're gonna get us a house!" I whispered, unable to contain my delight. "Oh, Gladys, he's just *got* to get this job."

"Now, don't count the chickens before they hatch," Gladys said without looking up.

I rolled my eyes. "He's got an interview on January 3rd. And Lonnie says it's just a formality and he's got the job if he wants it."

Gladys looked up at that. "Well, let's just hope he wants it then."

My jaw tightened. "Oh, don't you worry. He's *gonna* want it. I'll *kill* him if he doesn't."

***

Jake used the tip of a corn pone to push the last of yesterday's good luck black-eyed peas into his spoon. He shoved them into his mouth, and still chewing, got up from the supper table.

Mildly curious, I watched him. Usually, he didn't get up from the table until after Gladys had served him dessert.

"They's chocolate cake, Jake," Gladys said. "Sit yourself back down and I'll cut you a slice."

Jake headed for the door. "No time, Mama. I got to wash up."

My mouth dropped open. Now, where did he think he was going? Before I could say a word, though, Royce did it for me.

"Where you off to in such a hurry, boy?" he barked, shoveling in a big spoonful of mashed potatoes and black-eyed peas. "The least you can do is thank your mama for fixin' these vittles for you."

I looked away from the mess in Royce's mouth as he chewed with his big yellow horse-teeth, thinking, *yeah, you're one to talk, Royce Tatlow. You're always thanking Gladys for doing for you.*

Jake stopped in the doorway, wearing a look that was half-irritated and half-ashamed. "Good supper, Mama. Thank you." He turned to his father. "I told the boys I'd meet 'em down at the pool hall for a few minutes."

Alarm rippled through me. Jake's idea of "a few minutes" usually meant "three or four hours."

"Jake," I said. "You can't be serious!"

He heaved a frustrated sigh. "Don't start with me, Lily Rae."

Debby Ann, sitting on a stack of Sears & Roebuck catalogs, pointed a greasy finger at her father. "Daddy *go*! Debby Ann want to go, too!"

"You can't go, Debby," I snapped. "And Daddy can't either!"

Silence fell. Every eye at the table settled on me. The motor of the old Westinghouse refrigerator clicked on, unnaturally loud in the quiet room. The moment of silence stretched. Across from me, 14-year-old Inis shrank back in her chair, her brown eyes wide and fearful. Poor girl hated scenes, and Lord knew she'd suffered enough of them in this family. I hated putting her through yet another one, but this time, I just had to put my foot down. Royce, at the foot of the table, munched on a corn pone, his eyes gleaming in anticipation as they darted from Jake to me. He was just the opposite of his daughter; he loved a good knock-down, drag-out, and the uglier, the better.

Gladys, at the other end of the table, stared down at her plate, her lips stretched in a thin, stern line. It was the expression of the old Gladys—the one who wouldn't give me the time of day. And I'd actually believed I was making progress with the woman. Well, I should've known it wouldn't last. After all, her darling son could do no wrong.

I lifted my chin and met Jake's outraged gaze.

"What did you say, woman?" he asked. His tone was quiet, but the menace behind it was unmistakable.

I stared him down. "I *said* you're not going anywhere tonight. You've got that interview in Bowling Green tomorrow morning, and if you go out with your hooligan friends tonight, you'll get drunk and you'll either miss the interview or you'll go and make a blame fool of yourself and you'll throw away our only chance at a decent life. And I don't aim to let you do that."

I held his gaze defiantly. Across from me, I could almost feel Inis cringing in her chair.

Jake stared back, his jaw clenched. Finally, a slow grin spread over his face, but it was anything but pleasant. His eyes told the real story as they flared with rage. He looked at his father. "I *know* she ain't talking to *me*. 'Cause Tatlow women know better than to talk to their men like that, ain't that right, Daddy?"

Royce gave a snort of laughter and started to say something, but just then Gladys's head snapped up and she shot her husband a look that stopped him cold.

She turned to her son, and said quietly, "Jacob Royce Tatlow, you sit your behind back down in that chair, and have yourself another helpin' of supper. Or I can get you a slice of chocolate cake. But you ain't goin' *anywhere* tonight. The only way you're gonna take that car of yours out onto that dirt road leading to town is over my cold, dead body. You hear me, son?"

When Jake just stood there staring at his mother in total disbelief, her eyes narrowed and she barked, *"Move, I said! Sit yourself back down!"*

Two patches of red stained Jake's cheekbones as he moved back to his chair and fell into it. A shocked silence filled the room.

It was Gladys who broke it. "I reckon your wife knows what she's talking about," she said in a normal tone of voice as she reached for a platter of pork roast. "Tomorrow's a big day for you, son, and I reckon a few hour's extra sleep won't do you no harm."

No one said anything. Another moment of silence passed as Gladys calmly finished her supper. Finally, she looked up and gazed around at everyone as if she'd just noticed they were all there.

"Ya'all ready for a big slice of chocolate cake?"

***

Jake waited until we turned the lights out in the bedroom, then he turned to me as I climbed into bed.

"Don't you ever talk to me like that again in front of my folks, Lily Rae," he said softly. "If you do, I swear to God, I'll knock your teeth out."

I couldn't see his face in the darkness, but I knew what it looked like. Stone-cold. I knew better than to respond to him when he was this angry, so I simply got into bed and turned on my side away from him.

He didn't speak again, and a few minutes later, I heard his soft snore.

He was up the next morning and gone before I awoke.

CHAPTER THIRTY

Bowling Green, Kentucky
May 1955

I looked up from my magazine and glanced around the tiny back yard, still finding it hard to believe it belonged to us. Well…sort of. We were renting the house, but on a rent-to-own basis, so if we wanted to, we *could* own it someday.

It was just after four on a beautiful, summery May afternoon, and as the brilliant sunshine baked down on my Coppertone-slathered skin, I realized I'd never been happier in my life than I was at this very moment.

Jake had left for work at the iron factory 20 minutes ago, and Debby Ann was still napping. I hadn't wasted a moment after he took off. When Jake walked out the door, I'd been singing along with Pat Boone's new hit, "Two Hearts" as I ironed a basket of clothes. It was hotter than blazes in the house, even though I had the table-top revolving fan going at full-blast, and my sleeveless cotton blouse and shorts were splotchy with sweat. As soon as his car drove off, I turned off the radio, tip-toed into our bedroom and opened the dresser drawer as quietly as I could. I didn't want to wake Debby across the hall. After slipping into my swimming suit, I'd gone out the back door and dragged one of our brand new striped lawn chairs ($4.99 a piece at the 5 & Dime) from the concrete patio into the back yard. I'd settled into it with a glass of sweet iced tea, the bottle of Coppertone, a pack of Winston's, and the latest issue of **Housekeeping Monthly**.

But I was finding it hard to concentrate on the magazine. Every couple of minutes, I found myself looking around the back yard like I thought it was going to up and disappear or something. It was just that I was so confounded *thrilled* about the way everything had changed in the few short months we'd been here in Bowling Green.

A yellow butterfly flitted past my face, briefly landing on the wide daffodil-yellow stripe on my black swimsuit, and then darted off to inspect a rose bush growing along the side fence. The sight made my heart feel like it was about to bust with pride.

I grinned, reached down for my iced tea in its metallic-blue aluminum glass and took a sip. It surely was the *best* iced tea I'd ever tasted in my life. And that's how it had been with everything in my new home. Special. Even the scuffed up old furniture we'd bought at the Salvation Army and Mother's sun-faded blue gingham curtains at the kitchen window looked new and special here in our new house.

And I knew why. Because it was *ours*. No longer were we dependent on Jake's family...or even the military to provide a roof over our heads. We were on our own, and everything was just wonderful.

I glanced down at my Timex and saw it was almost 4:15. Debby Ann probably wouldn't be sleeping much longer, and my peace and quiet would be over. Especially if that durn Good Humor truck came by again at 4:30 like he had every blame day since the weather got good. Lord help me, if Debby Ann heard it, there would be no peace if I didn't scrounge around for a nickel to buy her something. Her reaction to the calliope music of that ice cream truck reminded me of what I'd learned in high school psychology about that Pavlov guy and his slobbering dog.

Well, maybe I'd be lucky today, and she'd sleep through the ruckus. It felt like a day that a miracle could well happen. I turned a page in the magazine and saw an article titled "The Good Wife's Guide." The picture showed a cheerful housewife in pearls and heels, stirring something on the stove, and a husband in a suit who'd obviously just arrived home, a newspaper under his arm, a smile on his face. At his feet were two well-scrubbed blond children, digging through Daddy's briefcase for the surprise he'd apparently brought them.

"Hmmmm..." I figured I was *already* a pretty good wife, but it wouldn't hurt to see if I could pick up a few new tips. Taking another sip of iced tea, I began to read the advice.

- **Have dinner ready.**

No problem there. I make Jake a big supper before he goes into work every day. But when he gets off at midnight and comes home, he's on his own. <u>This</u> wife is sleeping.

- **Touch up your make-up, put a ribbon in your hair and be fresh-looking.**

Well, with him working the second shift five blessed days out of the week, by the time he gets off work, I'm in bed fast asleep, and I ain't got a smidgen of make-up on, and I'm not <u>about</u> to wear a ribbon in my hair to bed.

I smiled. And I might not be all that fresh-looking at one in the morning, but it didn't stop Jake from kissing me awake and having his way with me if he was in the mood, so I reckoned I was fresh-looking *enough*.

- **Over the cooler months…light a fire for him to unwind by…catering for his comfort will provide you with immense personal satisfaction.**

I frowned at this one. *Now, <u>that's</u> interesting. I remember those days back in Texas, spit-shining his Army boots, laundering, starching and ironing his uniform and cooking three meals a day for him after being up all night, walking the floors with a screaming baby, and I never felt anything <u>close</u> to personal satisfaction.*

I shook my head and read on.

- **Listen to him…Let him talk first—remember, his topics of conversation are more important than yours.**

I rolled my eyes. *Huh? Who says?*

- **Don't complain if he's late home for dinner or even if he stays out all night.**

Well…guess I just flunked this test.

- **Don't ask him questions about his actions or question his judgment or integrity. Remember, he is the master of the house and as such will always exercise his will with fairness and truthfulness. You have no right to question him.**

Like hell I don't! I tried picturing Betty reading this, and what her reaction would be, but heck, I couldn't do it. Betty wouldn't be caught dead reading a magazine called **Housekeeping Monthly**.

But it was the last "rule" that really got my goat.

- **A good wife always knows her place.**

"*Agggggghhhhh!*" I threw the magazine halfway across the yard, which wasn't far, considering the lawn was only about ten feet long. "That's what I think about your idiotic 'good wife's guide!'"

The magazine landed face up on the grass, the warm breeze gently riffling its pages. I stared at it, chewing on my bottom lip. My good mood of moments before had disappeared. And I knew why. Guilt. That darn magazine article had made me feel guilty.

Because maybe I *wasn't* a good wife. Maybe that was why Jake had done all those awful things to me back in Texas. Sleeping around with whores. Going out and getting drunk all the time. Maybe if I wasn't so selfish, if I thought more about *him* instead of myself, I *could* be a good wife to him. Maybe instead of talking back and nagging and always putting my two cents worth in, if I just accepted the way things were supposed to be—the way **Housekeeping Monthly** said they *should* be--maybe then, I could keep Jake satisfied, and he'd settle down and be a decent husband to me.

Besides, hadn't he been sweet as pie lately? Having a steady job and a good paycheck every two weeks certainly had made a difference. Why, he'd even become friends with Lonnie Foley, even though, technically, he was his boss. The Foleys lived a few streets over in the subdivision. Once the twins had started sleeping through the night, Jinx and Lonnie had had me and Jake over for dinner and some card-playing a few times. Jake had actually seemed to enjoy himself, and I was pretty sure it wasn't just because of a couple of six-packs the two men put away through the evening. Once we got home that first night, he'd even made a remark about what a good time he'd had with them, and how we should do it again. I'd been pleasantly surprised. After all, in high school, he hadn't given the two of them the time of day.

Slowly, I got out of the lawn chair, and on bare feet, walked across the soft green lawn to retrieve the magazine. Now was as good a time as any to make a change, and I *did* want to be a good wife to Jake. I'd clip out that article and tape it somewhere where I could see it every day...and learn to live by it.

I grabbed the magazine, and as I straightened, I heard the first tinkling notes of the ice cream truck music from down the street. I held my breath, praying that Debby Ann would keep sleeping. *Just a few more minutes of peace, Lord.*

But it wasn't to be. As the ice cream truck approached and the music grew louder, I heard her calling out from her room. "Mommy, Mommy! Ice cream truck! Mommy, Debby Ann want ice cream! Mommy, *Mommy!*"

I sighed and headed for the back door.

Mother's Almond Delight Cake

1 cup shortening
1 ½ cup sugar
1 teaspoon vanilla extract
1 ½ teaspoon almond extract
2 ½ cups self-rising flour
¾ cup milk
8 egg whites, beaten stiff

Heat oven to 325 degrees. Grease and dust 10"
tube pan with flour. Cream shortening until light,
gradually add sugar and mix until fluffy. Add
extracts. Add flour and milk alternately, beginning
with flour, fold in beaten egg whites. Turn into
prepared pan. Bake 1 hour and 15 minutes. Cool in
pan 20 minutes, then remove to cooling rack. When
completely cooled, frost with almond icing.

Almond Icing

2 T butter, softened
1/3 cup milk
3 cups confectioner's sugar
1 teaspoon almond extract

Cream butter and gradually add milk, sugar &
extract. Beat until smooth, then spread on cake

CHAPTER THIRTY-ONE

July 1956

I heard the clink of the mailbox lid from the front stoop and quickly finished slathering peanut butter on a slice of white bread. Reaching for the jar of Welch's grape jelly, I replaced the cap. I glanced out the kitchen window to make sure Debby wasn't in the kiddy pool Jake had bought her at the beginning of summer—she wasn't; instead, she was torturing that poor cat the neighbors had given us in early May, carrying it around by its neck in a stranglehold that made its eyes bulge in futile panic.

"Debby Ann!" I yelled through the opened window. *"Put down that cat right now!* I've told you a million times not to carry him around like that!"

Lord Jesus, it's a miracle that animal hasn't gouged her eyes out by now. Must be her guardian angel in disguise.

Debby Ann, wearing a petal-pink sunsuit and white sandals, her blond curls tied up in twin pony-tails, looked at me through the window. The orange cat, held prisoner by her chubby little hands, also seemed to be looking at me with a forlorn expression that clearly said, "Please, lady. Save me from this monster child!"

"Debby *Ann*!" I yelled again. "*Did you hear me?*" Too late, I slapped my hand over my mouth. Dear God, Jake was sleeping! *When* was I going to learn to stop yelling in the middle of the day?

But at least my shout had the hoped-for effect on the headstrong child. Debby loosened her grip, and the cat seized the moment. With a disgruntled yowl, he scrambled out of her clutches and scurried off, finding refuge under a lilac bush. Debby Ann frowned and went after him.

"Debby Ann Kitty!" She squatted near the bush, trying to see under it. "Come here!" she ordered, having apparently caught sight of the cat. "Me *wuv* you, Debby Ann Kitty."

I sighed and slapped the jellied slice of bread onto the one topped by peanut butter. God save the unfortunate animals loved by a three-year-old little terror named Debby Ann Tatlow.

"Come on in and wash your hands, Debby," I called through the window, being sure to keep my voice down. I opened the new Norge Customatic refrigerator that Jake's company had installed when the old one died a few weeks ago, and grabbed a bottle of milk.

Once I got Debby settled at her little plastic table out on the patio a few minutes later, I placed my hands on my hips and gave her a firm look. "You sit here and eat your lunch. I'm going to go get the mail, and I'll be right back."

Debby Ann took a big slurp of milk, leaving a thick, white moustache above her upper lip. She nodded solemnly. "Okay, Mommy."

I turned to go into the house, but then hesitated. "That means no getting into the pool, no getting a-hold of Debby Ann Kitty, and *no* eating out of the cat bowl, you hear?"

Just last week, I'd caught her on all fours, meowing and eating the morning's leftover biscuits and gravy out of the cat's dish.

"Okay, Mommy," said Debby Ann, pie-eyed and innocent-looking.

I shook my head. *Lord, three years on this planet, and she's got that look down to a science.* One thing was for sure. No one could doubt there was Tatlow blood running through that one's veins.

I went into the house and moved quickly into the living room to get the mail at the front door stoop. Grabbing it from the box, I hurried back out to the patio. Incredibly enough, Debby Ann was still sitting at her table, munching on her PB&J, all the world looking like a little angel. I hoped she wasn't getting sick.

I sat down in a lawn chair and glanced through the stack of letters. It was a good mail day. Besides a couple of bills, there was a letter from Mother, and two light blue airmail envelopes, one postmarked Heidelberg, Germany, and the other from Honolulu. I quickly tore open the one from Germany. It had been weeks since I'd heard from Betty, and I was starved for news about her exciting life overseas.

Betty's letters were *almost* as good as a visit. Written on both sides of the stationery in her pretty, sweeping script, her letters told of fancy dining-ins where she wore sequined evening gowns and fur coats, weekend shopping trips to Paris and skiing in the German Alps. I unfolded her letter and began to read.

> *Dear Lil:*
>
> *I almost fell over when I saw that picture of Debby Ann you sent in your last letter. My God!!! You're going to have to stop feeding that girl, kid. Before you know it, she'll be as big as Davy.*

I smiled, recognizing the irony in Betty's voice. In the most recent picture she'd sent, Davy, nearly four, had looked like a miniature linebacker.

> *Well, girl, are you sitting down? No, I'm not pregnant. Heaven forbid! Eddie's leave is coming up and you'll never guess where we're going. GREECE! Can you believe it? Eddie has booked us into a gorgeous hotel on the island of Rhodes. Oh, Lil, I wish you were here. We could all go together…of course, the down side is that you'd have to bring that…husband of yours. How is the old snake-in-the-grass, anyway?*

I frowned. I supposed I'd never be able to convince Betty that Jake had changed. That he was a real family man now, holding down a steady job and buying kiddy pools for his daughter. A complete turnaround since Texas.

"Mommy, can I change into my swimming suit now?"

Debby Ann stood in front of me, looking so sweet that butter would have a heck of a time melting in her cute little rosebud mouth.

"Go ahead, but remember, you have to wait 30 minutes before you can go swimming. You don't want to get cramps."

Debby Ann was already halfway to the back door.

"You be quiet in there, you here?" I called after her. "You don't want to wake up your daddy."

Now that Jake was working the third shift at the factory, he didn't get up until two or three in the

afternoon. That had been hard for me and Debby
Ann to get used to, trying to keep the noise down in
the house. It had gotten better, though, once the
weather got nice and we could spend most of our
time outside. And it was swell having Jake home for
supper again, giving us some family time together.

Flicking a finger at an annoying ant crawling up
my arm, I went back to Betty's letter.

*The latest rage over here is what they call Swedish
Fitness Centers, and I joined one a few weeks ago. It has all
these work-out machines and a pool and a sauna. They offer
classes, too, in dance and yoga. I'm taking a belly dance class
right now. Trying to slim down so I can wear this hot pink
pair of short-shorts I bought in Milan this spring. I love
going to the fitness center, and I've already lost nine pounds.
What are you doing to stay in shape, Lil? Still watching
Jack La Lanne?*

I gave a wry grin. <u>No, I don't have time to watch
Jack anymore. I have my own personal fitness system. It's
called the Chasing Debby Ann Work-Out Program.</u>

Betty's letter continued:

*Well, kid, I've got to close now. I have an appointment
to get my hair cut before I have to pick up Davy. Oh, before I
forget, thanks for the pictures of your new living room
furniture. Your little house is so darn cute! Just adorable!
I'll bet it's a hell of a lot easier to keep clean than this huge
old monstrosity I live in. Thank God I have Gretta coming
in once a week to clean. Oh, I know how that sounds! But
really, all the military wives here in Germany bring in help,
even the enlisted wives. It's dirt cheap for us, and the local
economy expects it. Well, I'm going to be late if I don't get a
move on, and believe me, Beirgette is so popular with the
American women here, she'll fill my space if I'm 30 seconds
past my appointment. Take care, kid. Love you!*

Betty

I sighed and folded the letter back in thirds before slipping it back into its envelope. Betty was so very lucky! Her life just seemed so full of excitement; something happening all the time, it seemed--trips to Milan and Paris and Greece. Hair appointments, fancy parties, fun friends. And to think, if Jake hadn't been so durn anxious to get back to Russell County, *our* lives might be more like that. I might, at this very moment, be sitting on a beach in Hawaii instead of sweltering here in the back yard with nothing but a plastic blow-up pool to keep me cool.

I looked at the other airmail envelope—the one with the Honolulu postmark and Meg Tatlow's tiny, pinched script in the upper left hand corner. The return address was different than the one Jake's sister had had the last time she wrote. Instead of Fort Shafter, it had some oddball Hawaiian name--*Aiea*. I knew for a fact that Meg had re-upped in the Army for another two years, so why wasn't she living on post anymore? Well, I reckoned Jake would tell me. I always left letters from his family unopened so he could read them first.

"Mommy, I ready!"

I looked up to see Debby Ann coming out the back door, and I burst out laughing. "Honey child, you've got your swimming suit on backwards." But darned if she didn't look cute as a button with her hair up in those pony-tails and her pudgy baby legs all tanned from the sun.

Debby Ann could care less about her backwards swimsuit. She was already making a beeline for the pool. I got up and dropped the mail into the lawn chair. "Wait a minute! Let's get your bathing suit on right."

"*No!*" She'd already reached the grass. "I swim *now!*"

"No, you're not! You've still got ten minutes to wait!" I grabbed my daughter just as she reached the pool, and was trying to climb in. Debby let out a shriek that sent what felt like twin ice picks through my eardrums.

"*Hush, girl!* You're going to wake your father!" I pulled the straps of Debby's swimsuit off her shoulders and began to tug the garment down her body. It was like wrestling with a greased pig.

"*Noooooo!*" Debby howled, struggling like a little demon. "*Me want to swim now!*"

Debby wrenched herself away from my grasp and threw herself down on the grass, kicking and pounding the earth. Too late, I realized I shouldn't have pushed the issue. So *what* if the little brat had her swimsuit on backward? Who was going to see her in our own back yard?

But I'd gone beyond the point of no return, and war had been declared. Screaming at the top of her lungs, Debby fought me every inch of the way as I yanked off the swimsuit, my patience snapping like a worn rubber band. I turned the little girl over on the grass and gave her a smart smack on the buttocks.

"*That's* for being a big pain in the ass!"

Startled, Debby Ann caught her breath, and for a blessed second, she stopped screaming. But then she began again, louder than before. Exasperated, I stood up and glared down at her. "Okay, missy, just for this little drama, you can forget about going swimming this afternoon. You can just lay there on the ground and scream your heart out. But when you're done, you're going to go take a nap."

Debby Ann kept screaming, her face as red as a garden-ripe tomato. I stood with my hands on my hips, at my wit's end as to how to stop her. My eyes welled with frustrated tears, and I felt like bawling along with her. What kind of mother *was* I that I couldn't get control of the situation?

"*What the Sam Hill is going on out here?*"

I turned. Jake stood at the back door, wearing only a pair of checked boxer shorts.

"Oh, just the usual," I snapped, angry at my daughter, angry at myself for not being able to handle her. "Debby Ann is having one of her fits just because she can't get her way."

Jake's brows knitted together. "Well, maybe if you didn't spoil her rotten and mollycoddle her the way you do, she wouldn't do it." He stepped out onto the patio. "She's got you wrapped around her little finger, Lillian." He strode across the lawn, heading for the young hickory tree we'd planted just after moving in. "But I aim to put a stop to this behavior once and for all."

My stomach began to roil with dread. As angry as I was with my daughter, I hated what was coming. Debby Ann, naked as a jaybird, was still sprawled on the grass, pounding her heels into the earth; eyes squeezed closed, she was screaming like a banshee.

Jake tore a slender limb off the tree and headed toward her. He flashed a commanding look at me. "You better go on inside. I don't think you want to see this."

"Jake, please!" I protested. "It's not that—"

"Bad?" He stopped in his tracks. "You don't think her behavior is that bad? Lily Rae, if we let her get away with stuff like this, Lord help us when she's a teenager. We've got to start putting our foot down with her. You know I'm right."

I looked at Debby Ann who was still wailing. Yes, I *did* know he was right. The child was just too willful. And God knew the discipline I'd been using wasn't working.

I released a long, tremulous sigh. "Okay," I said. "But please, Jake, don't hurt her."

Jake nodded, and I could tell by his face that he wasn't looking forward to what he was about to do. "I won't. Not any more than I have to. But Lily, this child has got to be taught a lesson." He gestured toward the house. "Now, go on inside."

Every cell in my body screamed in protest as I stepped through the kitchen door. I was barely inside when I heard the first slash of the switch followed by Debby's outraged scream, more piercing than before.

I closed the door of the kitchen, then covered my ears with my hands, and burst into tears of my own.

***

Jake finished up the last of Mother's Almond Delight cake on his plate and drew away from the kitchen table with a contented sigh. "Lord, that's a good cake, Lily Rae. Put some in my lunch box for tonight, will you?"

I nodded. "I'll give you a few extra slices for the boys on your shift, too." I glanced over at Debby Ann with a worried frown.

Her plump cheeks were still splotched by the torrent of tears she'd cried after her whipping. And I knew for a fact that her little legs and buttock still bore the cruel lashes of the hickory switch. My heart just about broke when I saw them. But I supposed Jake was right. The child *was* out of control. It was time we let the little imp know who was boss around here.

And Lord knows Daddy hadn't spared the rod when it came to me and my siblings. The occasional whippings didn't seem to have left any permanent scars on any of us. In fact, we were probably all better people for having been disciplined with a firm hand. Landry, 24 now, had been working at the feed factory since graduating from high school and was saving almost every cent he earned. He'd been dating Tresia Tarter, a former Miss Russell County Fair, going on two years now, and I figured it was just a matter of time before they got married.

Edsel, at 16, wasn't going to be the best student Russell County High School turned out, but he sure was a hard worker on the farm. He was never happier than when he was on a John Deere, readying the Kentucky soil for planting.

At 12, Norry was pulling in straight A's in 7th grade, and every time I went back home for a visit, the girl constantly had her head in a book—not made up stories like the ones I liked to read, but big, boring books about marketing and economics. To be sure, we'd all four got our share of whippings, but we'd turned out okay.

So why did I feel so guilty every time I looked at Debby Ann?

The poor kid had barely touched her supper, and it was one of her favorites—pork chops and mashed potatoes with nice ripe tomatoes straight from the garden patch out back.

I sighed. I probably wouldn't feel like eating either if I'd just had my backside switched.

"Debby, honey," I said softly. "Just finish your mashed potatoes, and then you can have some cake."

Debby turned a pair of big sad eyes on me. "I's not hungee," she said.

"But sweetie—"

"Leave her be, Lily Rae," Jake cut in. "She'll be hungry tomorrow morning, I reckon. You can get down, girl. Go on and play now."

Debby climbed down from the stack of catalogs in her chair and plodded into the living room. My heart panged at the sight of the reddened welts on the backs of her legs, and again, doubts plagued me.

Jake reached for his pack of Winston's on the table near his plate. "Did you read Meg's letter," he asked, fishing out a cigarette and placing it between his lips.

"Yes, I did. I'll have one, too." I indicated the pack of cigarettes, and he slid it across the table to me. "Lord, I just don't believe she's living in a beautiful place like Hawaii. Her new house sounds just gorgeous! Can you imagine looking out your front window and seeing Pearl Harbor?"

Jake lit his cigarette, took a draw and shrugged. "I suppose if you don't mind looking at the spot where the Japs killed a shitload of American servicemen, it would be okay." He slid his lighter down to me.

"Oh, you know what I mean! It's just got to be a beautiful view is all." I lit my cigarette.

He sat across from me at the rectangular dining room table, looking devilishly handsome in cut-off dungarees and a white T-shirt, rolled up to expose his muscular biceps. He'd tipped his chair back against the wall and was contentedly smoking his cigarette, his blue eyes mildly amused.

I wondered what was so durn funny about what I'd said. He leaned forward and flicked ashes into his plate, then stuck the cigarette between his lips. "Well, one thing is for certain," he said. "My sister is—as my daddy would put it—riding to hell on a fast horse in a porcupine saddle!"

"Well, he would know all about riding to hell, wouldn't he?" I shot back, unable to resist the opportunity to get in a dig at Royce Tatlow. "But why do you say that?"

"Mommy!" Debby Ann's voice came from the living room. "Can I watch 'Captain Kangaroo?'"

"I don't know if it's on now, honey, but you can turn on the TV and see."

Debby must've been standing right in front of the television because before I'd barely finished speaking, the sounds of a Brill Creme commercial blared from the living room.

"Turn it down, Debra Ann!" Jake shouted. "The whole neighborhood don't need to hear it!"

"I don't know how," Debby wailed.

I jumped up. "I'll do it." I ran into the living room and turned down the volume. Then I turned to my daughter and was shocked by the look on her face. Stark fear.

My heart caught in my throat. "Oh, baby, come here."

She melted into my arms, and I hugged her tightly, kissing the top of her warm, blonde head. "Oh, sweetie. Don't look like that."

Debby Ann nestled in my arms, turning her lips so they were inches from my ear. "I's be good. Daddy don't spank Debby Ann no more, Mommy, okay?"

I swallowed hard, trying to dislodge the lump that had formed in my throat. "Oh, honey, I know you'll be good. We don't like spanking you, sweetie. But you've just got to stop throwing temper tantrums like that, okay?"

Debby nodded, her flushed face pressed up against my polka-dot halter top. I stroked her hair and gently pulled away. Jake would be wondering what was taking me so long.

"Let's see if we can find something on TV."

"Captain Kangaroo" wasn't on, but I found a puppet show. By the time I stepped back into the dining room, Debby Ann was curled up on the couch, her thumb in her mouth, her eyes on the TV screen.

Jake gave me an appraising look as if he knew exactly what I'd been up to, so I spoke before he got a chance to. "So, you gonna tell me why you think your sister is bound for hell?"

He released a thin ribbon of blue smoke. "I reckon I'll have to explain things to you, since you're so ignorant and all."

"Explain what?" I took my seat and reached for my cigarette in the ashtray.

"Meg and that woman she's moved in with. I reckon it hasn't occurred to you that they're living like a married couple?"

I stared at him blankly. "What do you mean, a married couple?"

He gave a sly grin. "They're sleeping together, Lily Rae. They're…doing things to each other…you know, the kind of things a man and woman do together. Well, except for what's missing."

My brows furrowed. "You're talking in riddles, Jake. Can't you just say what you mean?"

His chair slammed down to the floor. He placed his tanned elbows on the table and leaned toward me, his eyes glittering with amusement. Yet, there was something mean in them, too.

"They're fucking each other, Lily Rae! *Christ*! Is there anybody in the world more innocent than you? You mean you've never heard of lesbians?"

I just looked at him. Lesbians? Wasn't that some kind of actor? No, that wasn't right. The word I was thinking of was "thespians." I remembered that from drama class in high school.

"No, I guess I haven't ever heard of that word, Jake. And I reckon I *am* ignorant, but at least I have a high school diploma, which is more than you've got. Anyhow, what makes you think Meg is a...*lesbian* just because she moved in with another woman. Ain't you ever heard of roommates?"

Jake eased the back of his chair against the wall and took another long drag of his cigarette. "Hell, everybody knows that women who join the service are one of two things—whores or lesbians. When Meggie first joined the Army, I figured she must be a whore. Lord knows she's too ugly to get a man any other way. But after reading her letter today, my suspicions are confirmed. She's been talking about this Kay Waters ever since she got stationed at Fort Shafter. And now she's moved in with her." He nodded matter-of-factly. "They're lesbians, all right. Bound for hell in a hand basket."

I was still having trouble digesting all this. In the silence that fell, the high-pitched, cartoonish sounds of puppets engaged in an argument came from the living room. "But I still don't understand how..." My cheeks grew warm. "... how two women...you know...without the necessary equipment..." My voice trailed off, and I had to look away from Jake's laughing eyes.

"Well," he said slowly. "They use their mouths and their fingers."

"Oh." Cheeks burning, I stubbed out my cigarette, jumped up and began to clear the table.

"But then," he added, watching me. "You wouldn't know anything about using your mouth, would you?"

I stacked the dishes at the side of the sink and began filling the basin with hot, sudsy water, deciding to ignore that last ugly remark. Even after all these years, he still wanted me to do immoral things that no Christian couple would ever dream of.

I dropped the dishes into the water and began to wash them. And then a thought occurred to me. I paused and turned to Jake. "So, if there's such a thing as women who love other women, what about men? Are there men who…you know, love men?"

Jake's chair crashed to the floor. He reached across the table and grabbed my ashtray, stubbing out his cigarette. Then he got up.

"Yeah, they're called queers. And I'm not about to explain what they do because just thinking about it makes me want to vomit." He strode toward the threshold of the living room. "I'm going to get a couple hours of shut-eye before work." He paused and threw me a leering glance. "Why don't you get Debby Ann to bed and come in and join me?"

CHAPTER THIRTY-TWO

I'd just finished washing up the lunch dishes when the phone rang, and I rushed to answer it before the jarring sound woke Jake up. "Tatlow residence."

"Lily Rae, is that you?"

The voice on the other end of the line was one I hadn't heard in years, but I recognized it instantly. "Oh, my *Lord! Katydid!*"

Grinning, I took a step backwards, pulling on the cord of the phone so I could look out the window to check on Debby in the backyard. *Oh, good.* She was still playing in the sandbox Jake had bought with his last paycheck. "I don't believe it! Where are you calling from?"

"Right here in Bowling Green. I live here now."

"You *do?*"

"Just moved here a couple of months ago," Katydid said. "After I graduated from nursing school at Vanderbilt, I found a job here at City Hospital."

"Oh, wow! That's wonderful, Katydid! How's RJ?"

There was an odd silence on the other end, and then, "Oh, hon, you didn't hear? We're divorced. I caught him in a compromising position with a Vanderbilt cheerleader."

I felt as if someone had kicked me in the stomach. RJ Skaggs? With a cheerleader? Why, he'd worshiped the ground Katydid walked on in high school. Finally, I found my voice, "Oh, Lord, Katydid! I'm *so* sorry!"

"Don't be." Katydid gave a short, bitter laugh. "He did *me* a favor. I'm just grateful he did it while I'm still young and good-looking instead of waiting until I'm old and fat and unable to attract another man. But hey, that's old news. I'm doing fine. Anyhow, I was on my lunch break, and guess who I ran into at the diner on Main Street? Jinx Foley! I about died when she told me you live here, too. Before you know it, half the population of Bowling Green will be from Russell County."

I laughed, glancing back out the window to check on Debby again. Still playing in the sandbox like a little angel. Even Debby Ann Kitty had risked coming within ten feet of her and was curled up in the sun, dozing.

"Listen," Katydid went on. "I get off work at four, and I'd love to stop by and see you and the baby. Jinx says she's just gorgeous."

"Uh…" I thought quickly. Of course, I'd love to see Katydid, but the timing was terrible. Tonight was the big annual barbecue pool party given by the president of Jake's company. It was supposed to start at 6:00.

Katydid caught my hesitation and said, "If it's not a good time…"

"Well, now, it's just that we're supposed to be somewhere at six, and I'd hate to cut our visit short since it's been so long…"

"I know what!" Katydid said brightly. "Do you have a car? Maybe you could meet me for lunch one day next week. If you don't mind cafeteria food, we could stay right here in the hospital. The food's pretty good, believe it or not."

I thought about it. Well, why not? Jake would be sleeping, so I'd have the car. It would be a nice outing, and God knows I deserved a chance to get out of the house more often. When we first moved here, I'd figured me and Jinx would get together a lot, but the twins kept her so busy, she hardly ever could go out and do anything. So I'd pretty much stopped suggesting getting together, except for the occasional Friday or Saturday evenings when the four of us played cards.

"I'd love to do that," I said. "You just tell me which day is good for you, and we'll be there."

We settled on Monday, and I hung up the phone, smiling. It would be fun seeing Katydid again. I stepped out the back door, mentally preparing myself for the daily battle of putting Debby Ann down for her nap.

The sandbox was empty, and I felt a momentary anxiety until I saw Debby down at the back of the yard where trees and shrubbery grew up against the fence. She was on her knees, peering under a three-inch gap in the bottom of the fence.

"Debby Ann Kitty, come *back, I said*!"

I couldn't help but grin. It looked like Debby Ann Kitty had finally found a way to outfox her namesake. One of these days, if that cat had any sense at all, it would hi-tail it out of here and never come back.

***

I thought I looked right nice in my new strapless one-piece swimsuit--a bright red number with a wide white satin border along the bust line, which really emphasized...well, my bust. But when I walked into the living room to show it off to Jake, he barely gave me a second glance. "Nice, Lily. Better put something on over it and let's get going."

I put on a pair of navy pedal-pushers and a button-down red polka-dot blouse over the swimsuit, kissed Debby Ann goodbye (luckily, we'd got Lori, the teenage girl down the street to baby-sit), and grabbed the picnic basket of chicken I'd fried up for the potluck supper. According to Jinx, this summer barbecue/pool party at Lute Dawson's 40-acre estate northwest of Glasgow was almost as popular as the annual Christmas party. Just about all the employees and their wives showed up, she said. Kids were welcome, too, but most everybody left the younger ones at home because the party tended to go on well past midnight.

I'd been relieved to hear we weren't expected to bring our kids. I couldn't think of *anything* more horrible than having to keep an eye on Debby Ann near a swimming pool in a big crowd. That was a challenge I certainly wasn't up to.

The drive to Glasgow took about 45 minutes, and by the time we pulled up to the wrought-iron gates of the Dawson estate, it was almost seven. A guard at the gatehouse checked off Jake's name on a clipboard, and waved us through the elaborate gates. I caught my breath as we drove up a winding stone driveway toward a huge stone Colonial perched atop an emerald-green knoll.

"Oh, Lord! Would you look at that mansion!" My stomach tightened with anxiety. I wasn't used to going to places like this. What if it was too highfalutin' for me?

"Yeah," Jake said, his lips twisting in a smirk. "Old man Dawson sure knows how to live...while barely paying his employees enough to get by. Guess he figures a couple of parties every year will keep everybody happy."

I glanced at him in surprise. For the first time since we'd been married, we actually had a little money in a savings account. So why did he sound so bitter?

A man in a uniform directed Jake to park the car in a field past the horse stables. To me, it looked like a sea of cars were already parked there, and the butterflies in my stomach started having a field day. This was a much, much bigger deal than I'd expected.

It was a long trek back up to the house, and the red high-heeled sandals I'd chosen to go with my swimsuit kept sinking in the spongy ground. Once we got to the paved driveway, it was easier going, but I quickly realized I should've bought the next size up. A blister was already forming on my right little toe. And it was awkward carrying the big basket of fried chicken.

The sounds of merrymaking, live country music and splashing water grew louder as we approached the high stone wall that surrounded the manor house. The delectable aroma of grilling meat carried on the evening breeze. Instead of making me hungry, the smell had the opposite effect. I felt nauseous. Nerves, of course. Whatever had made me think this was going to be a down home kind of barbecue for ordinary folks?

"You think we should go around to the front?" I asked, uncertain of what to do.

"Nah, there's probably nobody in the house," Jake said. "There's got to be a gate somewhere."

I spotted a bouquet of brightly-colored helium balloons floating lazily with the evening breeze. "I'll bet it's right there."

I was right; below the floating balloons, I saw a black wrought-iron gate, a smaller replica of the one at the road. Jake opened the gate for me, and I moved through, my feet protesting in agony and my arms aching from carrying the basket of chicken. Who knew that three cut up chickens would weigh so much?

Once through the gate, I came to a stop and stared, my jaw dropping. Beside me, I could feel Jake's astonishment, too.

Why, it looked like something out of a Hollywood movie! Straight ahead stretched a stone walkway leading to a Japanese lantern-strung gazebo in front of the biggest pond I'd ever seen on a private property. It was much, much bigger than our pond back in Opal Springs. The back of the manor house was to my right, with three tiers of stone steps leading up to a huge stone terrace where a four-piece country band entertained the guests.

On the far side of the steps, a wisteria-curtained arbor perched on the lawn near an ornamental water garden complete with a small curved bridge and a romantic-looking bench made out of black wrought-iron.

On my left, and three wide steps down, the gigantic kidney-shaped pool with its rock waterfall was just about the most refreshing sight I'd ever seen. The deck surrounding it was made of the same beautiful, varied-colored stone that led to the gazebo and made up the tiers of steps to the terrace. And as if a water garden, a big pond—or lake—and a pool wasn't enough, on the near side of the pool, close to where me and Jake stood, a stone fountain topped with twin lion heads spurted arcs of water that cascaded into three basins. Beyond the pool deck, a gorgeous expanse of lush emerald grass stretched for probably 100 yards, ending in a grove of apple trees. It was just the most amazing back yard I'd ever seen—more like a park than a back yard.

The party appeared to be in full-swing. A bunch of people were in the pool, and they seemed to be having the time of their lives. Especially the men playing volleyball in one section. The game looked awfully rough to me. In fact, they looked like they were in danger of drowning each other. I decided then and there I wasn't about to get in that pool as long as those crazy men were in there. Swimming was one thing I'd never learned to do, and I didn't cotton to trying it with a bunch of maniacs around.

Dozens of tables had been set up around the pool, decked out with colorful umbrellas—each one a different color, pink, purple, red, blue, and yellow. Right now, they were coming in handy because the summer sun was still strong, even this late in the evening. Each table had six chairs, and most of them were filled with people eating and chatting and having a good time. Ladies in crisp, black uniforms circulated among the tables, delivering drinks and picking up used dishes.

Lah, it's so fancy, I thought, my stomach churning.

Alongside the stone wall, industrial-sized grills had been set up, and men in white aprons and chef hats were busy flipping big thick steaks—the source of the stomach-turning char-broiled smell. I glanced down at the dishcloth-covered basket I carried, wondering who on earth would want fried chicken when they saw those big steaks. Should I take the chicken up to the kitchen, I wondered? Where had everybody else put the food they'd brought?

Jake was no help. He was staring around, just as slack-jawed as I was. He'd never seen nothing like this, either. I felt so darn out of place, sort of like the bull that wandered into the china shop. Especially since people were now giving us odd, sidelong glances like they were wondering who let the riff-raff in. Not a soul lifted up a hand to greet Jake and call him over.

"Don't you see anybody you know?" I muttered, shifting my weight to ease the pain in my feet.

He shook his head. "Not yet."

"Well, I've got to find something to do with this chicken. I can't stand here and hold it all night."

I caught the gaze of a tall, slender brunette sitting at one of the nearby tables. The woman stared at me for a moment, one perfect black brow arched in curiosity, then stood and came toward us. She moved graciously through the crowd, almost as if she were skating instead of walking in her outrageously spiked stiletto sandals, at least an inch higher than mine. The pleats of her red and white-checked halter dress swirled around Betty Grable-slim legs, so tanned I suspected she'd just got back from the tropics.

"Hello!" Smiling, the woman stopped in front of us and stuck out a slender hand adorned by movie-star length crimson nails and a diamond ring big enough to choke a python. "I'm Roxanne Dawson, and who might *you* be?"

Up close, the woman looked older than she had from the table. I guessed she was in her mid-40's, judging by the tiny crow's feet at the corners of sapphire eyes rimmed with false-eyelashes. And that was *definitely* not a Kentucky accent she had. More like from somewhere further south--not hillbilly—but a cultured southern accent.

I adjusted my grip on the basket so I could shake the woman's hand. "I'm Lily Tatlow, and this here is my husband, Jake. He works for your husband."

"Hello, ma'am," Jake said politely, looking decidedly uncomfortable as he stuck out his hand.

Roxanne Dawson looked at Jake, and I watched her turn into a sex kitten right in front of us. She took his extended hand, her gaze flicking over him, drinking in every detail of his tan dungarees and crisp short-sleeved shirt, then lingering for an obvious moment on the gap at his neck that gave her a tantalizing glimpse of chest hair.

Her lips parted in a seductive smile and her voice lowered to a purr, "Hello, Jake. I'm so glad you could come to our little pool party. It's especially nice when we have new faces here."

Her expression of obvious appreciation told me it was the new *male* faces that made the most impression on Mrs. Roxanne. Why, the woman was almost drooling.

"Uh, what would you like me to do with this?" I asked in my nicest voice, gesturing with my basket of chicken.

The woman drew her hungry eyes from Jake long enough to look and see what I was talking about, and slowly released his hand. "What is it, dear?"

I saw right through her phony smile. The woman was annoyed at having to turn her attention away from a potential conquest. "Fried chicken," I said, and then added pointedly, "It's *my husband's* favorite recipe--a family specialty."

Roxanne Dawson looked at the basket in my hands as if it were a rattlesnake, coiled to strike. But she recovered quickly. "How nice! But you shouldn't have bothered! We have plenty of food." She turned toward one of the men grilling steaks and called out, "James, come here!"

I frowned. Jinx had told me to bring a potluck dish. I was sure of it.

A beefy, red-faced man hustled over, still holding a barbecue fork in one gigantic hand. "Yes, Mrs. Dawson?"

She gave him a cool smile, nothing at all like the chili-peppered one she'd bestowed on Jake. "Please take this lovely fried chicken our guest here prepared and add it to the buffet table. No doubt it will be appreciated by those that don't care for red meat."

With relief, I gave up the basket of chicken to James.

Closing a possessive hand around Jake's upper arm, Roxanne Dawson cooed, "Come, both of you. Let me introduce you around." And drawing Jake with her, she towed him over to the table she'd just vacated. Gritting my teeth, I followed behind, feeling like an unwanted puppy dog.

I had a feeling it was going to be a long, uncomfortable evening.

***

"Would you look at that, Jinx? Have you ever seen anything so outrageous in all your life?"

"No, I haven't," agreed Jinx. "And if it were *my* husband, I swear, I'd jump in that pool, and pull him out of there by his damn balls!"

I looked at her in astonishment and could just make out the outraged look on her face in the fluttering light of the Japanese lanterns hanging under the umbrella at our table. Why, Jinx was as mad as a hive of wasps.

"Well, I'm not about to make a scene," I said lightly. "And I don't think *you* would either if that were Lonnie she'd latched onto. After all, she *is* the boss's wife."

"Humph!" Jinx snorted, taking a sip of the Mai Tai a waitress had placed in front of her. "She's a Jezebel! And everybody knows it. You know where Lute met her, don't you? In a New Orleans cathouse. She's nothing but poor white trash!"

I looked over at the pool where Jake was engaging in flirtatious horseplay with Roxanne Dawson. He grabbed her by her sleek, tanned shoulders and playfully tried to dunk her as she squealed and tried half-heartedly to escape his clutches. He'd certainly lost his initial shyness with the woman, I thought dryly.

It was after eleven, and the party had quieted down a bit. The people who'd brought kids had gone on home, leaving only the serious party-makers to finish off what was left of the food and the still plentiful flow of alcohol. I hadn't thought that me and Jake would be in that company, but when I'd tried to get him to leave about ten o'clock, he'd flat-out refused, saying the party was just getting started. That was about the time he'd had enough booze to make him strip down to his trunks and jump in the deep end of the pool.

Not more than five minutes later, Roxanne Dawson got up from the table where she'd been watching Jake like a hungry lioness. She untied the waistband of her pleated skirt, allowing it to fall to the stone patio, and with a flick of her wrist, released the back of her halter top, and it, too, went fluttering to the ground. By this time, the woman had an audience watching her. Every eye in the vicinity, male and female, was glued to her...or rather, to what she had on.

It was like nothing I'd ever seen before. And I'd thought *my* new bathing suit was daring! Roxanne wore a two-piece swim suit in a red and white check print, and the bottom was shorter than even the short-shorts those European women wore in the magazine ads Betty had recently sent me—they were cut pretty low at the top, too, because Roxanne's belly button was clearly visible. The top, though, was just pure scandalous, revealing so much of Roxanne's cleavage that it was durn-near indecent. And as if she knew—and reveled in—the appreciation of every man near the pool, Roxanne lifted one magnificent leg, placing her foot on the bottom of the chair and leaned down to unbuckle the strap of her stiletto sandal, giving everyone who wanted it a perfect view of her firm backside. Discarding her shoes under the table, Roxanne turned, her gaze seeking out Jake in the pool. Locking eyes with him, she tucked her hair beneath a rubber swimming cap, and with everyone watching, jiggled her way over to the edge of the pool nearest him. She eased down onto the deck, and slipped her feet into the water, making coquettish squeals as to how cold it was.

Me and Jinx both watched in astonishment as she playfully kicked water at Jake and did everything short of begging him to pull her in. And of course, he did. And they'd been in there fooling around for over 45 minutes now.

The only lights in the area were the Japanese lanterns and the blue-green glow of underwater pool lights. And sometimes, Roxanne and Jake disappeared into the far end of the pool near the waterfall where it was darker, and I tried not to think about what could be going on there. But surely even Jake wasn't brazen enough to cavort with another woman right under my nose!

Then I remembered Texas and the harlot he'd brought home to give me instructions on how to love a man. I grabbed the half-finished sloe gin fizz in front of me and downed it.

"*God!* Look at her rubbing up against him," Jinx snarled, sounding even more indignant than I could drum up the energy to feel. "Why don't you put a stop to it, Lily?"

"What do you suggest I do?" I asked. "Get in there and drag him out by the hair?"

Jinx took a gulp of her Mai Tai and slammed the glass back down on the table. "*My* suggestion was his balls. Much more efficient."

I sighed. "I want to know why her husband lets her get away with it? Where *is* he, anyway?"

"In the house. He and the managers are playing Texas Hold 'Em. Another annual tradition. Believe me, you've seen the last of Lute tonight."

Not that I'd seen a lot of the company president at all. Just as we'd filled our plates from the buffet table (which, strangely enough, had been missing my fried chicken), we'd come face-to-face with the head honcho, a scrawny-looking weasel of a man whom Jake had fumblingly introduced me to. I'd had a hard time picturing him as the powerful tycoon from Ashland, Kentucky, who'd single-handedly built his iron factory into a million dollar business before he turned 25—and even more incredible—had married a woman who looked like a pin-up girl, and if Jinx could be believed, worked in a New Orleans brothel before becoming lady of the manor.

Suddenly I realized that the "lady of the manor" was getting out of the pool. Jake watched her every move as if hypnotized. Like magic, one of the house servants appeared with a large, thick towel and wrapped it around Roxanne's elegant shoulders. She took off her bathing cap and shook her head, allowing her dark brown curls to tumble charmingly around her flawless face.

"Lily, take Jake his towel," Jinx said in a low, firm voice. "*Hurry!*"

I did as ordered. As Jake hefted himself up out of the pool, I held out his towel, and said, "We've got to be getting home, Jake. The babysitter is going to cost us a fortune."

Jake stared at me. My heart sank at the crestfallen look in his eyes.

Before he could respond, Roxanne spoke in her silky New Orleans accent, "Oh, dear. I've promised to show your Jake my mask collection. You will excuse us, won't you? We won't be more than a few minutes."

I stared at Roxanne, dumbfounded. How stupid did this woman think I was? *A mask collection?* I looked at Jake. His cheekbones were flushed, his eyes glittering. I knew that look. He was aroused. What nasty little suggestion had Roxanne whispered into his ear as they frolicked in the pool?

"A mask collection?" Suddenly, Jinx was at my side; she gave Roxanne and Jake a brilliant smile.

"From New Orleans? Oh, I'd simply *love* to see it, Roxanne. It sounds *divine!*"

Roxanne frowned, clearly put out that her little plan had back-fired.

Jake took the towel from me and began to rub it over his hair. "Some other time, Mrs. Dawson. Lily's right. We've got to get going."

I exchanged a glance with Jinx, mouthing the words, "thank you." She gave a shrug, and although her blue eyes blazed fury, she turned to Roxanne Dawson with a big smile. "Well, I guess that leaves you and me, Mrs. D. Lonnie will be in there all night playing poker with your husband, so I've got all the time in the world. And I just can't *wait* to see your mask collection."

I watched the two women walk toward the steps leading to the terrace, and hoped with all my might that Jinx would manage to break something really expensive.

***

Jake pressed his foot down on the accelerator, and we sped through the summer night down Rt. 90 towards Glasgow.

"So, what's got your panties in such a wad?" he finally asked. "You ain't said more than two words to me since we got in the car."

I stared out into the darkness, blinking back tears. I didn't want to get into this now. What was the point, anyway? He could tell me until he was blue in the face that nothing was going on, that it was all in good fun. But I knew better. I'd seen his face. And I knew what they would've done if they'd gone into the house. Right there under the roof where her husband sat playing cards. How could anyone be so shameless?

"Hey, she was making eyes at *me*, Lily Rae," Jake said, staring at the dark highway ahead. "What was I supposed to do? Be rude to her? She's my boss's wife, for chrissake!"

Still, I didn't speak. But my tears burned hotter behind my eyelids. The lump in my throat grew larger.

"*Goddamn it*, Lily Rae!" He banged the palm of his hand on the steering wheel.

I flinched, but steadfastly kept my gaze out the side window.

"What did you think I was going to do? Fuck her right there in the pool?"

My resolve shattered. Wildly, I twisted in the seat to face him. "*No!*" I screamed. "You were going to take her in the *house* and *fuck her!*"

It was the first time in my life I'd ever uttered such a foul word. But it was the only way to describe what he would've done if Jinx hadn't stopped him.

The blood drained from Jake's face. I could see that even in the darkness of the car. Slowly, he took his eyes off the road and looked at me.

I stared back, my stomach curling in fear of what he'd do. And even then, I wasn't prepared.

His right hand released the steering wheel and curled into a fist. His punch hit me in the mouth like a slab of cement. Pain rocked through my jaw, and a gush of warm, salty blood filled my mouth. It ran down my chin and spilled onto my blouse, heedless of the hands I cupped to my lips. I spit out something sharp, and realized with a dull sense of irony that it was my right front tooth.

"Maybe *that'll* teach you not to talk like a goddamn sailor," Jake said.

And we drove on down the highway,
heading for home.

CHAPTER THIRTY-THREE

On Monday afternoon, a knock came at the front door just after four o'clock. I jumped up from the couch to answer it, thinking Jake had forgotten his key. He'd left the house shortly after getting out of bed this afternoon, giving no explanation as to where he was going, and I'd asked for none. True to form, he'd been filled with remorse on Saturday morning, begging my forgiveness with his usual excuses—he'd had too much to drink, he didn't know what he was doing—and my favorite, "you pushed my buttons and I just lost my temper." I'd responded by ignoring him. I could barely stand to look at the man, much less accept his so-called apology for his brutal attack.

And of course, my response—or non-response—to his entreaties finally pissed him off, and he hadn't spoken a word to me since.

The knock came at the door again, louder this time, just as I reached it. Cradling my throbbing jaw, I opened it and saw, not Jake, but a pretty young woman in a nurse's uniform. Despite her hair color—strawberry blonde instead of the dark brown of the old days—Katydid looked just like she had in high school—cute as a bug's ear. When she saw me, her blue eyes widened in dismay.

"Dear Lord, Lily," she said, stepping inside. "What happened to you?"

I closed the door and spoke through still numb lips, "I told you when you called that I had a toothache."

Katydid untied her navy cape and slipped it off her shoulders, examining me with eyes that seemed worldlier than they'd been in high school. "Honey, a blind monkey could see you've got more than a toothache. You look like you've been in a bar fight!" And then her eyes widened. "Good God! Jake hit you, didn't he?"

My eyes filled with tears. I'd been successful at holding them in through the weekend, determined not to let Jake think he'd broken me. Even when I'd gone to the dentist this morning, giving them a rooster tale about getting hit in the mouth by a flying rock—which they didn't believe for a second, I was sure—I'd remained strong, determined not to break down. Even the look of pity on the dental assistant's face as I'd unfolded the square of tissue paper in which I'd wrapped my tooth hadn't fazed me. Of course it hadn't been salvageable. And worse, the two adjoining teeth on either side of the missing one were loose, and would have to be pulled. The dentist had shot me up with Novocain and put in a temporary cap until it could be replaced by three false teeth and a bridge.

"Oh, Lily, come here." Katydid held out her arms.

I collapsed against my old friend, sobbing out all my pent-up emotion—the hurt and rage and helplessness. Finally, when I was all cried out, I drew back and gave her a watery smile. "Heck of a way to renew an old friendship, isn't it?"

She just smiled. "Where's the kitchen? I think we both could use something cold to drink. Iced tea? Or maybe a Pepsi-Cola?"

I led her into the kitchen, and opened the refrigerator to grab a couple of Coca-Colas. "Let's go out on the patio. Debby Ann will be waking up from her nap soon, and I don't want her hearing this."

A few minutes later, we settled into lawn chairs, the ice clinking in our aluminum glasses of soda pop. And I told her the whole story. After I finished, Katydid crossed one white hosiery-clad leg at the knee and swung her rubber-soled white shoe back and forth, staring off toward the western sky where a line of thunderheads had gathered like an army on the march.

Finally, she spoke in her soft, matter-of-fact, Katydid way, "Lily, RJ and I were married a little over two years. And up until he had a fling with that little Vanderbilt cheerleader girl, he was a good husband. With both of us going to school, we were on crazy schedules, and there were times we didn't lay eyes on each other for days." She reached up, unpinned her cap from her head and laid it gently on her lap. Giving her head a shake, she ran strong-looking fingers with neatly trimmed nails through her gold-red hair, and the faraway look in her eyes disappeared as they focused on me.

"I reckon some folks would say he fell in bed with that cheerleader because he was lonely. My own mama thought I should give him another chance. And you know what? I actually considered it."

She reached down for her drink and took a long sip. In the neighbor's back yard, a screen door slammed, and I glanced over to see Bill Adams carrying a bag of charcoal toward a grill on his patio. He glanced at me and waved.

"Looks like a storm brewing," he called out with a grin as I waved back. "Guess I better rustle up these hamburgers for my hungry boys pretty quick."

"I reckon so," I called back, wincing at the pain searing through my jaw. It was almost time for one of those painkillers the dentist had prescribed. "So, did you give RJ another chance, Katydid?"

"Sweetie, do me a favor..." Katydid placed a hand on my knee, giving me a wry smile. "Call me Kate. That old nickname just doesn't fit me anymore. It belongs to that naïve, sunshiny, Pollyanna girl I used to be. Not who I am today. You know who that is? A smart, accomplished gal who's done her part in saving at least a couple of lives since I got that nursing degree. A woman who demands respect, not because of my gender, but because I'm a member of the human race. A woman who said wedding vows in a Baptist church in Russell Springs, promising to love and obey a man who'd been the love of my life since I was 14. *He* was the one who broke those vows, Lily, not me. No, I couldn't give him another chance. I knew I deserved a husband who'd love me unconditionally, through thick and thin. RJ proved he wasn't that man. And as much as my family—and his—tried to convince me that 'boys will be boys,' that I should just put his 'little mistake' behind me and start over with him, I just couldn't do it. And I've never once regretted that decision."

I didn't know what to say. In the silence, thunder rumbled in the distance, still too far away for concern. Katydid—Kate—lifted her glass to her lips and took a sip. Over in the Adams's back yard, Bill had the fire going in his grill. The smell of charcoal drifted toward us, and my mouth began to water. I closed my eyes and pressed a hand to my mid-section.

"So, I guess my question for you, Lily, is…" Katydid turned and looked me square in the eye. "How long are you going to put up with this barbaric caveman who vowed to love you 'til death do you part?"

My stomach spasmed. Bile rose in my throat. Cupping my hands over my aching mouth, I jumped up from the lawn chair and ran into the house. A moment later, I sank to my knees in front of the toilet bowl, retching. The clear chicken soup I'd had for lunch—the only thing I'd been able to eat for the past three days—came up.

I was still on my knees in the bathroom when I heard the rustle of a starched uniform, followed by the gush of water in the sink. And then I felt the blessed coolness of a wet washcloth pressed against my forehead. Katydid didn't speak; she just stood there patiently, waiting for my nausea to pass.

Finally, it did. I lowered my body to the bathroom floor and wiped my tender mouth with the washcloth. Weakly, I lifted my head to look at Katydid. "How long will I put up with him?" I said softly. "Well, seeing as how I'm pretty sure I'm pregnant, and I ain't got a pot to piss in without Jake, I reckon I'll just have to put up with him for the rest of my life." My lips twisted in an ironic smile. "Like my mother once told me ...I've made my bed. Now, I have to lay in it."

CHAPTER THIRTY-FOUR

January 1957
Bowling Green, Kentucky

I looked in on Debby Ann, saw that she was
sleeping, and closed the door to her bedroom. With
a relieved sigh, I lumbered into the living room,
grabbed my library copy of **Peyton Place**, the
scandalous new novel Betty had written me about,
and plopped down on the couch to read a few more
pages until Jake got home from work. That is, if my
darn bladder would let me. It felt like the baby
inside me was taking its tiny little hands and
squeezing it like it was a ripe melon.

Lord, was I *ever* going to give birth to this child?
I felt like I'd been pregnant forever. But it's only
three days past my due date, I reminded myself as I
opened the novel to where the bookmark held my
place. Releasing a contented sigh, I glanced out the
sheer-curtained window to make sure the snow was
still falling. It had started just after noon, and now, I
could see it was coming down thicker than ever.
Across from the sofa, the black pot-bellied stove
crackled and popped, sending out a comforting
warmth on this cold winter's afternoon—a perfect
afternoon for reading! With a smile, I turned back
to my book.

Despite my interest in this potboiler, though, my eyelids began to grow heavy after reading only a few pages.

I'll just close my eyes for a few minutes. Debby Ann will be up from her nap soon...and now that Jake is on the day shift, I'll have to get up and start supper...not that there's a lot to do to make soup beans and cornbread...

My thoughts began to drift...

"Mommy...*Mommy*! I made poo-poo in my potty. You come see."

At first, I thought I was dreaming. But when Debby Ann's sharp little fingernails dug into my arm, I bolted up from the couch. "*Ouch*!!! Lord, Debby Ann! What *are* you, part *cat*?"

"Come see my poo-poo," she insisted, tugging at my arm, her dark eyes guileless.

I sighed and swung my feet to the floor. Lately, my daughter had shown an inordinate amount of interest in her bowel movements, another pleasant stage of childhood, I presumed, one that, oddly enough, *I* didn't find all that delightful.

"Did you wipe?" I asked, following her to the bathroom.

"Uh huh!" On bare feet and wearing only a pair of pink terrycloth training pants and a T-shirt, she toddled ahead, almost tripping over Debby Ann Kitty who jumped a foot into the air and scampered off into the safety of my bedroom. Inside the bathroom, Debby Ann pointed in triumph at her Minnie Mouse potty-chair. "Look, Mommy! *Poo-poo*!"

Oh, she'd wiped all right, I saw. What looked like half a roll of toilet paper was scattered across the bathroom--some in the potty-chair, some in the toilet, and most on the floor.

Debby Ann beamed up at me. "See, Mommy?"

"That's a good girl. Next time, though, call Mommy before you go so I can help you with the toilet paper. You don't have to use so much, you know."

Debby clapped her hands and stamped her feet on the tile, a proud grin on her face. "I did poo-poo, I did poo-poo," she sing-songed.

Lord a-mighty, I thought. You'd think she'd just pooped out the Hope Diamond.

A sound came from the living room--the front door opening. Oh, damn, I thought. *Jake's home. And I'll bet* **Peyton Place** *is laying right out there in plain sight*. Not that it had a lurid cover. But still, Jake might've heard about it, and he certainly wouldn't approve of me reading "such trash."

"We're in the bathroom, Jake," I called out. "Be right out!" To Debby, I muttered, "Let me check and make sure you wiped good, sweetie. Not that I don't trust you..." I tucked an index finger under the elastic of her training pants for a quick peep.

Debby pulled away, giving me an indignant look. "I *did!*"

"Okay, I guess you did." I gave her bottom an affectionate pat. "Now, go get your clothes on, girl. It's January, not July. I swear, you'd go naked year round if I let you!"

"*Lily Rae!*" Jake called from the living room.

I frowned. He sounded mad. "Butter my butt and call me a biscuit," I muttered, stepping out of the bathroom. He'd found the book, sure as H-E-double hockey sticks. Well, if it was a fight he was rarin' for, I'd give him one. Being nine months pregnant with an aching lower back, swollen feet and a bladder that felt like a 400-pound hippo was sitting on it, hadn't done a thing to put me in a good mood.

"What?" I snapped, stepping into the living room.

Jake stood just inside the front door, wearing his heavy wool coat, splotched with melting snow. His face looked as gray as the waning daylight through the window. My gaze darted to the book still lying facedown on the floor where it must've dropped when I fell asleep. Whatever his problem was, it wasn't that, thank the Lord.

"What's wrong, Jake?" I asked. "Why are you home from work so early?"

He stared at me a long moment without speaking. And I felt the first icy fingers of fear crawling over my spine.

He swallowed hard and said, "You better get on over to Jinx's, Lily. She's gonna need a friend tonight."

My mouth dropped open. "Why? What happened?"

Jake stared out the window at the falling snow. "There was an accident at the plant." His voice was so soft, I could barely hear him. "A forklift went out of control and pinned Lonnie against a steel girder."

"Oh, my Lord," I gasped, my stomach dipping. "Is he okay?"

Jake turned his head and looked at me. "No, Lily. He's not. The poor bastard was killed instantly."

***

The six inches of snow that had fallen on the day of Lonnie Foley's death had barely begun to melt by the morning of his funeral. But on the night

before he was to be laid to rest in the Poplar Grove
Baptist Church graveyard near Webb's Crossroads in
Russell County, the cold spell broke with the onset
of an unusually warm air mass that brought steady
rain to the region. I was huddled beneath an
umbrella, dressed in a double-breasted wool coat
that couldn't be buttoned over my distended belly
and a black soft-brimmed hat, watching as Lonnie's
casket was lowered into the yawning grave carved
out from the red Kentucky clay. Jake stood next to
me, holding the umbrella, one arm wrapped around
me tightly. A few feet away, Jinx Foley leaned
against her father and sobbed as the gray casket
disappeared into the earth.

My heart ached for my friend. I'd never seen
her this bad off—eyes reddened from crying, her
face without make-up, as pale as what was left of the
dingy snow on the ground. I could only imagine
how awful it must be for her to see her husband
dead and buried. And once that shock wore off,
she'd have to deal with the other one—the sudden
change in her life.

Of course, the company had been good to her.
Since Lonnie had been killed on the job, word had
come down from Lute Dawson that Jinx could stay
in the house, rent-free for six months in order to
figure out her future plans. I supposed that was a
generous offer, but it still left a funny taste in my
mouth. After all, the poor guy had been killed on
the job, and it hadn't been his fault. It seemed to me
that Dawson Ironworks should sign over the deed to
the house, free and clear, especially considering the
paltry pension she'd be living on.

Over in front of the grave, Brother Joe Bob led
the gatherers in a warbling verse of "Amazing
Grace," ending the service. As the mourners turned

away and headed back to their cars, I heard a voice call out my name and I turned to see Glenodene Cook, Jinx's mother, picking her way across the soggy grass toward me. I felt Jake stiffen.

"Here." He thrust the umbrella in my hand. "Take the umbrella. I'll be in the car." And he loped off.

I understood why. Glenodene was one of the most long-winded talkers in the county. And just because she'd just watched her son-in-law being buried didn't mean she'd be at a loss for words.

"Lawsy, me," she moaned even before she reached me as her high heels sank in the muck. "Have you ever seen the like of this weather? I swan! It just takes the cake. All that snow the other day, and now this."

"I know. It's just awful." When the woman finally reached me, I reached out a sympathetic hand. "I'm just so sorry for your loss, Glenodene."

The woman blinked reddened dark eyes behind thick-lensed spectacles, her ruby lips twisting in anguish. "Thank ye, kindly, Lily Rae. I know Jenny Lynn appreciates all of you've done for her since Lonnie's passing."

"I just wanted to do something. It wasn't much."

In addition to taking over some fried chicken, an oatmeal cake and a freshly-baked apple pie to the Foley home, I'd brought the twins over to the house while Jake helped Jinx with the funeral arrangements.

"I just don't know what's to become of her," Glenodene said, dabbing at her eyes with an embroidered handkerchief. "You tell me…what's that girl supposed to do now? Here she is with them two-year-old rambunctious twins and another baby on the way, and all she has to live on is that measly little pension Lonnie left her. How is she supposed to survive on that, I ask you? And Lord knows Festus and me ain't got an extra dime to our name to help her out. I'm just worrying myself sick over it, I tell you."

She paused to snatch a breath, and I grabbed the opportunity to get in a word edgewise. "I didn't know Jinx was expecting, Glenodene." I squeezed the woman's hand in sympathy. "Oh, this just makes it even more tragic. But you know Jake and me will help out just as much as we can. I reckon, though, she'll probably want to move back to Russell County?"

Glenodene shook her head as fresh tears gathered in her eyes. "I just don't know what my girl will do. She's too upset to think, much less make plans. Oh, Lord! Lonnie was just too young to go. A man in his prime, he was. Well, none of us knows the will of the Lord, do we? And it's not our place to question it, I reckon."

I nodded and tried to pull my hand away from her clutches. "Well, Jake's waiting for me in the car so..." Suddenly I stiffened as a pain knifed through my lower back and then radiated around my belly, tightening like an iron vice.

Oh, I remembered that pain well. *Too* well.

Clutching my bulging tummy, I turned away from Glenodene. "I think maybe Jake better get me to the hospital."

Of course, I'd planned to have the baby at City Hospital in Bowling Green where Katydid worked, but it didn't look like that was going to happen now. Oh, well. I supposed Glenodene was right about the will of the Lord.

She immediately realized my predicament, and helped me to the car.

"The baby's coming," I said to Jake, slumping into the front seat as a new labor pain began in the small of my back. "I reckon you better get us to Columbia Hospital as fast as you can."

CHAPTER THIRTY-FIVE

"**I**'m sorry, Mrs. Tatlow," said the pretty redheaded nurse, approaching my bed with an apologetic smile. "It's time to take your baby girl back to the nursery."

I looked up from Kathy Kay's sweet little face with a worried frown. "I think something's wrong with her. She barely took any formula before she fell asleep." With the baby cradled in my left arm, I picked up the four-ounce glass bottle of formula with my free hand and jiggled it back and forth. "You see? Not even half of it's gone." I knew I was probably being silly, but after what had happened with Debby Ann, I wasn't taking any chances.

The redheaded nurse—Enola Huddleston, her name tag said—reached over and took the baby from my arms. "Now, little mother, don't you be worryin' about this youngun. She's only a day old.

It usually takes two or three days before they really start eatin' good."

I gave the girl a do-you-know-what-you're-talking-about look. How old was she, anyhow? Maybe 18? She sure didn't look old enough to have graduated from college with a nursing degree. Not only that, but there was something awfully familiar-looking about her. I narrowed my eyes as the nurse placed Kathy Kay into the plastic basket of a steel cart and tucked the blanket around her.

"Well, I'll *be*," I murmured as the light dawned. "I know who you are now. You're Pat-Pea..." I caught myself, realizing that the girl had probably never heard the nickname of her big sister. "You're Patty Huddleston's little sister, aren't you?"

The nurse flashed a big smile. Lord, she was pretty! Much prettier than Pat-Peaches in her wildest dreams. I wondered if Enola was as much of a tart as her sister had been.

"Why, yes!" Enola said. "You know my sister?"

"I did. We went to Russell Springs High together."

"Well, what do you say?" Her grin widened. "I went there, too! Small world, huh?"

"Sure is," I agreed, but thinking it wasn't that big of a deal. After all, we were here in the hospital in Columbia, only about 16 miles away from Russell Springs. I supposed a good portion of the employees at the hospital came from Russell County, which meant they'd graduated from RSHS.

Enola flashed me another smile and began to push the baby cart out of the ward. "You get some rest now, Mrs. Tatlow. Feeding time will be here again before you know it."

"Wait! How is Patty and...Chad doing?"

The girl's brown eyes lit up. "Oh, they're just fine," she gushed. "They have three younguns, two boys and a girl. Charlie just turned four, Jimmy is two, and the baby, Maggie, is seven months. Just precious as all get-out! And they have this beautiful house down in Myrtle Beach, South Carolina. Chad bought this golf course down there and fixed it up, and from what I hear, business is really booming. I go down there for vacation every summer, so I'll be sure and tell them you said 'hey,' okay?"

"Yeah, that would be nice," I said, thinking of Chad and Pat-Peaches living down there near the beach—a life of sunshine and ocean breezes.

With a little wave, Enola disappeared with the baby, leaving me to stare vacantly into space. *It could've been me.* But it seemed Chad and Pat-Peaches were happy together. The Big Man On Campus and the School Slut. Who would've thought?

"Well, you look about a million miles away."

I jumped and looked over at the door. Jake stood there, leaning nonchalantly on the doorframe of the ward. He walked over to my bed and gave me a peck on the cheek.

"How come you're in here all by yourself?" he asked. "This here's the maternity ward, right? Where are all the other mothers?"

"You're looking at the only one, I reckon. That little black-haired gal went home this morning, and I can't say I'm sorry. She like to worried me to death...always whining about her burning stitches or what-not. I sure feel sorry for her husband; he's gonna have *two* babies to take care of." I gave Jake a sharp look. "And speaking of babies, you just missed seeing yours. The nurse picked her up and took her to the nursery not more than a minute ago."

Jake shrugged. "Bad timing, I reckon."

I stared at him a moment. "You're disappointed, aren't you, Jake? That you didn't get a boy this time?"

Instead of answering me, he strolled over to the window and looked out. "'Pears like it's gonna snow again. I reckon I ought to hit the road and head back to Bowling Green."

"You have to go back? I thought the factory was giving you a few days off?"

"They are. But I told Jinx I'd go over the insurance papers with her to make sure they're all in order." He turned away from the window and met my gaze. "She's barely holding it together, Lily Rae. I just hate seeing her so tore up."

"I know." I nodded glumly. "I do, too. Jake, you're doing a real sweet thing—helping her out like this. I wish they'd let me out of the hospital so I could do something."

"You'll be out by the weekend."

"I know." I gave an exasperated sigh. "But I'm so dadburn *bored*. I don't know why they won't let me go home sooner. I feel fine."

My labor had been a little longer with Kathy Kay than it had been with Debby Ann, but the ordeal hadn't been all that bad. Not nearly as bad as when the dentist had to pull those two teeth loosened when Jake knocked out my front one. We'd arrived at the hospital in Columbia just after 1:00 PM, and Kathy Kay was born just before suppertime.

"Well, I'd better head on out," Jake said, glancing longingly at the door. "Especially if there's snow on the way."

"You aren't going to stop by the nursery and see Kathy Kay?"

"I'll look in on her at the window." He gave me a wink. "I reckon I'll get to know her when she comes home."

I chewed on my bottom lip. "Jake, I'm sorry…I know how much you wanted a boy." Even as I said it, I felt ashamed. I wasn't sorry. Not really. Kathy Kay was a sweetie-pie. But I couldn't help but wonder if Jake would show more interest in his children if he had a boy.

"Don't worry about it," he said. "There's always next time." He came over to the bed and brushed his lips against my forehead. "I probably won't make it back here until day after tomorrow."

I reached out for his arm as he turned to go. "Jake, do me a favor, huh? I have a stack of library books sitting on the end table in the living room. Can you bring them on Thursday? I need something to read." I didn't add that **Peyton Place** was one of them. I'd purposely placed it on the bottom of the stack before we'd left for Russell Springs. Maybe he'd just bring them without looking at them. I was dying to get back to the exciting story about the tiny New England town.

Jake nodded and pulled away. "I'll try to remember."

***

Of course, he didn't remember.

He arrived empty-handed on Thursday afternoon—not like the husband of the Doris Day look-a-like in the next bed who'd shown up this morning with a big bouquet of fresh roses and a two-pound box of Whitman's Chocolates. The labor & delivery staff had rolled "Doris" into the ward about ten o'clock on Tuesday night after she gave birth to a ten-pound baby boy—quite a feat since the new mama wasn't any bigger than a minute. I'd guessed it was a first baby even before the mother told me so. That was evident by the proud grin on the daddy's face and the melting look in his eyes when he held his new son--a look I'd never seen on Jake's face. Not once.

And because of that, I wasn't in the best of moods. "Where are my books?" I asked, knowing and not caring that I sounded grumpy after he bestowed a perfunctory kiss on my lips.

A pained look crossed his face. "Oh, damn, Lily! I clean forgot about them."

I bit back my exasperation. One little favor! "Doris" over there got chocolates and roses, and *I* couldn't even get my blame library books to help me pass the time in this lonely old mausoleum!

Well, I reminded myself, Jake had a lot on his mind, helping out poor Jinx with her affairs and taking care of things around the house while I was gone. Still, the mean little voice in my mind just wouldn't stay quiet. *It's not like he's got a lot to do.* I'd left the house spick and span before the trip to Russell Springs, and Mother, of course, was taking care of Debby Ann. So why was it so hard for Jake to follow through on my one little request?

He didn't stay long. Shortly after his arrival, the nurses brought in the babies, and he held Kathy Kay for a few minutes after I fed her. But as soon as they were taken back to the nursery, he became so fidgety and bored-looking that I finally snapped, "Why don't you just go on home, Jake. It's clear you don't want to be here."

And to my complete disgust, he stood and gave a big yawn. "Well, to tell you the truth, I think I will go on back to Opal Springs and take a nap before Mama gets supper on the table. I haven't been sleeping too good…" He gave me a wink. "…without you in the bed."

Well…" I rolled my eyes, but couldn't hide a smile. It wasn't often Jake threw me a bone like that. But still, I had to get in another shot. "You might want to stop in at Mother and Daddy's and see how your daughter is doing. Daddy brought Mother by to see me yesterday, but Debby Ann had to stay with Norry down in the waiting room. I know the poor little thing is missing us."

"Yeah, I'll try to do that." He leaned down to give me a kiss. "I'll stop by here tomorrow sometime. You take care, hear?"

"Yeah," I muttered. "What else have I got to do?" I glanced over at the other occupied bed, and saw the doting couple with their heads close together, chatting softly. A wave of jealousy swept through me. *Why can't my man look at me that way?* The woman looked up and caught my gaze, and embarrassed, I turned away, but not before noting the look of pity on her face. Even a stranger could tell how disinterested Jake was in his wife and new daughter.

When I looked back at the door, he was already gone. I threw back the covers on the bed and swung my legs over the side. If I didn't get out of this ward for a few minutes, I'd surely lose my mind. Besides, "Romeo & Juliet" over there was making me feel nauseous. Drawing on my robe, I stepped into my slippers and shuffled down toward the nurse's station.

As I passed a small supply room, I heard a giggle, and glanced inside. My cheeks grew warm as I recognized Pat-Peaches' little sister, pressed up against a counter by a handsome man in surgical scrubs. He was laughing down at her, one hand caressing a long red curl that had escaped from her French roll.

I looked away and quickened my step. Apparently, little Enola was following in the footsteps of her big hussy sister. Still, there had been something really romantic about the scene. It was almost as if Enola had stars in her eyes as she gazed up at the handsome doctor.

And that gave me an idea.

At the nurse's station, I asked if someone could find me a notebook and a pen. Seconds later, I was on my way back to the ward, the items in hand. Back in bed, I thought for a moment and then wrote on the first page of the notebook:

The Healing Love—A Nurse Romance
By
Lily Rae Tatlow

And then I began to write, the words flowing from my brain through my fingertips and onto the lined paper like the fresh, clear water of Opal Springs as it emptied into the pond.

"Do you know what happened to my library books?" I looked over at Jake from where I sat at the kitchen table, feeding Kathy Kay her bottle.

I'd noticed the books were missing as soon as I'd stepped into the house after my discharge from the hospital, but I just figured Jake had moved them for some reason. But when I couldn't find them anywhere in the house, I finally decided I might as well come right out and ask him.

"Mommy, when can I hold the baby?" Debby Ann asked, standing at my elbow. Instead of being jealous as I figured she might be, she seemed fascinated with her new baby sister.

"Later, maybe. She's eating now," I said, then looked back at Jake. "Did you hear me, Jake?"

He looked up from the tuna casserole Jinx had brought over for my first night home from the hospital—a meal I was sure had come from one of the mourners at the funeral. I hoped it was still safe to eat.

He took his time chewing his food and following it with a gulp of milk before answering my question. "I took them back to the library," he said finally.

I stared at him. "You did what? But...you told me...you said you forgot them."

He shrugged. "I lied." Then he skewered me with his eyes. "Lily Rae, I wasn't about to bring that trash into a hospital. That's nothing but smut you're reading. Especially that **Peyton Place**. I've heard about that filthy book, and I'll be damned if I let my wife read trash like that, especially out in public."

I couldn't believe my ears. I felt my blood start to simmer, but forced myself to remain calm.

Turning to Debby Ann, I said, "Sweetie, why don't you go watch TV for a while, and as soon as Kathy Kay here is done eating, I'll bring her in and let you hold her."

Debby Ann's face brightened, and squealing with delight, she ran out of the room. I waited for the sound of the TV coming on, and then looked back at Jake. "What I read is smut, you say? Well, what do you call them detective stories *you* read? The ones with the gory pictures of women's naked bodies with their blood splashed all over the place? Or what about them girly magazines I sometimes find under our bed? You know the ones I'm talking about—the ones with the naked girls and the dirty stories about sex. If you ask me, Jake Tatlow, those are pretty damn smutty! They make **Peyton Place** look like **Rebecca of Sunnybrook Farm**."

Jake put down his fork and pushed his plate away. "Big difference," he said. "I'm a man, and everybody knows men like stuff like that. But a lady..." He looked at me. "...which is what you're *supposed* to be...should have higher standards. Besides, you're raising up two daughters. You want to set a good example for them."

I stared at him for a long moment, totally flabbergasted. And then I couldn't help but laugh at the irony of Jake preaching about good examples. This, from the man who'd brought a slut into our home to give me sex lessons.

"Well, you know what?" I drew the nipple from Kathy Kay's lips and placed the bottle on the table. Positioning the baby against my shoulder, I gently patted her back to burp her. "It doesn't matter a bit about the library books. I can always check them out again. Besides..." I looked Jake square in the eyes. "I've started writing my *own* book. And yeah, you just might call it smut, but I call it a nurse romance. And I wrote three whole chapters on it in the hospital." I gave him a triumphant look, just daring him to shoot me down.

"You're kidding, right?" he said.

I shook my head. "Not even a little bit. And you know what else? When I'm finished with it, I'm going to get it published…turned into a real book. You just wait and see if I don't."

As if adding an exclamation mark to that statement, Kathy Kay let out a gigantic burp.

"Good girl," I said, and got up from the table. "I reckon you'll take care of the dishes." It was a statement, not a question.

Without waiting for a response, I walked out of the room.

***

"Just as I expected. Crap. *Pure crap.*"

His voice came from far away. I felt something flutter against my face. I dragged myself from a dream, already half-forgotten, and opened my eyes to see Jake standing over the bed.

He gave me a mean grin and dropped another sheet of notebook paper on my face. "I wouldn't use this to wipe my ass."

Realizing what he was talking about, I scrambled up to a seated position and began to gather up the notebook sheets of my novel he'd already dropped. *"How dare you!"* I sputtered. "You had no right to read that. How did you even find it?"

His grin widened. "There's only so many places you can hide something in this little house, Lily. A shoebox in the closet? Not very original."

My eyes burned with tears. "Why are you so dad-blasted mean? It's something for me, don't you get that? Something that ain't got anything to do with you and them babies in there. It's just for *me*. And all you want to do is tear it down."

"Aw, come on, Lily Rae. You can't really believe someone will actually publish that syrupy pig-slop, do you? If you do, you're more of a fool than I ever thought." He turned away with a look of disgust. Then he whipped back around. "What makes you think you can write a book, anyhow? You're just a little hillbilly out of Russell County...barely graduated from high school. You ain't got no training to write books!"

Tears of fury flowed down my face. "What do you mean, *barely* graduated from high school? I was a B-average student. Just got C's in math and science. Anyhow, it's more than *you* did! And maybe I don't have any training in writin' books. But that don't mean I can't *try*. And what has Russell County got to do with it? Look at Janice Holt Giles over in Knifley? That's Adair County, I know, but close enough. She's got probably a half-dozen books out, and she doesn't live more than a few miles from Opal Springs."

He shook his head and began to unbutton his shirt. "She wasn't born and raised here. She's not a hillbilly like you. Face it, Lily Rae. You're not *ever* gonna be nothing more than what you are right now. A mother and a housewife. So you might as well get used to it." He turned to the door, muttering, "That damn Betty Kelly...putting foolish notions in your head."

Over in the corner of the bedroom, Kathy Kay began to fuss in her bassinet. It was time for her three o'clock feeding. Jake grinned. "And there's your wake-up call, Mama."

My tears had dried by the time Jake left for work a few hours later. When I staggered into the kitchen to warm up a bottle for Kathy Kay's morning feeding, I saw the dirty dishes on the counter, and the remnants of last night's meal still on the table.

I stood staring at the mess for a long moment, wanting to do nothing more than sink to the floor and bawl my eyes out. Instead, I turned and plodded back to the bedroom, pulling open my lingerie drawer. Digging beneath the bras and panties, I pulled out the rumpled pile of notebook paper I'd retrieved from the bed a few hours before. Taking them back into the living room, I carefully opened the door of the black pot-bellied stove with its briskly burning fire, and threw the pile of papers inside. I closed the door, and stood there a moment, listening to the sizzle of the flames, feeling a curious detachment. Not at all like I thought I should feel at the death of my dream.

I peeked in on Kathy Kay and saw she'd gone back to sleep. Then I turned and went into the kitchen to do the dishes.

CHAPTER THIRTY-SIX

August 1960
Myrtle Beach, South Carolina

Looking up from my book, I lifted my sunglasses to check on Debby Ann and Kathy Kay, making sure they hadn't broken my rule and wandered out past ankle-deep surf. Those two little dickens were braver than smart in the water, and oh, they *did* love the ocean. *Had*, since they'd caught their first sight of it four days ago.

Much to my relief, neither child was in the water right now. Debby Ann was on her knees in an eddying pool of seawater, building another sandcastle, and Kathy Kay, who'd turned three in January, sat at the edge of the surf, her tanned little legs stretched out seaward, a look of intense concentration on her fine-boned face as she sifted through the wet sand.

I smiled and returned to **To Kill a Mockingbird,** one of the best books I'd ever read in my life. On the blanket next to me, a transistor radio played The Everly Brother's "Cathy's Clown." I thought about calling to Kathy Kay that her favorite song was on, but decided against it. It would just make Debby Ann mad, and she'd start in about how come the radio didn't play any songs about *her.* Besides, the heat of the afternoon sun had made me feel so lazy, I wasn't sure I could summon up the energy to use my voice.

Instead, I reached for my can of Coke and took a sip, grimacing at how warm it had become. I thought about sending Debby Ann back to the cottage to get me a cold one, but decided against that, too. It was after four, and we'd soon have to go in anyway, and get showered and try to decide what to do about supper. Maybe Jake would take us out to eat. We'd been barbecuing every evening except the night we arrived, and I was getting sick and tired of undercooked hamburgers and charred hotdogs.

I still couldn't believe I'd actually talked him into coming here to Myrtle Beach for vacation this year. It was the first real vacation we'd ever had, if you didn't count those two days we'd spent in the

Smoky Mountains a few years back, and that one overnight trip to Nashville to see the Grand Old Opry. Of course, I hadn't dared mention to Jake that Chad and Pat-Peaches lived here.

The radio began to play Chubby Checker's "The Twist" for probably the hundredth time since I'd parked myself on my beach towel, and I put down my book and sang along, resisting the urge to stand up and do the new dance that **American Bandstand** had made famous. That would be cute, wouldn't it? I'd be a spectacle for everybody on the crowded beach. Oh, wouldn't Jake just *die* if I did? But he was back at the cottage, probably either taking a nap or drinking a beer in the little yard that faced the beach.

Wonder what Chad is doing right now?

On the late afternoon we'd arrived, I'd looked intently at each golf course as we drove down Rt. 17 on the way to our rental cottage, wondering which one Chad owned. Of course, Jake didn't play golf, so I'd never know...never have a reason to stop by one and ask if they knew Chad.

The Chubby Checker song ended, and Dante & the Evergreens' "Alley-Oop" began to play. I glanced over at Kathy Kay, my brow furrowing. What on earth was so fascinating about the sand she was sifting through? It looked like she was searching for something.

Poor little thing. She'd cried her eyes out on the day we'd left home for vacation because she hadn't wanted to leave her best friend, Paul John, Jinx's youngest boy. It was funny, the way those two had bonded from the time they were babies. Kathy Kay was only six months older, and since they were able to sit up and take notice of each other, they'd been like two peas in a pod. I marveled at how adorable they were together, both of them looking like little cherubs with their blond curls and guileless blue eyes.

But I hadn't been prepared for Kathy Kay's sobs as we'd driven away that morning. If they were so inseparable now, what would it be like in ten years when the two of them would be hovering on the threshold of adolescence? Trouble, I suspected, with all those teenage hormones raging. It didn't bear thinking about.

I got to my feet, brushed the sand off the seat of my black strapless swimsuit and ambled toward the shore. As I approached Debby Ann, she looked up and grinned, revealing a gap where her right eye-tooth used to be. Her new permanent tooth was just visible. She looked adorable.

"Like my sandcastle, Mommy?"

"It's beautiful, honey." I placed a hand on top of her sun-warmed head. At seven years old, Debby had lost all her baby fat, and was pretty much all gangly arms and legs with a pixie face and big brown eyes. Her blond hair had darkened to a rich, golden-brown, and in the summer, was streaked with blond from the sun—just like Jake's.

I stroked her tanned shoulder. "You need to put some more Coppertone on, girl. Go on, now. It's in my bag on the blanket. I'll get your back in a minute, okay?"

Debby Ann's bottom lip poofed out. "But Mommy! I *need* to get a suntan!"

"But you don't *need* to get burned. Now do what I say!"

With an exaggerated roll of the eyes, Debby got to her feet and plodded toward the beach blanket, kicking sand and muttering about how nobody—meaning Mommy–would let her get a decent tan.

Cantankerous little squirt, I thought. *It could be raining cats and dogs with thunder crashing and lightning flashing and the girl would look you in the eye and insist that the sun was shining.* That was Debby Ann.

I walked on toward Kathy Kay, the complete opposite of her older sister. There wasn't a child on the face of the earth with a sweeter disposition than this one. And I swear, with her big blue eyes and blonde curls, she was the spitting image of my long dead little brother, Charles Alton. I sat down on the wet sand next to her, bracing as a wave washed around us. "Hey, Sweetie. What ya doing?"

She looked up and smiled, her golden ringlets gleaming in the sun. "Lookin' for a starfish."

"But honey, you've been sitting in that same spot all morning. Don't you want to come help Debby Ann build a sandcastle?"

Kathy shook her head emphatically. "No, Mommy. I told you...I *got* to find a starfish."

I ran a hand down the silk of her damp hair. "Sweetie, I don't think starfish wash up on the beach. You probably have to go out into the deep water and dive down to find one."

Kathy glanced out at the waves, the expectant look on her face unchanged. "They do *too* wash up on the beach, Mommy," she said. "Remember the story book you read us? The Bobbsey Twins? They found a starfish on the beach. So...I'm going to wait right here until the sea brings *me* a starfish. And when I find one, I'm going to give it to Paul John."

I sighed. "Well, honey, that's very sweet of you, but you can't wait here forever. We have to go in pretty soon, get washed up and changed. Maybe Daddy will take us out to supper tonight. You want to go to that restaurant with the doors that look like you're walking into a big old shark's mouth?"

Kathy Kay shook her head solemnly. "No, I don't want to go into a shark's mouth." She turned and fixed serious blue eyes on me. "And I *can't* leave until I find my starfish. I promised Paul John I'd bring him one!"

I thought for a moment. Kathy Kay had never thrown a fit in her life, but there was always a first time for everything.

"You know, honey, the ocean tides work on a schedule. There's low tide and high tide, and they both happen a few times a day. This here, I reckon, is high tide. And I'm pretty sure it's *low* tide that you can find the treasures from the sea...things like sand dollars and big seashells...*and* starfishes." I hoped to God I had it right, and it wasn't the other way around. Not that it really mattered. Kathy Kay could look her little heart out and never find a starfish. "I think maybe if we come down here at low tide, you'll have a better chance of finding one."

"When will that be?"

"Well, I'm not exactly sure, but maybe later tonight. After we get back from supper."

Kathy Kay nodded as if that made perfect sense. She got to her feet and brushed the sand from her cute little polka-dotted bottom. "Okay, Mommy. Let's come down here at low tide." Her hand curled around mine.

Debby Ann had just settled back into the pool of water in front of her sandcastle when we approached. "I don't need no more suntan lotion on my back," she said defiantly, removing her sand pail from a cone of wet sand to form a new wing to her castle.

"Just as well," I said, mentally preparing myself for World War III. "Because it's time to go in."

Debby Ann's brows lowered like the onset of a particularly violent thunderstorm. "But *Mommmmmmmeeeee!*"

"Don't start, Debby Ann," I warned.

"Come on, Debby Ann." Kathy Kay calmly gazed down at her big sister, for all the world like *she* was the big sister, not Debby. "Mommy says we can go to that big shark's mouth for supper."

Debby Ann stared at Kathy, her mouth open in what I figured had been—or was going to be–a protest. It clamped shut as her gaze darted to her me. "Really, Mommy? We're going to the big shark for supper?"

I grinned. "I'm sure you can talk your daddy into it. But it has to come from you two, not me."

"Okay!" She began to gather up her sand toys, and Kathy Kay bent down to help.

The girls raced in front of me toward our rental cottage. By the time I reached the door, my arms full with the beach bag, wet towels and blanket, they were already inside, begging their father to take them to the restaurant with the big shark's mouth.

"We'll see," he said, looking up at me as I came through the door. "Ya'all go wash up now. I've got to talk to your mommy."

"What's going on?" I asked as the girls ran off to the bathroom, Debby Ann shouting that she had first dibs on the shower.

"I just got off the telephone with Jinx," he said, his expression unreadable.

"Nothing's wrong with Debby Ann Kitty, I hope."

Jinx had offered to come over to the house to feed the cat and clean out the litter box while we were gone. Even though Debby Ann Kitty was an outside cat, I'd thought it best to keep her in the house while we were gone for the week. She might not like it, but at least she'd be safe.

"No, it's not the cat," Jake said. "It's Paul John. He's in the hospital."

I drew in a sharp breath. "Oh, no! What happened?"

Jake shook his head. "They don't know what's wrong with him. He's running a high fever, and they're doing all kinds of tests."

"Oh, poor Jinx. She must be beside herself." I placed the beach bag on the floor and stepped back outside to drape the wet beach towels on the squat stone barrier separating our cottage from the one next door.

Paul John had been born just six months after Kathy Kay, the last legacy of poor old Lonnie. It was just Jinx and her "men" now—the twins, David Lee and Douglas Dean, and little Paul John. Since Lonnie died, they were pretty much all Jinx lived for. And now, to have her youngest in the hospital, not knowing what was wrong with him, must be worrying her to death.

I went back into the cottage. "Well, I sure hope it's not serious. Poor Jinx! It's always something, isn't it? I think we should be careful about what we say to Kathy Kay about Paul John. You know how she is. She'll worry herself sick about that boy." When Jake didn't say anything, I went on, "So...what do you think about the girls' idea? Going to that Calabash seafood place?"

"I reckon we could do that." He stood at the picture window, staring out at the ocean.

"Great!" I smiled, relieved at how easy that had been. "I'll go make sure the girls are getting ready. You've already showered, I see. It'll only take me a few minutes. I'll just leave my hair wet, and pull it up in a pony-tail. Hey, should I wear the new pink-flowered sundress I bought in that beach shop the other day?"

"Yeah, why not? But wait a minute, Lil."

Already half-way down the hallway, I hesitated. "Yeah, what?"

He turned away from the window. "I think we should head back tomorrow."

"What?" As his meaning hit me, my heart dropped. I returned to the living room. "But Jake, we've got two more days here."

"Jinx needs us, Lily Rae," he said quietly. "She's worried sick about Paul John, and she's got them twins to deal with. She told me she's paying a babysitter fifty cents an hour to watch them so she can go to the hospital. And you know she can't afford that. I think the decent thing to do would be to go home and help her out."

My mouth dropped open, and I spoke without thinking, "Well, can't she just take the twins to her mother's in Russell Springs? For the life of me, I don't understand why she doesn't just move on back there, anyway!"

He frowned. "Now, you know damn well why she doesn't. She's got that job in the front office at the iron factory, and she needs it. Lonnie's pension doesn't pay for jack-shit, and you know it."

"Well, I know for a fact that the sewing factory in Russell Springs is hiring because Norry has been working there for the summer. So, it seems to me it would make sense for Jinx to move where she has family, and that way, she doesn't always have to depend on us, and maybe then we could have a decent week's vacation to ourselves." Even as I spoke, I knew how mean and selfish it sounded. But I just couldn't help it.

Jake's face had turned to stone. "Well, I reckon it's too much to ask for you to stop thinking about yourself for a minute, and instead, concentrate on that poor sick baby in the hospital. But hell! It's not one of yours, is it? You know what? Forget it." He turned back to the window. "We'll stay here until Saturday just as we planned. Have ourselves a fun old time here in Myrtle Beach, and just let Jinx fend for herself. And maybe we'll get lucky, and Paul John won't up and die while we're gone."

I knew he was manipulating me, but even as I realized it, my cheeks burned with shame. I thought of that poor little boy in a strange hospital bed, burning up with fever. It reminded me of Charles Alton, and the anguished look on Mother's face that sweltering May night as she rocked his lifeless body in her arms.

I stood there a moment, staring at Jake's broad shoulders covered in blue cotton. He'd joined the factory boxing team last winter, and his body showed the effects of daily work-outs in the company gym. But his body wasn't the only thing about him that had changed in the past few years. A dramatic change had come over him after Lonnie Foley's death. He'd cut down on the drinking, limiting himself to a beer or two on the weekends. He'd become a decent husband and father. He'd learned to think about others and what they needed, rather than his own needs. In short, my husband had finally grown up.

This vacation, for example. He'd saved for two years for it, faithfully putting money aside so we could really treat ourselves. And he'd actually been having a good time, playing in the ocean with the kids. Taking them to the miniature golf course nearby in the evenings. Paying attention to me, too.

We'd made love almost every night here, and he'd been unbelievably sweet and romantic.

And now, here I was, acting like a spoiled brat because we had to end our vacation a couple of days early.

I approached him quietly and slipped my arms around his waist, resting my head on his back. "I'm sorry," I whispered. "You're right, Jake. We'll go home tomorrow."

***

As Jake checked the oil, I put the last bag into the car and went back into the cottage to tell the girls to go to the bathroom so we could get on the road. It was then that I realized Kathy Kay wasn't in the cottage.

I stood in front of Debby Ann, my heart pounding. "Where's your sister?"

Debby Ann shrugged and didn't answer. She was still sulking because we were leaving early, having parked herself on the couch while me and Jake packed up, and there she still sat with her arms folded, an expression on her face like a mule eating briars.

I lost my temper. "Damn it, Debby Ann, you'd better wipe that frown off your face before I do it for you! *Answer* me! Do you know where your sister went?"

"Down to the beach," Debby snarled, eyes shooting daggers. "What do *you* care? You hate us anyway!"

I ran out the door. "*Kathy Kay!*"

Oh, Lord! What if she went into the water and a big wave washed her out to sea? That child wasn't afraid of anything. Why, it was even possible she'd wandered toward the highway. Oh, *God!*

On the edge of panic, I stumbled past the swaying sea grass on the dunes, my gaze sweeping the crowded beach for a tow-headed little girl. *Oh, God, oh, God, oh God...*

And then I heard it.

"*Mommy, Mommy!*"

I turned to my left. And there she was, Kathy Kay, running toward me, as fast as she possibly could in the sand, blond curls streaming behind her like a mermaid in a fairy-tale. Her little face was as bright as the orb of sun beaming down out of a crystal blue sky.

"Look, Mommy! I found it!" she shouted gleefully. "*I found my starfish!*"

I ran to her, fell to the sand and pulled her into my arms. Thankfully, I buried my face in her silky, sunshine-scented hair. "Oh, honey, you scared me to death. Don't you *ever* do that to me again!" I pulled away to look into her eyes. "You hear me? You don't run off like that again."

"I'm sorry, Mommy." She looked contrite, yet, still excited. "But I couldn't leave 'til I found my starfish for Paul John. And *look*! Here it *is*!"

She held out a small hand and uncurled her fingers.

It was tiny, not more than an inch wide—but Kathy Kay *had* found her starfish.

CHAPTER THIRTY-SEVEN

August 1962

"**K**atydid, would you look at who's getting out of that fancy Cadillac? If that's not Jewell May Foley, I'll eat my hat." I stared at a gangly plain-faced woman in an expensive-looking tailored suit.

Katydid pulled into a parking space at the Holiday Inn in Somerset. She turned off the ignition and tossed me an amused grin. "Eat your Jackie pillbox? I think *not*! And yes, that *is* Jewell. She's a high-end lawyer in Louisville, I hear. Still single and proud of it, I bet."

"Well, that doesn't surprise me at all—not the high-end lawyer part—the fact that she's still single." I adjusted the rearview mirror so I could re-apply my lipstick. "Didn't the boys call her Mud Fence back in high school?"

"Yeah." Katydid reached for her pocketbook on the seat between us. "And it looks like she's still crying all the way to the bank. You ready?"

I smoothed a hand over my new hair-cut. It had cost me $20 to get it cut in a bob like Jackie Kennedy's—and Jake would just die if he ever found out I'd skimmed off the grocery money to pay for it. But it wasn't every day a girl went to her 10-year high school reunion, and I wanted to knock Chad's socks off when he saw me. If he was even here.

"Do I look okay?" I asked Katydid, adjusting the bow on my sage-green hip-banded dress.

"Honey, you look like you just stepped out of Vogue." Katydid opened the car door. "Come on. Let's go in."

My heart raced with anticipation as we walked across the parking lot toward the hotel lobby. The flared hem of my dress swirled playfully just at my knees, and despite the heat of the afternoon, I was glad I'd worn pantyhose. Not only did they make my legs look nicely tanned and trim, I could walk in my black leather stilettos without looking like I was in agony—which I was, but not as bad as I'd be if I were in them bare-footed.

Jake had refused to come with me to the reunion. Not that I'd been surprised about that. And to tell the truth, I was glad he hadn't. How else would I get a chance to get a few minutes alone with Chad?

If he was here.

"I just can't believe Jinx isn't going to be here," I said as we stepped into the lobby, then immediately wanted to bite my tongue. I'd seen the tightening of Katydid's mouth at the mention of Jinx.

My two friends had had some kind of falling-out this summer, but neither one would talk to me about it. I'd tried my best to get them to work it out, whatever the problem was, but neither one would budge. So, I tried to just leave it alone, hoping that sooner or later, they'd patch up their quarrel. Meanwhile, I sure hated being caught in the middle of them. And having to be careful about bringing up one of their names in front of the other.

Inside the lobby, a sign on an easel directed us to Ballroom # 1. As we neared the room, I thought I might faint, my heart was pounding so hard. *What if he isn't here? What if he is? What if he's here, and he acts like he doesn't even remember me? Or worse—what if he really doesn't remember me?*

I stepped into the room with Katydid and saw a large crowd had already gathered. Former classmates stood in small groups, sipping punch from tiny cut-glass cups and catching up with each other, contributing to a loud buzz of conversation throughout the cavernous room. Most of the faces were familiar, yet, ten years had made a difference. Teeth had been capped, scrawny bodies had filled out. There were new hairstyles and modern clothing, stilettos instead of bobby sox and saddle shoes, Italian suits instead of plaid shirts and blue jeans. Crew-cuts were a thing of the past, now replaced by "the duck's ass," a hairstyle made popular by Edd Byrnes's character, Kookie, on "77 Sunset Strip." The women, though, like me, were all trying to look like Jackie with their pillbox hats, flared skirts and three-quarter-inch sleeves.

I was making my way through the crowd when a familiar voice called out from my left. "Oh, my *lord!* As I live and breathe, it's Lily Rae Foster!"

I recognized the voice immediately, even before I spied the plump brown-haired woman with the

Texas-sized grin. "*Daisy!*" I cried out in delight. "I was *hoping* you'd be here!"

"Wild horses wouldn't keep me away, honey!" Daisy held out a pair of fleshy arms. "Come here and give me a *hug!*"

I embraced my best friend from high school, regretting that we hadn't kept in touch like I'd always thought we would--just the usual Christmas cards and an occasional letter. After graduation, Daisy had married Lawless Russell and moved to Indiana. Three kids later, her face was just as cute as it had ever been, but she'd put on about 30 extra pounds since high school. Lawless was with her, and I saw he'd put on some weight, too. Apparently, Daisy had learned how to cook, something she'd always sworn she'd do only when Hell froze over.

"You've just *got* to come up and visit us in May next year, Lily Rae," Daisy gushed, brown eyes dancing with excitement. "Law and I would just be tickled to death. You know, there's nothing in the world like being in Indianapolis during the Indy 500 madness. It'll be a blast."

"That's what I hear." I nodded, adding, "You know, my sister, Norry, just got a job with the Speedway people."

A buxom woman with a platinum blond bouffant caught my attention as she edged her way through the crowd with two cups of punch. I focused on the woman's name-tag, and my eyes widened. It was Justine Franklin (nee) Duba, whom I remembered as a skinny little wallflower with bad teeth, so timid she flinched when anyone looked at her cross-eyed.

Daisy saw the blonde, too, but instead of remarking about the startling transformation, she frowned, her eyes filling with sadness. "Isn't it just *awful* about poor Marilyn Monroe?" she whispered, leaning toward me as if she were sharing a horrifying secret. "You know, she was *naked* as a *jaybird* when they found her. Doesn't that just beat all?"

I was still trying to adjust to the quick change of subject when I heard his voice, and my heart gave a jolt.

"Lily Rae?"

Hot blood rushed to my cheeks. Slowly, I turned and looked up into the expressive brown eyes of Chad Nickerson.

***

It was awkward at first—exchanging small talk with my first love, especially with those knowing eyes of his peering into my soul, or so it seemed.

I told him about my daughters and life in Bowling Green, barely mentioning Jake except to say he worked at the iron factory, and that's why he wasn't here. Chad told me about the latest golf course he'd taken over in Pawley's Island and the house they were having built in Murrells Inlet overlooking the marsh.

Not even close to where we'd been staying two summers ago.

He was as handsome…no, *more* handsome than he'd been in high school. His shoulders, under an expensive-looking suit jacket—probably Italian—were much broader than I remembered, and it was clear by his trim waistline that he kept in good shape, probably with all that golfing he did. His dark brown hair, though no "duck's ass," was longer than he used to wear it, revealing a natural curl I'd never noticed before. And when he smiled…yes, there were those same deep dimples I'd loved to trace with a finger back in the old days.

He spoke with pride about his three children, his eyes sparkling as he described each of them. I wondered what it would be like to see Jake that excited about his two girls. They were both growing like weeds. Debby Ann would be starting 4th grade in the fall, and Kathy Kay was mad with excitement at going off to kindergarten. Not that Jake barely noticed what was going on with his daughters. I bet Chad, as busy as he was with his golf courses, never had "something come up" so he couldn't be there for his kids.

Chad's conversation was littered with "Patty this" and "Patty that," and with a little shock, I realized he spoke about his wife with genuine affection. Why, it was almost as if he'd fallen in love with her!

"Well, speak of the devil," he said in the soft, Carolina drawl he'd acquired, his eyes crinkling with a smile. "Hey, Patty, you remember Lily Rae Foster, don't you? It's Tatlow now, though."

I turned to face Chad's wife, steeling myself for an ugly scene. I'd never forgotten that night over 10 years ago when I'd caught the two of them kissing in Katydid's living room—the mocking smile on Pat-Peaches' face as she clearly enjoyed my pain.

But when our gazes met, Pat-Peaches' face revealed nothing but warmth. She extended a slim hand to me and smiled, exposing a mouthful of even, white teeth. Hadn't they been *decaying* in high school?

"Hello, Lily. You're just as beautiful as you were in high school," Pat-Peaches said in a rich southern accent, sounding more like the genteel mistress of a South Carolina plantation than a little gal raised in the hills of Kentucky. But there wasn't a hint of snobbishness in her manner, I realized. And if she felt threatened by Chad talking to an old girlfriend, she sure didn't show it.

"Thank you," I said, my gaze sweeping over the woman. "And you look just..." I shook my head, searching for the right word. "Drop-dead gorgeous."

The last time I'd seen Pat-Peaches had been in Grider's Drug Store the winter Jake had gone off to boot camp, and she'd been as big as Mammoth Cave in her maternity dress. I'd taken a lot of satisfaction in that, sure that once she had the baby, she'd be a fat old housewife forever. But not only had that not happened, Pat-Peaches, after giving birth to *three* babies, was as slim as a young willow tree, and absolutely radiant. Gone was the thick pancake make-up and over-done eyes. The trampy clothes were a thing of the past, too. Instead, standing there at Chad's side, Pat-Peaches...Patricia Nickerson (nee) Huddleston...looked like the ideal wife of a successful young businessman in a silver-blue pleated dress of Tricel with a blouson bodice and banded waist. Her hair, russet-red as when she'd been a teenager, was caught up in an sophisticated French roll, revealing a long, slender neck that reminded me of an elegant swan.

Chad smiled down at his wife, and my heart gave a twinge at the obvious adoration in his eyes. "She *is* drop-dead gorgeous, isn't she?" he said softly, devouring her with his gaze.

Pat-Peaches blushed and with an abashed smile, gave him a playful swat on the bicep. "Oh, stop it, you Irish devil! Look! They've opened the buffet line. Shall we go fill our plates?"

He nodded, and then turned to me. "Will you join us, Lily?"

"I...uh..." My gaze darted around the room, searching for Katydid or Daisy—*anyone* that could rescue me. I couldn't take another moment of this, watching those two together. Dealing with the feelings triggered by their happiness.

It could've been me. It should've been me. If I had stayed with Chad...if I'd given in to him and let him make love to me, I'd be where Pat-Peaches is now. In a happy marriage. With a man who loves me. Really loves me.

"I can't," I said, then rushed on to cover my bluntness, "I came with Katydid, so I've got to find her. We promised to sit together."

Chad glanced at Pat-Peaches. "Hon, go on and get in line. I'll get us a table."

"Okay, baby." With another warm smile at me, she turned to go, then hesitated and added, "It was lovely seeing you again, Lily."

I watched her move through the crowd, smiling graciously at everyone and engaging them in conversation just as if she'd never been the class whore at all. And the way everyone was responding to her, it was like *they* hadn't remembered it, either.

"Lily," Chad said.

He reached out and took my hand, sending electric sparks skating up my arm and straight into my heart. I gazed up at him, my throat tightening. For a long moment, he stared down at me, a solemn expression on his face.

"Are you happy?" he asked, his voice graveled with emotion.

The knot in my throat began to swell. I was seconds away from tears, from falling apart.

Happy? How can I be happy when I'm supposed to be the one you love? The one you were supposed to live your life with?

What would he say if I just blurted that out? I imagined him sweeping me up in his arms and strolling out of the Holiday Inn, away from Pat-Peaches and the life he'd built with her. Walk away from it all, from his wife, his kids, his golf courses.

He squeezed my hand, still peering deeply into my eyes. "I know it's none of my business," he said. "But I think about you a lot. I mean, it's funny how life worked out, isn't it? I always thought you and I...well..." He gave a shrug. "I know I was the one who screwed things up between us, putting pressure on you, and then turning to Patty because you wouldn't..." He shook his head. "All water under the bridge, isn't it? And you know, I can't imagine life now without Patty and the kids..." His voice trailed away. He held my gaze for a long moment.

I managed to bring a smile to my lips. "Of *course* I'm happy," I said, hoping the catch in my voice wouldn't betray me. "Everything worked out *exactly* as it was meant to."

CHAPTER THIRTY-EIGHT

November 1963

*D**ear Lily,*

Can you believe it's been <u>nine years</u> since we've seen each other? It's a damn shame, isn't it? You'd think Eddie could get transferred to Fort Knox, wouldn't you? But <u>no</u>. I swear the Army searches out the most <u>god-awful</u> places they can find to send us. Except for Germany, it's been one hell-hole after another—Fort Sill, Oklahoma...Fort Polk, Louisiana. Not to mention <u>Texas</u>, for God's sake. And now, here we are at "Fort Lost in the Woods." That's what everyone calls Fort Leonard Wood. And believe you me, that's <u>not</u> an exaggeration. We are deep in the boonies out here. Not a decent department store within a hundred miles, I tell you!

Well, enough about my incredibly boring life these days. At least, <u>Davy</u> seems to like it here in the boondocks. He's playing Little League on post, and as long as he's got some *kind of ball in his chubby little hands, he's happy as a pig in shit.*

So...I guess you're wondering about the book I've sent you-- Betty Friedan's "The Feminine Mystique." Honey, it will <u>blow your socks off</u>! Talk about a wake-up call for American women! This Friedan chick tells us we don't have to settle for being just a housewife or mother anymore. Not that I have, of course. You know me...I've always been something of a rebel, and thank God, Eddie has never tried to force me to be something I'm not, but I couldn't help but think of you as I read this book. If any woman in the world needs to read it, it's <u>you</u>, my dear, Lily. I kept thinking about that letter you wrote me a few years ago when you'd started writing that romance novel. And then that idiot-husband of yours said something to make you shove it into the trash or something. That's such <u>bull-shit</u>! I get furious all over again, just <u>thinking</u> about it. I mean it, Lily, you <u>need</u> to read this book!!! I'd bet my eye-teeth that as you're reading this letter right now, you're ironing clothes or changing a diaper or washing dishes...something like that, anyway. Well...maybe not changing a diaper...unless you've got news you haven't shared with me. Anyway, <u>whatever</u> it is you're doing for that husband of yours, stop it, sit your ass down on the sofa and start reading Betty Friedan's <u>hot damn</u> good book.

Seriously, Lily, you owe it to yourself to go after your dream, hon. And if that dream is to be a romance writer, more power to you. I promise, when your first book comes out, I'll be <u>first</u> in line to buy it. XOXOXO

Love ya,
Betty

I smiled and shook my head. That Betty! She hadn't changed a bit. Such a know-it-all! I folded up the letter and tucked it into the pocket of my jeans, then turned back to the ironing board, my gaze skating over the laundry basket of clothes to rest on the book on the coffee table.

Betty's letter *had* aroused my curiosity. I'd dearly love to sneak in a chapter right now, but it was going on one o'clock, and Jake, on the day shift now, would be home shortly after four. Half of what was in the basket were his work clothes, and I had to get them done. If I hurried, maybe I could find time to read a few pages before the girls got home from school at four. If not, who *knew* when I'd get any free time? There was supper to prepare and the grocery list for Thanksgiving I needed to start on.

For the first time since we'd moved back to Kentucky, Mother and Daddy were coming to Bowling Green for Thanksgiving dinner. It was going to be extra special because my brothers and Norry were coming, too. Landry had called from Louisville last night, and said he was bringing his girlfriend, Annette. And even before he told me his exciting plans, his voice had said it all. My big brother was in love. And about time—he would soon be turning 32.

With one more longing glance at the book, I turned back to the basket of wrinkled clothes. "Well, Betty—*both* Bettys--you're just going to have to wait." I grabbed one of Jake's tan work shirts and placed it on the ironing board.

The hot iron hissed as I moved it over the dampened collar, and the starchy-pleasant scent of cotton floated up from the board. Actually, if I were to be honest, I sort of liked ironing because it was a good opportunity to watch television while I worked.

I'd become hooked on "As the World Turns," and faithfully watched it every day. Keeping my gaze fixed on the TV screen, I deftly flipped over Jake's shirt to iron the back.

On the TV screen, Nancy was sipping tea with Grandpa in their living room. "I have some very interesting information," she said.

I sighed. I knew what was coming. Bob had invited Lisa to Thanksgiving dinner, which meant nothing but trouble for the Hughes family.

"I'd rather entertain a rattlesnake," I muttered, pressing the iron over a particularly stubborn wrinkle in the tail of Jake's shirt.

Suddenly, an odd whistle cut off Nancy's voice, and startled, I looked up to see the soap opera had been replaced by a CBS News Bulletin. A male voice began speaking—Walter Cronkite, it sounded like.

"Here is a bulletin from CBS News. In Dallas, Texas, three shots were fired at President Kennedy's motorcade in downtown Dallas..."

I gasped, clutching my stomach as it dropped in free-fall to my feet.

"...the first reports say that President Kennedy has been seriously wounded by this shooting."

Walter Cronkite appeared on the screen. "This is Walter Cronkite in our News Room. There has been an attempt, as perhaps you know now, on the life of President Kennedy..."

Oh, no! Not our young, handsome JFK! Walter Cronkite went on to talk about the few facts they knew, which wasn't much. Governor Connelly of Texas, had also been wounded, and both he and the President had been taken to Parkland Hospital.

I shook my head, tugging anxiously at my hair, my stomach churning as I waited for more news. But then, incredibly, CBS returned to "As the World Turns."

As if everything was still normal. As if nothing had happened to rock the world on its atlas.

On wooden legs, I walked over to the sofa and sank into it, my gaze fastened on the television screen where the soap opera continued. Cold, despite the heat of the wood stove and the knitted wool cardigan I wore, I rubbed my hands up and down my arms. Tears blurred my eyes. *Dallas.* It figured something like this would happen in Texas. Those hotheads down there had hated JFK from the get-go.

The phone shrilled out, and I jumped. It was Jinx. "Oh, God, Lily, did you hear?"

"Yes, I just can't believe it. It's just so awful! Why would anyone want to kill JFK?"

"The Communists are probably behind it," Jinx said grimly. "Cruel bastards! Have you heard from Jake? Do you think he knows?"

I shook my head. "I don't know. Unless the foreman heard and told the guys in the factory. Maybe I'd better call him?"

"Yes, I would. This is a national crisis. He needs to be home with you. I wish..." She stopped, and I sensed she was choking back a sob.

"Jinx, bring the kids and come over here," I said. "You shouldn't have to watch this alone. And if he..." I stopped myself. *No, JFK won't die. He's got to be okay. He's our president.*

"Are you sure you don't mind?" Jinx asked, her throat sounding thick with tears.

"Of *course* I don't mind. Come on over as soon as the kids get off the school bus, okay? I bet they'll be let out early."

When I hung up the phone and turned back to the TV, I saw that the soap opera had been interrupted by taped footage of JFK's motorcade leaving Love Field in Dallas. Probably just moments before the shooting happened. Jackie looked so

pretty in her light-colored suit and boxy hat.
And they both looked so happy.

Oh, poor, poor Jackie.

***

Just as I reached for the phone to call Jake
again—the lines had been busy when I'd tried
before--Walter Cronkite slipped his glasses on and
read from a sheet of paper, "From Dallas,
Texas...the flash, apparently official...President
Kennedy died at..." He took off his glasses. "...one
p.m. Central Standard Time..." He glanced up at an
unseen clock on the wall. "...two o'clock Eastern
Standard Time...some..." He glanced up again.
"...38 minutes ago." He then put his glasses back
on, and seemingly overcome with emotion, looked
down with a slight shake of his head.

I slowly hung up the phone and sat on the edge
of the sofa, my trembling hand covering my mouth
as tears streamed down my face. I'd known the
announcement was coming. I realized now I'd
known it from the beginning, from the very first
announcement about the shooting. But still, when
Walter Cronkite said the word, "died," my stomach
had plunged, and now, my heart felt as if it had
crumbled into dust.

My tears were not just for Jackie and those poor
little ones, Caroline and John-John. But for the
world. What kind of world did we live in that would
murder the best leader America had ever had? One
thing was for sure, and it didn't take a scholar to
figure it out. This was more than the murder of a
president. It was the murder of a country's
innocence.

I heard Jake's key in the lock as footage from
Dallas continued to run across the TV

screen—dazed-looking policemen, dismayed onlookers, shots of the Texas School Book Depository, from which authorities believed the lethal gunfire had come. It was a nightmare. A national nightmare.

Without any memory of actually walking across the room, I found myself at the door as Jake stepped inside. I saw by his face that he knew. His skin was pale as milk, his eyes haunted.

"Oh, Jake…" I broke into sobs, throwing myself into his arms. "It's just so awful! *Why*? How could anyone do such a horrible thing?"

He wrapped his arms around me, silently holding me close. I felt his lips touch the top of my head, and despite all the pain and horror this day had brought, I was comforted by the warmth of him, the even thud of his heartbeat beneath my ear. As I clung to him, my heart welled with love. He might not be perfect, but he was mine. And when the chips were down, he was here for me. The thought brought Jackie to mind again, and I sobbed harder. *Oh, that poor, poor woman. The horror she must've felt as those bullets ripped into her husband, splashing her with his blood.*

After a long moment, Jake drew away from me and gently tilted my chin up so he could look me in the eyes. "Lil, hon. You've…" He cleared his throat once, and then again, staring off at the wall as if he couldn't quite meet my gaze. "Sweetheart, you've got to be strong for me. I've got something to tell you. Something bad."

"I kn…know!" I stuttered. "I've been watching it since it happened. Oh, Lord, Jake! The *kids*! Do you think they know? Surely the school will let them out early. They let *you* out early." I saw then that Jake had tears in his eyes. Tears! My heart gave a twinge. He hadn't even *voted* for JFK. Thought he was too damn liberal. But yet, here he was *crying* at the news. "Oh, honey…" I hugged him to me. It was my turn to do the comforting.

Gently, but firmly, Jake pulled away, took me by the arm and led me over to the sofa. "Sit down, Lily Rae. This isn't about JFK." He sat down next to me and took my hands in his.

I stared at him. "Then what is it?" When he didn't say anything, terror stabbed through me. "Has something happened to one of the girls?"

He shook his head. "No, they're fine. I called Jinx and asked her to pick them up at school. We've got to head to Russell Springs."

I shook my head before he finished speaking. "Why? What's going on? Wh…?"

Jake pressed two fingers to my lips to stop me. "Shhhhh…you've got to listen to me, Lillian." His eyes were pleading, his mouth a thin, bleak line.

Lillian. My heart plummeted. He never called me Lillian unless he was dead-serious. I met his gaze. "I'm listening. Tell me what's wrong."

"I got a call at the factory from your father. Landry was in a car accident early this morning outside of Elizabethtown. He was on Rt. 61 on his way home to Opal Springs when a drunk driver crossed the center line and hit him head-on. I'm sorry, Lily. He was killed instantly."

I blinked. Landry? *Landry?* I began to shake my head. No. Jake was wrong. He had his signals mixed up. *JFK* died today, not Landry. Not sweet-tempered, good-hearted Landry.

"You're wrong," I said. I wrenched my hands out of his and jumped up from the sofa. "Daddy is wrong! Someone's got their signals mixed up, that's all."

403

On legs that felt like toothpicks, I paced the small living room. I whirled around. "I just talked to him last night on the phone. Why would he be heading home today? He's coming for Thanksgiving *next* week! You know why?" I glared at Jake, suddenly furious at the look of pity on his face. "He was going to ask Annette to marry him this weekend. He had a special night planned...dinner at this fancy restaurant. He *bought* the *ring*, Jake! He told me he's going to order a bottle of wine and drop the ring in her glass, just like in the movies..."

"Lily, hon..." Jake said softly, taking a step toward me.

"*No!*" I stamped my foot in fury. "God*damn* it! Quit looking at me like that. It's not *Landry!* My brother is not *dead!*" My stomach churned. My blood had turned to ice water.

Jake came closer, his hand outstretched, his face etched with sorrow. I wanted to scream, but the lump thickening in my throat wouldn't allow it.

Slowly, Jake took me in his arms, his hand cupping the back of my head. I sucked in a ragged breath. "He was going to ask Annette to marry him," I whispered.

And then I began to cry softly against his work shirt.

***

Another gravesite at Poplar Grove. Last time, it had been Lonnie, Jinx's husband. Last time, Landry had been one of the mourners. Impossible to believe he was gone now, his broken remains relegated to that gleaming blue casket resting over a yawning hole dug out of the red Kentucky clay, waiting to be lowered after the mourners finished the second verse of "Rock of Ages."

It was a beautiful late autumn day with sunshine and a cold gusty wind that stirred up leaves of orange and crimson and sent them dancing across the graveyard in frenzied dervishes. The skirts of the female mourners billowed and whipped, and the men and women who were foolish enough to wear hats had to hold onto them for dear life.

Dry-eyed, I watched Landry's coffin being lowered into the ground next to Charles Alton's grave. I knew I should be crying. That's what you were supposed to do at funerals, after all. But I couldn't cry anymore. I'd always heard that pain was sometimes too deep for tears, but I'd never believed it.

I believed it now.

The entire country was in mourning, I knew. President Kennedy had been buried at Arlington Cemetery yesterday. The day before, Lee Harvey Oswald, the accused assassin of JFK, had been shot on TV before my tear-stained eyes, and I'd barely comprehended it. On Friday when Walter Cronkite broke into "As the World Turns" to deliver the horrifying news about the assassination, I couldn't have imagined how things could get worse.

Now, I just wanted to go back in time. Back to my grief for a beloved, but distant man, the leader of my country. The grief I'd felt for him was nothing to what I felt for Landry. My sweet, tender-hearted brother, the rock that had been there for me throughout my childhood, was gone forever.

Brother Joe Bob, looking like he was at death's door himself, wheezed his way through one last prayer for Landry's soul, and with a mumbled "amen," I looked up and saw that Daddy was already leading Mother back toward the line of cars parked along the south side of the graveyard. Edsel and Norry, their faces pale as winter, filed behind them. An irrational anger swept over me.

What was *wrong* with my parents? It was their *child* they were leaving behind here. How could they be so damn accepting about death? I wanted to rush over to Mother, grab her by her frail arm and give her a shake. *How can you lose two children, Mother, and still maintain your faith in God? What gives you that kind of strength and courage?*

But I already knew what her answer would be. She would say something about God's will and how He never gives you more sorrow than you can take. Same old mumbo-jumbo Southern Baptist bull-crap, I thought bitterly.

Jake's hand tightened on my arm. "You ready to go, Lily?"

I glanced over at the church to my right—the church of my childhood. So many memories inside that clapboard building—Sunday School classes, Vacation Bible School afternoons, Christmas programs with the choir, giggling with Daisy during the god-awful tedious sermons on those sweltering August Sunday mornings. I hadn't stepped foot into the place since Lonnie's funeral—until today. And I knew in my heart that the next time I walked through those doors, it would be to attend another funeral. I refused to even think about whose it would be. One thing I was sure of, though. There was nothing inside that church for me.

"Hon?"

I turned slowly and looked at Jake. A gust of wind pierced through my wool coat, and I shivered.

"Let's go," Jake said, guiding me toward the car. "There'll be hot coffee on at your mother's."

"No." I stopped and turned to him. "I want to go pick up the girls, and then I want to go home. Not to Mother's. Back to Bowling Green."

Arrah Wanna's Melt-in-Your-Mouth Cookies

1 cup white sugar
1 cup powdered sugar
1 cup butter
1 cup oil
2 eggs
4 cups flour
1 tsp. cream of tartar
1 tsp. soda
2 tsp. vanilla
1 tsp. salt

Mix dry ingredients and add the rest. Chill one hour. Roll 1 teaspoon dough into a ball. Press down with glass dipped in sugar. Bake 8-10 minutes at 375 degrees.

CHAPTER THIRTY-NINE

July 1969

I tapped furiously on the Smith-Corona I'd
rescued from a yard sale last August, breathing in its
oily, inky scent—a scent that never failed to put me
into a state of excitement. If someone asked me
why, I probably wouldn't have been able to explain
it, but I figured it had something to do with
freedom. I felt free when I typed on the Smith-
Corona, free to unleash my creativity and get it
down on paper.

I'd started the new romance novel last
September when the girls went off to school, and
every afternoon between 1:30 and 3:30, I'd worked
on it. By the time Debby Ann and Kathy Kay got
off the school bus at 4:00, the typewriter was put
away in its case in my closet, and I was in the kitchen
preparing their after-school snack.

The novel had been inspired by a week-long
visit with Norry who worked in the business office
at the Indianapolis Speedway. At 26, Norry was the

only female public relations representative in the Speedway office, and was quickly building a name for herself in the racing world. Last August, she'd invited me and the girls up to stay in her gorgeous apartment in Speedway, complete with a community swimming pool, which might as well have been Disneyland as far as the girls were concerned. It hadn't been easy dragging them out of the pool, even for the tour of the Indianapolis 500 track that Norry had arranged for us. But that day at the track had been the first glimmer of a novel idea for me. I hadn't said a word about it to anyone, but a week after returning home, I found the Smith-Corona at a yard sale, and knew it was a sign. I had to write that romance novel!

Up until May, the only two people in the world who knew about it were Norry and Betty. It only came out into the open when a registered letter with the return address of The Indianapolis Motor Speedway arrived one morning containing four tickets to the race on Memorial Day Weekend. The girls had been beside themselves with excitement, and even Jake had been impressed. But when Norry wanted us to come up early so I could have a tour of Gasoline Alley, it all came out about the novel. Jake's reaction had been pretty much what I expected—amazement followed by patronizing amusement—but I'd been prepared this time, and easily deflected his condescending remarks with an acid retort.

"Ridicule all you want, Jake Tatlow, but I'm going to do what I've been wanting to do all these years, and this time, your mean little remarks aren't going to stop me. And you just wait and see. I'm going to get a book published. There's a romance publisher in Canada called Harlequin, and that's where I'm aiming to sell to...or I'm going to die trying."

He'd been so flabbergasted at my outburst that he hadn't uttered another word about it. We'd all gone to the Indianapolis 500 and sat on the main straightaway in seats that usually sold for $50 a piece to watch Mario Andretti get the checkered flag. But even that hadn't been as exciting as the tour around Gasoline Alley that Norry took me on a few days before the race. There, I'd got to meet famous drivers like Peter Revson and Dan Gurney...and even the handsome Italian, Mario himself—and although I could only talk to them through a fence because of the "Men Only" policy of the famous garage area, it was still thrilling. Actually getting to see the workings of the drivers' garages had been enough to fire up my imagination so I could add vivid new scenes to **Swedish Passion**, my story about a Swedish race car driver and a journalist from Indianapolis.

And now, here I was, writing the final chapter. From the radio on top of the refrigerator, Neil Diamond's "Sweet Caroline" came on. I glanced up at the Corvette clock on the kitchen wall and began to type faster. Betty would be here within the hour, and I wanted to be able to type "The End" and have the stack of manuscript pages ready to hand over to her. Of course, Betty would be my first reader.

Brad sighed and his eyes re-focused on the bright blue race car as it pulled into Victory Lane at the Indianapolis Motor Speedway...

The back door squeaked open, and 16-year-old Debby Ann sauntered into the house, long-legged and trim in her paisley purple bikini, her body slathered in baby oil mixed with iodine in the hopes of attaining a tan just like the ones sported by the California girls in **Teen Magazine.**

Casting a glance over at me, she blew her bangs out of her eyes, ala Sally Field in "Gidget" and made a bee-line for the refrigerator. I hid a smile and kept typing. Although Debby Ann's new heroine was Peggy Lipton from "The Mod Squad," she couldn't quite shake the mannerisms she'd picked up from Sally Field.

Grabbing the Tupperware container of iced tea, Debby said, "How's the book coming along, Mommy?"

"Almost done," I muttered, my eyes fixed on the tiny keys splatting onto the paper. "Be sure and put that top back on the pitcher the right way. Last time, I spilled it all over the cabinet because it was loose."

"I didn't do it," was Debby Ann's automatic reply, accompanied by a *Geez-aren't-you-an-idiot* roll of her eyes. "When's your friend coming?" From the decorative bunny rabbit cookie jar on the counter, she grabbed one of Great-Aunt Arrah Wanna's sugar cookies and began munching.

"Soon."

Debby Ann took a long draw of iced tea from a pale pink Tupperware tumbler and ran her fingers through her long, stick-straight brown hair. "I can't wait to meet Davy. I just hope he's not a drag. Did I like him when we were babies?"

I suppressed a sigh, stopped typing and looked up. "You got along fine with Davy when you were babies. Maybe it was because you were both brats."

She rolled her eyes again and tried to hide a grin. "Well, *God!* Tell it like it *is, Mother!*"

"That's what I just did."

She put the top back on the pitcher and shoved it back in the refrigerator. "Well, I'll be in the back. Call me when they get here."

I eyed her curvy little bottom as she sash-shayed toward the back door. "I don't suppose I can convince you to put some clothes on before they get here?"

She glanced back, her eyes big and brown under her thick, long bangs and gave me a saucy smile. "Are you *kidding*, man?"

"I'm *not* a man!" I shouted, wincing as the screen door slammed behind her. If Jake were here, he'd jerk a knot in her pretty little behind and make her change clothes. But I didn't have the time or the energy to argue with my eldest. I had to get this book finished.

I began to type again, but before I could finish one sentence, the front door opened, and a shrill scream erupted from the living room, followed by the sound of thumping footsteps. It was as if a herd of elephants were being driven through the house.

Blond-headed Paul John burst into the room, his grinning face grimy with dirt. "Miss Lily, tell her to stop! She's got a lizard!"

Twelve-year-old Kathy Kay appeared behind him, her face just as filthy and her eyes sparkling with glee. In one hand, she held a wriggling lizard. "Ooooh, *ooooob*," she taunted. "Mr. Big Shot is afraid of a itty-bitty little lizard!"

"Get that thing away from me!" Paul John screamed, running out the back door.

Kathy Kay followed behind, laughing uproariously. Nothing had changed between those two, still best friends despite their gender difference. Probably because Kathy Kay was such a tomboy. Or maybe it was because Paul John was such a sissy.

I typed faster.

...Oh, but there is another lovely lady here who is waiting for her kiss. Sven's wife, Laura."

The phone rang. I ignored it.

"Sven Johannsen is also joined in the winner's circle by his young adopted son, Stephen, and of course, it was announced here last week that there is going to be a new addition to the Johannsen family in mid-December. Won't that be a nice Christmas gift? Word has it that Sven is hoping for a girl who'll look just like her mother..."

It kept ringing. Finally, my fingers stilled on the typewriter keys. *"Damn!"*

If it's a salesman, I'm going to have a conniption fit! I got up from the kitchen table to answer it.

"Hello!" I barked. "Oh." The sound of Mother's voice on the line brought immediate regret, and my tone gentled. "Hi, Mother. Is everything okay?"

"Well, now, I thought you'd like to hear the bit of news I heard at the Key Market this mornin', Lily Rae," Mother said. "Bit of sad news, though, I reckon."

"What is it?" I longingly eyed the sheet of paper in the typewriter. So close...one more paragraph and I could type "the end." But if Mother had bad news, and needed to share it, listening was the least I could do. No doubt, one of the old folks on the ridge had died in their sleep.

"Remember that boy you used to go with in high school? That Nickerson feller?"

My heart froze and my throat went dry. "Ch...Chad?" I croaked.

"That's the one," Mother said. "Poor feller. Geraldine Coffey told me that his wife, a Huddleston girl, I recall, died yesterday, and they're bringing her back home to be buried in Russell Springs."

Relief surged through me, followed immediately on its heels by remorse. Pat-Peaches, *dead?* I remembered the couple at the high school reunion—mutual adoration shining on their faces.

"Oh, that's awful," I managed to say. "What happened? Do you know?"

Mother's voice lowered as if she were sharing a shameful secret, "Breast cancer, I reckon. It took her fast. Geraldine said they opened her up, and it had already spread all over her insides. There wasn't nary a thing they could do for her."

I shook my head, a hollow feeling in the pit of my stomach. "Oh, those poor kids. And Chad! Lord, he must be torn apart."

"I reckon so," Mother said. "Well, there's apt to be a notice in the **Times Journal**. Once we find out where they're laying her out, we can send flowers, I reckon. Lily Rae?"

"Hmmmm?" I thought I'd heard a car pull up out front. I walked around the table, pulling on the phone cord so I could see out through the picture window. Sure enough, a red Dodge Charger had parked in front of the house.

Mother cleared her throat and then said briskly, "I reckon there's something to them exams…the ones you do yourself. I don't truck with folks using their bodies like it's a playground, but I reckon you oughta start doing that exam, Lily Rae." She lowered of her voice. "They say the best time is after your monthly friend is done with its visit."

I smiled. "Yes, Mother. I've been doing a self-exam for a couple of years now." I watched as a tall, flaming redhead unpeeled herself from the driver's seat. Could that be Betty with that lop-sided short haircut? Why, she looked like she'd just stepped out of a Carnaby Street fashion magazine.

The passenger door opened, and a gangly teenage boy dressed in blue jeans and a tie-dyed T-shirt crawled out of the car. His dark brown hair fell in luxurious waves to his shoulders. David. The last time I'd seen him, he'd still been in diapers.

"Well, alright then," Mother said. "I'll let you go now."

"Thanks for calling, Mother," I said, and then added quickly, "I love you."

There was a slight hesitation on the other end of the line, and then Mother said, "I love you, too, Lily Rae. Bye, bye, now."

Torn between sadness for Chad and his family, a welling of love for Mother, and excitement at seeing Betty after all these years, I hung up the phone and rushed into the living room.

By the time I opened the front door, Betty was halfway up the sidewalk, looking young and beautiful, dressed in a Mod hot-pink paisley top, white hip-hugger shorts and strappy vinyl sandals--just as full of spit-fire as she'd ever been, I could see, even more now that she was a fiery redhead instead of a strawberry blonde.

"Come here, you!" I called out with a delighted grin.

And we were in each other's arms, shrieking and squealing like teenagers.

***

The sun had just come up when I tip-toed out of the bedroom on my way to the kitchen to make coffee. I'd had a horrible night's sleep. Well, make that simply a horrible night. There had been very little sleep involved.

I walked as quietly as I could through the living room to the front door, mindful of the three lumps of teenage bodies on the floor in sleeping bags…well, two teenage bodies and one 12-year-old body. With such a tiny house, there hadn't been any other way to figure out the sleeping arrangements. I'd given the girls' room to Betty and made two separate beds on the living room floor—Debby Ann and Kathy Kay in one, and Davy…David, he now insisted on being called…in the other. Of course, the kids had spent half the night talking, and with the thin walls, I'd heard every topic of conversation ranging from how cool the movie "Easy Rider" was to whether or not Twiggy was beautiful. It was just a good thing Jake was working nights this week or he would've surely raised the roof.

But it wasn't only the kids who'd kept me awake. It was anxiety. Just before turning in last night, I'd hauled the Smith-Corona out of its hiding place and finished that last paragraph, typing "the end" with a feeling of satisfaction that must've rivaled what Hillary felt when he planted that British flag on the top of Mt. Everest.

Betty's light was still on, so I'd picked up the stack of manuscript pages—all 250 of them—and tapped on her door. "Well, here it is. I don't know if it's any good or not, but you know what? At this point, I just don't care. I love it. I love the characters and I love the story. But if you don't, I want you to tell me, Betty. Tell me what's wrong with it, and I'll fix it." I paused, and looked Betty in the eye. "I aim to make writing my career, come hell or high water. And I trust you to tell me whether it's worth sending out or not."

For once, Betty hadn't made a joke. She'd taken the manuscript, a serious look on her face. "I'm honored to be the first to read your book, Lily. And I *will* be honest with you. Even if what I have to say isn't something you'll want to hear. Okay?"

I nodded and left the room. And that's why I hadn't slept the night before. Because I kept picturing Betty reading my book, and I couldn't help but stress over what she was thinking of it.

I grabbed the newspaper from the sidewalk and opened it to the front page, only to see the glaring headlines about more casualties in Vietnam. So senseless! All those American boys dying over there. *Hey, hey, LBJ, how many kids did you kill today?* Maybe those anti-war marchers had the right idea. If I were 15 years younger, I'd join them, by golly.

I quietly made my way back through the living room and stepped into the kitchen, then froze at the sight of my manuscript on the table. Heart thumping, I walked over to it, and placed the newspaper down beside the stack of paper. A sheet of notebook paper lay on top of the title page, and I immediately recognized Betty's scrawl. I sank down into a chair and grabbed the note with trembling fingers.

Lily!!!!! Or should I just call you the next Jacqueline Susann? I knew you'd be up before me, and I also knew you'd be about to shit your pants, waiting to hear my verdict on "Swede's Passion." Well, honey, you can stop worrying. THIS BOOK IS FANTASTIC!!!! I swear to God, Lily, I couldn't put it down. It was three AM when I read the last page. Where did you learn to tell a story like this? Honey, how do you know so much about Swedes? My God, that man just jumped off the page! And Laura! She wasn't your typical beautiful but stupid heroine. She was an ordinary woman with spunk! Oh, Lily, I don't know what more I can say to convince you that you've got to send this book to Harlequin. As soon as possible. If you don't, I swear to God, I'm going to have one of your famous conniption fits. Now, I'm going to bed. Don't wake me until at least ten.

And remember, Goddess of Excellent Romance, I like my coffee strong and black.

Love, Betty

By the time I'd finished reading, I had tears running down my face. But I was grinning like an idiot.

Lily's Meat & Cheese Loaf

2 lbs. ground beef
1 ½ cup diced Velveeta cheese
2 eggs, beaten
1 large onion, chopped
1 large green pepper, chopped
2 teaspoons salt
1 teaspoon pepper
1 teaspoon celery salt
½ teaspoon paprika
3 cups milk
1 cup dry bread crumbs

Combine ingredients in order given. Mix well.
Press into 2 greased loaf pans and bake at 350
degrees for 1 ½ hours.

CHAPTER FORTY

"So, you've barely said a word about Jake," Betty said, lighting a Virginia Slim and inhaling a deep lungful. "Is everything okay between you two?"

On the asphalt between our lounge chairs, a transistor radio played Three Dog Night's "One." It was a cloudless day with temperatures in the nineties. The sounds of summer were all around us at the public swimming pool—Top 40 music, kids shrieking, the thumping spring of the diving board, splashing water—and always, somewhere, the sound of childish voices calling out "Marco" followed immediately by "Polo!"

I took a sip of my Fresca before answering Betty's question. "Oh, it's been fine. Jake is a different person than the one you knew back in Texas."

I glanced over at Debby Ann and David just to make sure the two horny teenagers hadn't slipped off somewhere to be alone. I figured if Betty and I kept the two teenagers where we could keep an eye on them, we'd save ourselves some grief later. Betty and David had been here less than 48 hours, and already, there were signs of a romance budding between him and Debby Ann.

I frowned. *Just look at that little flirt!* Debby sauntered over to the snack bar in her skimpy bikini, flipping her long brown hair and laughing back at David who followed her like an eager puppy, his long, wet hair pulled back into a sleek pony-tail.

Down on the other end of the pool, Kathy Kay and Paul John engaged in horse-play rough enough to frequently catch the attention of the teenage lifeguard, forcing him to give a harsh blow on his whistle and cast a dark scowl their way.

I reached for my Coppertone. Feeling Betty's gaze upon me, I turned to her. "What? You don't believe Jake's changed?"

She lifted her gold bug-eye sunglasses, cocking one neatly-plucked brow. "Oh? You mean he hasn't brought any girlfriends home lately?"

I felt a flash of irritation, but it faded away as fast as it came when I saw the teasing light in my best friend's eyes. Typical Betty. She couldn't help but say whatever came to mind. And it wasn't as if she was going to forget what had happened in Texas.

"Not a one," I said with a grin. I rubbed Coppertone onto my already tanned legs. "Come on, Betty. You've got to admit you see the change in him, don't you? Wasn't he nice to you last night?"

"He was a perfect gentleman," she agreed, taking another draw on her cigarette. "And much more personable than I remember. Maybe you're right. Maybe he *is* finally growing up."

"Well, I should hope so," I said dryly. "After all, he's 37. So, how is Eddie? I was sorry he couldn't take leave to come with you."

Her smile faded. "Well, he *did* take leave, but he went to California to see his parents. When I first planned this trip, he *was* going to come with me, but then…well, the military has a way of changing your plans." She looked at me. "He has orders for Vietnam, Lil. He ships out two weeks after we get home."

Fear rippled through me. "Oh, no. I'm sorry, Betty."

She shrugged and glanced away. "What can you do? It was bound to happen. I'm actually surprised it took them this long to send him there. And it's not like I haven't been through this before. You remember."

I nodded. "Are you staying on at Fort Benning?"

"Oh, yeah. Why uproot Davy for a year? And as busy as I am with the Officer's Wives Club and all the jock stuff he's involved in, the year will go by in a flash."

I reached out and squeezed her hand. "I know you'll be fine. And I'll pray that Eddie gets back safely."

"Thanks. I just hope this stupid war ends soon," Betty said. "There's way too many young guys dying over there. But I'm not worried about Eddie. With his rank, he won't be on the front lines."

Just then Creedence Clearwater Revival's "Bad Moon Rising," came on the radio, and I couldn't help but think it was a bad omen. But that was probably the Irish in me. Apparently, Betty didn't feel the same way because she started singing along with it, interrupting herself in mid-line to say, "Oh! Here comes Debby and Davy with our hamburgers, and thank God! I'm starving!"

A few minutes later, halfway through her burger, Betty glanced over at me. "So, this barbecue thing is tomorrow night? And where is it?"

I licked a smudge of mayonnaise off my finger. "Near Glasgow. It's an annual tradition at Jake's company. The boss opens up his mansion for the peons. Gives us a chance to see how the rich people live. But it's actually kind of fun. Wait'll you see Roxanne Dawson. That's the boss's wife. Every year the employees take bets on which young stud she'll set her sights on. It was Jake the first year we went." I shook my head, reaching for my Fresca. "Funny thing is…she's not getting any younger. But she still thinks she's Ann-Margret or something. I almost feel sorry for her. It's really pathetic to watch her flirt with these young guys."

"More power to her," Betty said, crumbling up her hamburger wrapper and tossing it into her beach bag. "It's probably the highlight of her year. And you said your friend, Jinx, will be there? I can't wait to meet her."

"Oh, yeah, she'll be there. I told you, didn't I? About her husband getting killed on the job? I guess the boss still feels guilty about it because Jinx is invited every year. Hey, I'll have one of those, too, if it's okay?" Betty held out her package of Virginia Slims and I took one. "I think you'll like Jinx." I inhaled as Betty lit my cigarette, and then released a stream of smoke. "She's fun…but not as fun as you, of course."

"Well, I would think not." Betty grinned and lit her cigarette. Blue smoke ribboned out of her nostrils. "But hey, how could I *not* like a girl with a name like Jinx?"

***

Midway through the barbecue, I realized I'd been right about one thing and dead wrong about another. It hadn't taken Roxanne Dawson long to corner one of the new guys in the pool and play her special version of Tic-Tack-Toe on his bare chest, all the while with his pregnant wife looking on, nearly in tears. I wanted to go to the young girl and tell her not to worry, that Mrs. Dawson was just joking around like she always did; it was all in good fun.

But I'd be lying, and I just couldn't do it. To this day, I still wondered if Jake had had a little fling with Roxanne. If not, it wasn't because he hadn't wanted to. The memory of what had happened on the way home the night of that first barbecue was lodged in my mouth where a permanent bridge now took the place of three teeth.

I have you to thank for that, Roxanne. I glared at the woman, and then looked back at Jinx and Betty, sitting at the poolside table with me.

And here, I thought, *is what I was dead wrong about.*

Jinx and Betty couldn't stand each other. That had been obvious almost as soon as I'd introduced them. Just after I arrived at the Dawson mansion with Jake, Betty and all the kids, Debby Ann and David had headed straight for the buffet table. So the teens weren't with us when I saw Jinx and led Betty over to introduce her. The three of us were engaged in small talk when a scruffy-looking young man with waist-length blond hair, a handlebar moustache and a goatee ambled by us with a brimming plate of barbecued pork and potato salad.

Jinx, who'd grown more politically conservative with each passing year, gave him a dirty look and said loud enough for everyone nearby to hear, "Who let the damn hippies in?"

"Shhhh!" I hissed. "That's the Dawson boy. Home from UK for the summer."

The Dawson kid either hadn't heard or was used to his appearance causing a negative reaction in the older generation. He'd moved on, oblivious.

Jinx looked mildly embarrassed, but barely lowering her voice, added, "I don't care. He's still *disgusting*! Those long-haired beatniks make me sick. Only reason he's in college in the first place is to dodge the draft, I'll bet. He's probably majoring in how to overthrow the country and burn American flags."

A strained silence followed Jinx's outburst. My cheeks burning, I tried to think of a way to fill it, but before I could say a word, Betty turned to Jinx with a cool smile. "Well, you surely don't expect the *rich people* to send their sons to Vietnam, do you? Not when we have blue collar boys and blacks to go fight for us. Why, that wouldn't be the American way, would it?"

Confusion crossed Jinx's face, and I could see she was wondering whether to take Betty serious or not. But just then David and Debby Ann walked up with their filled plates.

Betty smiled and put an arm around her son. "Jinx, I'd like to introduce you to my son, David."

Jinx, taking in David's long dark hair, stiffened, and a blush spread across her cheekbones. Seeing her discomfort, Betty widened her smile, but her blue eyes remained chilly. "He's a little too young to be a draft-dodger, but give him a couple of years. If this damn war is still going on, and he's made up his mind not to fight, I'll drive him to Canada myself."

Oh, God, I thought, taking a hurried sip of rum-spiked tropical punch. *Let the fireworks begin.*

"*Mom!*" David shrugged off her arm and gave her a disgusted look. "I *want* to fight for my country!"

Jinx's face had paled at Betty's statement. She gave David a tight smile. "Good for you. I guess you're more like your daddy than your mama." She gave Betty a scornful look, then turned back to David. "You might want to think about getting a hair-cut, though, young man. If you want people to take you seriously."

"I *like* his long hair!" Debby Ann said hotly, glaring at Jinx. "Come on, David." She grabbed his arm. "I don't want to talk about that stupid war! That's all grown ups talk about anymore." She led him away.

I watched her go, torn between calling her back to reprimand her for sassing Jinx or to try to defuse the tension between my two friends. I decided on the latter. "Well, I'm starving!" I said brightly. "Who wants to go with me to the buffet table?"

Both women ignored me. Jinx, her jaw tight, locked gazes with Betty. "Lily tells me your husband is a lieutenant colonel in the Army. What does *he* think when you talk all that anti-war stuff?"

I held my breath. If Jinx wasn't careful, Betty just might knock her block off. Jeez, they'd just met! How could things have gone downhill so quickly?

But Betty maintained her cool, giving Jinx a brittle smile. "You don't know my Eddie. He's a breed apart from most men. He actually *encourages* me to have my own opinions and speak my mind about them."

427

"Even if your opinions are anti-American?" Jinx shot back.

Betty's eyes narrowed. "Is it *anti-American* to be against American teenagers dying in rice fields while rich politicians play their power games in Washington? I don't think so."

That did it. I knew I had to do something or it was very possible one of my friends would end up in the pool, fully-dressed. I grabbed Betty's arm. "Jinx, why don't you find us a table while we go scout out the food?" And I practically dragged Betty away.

"Why didn't you tell me she's a goddamn Republican?" Betty hissed. "God! You'd think she's got a cattle prod stuck up her ass."

I sighed. "So much for you two liking each other."

***

It was a beautiful summer night. At least, Betty and Jinx could agree on *that*, I thought, gazing up at the millions of stars glimmering like diamonds on a black velvet tablecloth. Nowhere else in the world could compete with Kentucky when it came to a star-lit night. Even Texas, as open and barren as it was, couldn't produce a star show like the Blue Grass state could. And somewhere up there...

My gaze turned to the crescent moon hanging over the lake, looking like one of those whimsical photo sets at the county fair. Somewhere up there, Astronauts Buzz Aldrin, Neil Armstrong and Michael Collins were rocketing their way toward that moon, and if everything went according to plan, would be landing on it. Somehow, that thought made me feel very small, just a spec of inconsequential life on this planet in the middle of a vast universe.

Uneasiness filled me. What on earth did I think I could offer this world with my silly little love story? Who did I think I was for even *trying* to get a book published? Maybe Jake was right. Maybe I was reaching in vain for those stars.

Betty, at the table next to me, must've sensed my thoughts. "Why so quiet, Lil? Are you plotting a sequel to 'Swede's Passion?'"

Before I could answer, Jinx, on my left, leaned toward me, grinning. "Oh, did you finish it, Lily Rae? I remember you were close. When do I get to read it?"

"Well, I…" I didn't remembering offering to let Jinx read it. And I wasn't sure I wanted to. Much as I considered her a good friend, Jinx had a tendency to always try to "one up" me, and something told me if I got the book published, she wouldn't be able to contain her envy. So, if she read the novel before I sent it off, she'd probably find all kinds of things "wrong" with it.

"I read it," Betty said, and even to my ears, she sounded smug. "And it's wonderful."

Uh oh. Here we go again. The last hour had been tolerable, with only a slight undercurrent of tension between my two friends. A pop band had begun to play on the upper terrace, and couples were dancing on a plywood floor that had been set up on the other side of the pool. Jake and many of the other men had excused themselves at nine o'clock to head into the house for the annual poker game. Of course, the young man Roxanne Dawson had set her sights on tonight wasn't one of them; he was dancing with her to a cover of Deep Purple's "Hush" as his wife sat at a table with several other young wives, wearing a stiff smile and pained eyes.

The pool had been taken over by teens and the younger kids, among them all of our kids. It was just past ten o'clock. The poker game would probably go until well past midnight, so that meant at least two more hours left to referee between Betty and Jinx.

"Well, if you let *her* read it, you've got to let me read it, Lily," Jinx said, trying to inflect a teasing note in her voice. But it didn't come across that way at all.

"I'm sure she would, Jinx," Betty cut in before I could respond, "…if it wouldn't be terribly bad luck. I know a thing or two about the publishing industry, and it's a well-known fact that if you let more than one friend read an unpublished manuscript, it'll never get published."

I stared at her. "What?"

Betty gave me a look that screamed out *shut up and go along with me on this, birdbrain!* "You remember, Lil. It was in that writer's magazine I gave you. The interview with Philip Roth. Or was it Kurt Vonnegut? I forget. Anyway, it was one of those big name writers who said it."

I looked at her, impressed, almost believing her myself. "Yeah, I forgot about that." I turned to Jinx with a contrite look. "I'm sorry, Jinx. It might be a stupid superstition, but…well…" I shrugged. "I need all the good luck I can get. But when the book comes out, I promise, you'll be the first to get a free autographed copy."

"Oh, great." Jinx rolled her eyes. "And if it *doesn't* come out, I just don't get to read it, right?"

Fear rippled through me. Jinx obviously didn't believe I'd get the book published.

"Have a little faith, Jinx," Betty said, her eyes shooting daggers. "She'll get the book published.

Like I said, it's wonderful. It's as good as anything Jacqueline Susann puts out."

Jinx's mouth gaped. "Oh, Lord! It's *that* steamy?"

Hot blood rushed to my cheeks. "*No!* It's not at *all* like Jacqueline Susann's books." I'd read **Valley of the Dolls** two years ago, and loved it. But I could never *ever* write sex scenes like that! "Betty is just pulling your leg."

Betty snickered. "Well, that kissing scene between Sven and Laura was pretty yummy. I'm betting you'll be giving Miss Jackie a run for her money one day."

Jinx gave me a searching look. "Out of all the people I know, I'd say you're the least likely to write steamy novels, Lily Rae. You always seem so prim and proper."

Betty gave me a wink. "That's because you're not privy to her sex life with Jake."

"And I don't *want* to be," Jinx snapped, sending a dark scowl in Betty's direction.

I sighed. Leave it to Betty to say something to get under Jinx's skin. Would this night *ever* end?

"*Mommy!*"

I turned toward the voice. A towel-wrapped Kathy Kay ran up to the table, Paul John close behind her. They looked so cute with their wet blond curls matted to their heads, blue eyes dancing with excitement.

"Mommy," Kathy Kay burst out in excitement. "This maid lady said we can make our own sundaes over in the summerhouse...just for the kids. Can we go, huh?"

"Yeah, Mom," Paul John echoed, his eyes pleading with Jinx. "Make-your-own sundaes! For *free!*"

The two children waited breathlessly for permission, and their identical expressions of yearning looked so comical that the three of us couldn't help but burst out laughing. Once the two kids got our permission, they let out simultaneous "Yays!" and ran off in the direction of the summerhouse.

Betty followed them with her eyes, an amused smile on her face. "Now, there goes two peas in a pod. If I didn't know better, I'd swear they were brother and sister."

I laughed. "Oh, *please*! Kathy Kay better not hear you say that. She's planning on marrying Paul John someday." I signaled a waiter circulating through the tables with a tray of tropical drinks.

It wasn't until I chose a pina colada and lifted the glass to my lips that I noticed the odd silence. Only the sound of the band singing "Along Comes Mary" floated in the summer night. I looked from Betty to Jinx. "What's wrong?"

No one spoke. Betty wore an odd expression on her face as she stared at Jinx, a speculative gleam in her eyes. Jinx seemed to be having trouble looking at either one of us, and her face was as white as paper. Not only that, but she'd become fidgety, twisting a diamond ring on her finger, her eyes darting around the pool area, almost as if she were searching for an escape route.

"Did I miss something?" I said.

Jinx shoved her chair away from the table, making a horrible scraping sound on the flagstone deck.

"Excuse me," she said. "I've got to go to the restroom." And she hurried off in the direction of the terrace.

I stared after her, and then turned back to Betty. "Do you know what the hell just happened?"

Betty studied me a moment, then looked away. "How long ago did Jinx lose her husband?"

I didn't even have to think about it. "Twelve years ago. I was at Lonnie's funeral when I went into labor with Kathy Kay. Why?"

Betty toyed with the straw in her tropical drink. "So, Paul John was born after his father died?"

"Yeah, that's right. I remember finding out she was pregnant the day of the funeral." I studied her. "Betty, why are you so interested in Jinx and Paul John?"

She looked away. "Nothing I can put my finger on. I just..." She shook her head. "I'm just not crazy about her, Lil. I don't trust her. I don't feel like she has your best interests at heart."

"Oh, come on, Betty!" I protested. "Just because she doesn't share the same political viewpoints you do doesn't mean she's a bad person. I've known the girl since grade school! I think I can trust her."

Betty was silent for a long moment. The band on the terrace started singing The Box Tops' "The Letter." Betty stared at a lone couple locked in each other's arms in the pool. Her straight white teeth nibbled on her lower lip as if she were deep in thought.

Finally, she turned and met my gaze. "Just be careful around her," she said, her blue eyes solemn. "I've known women like her, Lil. They'll stab you in the back the first chance they get. Especially..." she hesitated, and then went on, "...if you have something she wants."

Great Aunt Ona's Sweet Potato Cake

1 ½ cups raw grated sweet potatoes
1 ½ cups vegetable oil
2 cups sugar
4 eggs, separated
4 tbsps hot water
2 ½ cups sifted flour
3 tbsps baking powder
¼ tsp salt
1 tsp vanilla
1 small can crushed pineapple

Combine oil and sugar and beat until smooth. Add egg yolks and beat. Add hot water and flour which has been sifted with baking powder and salt. Stir in sweet potatoes, vanilla and pineapple. Beat egg whites until stiff, fold in mixture. Bake in two 9-inch pans at 350 degrees for 25 or 30 minutes.

Coconut-Walnut Icing

1 large can evaporated milk
1 stick Oleo
1 cup sugar
3 egg yolks, beaten
1 tsp vanilla
1 cup coconut
1 cup chopped walnuts

Combine milk, Oleo, egg yolks and sugar. Cook about 12 minutes, stirring constantly over low heat. Add coconut, nuts and vanilla.

CHAPTER FORTY-ONE

"**H**ere it is." I ran a hand over the cool, smooth rock face in front of me. "He painted it the day before Valentine's Day to surprise me." I smiled, my index finger tracing the large red heart inscribed with "Lily Rae & Chad, February 14, 1951."

"He sounds like he was a real romantic guy," Betty said. "That's so sad about his wife."

My smile faded. "Yes. Poor guy. My heart just aches for him."

"Life is hard sometimes," Betty said. Then, as if to shake off the gloom that had fallen, she took a step backward and glanced around at the enormous rock formation arching over us. "This is an amazing place! Thanks for bringing us here."

I grinned, my heart filling with pride. "Everybody says that about Rock House Bottom. Isn't it just gorgeous?"

On the drive home from Glasgow last night, Betty had expressed an urge to see Russell County, and since this was their last day here, all of us had gotten up at the crack of dawn and headed for Opal Springs, but not before dealing with a tantrum from Debby Ann, the silent treatment from David and an unusual snappish mood from Kathy Kay. The teens had begged to stay home because they couldn't *possibly* miss **American Bandstand**; Andy Kim-somebody was supposed to be on it, and Debby would just *die* if she missed it, and everybody knew that Mother and Pa Pa didn't get good reception on their TV out in the Russell County sticks. Her pleas hadn't fooled me one bit. I knew the *real* reason they wanted to stay home. Jake was doing some over-time at the factory, and the two teenagers would have the house to themselves. **American Bandstand**, my hind-end. They just wanted an opportunity to neck. Or do *more* than neck. I had no intention of giving them that opportunity.

The teenagers weren't the only ones disgusted with me. Kathy Kay was upset because she hadn't got the chance to ask if Paul John could come along to Opal Springs; it was way too early to call over at Jinx's before we left. Needless to say, there had been a lot of sullen silence in the back seat for the hour and a half drive. But once we arrived at my old home, Mother's chocolate gravy over hot biscuits had cheered everyone up.

Betty had been on her best behavior with Mother and Pa Pa, having realized from years of conversation with me just how conservative they were. She hadn't uttered one cuss word the entire morning in Mother's presence—a record for her, I guessed.

Mother seemed to have aged since I'd last seen her. Had there been that much gray in her hair two months ago? Every time I came home and saw how my parents were aging, it brought a twinge to my heart. It had been 17 years since I'd left this place I'd once called home. Debby Ann was only three years younger than I'd been on the day I'd married Jake and made my way with him through the woods to his parents' home. A life-time ago, it seemed.

After washing the dinner dishes, I suggested we drive out to Rock House Bottom, a natural arched bridge in the southern end of Russell County, carved thousands of years ago by the force of the Cumberland River. It was the most beautiful place I could think of within an hour's drive, not to mention that it held a lot of memories for me from high school.

Rock House Bottom, known as a local "lover's lane," was frequented back then—and probably still--by hormonal Russell County high school students looking for romance; I'd spent lots of memorable hours there with Chad. Good memorable hours, mostly, except for the night we'd broken up.

I turned back to the heart Chad had painted on the rock wall so many years ago. Smiling, I traced my hand over it, my eyes misting with tears. So much time gone by. Two teenagers, so in love back then, had grown up and gone their separate ways. I felt sad for them—those teenagers. They'd been so idealistic, so sure their love would last forever.

That Valentine's night when he'd brought me here to see the heart—the memory of it was still vivid. That night had been the first time he'd tried to do more than kiss and engage in light petting. And I'd *wanted* to do more. If I hadn't been such a "good girl," I might've given in that night. Instead, a year later, after the break-up with Chad because I wouldn't "go all the way," I'd turned around and given my virginity to Jake without barely a thought—and that had set the course of my life, bringing me to this moment.

The moment of truth.

I glanced over to check on Kathy Kay. The 12-year-old squatted at the edge of Jim Creek, tossing stones into the water, an expression of deep concentration on her heart-shaped face. Debby Ann and David had climbed onto an automobile-sized rock, and sat with their bare legs dangling, holding hands and talking quietly. Betty stood a few feet away, her hands planted on her hips, gazing off at the Cumberland River making its slow, tranquil way toward Tennessee.

I took a deep breath. It was time to ask the question I wasn't sure I wanted an answer to. All night long, I'd tossed and turned next to a gently-snoring Jake. Wondering. Thinking back. Remembering things that hadn't seemed all that significant before, like Jinx's anger at that very first Danson barbecue as she watched Roxanne flirting with Jake. Even then, through my pain, I'd been surprised at how livid she'd become. Almost as if *she* was the betrayed one, not me.

And then, there was the time in Myrtle Beach when Jinx had frantically called Jake about Paul John's sudden illness, and we'd had to cut our vacation short. I remembered being outraged at her gall, wondering why she hadn't called her parents in Russell Springs for help.

And finally, there was Katydid, and the falling out she'd had with Jinx seven years ago. What had caused it? Could it be that Katydid had found out something that she couldn't bring herself to share with me? Something about Jinx and Jake?

A pleasant breeze wafted off the river, sifting through my shoulder-length hair, cooling the sudden heat on my face. Could I have been so stupid not to have seen what was happening under my nose all these years? Could I have been so *blind*? It was time I faced the truth.

I looked over at Betty. Her lop-sided, Aqua Net-sprayed, Irish Setter-red hairstyle hadn't budged in the breeze. She was looking down, rummaging in her handbag for her cigarettes.

I cleared my throat. "Betty, I need you to be straight with me."

She looked up, her hand growing still in her bag. The darkening of her eyes told me she knew exactly what I meant. I waited for her answer, barely breathing.

She glanced over at Debby and David, and then to Kathy Kay. A resigned look crossed her face and she gave a sigh. "Okay. Just let me grab a cigarette, and we'll talk."

A moment later, we'd situated ourselves on another big rock far enough away from the kids that they couldn't overhear, yet close enough so we could keep an eye on them. Betty lit cigarettes for both of us. I sat quietly, waiting for her to begin.

She took a drag on her Virginia Slim, fastened her eyes on the moss-covered river, glinting in the afternoon sunlight. "Okay. What is it you want to know?"

I gazed at the lit cigarette in her right hand. It trembled in her grasp. "What did you mean with that remark about Jinx? About not trusting her. What is it you suspect?"

Betty studied me, eyes wary. "Hon, it's probably nothing. You know how I am. I always think the worst of everyone. And you know Jinx and I didn't get off to a good start. It's probably my dislike that's affecting my thinking."

I bit down hard on my bottom lip and then said bluntly, "You think Jinx and Jake are sleeping together, don't you?"

I watched Betty absorb the question. Laugh, I silently urged her. *Laugh it off and tell me that's the most ridiculous thing you've ever heard. That I'm over-reacting.*

She didn't laugh. She looked away from me and stared out at the river, lifting her cigarette to her lips. Instead of taking a draw on it, though, she held it motionless for a long moment. Finally, her hand dropped, and she turned to me.

"Lil, the last thing in the world I want to do is hurt you. You know that, don't you?" Her eyes glimmered with sadness.

The knot in my throat thickened. My stomach felt as if a bowling ball had lodged inside it. I tried to speak, but found there wasn't enough air in my lungs to drive the words. Betty reached out and took my hand, squeezing it hard.

Finally, I found my voice. It came out scratchy and hoarse. "I know you don't want to hurt me. I'm sure Katydid didn't want to hurt me, either. She knows. That's why she and Jinx haven't spoken to each other in seven years." I looked up and met Betty's gaze. "I need a friend who'll be straight with me. No matter how much it hurts. I *need* to know the truth, Betty…even if it destroys my life."

"You can't get the truth from me," Betty said softly. "You know there's only one person you can go to for the truth."

"But you *do* believe it, don't you?" I said. "You think Jinx is having an affair with my husband."

Slowly, Betty nodded. "Yes, that's what I think. But I hope I'm wrong."

I swallowed hard. It was all or nothing now. I might as well get it over with. "And you also think...that Paul John is Jake's son, don't you?"

"Oh, *God*, Lil!" Betty jumped down from the rock and strode a few feet away. She whirled around and stared hard at me. "You've *seen* Paul John and Kathy Kay together. They look like *just alike!* The blonde hair, blue eyes. Even their *noses* are identical. Yes, Lil. *Yes.* I think it's likely that Jake is Paul John's father." Tears welled in her eyes. "I'm *sorry!* I never should've said anything last night. I should've just kept my big mouth shut."

I felt a strange calm settle over me. I climbed down off the rock and went to her, slipping my arms around her. "Thank you," I whispered. "For being honest with me."

She hugged me tight. "We don't know it's the truth," she said softly. "Maybe I'm letting my imagination run away with me. Maybe if you talk to Jake, he'll..." Her voice faded away.

I gave a soft, bitter laugh. "What? Deny it? Yes, I'm sure he will."

Our gazes locked. Betty's eyes were still filled with tears. "I'm sorry," she said again.

I shook my head. "Don't be. You tried to tell me 15 years ago that I needed to leave him. That I deserved better. And I chose not to listen." Betty's face blurred in front of me. I blinked away my tears. "Maybe it's time I started listening."

***

To everyone else, it was a Sunday afternoon like any other. Well, that wasn't quite true, I realized as soon as the thought went through my mind. It wasn't just *any Sunday* that an American space ship had entered the moon's orbit and was getting ready to land on its dusty gray surface. And it wasn't just *any Sunday* that my 16-year-old daughter had spent most of the day in her bedroom, crying her eyes out because the boy she loved had gone away.

And it definitely wasn't just *any Sunday* that I would confront my husband, asking him if he'd been carrying on a 12-year affair with a childhood friend and classmate. I still wasn't sure I could do it.

It was now just after five p.m., and me and Jake, like millions of other Americans, were sitting in the living room, our eyes glued to the TV as the Apollo 11 lunar lander, manned by Commander Neil Armstrong, descended toward the moon's Sea of Tranquility.

"Seventy-five feet…" reported the crisp, calm voice of Buzz Aldrin, the lander's co-pilot. "Lights on…down two and a half…40 feet…picking up some dust."

Jake looked toward the hallway and yelled, "Debby Ann, get the hell in here! History's happening! You need to see this!"

Debby Ann's door opened, and the voice of Lesley Gore spilled out from her record player. *It's my party and I'll cry if I want to…* For some reason, every time Debby Ann went into a funk, she played Lesley Gore.

"I'm *busy!*" She called out, her voice slightly hoarse from all the crying she'd been doing. "Besides, I don't *care* about any *stupid astronauts* and whether or not they land on the *stupid moon!*"

Jake's mouth dropped open. It took about two seconds for him to understand what he'd just heard. *"Get your ass in here right now, Debby Ann!"*

I tried to defuse his anger. "Jake, she's upset." I placed my plate of barely-eaten Cheez-Whiz and crackers on the coffee table, my stomach roiling. So much for pretending the afternoon was a normal one.

He threw me a dark look. "*Your* fault! Didn't I tell you it was a mistake to invite that highfalutin' Kelly woman and her horny little son to stay with us?"

I stiffened and glared at him. "You did *not*! And if you had, do you think I would've listened to you?" I looked back at the grainy images on the television, half expecting Jake to explode.

But his gaze was fixed upon the hallway as Debby Ann stomped toward the living room. She entered with the latest issue of **Teen Magazine** in her hand and a black scowl on her face. "*God*! What *is* this, a dictatorship or something?" She threw herself onto the sofa on the other side of me, just as far away from her father as she could possibly get. "How come you're not forcing Kathy to watch it? What makes *her* so special?"

"You're not too big for me to set your britches on fire, girl," Jake growled, reaching for his glass of whiskey and Coke on the coffee table. The ice rattled as he took a long draw from it.

"I'm sure she's watching it over at Paul John's, Debby," I said quickly, still trying to keep the peace. I'd had second thoughts about Kathy going over to Jinx's, but had decided to go ahead and let her. After all, if my suspicions were true, there wouldn't be many days left together for the two best friends.

"Now, look here, girl." Jake pointed at the TV. "We're about to witness history in the making, and one day, your grandchildren will ask you what it was like to watch the first moon landing, and you'll be able to tell them all about it."

I glanced at Debby Ann. She'd defiantly opened her magazine and was leafing through it, her jaw rigid. Stubborn as a mule, that one. A younger female version of Jake.

"Honey," I placed a hand on her bare knee. "Daddy's right. This is one of those times you'll remember all your life. Like what you were doing when JFK was assassinated. You don't really want to miss it, do you?"

She shrugged and flipped a page in the magazine. "When are we going school shopping?" she asked sulkily.

"*Hush!*" Jake threw her a dark look. "Can't hear the goddamn TV!"

Buzz Aldrin's voice came from the television. "...contact light...okay. Engine stop." He paused, then said, "Houston, Tranquility Base here. The *Eagle* has landed."

The grainy images on the TV screen looked as if they were being broadcast from...well, the moon.

Debby Ann shut her magazine with an audible smack and stood. "Well, they've landed. Can I go back to my room now?" She glared at her father, waiting for his response.

"*Jesus Christ!*" he snarled. "Get the hell out of here, then!"

Lifting her chin haughtily, she turned and headed toward the hall.

"She's turning into such a little bitch," he said, loud enough for her to hear. He reached for his Winston in the ashtray on the coffee table. "That girl is becoming one huge pain in my ass."

I looked at him for a long moment, and then said quietly, "I wonder if your son will be a pain in your ass when he's her age?" I studied him, waiting for his reaction.

He stared at the TV, still showing grainy, ghostly images of the United States landing craft on the moon's surface. He held his cigarette suspended between the table and his lips, and for a second, I thought I saw his hand tremble. His Adam's apple bobbed as he swallowed, and slowly, he turned his head and looked at me.

"What the hell did you say?"

A cold blade of despair sliced through the pit of my belly. Until this very moment, somewhere deep inside, I'd held onto a tiny shred of hope that I was wrong. That Betty was wrong. Now, looking into Jake's wary blue eyes, that hope dissipated like a thin stream of smoke. I knew in my heart I was looking at the face of a guilty man—a man who knew he'd done wrong, and had been found out.

"You heard me," I said, my voice barely above a whisper. "Your son. Paul John. You know...the baby you conceived with Jinx."

The blood drained from his face. He stared at me silently. Finally, he jabbed his cigarette into the ashtray, grinding it viciously into the glass. "What did that bitch Betty put into your head?" he said, his voice thick with fury. He grabbed his glass and got up from the sofa. At the doorway to the kitchen, he stopped and gave me a scornful look. "I don't know what you've been drinking, Lily Rae. Or what kind of fairy tales Betty Kelly has been telling you, but she's about as full of shit as that old outhouse we used to have on Opal Springs Ridge." He gave a harsh laugh and disappeared into the kitchen.

I sat on the couch, my eyes fixed on the TV screen. From the kitchen, I heard ice clinking into a glass. I knew what he was doing. Buying himself some time. Trying to come up with a good story to cover his ass. Well, that was fine. I'd give him enough rope and let him hang himself.

He returned with a fresh drink and a shit-eating grin on his face. "Christ!" He shook his head.

"You're really something, you know that? That trouble-making Women's Lib witch comes here for a few days, and tells you some bull-shit story that she makes up out of thin air, and you believe her without batting an eyelash. What does that say about our marriage? What does that say about trust?"

I pressed my lips together, forcing myself to remain silent, and stared at the TV, even though there was nothing to see except **The Eagle** sitting there on the barren landscape of the moon. I understood what he was trying to do—trying to deflect the blame from himself and turn it onto me. My only defense was to be silent.

He took a long swallow of his whiskey and slammed the tumbler onto the end table. "I suppose you went running to Jinx as soon as Betty Boop put the idea in your scatter-brained little head. I'll bet she thinks you've finally lost your marbles, doesn't she?"

Here it was. The rope. I turned and looked him dead in the eye. "And if I did? You really don't think she denied it, do you? When she's been in love with you all these years?"

His face paled. He reached for his glass and downed the remainder of his drink. This time, I was certain I saw his hand shaking. "Aw, shit." He ran his hand through his hair. "What kind of crap did *she* put in your head? That girl is crazy as a loon."

Deciding to gamble, I looked at him pointedly. "You tell *me* what she said. You apparently know her so well."

Jake dropped his head into his hands. "Jesus," he muttered. Slowly, he looked up at me. "She doesn't love me, Lil. She loves the excitement of sneaking around. If it hadn't been me, it would've been someone else."

I got up from the sofa. Amazing, I thought. I should be screaming and crying and hurling accusations and threats. That's what the old Lily would be doing. But this one...the one I'd grown into...was just too tired—and too disgusted.

"It only happened a few times, Lil. I haven't touched her in years!"

I headed for the door to the hallway.

"Where are you going?" Jake shouted. "We've got to talk this out."

I felt his gaze on my back, and imagined it to be pleading. But I wouldn't look to confirm it. "I don't think there's anything left to talk about."

"She came on to *me*, Lil. She wouldn't leave me alone. And even after she got pregnant with Paul John, those first months after Lonnie died, she kept calling me...just wouldn't take no for an answer. Lily! Don't you walk away from me!"

I'd reached the hallway. His footsteps approached behind me.

"Lillian, goddammit, listen to me! It didn't *mean* anything!"

That stopped me. Slowly, I turned around and my eyes swept over him.

At 37, he looked even more handsome than he had at 20. His face had filled out, the creases along his mouth deepening into attractive grooves. Tiny crinkles at the edges of his sparkling blue eyes—laugh lines, some people called them—gave him a Clint Eastwood movie-star-ish kind of appeal. His brown hair, grown out from the duck-tail he used to wear now sported long sideburns and longer layers on top. Even Jake wasn't immune to the fashions of The Love Generation.

With a curious detachment, I realized his eyes were sparkling with unshed tears.

He lifted a hand toward me. "You've got to believe me, Lily. It didn't mean *anything*."

I stared at him for a long moment. From Debby Ann's room, Lesley Gore sang "You Don't Own Me"—a song that, under the circumstances, seemed uncannily appropriate.

I nodded. "You're right," I said. "It didn't mean anything. And *that*, Jake, is the problem. *Nothing* means anything to you. Not Jinx, not Paul John. Not me, not the girls, and most of all, not our marriage. In fact, I'd venture to say…there are only two things in this world that mean anything to you. One of them is booze…and the other one is your dick. And I'm tired of playing second fiddle to both."

I turned and walked on down the hall.

There was a brief silence, broken finally by Jake's voice, angry now. "Well, *fuck* you, then, *bitch*! Who needs you? I'm better off without you, anyway. Always *have* been! You're the one who trapped me into marriage—getting knocked up like you did. Don't you forget that! You were just an easy lay for me, and if it hadn't been for your daddy and your sanctimonious brother, I would no more have married you than I would've married my mama's old sow in the pig-sty."

My step faltered, and my heart contracted as if his words were bullets piercing into my flesh. I wanted to turn and slap him for talking about poor dead Landry like that. But some sane part of my brain told me it would be counterproductive to my next step. I straightened my shoulders and kept walking. Outside of Debby Ann's door, I hesitated a moment, taking a deep breath to calm myself, then tapped on it.

"Come in." Debby's voice sounded muffled.

I opened the door. She was face-down on her bed, her face buried in her pillow. "Honey?"

She turned over. Her anguished eyes stared at me from a face streaked with tears. And I knew she'd heard everything.

***

Jake was gone when I stepped back into the living room a half-hour later, and so was his pick-up truck. Either he'd gone to one of his favorite drinking holes, or maybe over to Jinx's house to have it out with her. I didn't care. I was glad he was gone. It would be easier to leave if he wasn't here to stop me.

An hour later, the three of us were packed up and ready to go—Kathy Kay, confused, asking one question after another, and Debby Ann, morose and silent. I tried to placate Kathy with the promise of a stop at White Castle on our way out of town. I couldn't tell her the truth now. Time enough for that, later.

The last thing I did before hustling the girls into the car was to go into the armoire in our bedroom and draw out the old cedar jewelry box from my childhood. I opened it and gently took out the bit of cloth that held the ring of blackberry twig Jake had first given me when we were children. I'd kept it safe all these years. Taking it out of its protective wrap, I gazed at it until the tears in my eyes made it impossible to see. I left it on my dressing table on top of the cloth—along with the gold band he'd bought me in Korea.

It was just starting to get dark after we pulled out of White Castle onto Highway 31 heading toward Russell Springs. That's when I saw it—the quarter moon shimmering above the trees to my right. It wasn't a Shepherd Moon. Not at all like the one me and Mother had gazed at that night on the wharf so many years ago.

All the same, it was calling me home.

Mother's Orange Slice Cake

3 ½ cup sifted flour
½ teaspoon salt
A pound of orange slices candy, cut up
An 8-ounce pack pitted dates, chopped
A cup of margarine or butter
2 cups sugar
4 eggs
1 teaspoon soda
½ cup buttermilk
1 3 ¼ ounce can flaked coconut
2 cups chopped walnuts or pecans

Sift together flour & salt. Combine orange slice candy, dates, walnuts, coconut and add the ½ cup flour. Cream butter or margarine until light; gradually add the sugar while beating. Beat well. Add eggs, one at a time, beating thoroughly after each addition. Combine soda & buttermilk. Add alternately with the flour mixture. Blend well after each addition. Add candy mixture, mixing well. Turn into large tube pan which has been greased & floured. Bake in 300 degree oven for 1 hour and 45 minutes. Combine a cup orange juice and 2 cups sifted confectioner's sugar, pour over hot cake. Cool, then let stand in refrigerator overnight before removing from pan.

EPILOGUE

May 1972
Plainfield, Indiana

"But *Mommy, y*ou absolutely *have* to go to this! You're the local celebrity. How can you *not* go?"

Out of the corner of my eye, I saw Debby Ann at my side, hands on her slim, boyish hips. Her long hair was pulled back into a single braid, and she wore white hip-hugger shorts with a midriff-baring ruffled top of blue and white-checked gingham.

I ignored my daughter's glare and continued typing on my new electric Smith-Corona. From the girls' rooms down the hallway, Pink Floyd's "Dark Side of the Moon" competed with Gilbert O'Sullivan's "Alone Again, Naturally." At the moment, Pink Floyd was winning because Debby

Ann had left her door open when she came out to check the mail. Instead of whatever she'd been looking for, she'd found the letter from Russell County High School announcing the 20th Reunion for the Class of 1952—and the box I'd checked on the RSVP card—"Unable to Attend."

"*Mother!*" She gave an exasperated stamp of her foot. "You're ignoring me!"

With a sigh, I stopped typing and looked up at her. Nineteen years old, and she was still stamping her foot like a two-year-old. It was clear that graduation from nursing school at Ball State University hadn't done a thing to improve her maturity level.

Always the brilliant student, she'd graduated early from Plainfield High School, and without taking a break, entered the two-year nursing program on a full scholarship. Just last week, I'd attended her capping ceremony in Muncie.

I looked at her clenched jaw, and groaned, "I'm on a deadline here, Debby. This manuscript has to be delivered by mid-June, and I'm barely past the first third of it."

Debby rolled her eyes. It was a habit that growing up hadn't broken her of.

"Oh, come *on!* You can't take one measly weekend off to go back to your hometown for your class reunion? Mommy! You haven't seen any of your old friends since we moved here."

And I don't need to, I thought. *Life is just fine and dandy without faces from the past to show up and remind me of what I've left behind.*

It hadn't been easy, those first months on my own. Thank God for Norry. She'd built a house in Plainfield, about ten miles from Speedway—a three bedroom, two bath home—more than enough room for me and the girls to move in with her, and on her

CAROLE BELLACERA

insistence, that's what we'd done. We'd lived there until I saved enough money from my job at the local newspaper—and the advance for my first book with Harlequin—to get our own apartment. Now, six books later—and working on the 7th—I'd put a down payment on a small three bedroom ranch house on the outskirts of town, and along with Kathy Kay, a freshman in high school, we'd moved in March. There were still boxes to be unpacked, but I was under the gun with this latest book. And that was why the class reunion was out of the question.

"Mommy!" Debby Ann dropped her hands from her hips and approached, her expression changing from exasperated to concerned. "Seriously, I'm worried about you. You've been working non-stop since I got home from Muncie. You need a break. And besides, I haven't seen Mother and Pa Pa in ages. Let's just go down to Opal Springs for the weekend, and you can go to the reunion and Kathy can visit Daddy. God knows why she wants to, but that's *her* problem, not mine."

I eyed her. "You should visit him, too. He always asks about you when I talk to him on the phone."

Her brows lowered in a scowl. "Big deal! If he really cared about me, he would've made it to my graduation, don't you think?"

"Come on, Debby. He barely leaves that shack he lives in, much less the state." I pushed away from my desk in the corner of the kitchen and stood. "You want a Coke?" I headed for the refrigerator. "Besides, he sent you that card."

"Big *whoop*! I'll bet Grandma Gladys made him send it."

She was probably right, I thought. Thank God for Gladys. If it weren't for my ex-mother-in-law, I doubted we would've ever seen the monthly child support payment Jake managed to scrap together. After the divorce, he'd quit his job at the iron factory (to avoid alimony payments, I suspected) and moved back to Opal Springs where he'd taken up residence in an old ramshackle log cabin once owned by Gladys's hermit uncle, and was living off welfare and, apparently, drinking himself to death.

"So, come on, Mommy. Will you at least *think* about it? The reunion? I'll bet it'll be a groove. You're a celebrity down there, you know."

"Stop saying that! I'm not a celebrity!" I handed Debby a can of Coke and popped the tab of my own. It opened with a soft hiss.

Debby Ann opened her soda, took a sip and grinned. "You just signed a new three-book deal. Your books are in every drugstore I walk into. Have you already forgotten about that big poster of you and your book cover Grider's Drugs had up last winter? I wouldn't be surprised if they name a street after you in Russell Springs one of these days."

"Oh, hush." Trying to suppress a grin, I moved back toward my desk. "A street named after a romance writer? I doubt it!"

"So, will you think about it, Mommy? *Please?*"

Suddenly the Gilbert O'Sullivan song grew louder as from down the hall, Kathy Kay's door opened. A moment later, she plodded into the kitchen.

The gangly 15-year-old glanced at us from beneath her straight blonde bangs. "What's going on?" She reached for an apple from a bowl on the counter and sunk her perfect white teeth into its tender flesh.

Kathy Kay had turned into a real beauty, a younger version of Cheryl Tiegs, some folks said. People were always telling her she should be a model, but Kathy didn't have the slightest interest in that. Unlike Debby Ann, she'd never owned a copy of **Teen Magazine**, and from the time she'd turned nine, she'd talked about becoming an oceanographer, and as far as I knew, that was still her intention.

Despite all that had happened, she and Paul John had kept in close contact with each other, writing letters back and forth and visiting whenever we made it down to Kentucky. The discovery that they were half-siblings had been a shock that had taken some adjustment, but once they'd come to terms with it, they'd grown closer than ever. I was glad about that. Paul John was a sweet boy, and even though his existence had been the final straw that ended my marriage, I couldn't hold it against him—an innocent child.

"Oh, nothing," I said, fingers poised on my typewriter keys. "Your sister is just trying to bully me into something."

Kathy Kay rolled her eyes and ambled back toward the hallway. "So what *else* is new?"

***

I took a deep breath, smoothed my hands down the creamy white crocheted A-line dress I'd ordered from the Montgomery Wards catalog. My fingers nervously toyed with the strand of pearls I wore around my neck, imitation but good-quality fakes I'd bought at the costume jewelry counter at Blocks department store. I saw my reflection in the glass double doors of the hotel in Somerset, and smoothed an errant strand of hair that had come loose from my top-knot.

Well, here goes, I thought, and pushed the door open. A sign in the lobby directed the Russell Springs High School Alumni to Ballroom A. Why am I doing this, I asked myself as I walked down the richly carpeted corridor. *This is silly. I should never have let Debby Ann talk me into this.*

The last person in the world I wanted to run into was Jinx, and surely, she'd be here. She never missed a party. Rumor had it that she'd married again. A Southern Baptist preacher, of all things. It was a good thing he was a praying man, I thought. He'd be needing a lot of prayers.

Katydid wouldn't be here. She'd up and moved to San Diego after meeting a marine biologist while on vacation out there. They were on their honeymoon right now in Hawaii.

Daisy would probably be here, though, and I was prepared to get my ear talked off, even though she lived close enough to me for us to get together for lunch once or twice a month in Speedway.

Chad? My heart gave a lurch. I was trying not to get my hopes up. He probably wouldn't come. After all, it was the height of the golf season down in South Carolina, and he was probably way too busy to take time out for a stupid class reunion.

Music from the 50's filtered from up ahead—Debbie Reynolds singing "Tammy." I stepped into the ballroom and looked around. Heads turned at my entrance, and I could feel their curious gazes. Was it my imagination, or could I hear muted whispers? Not one face looked familiar. Had they all aged so much in 20 years? Or had I wandered into the wrong room by mistake?

Their stares felt hostile, unwelcoming. Uncertainly, I turned back to the door.

"Lily?" His voice came from behind me in the brief silence between songs. My heart jolted. Slowly, I turned.

Chad stood there, staring at me with his soulful brown eyes, looking a little older and more world-weary than when I'd last seen him 10 years before. But even with his graying temples and the laugh lines at the corners of his eyes, I could still see the high school basketball player I'd dated so many years ago.

"Hello, Chad."

His hand closed around mine. "I was hoping you'd be here," he said with a warm smile.

"I almost didn't come," I said softly. "My daughter made me."

His eyes crinkled, his hand squeezing mine. "Your daughter sounds like a force to be reckoned with...just like another girl I used to know."

As he slipped his arm around my shoulders and maneuvered me through the crowd, a memory drifted through my mind—one of a hot summer's night, the sound of bullfrogs croaking...my feet dangling in the cool pond water of Opal Springs...and the sound of Mother's soft, sweet voice in my ear.

Trust in the Shepherd Moon, Lily Rae. It'll always lead you home.

The End

Meet Carole Bellacera

Carole Bellacera wrote her first novel, "The Vaughn's Daughters," in a loose-leaf notebook, drawing her own illustrations for it at the age of 12. Summers were really boring in a rural area of Indiana in the days before driver's licenses. With both parents working, Carole and her younger sisters, Kathy, and Sharon, had to drum up their own entertainment to while away the hours of the long, hot summers. Kathy and Sharon liked the outdoors, but Carole preferred making up stories in her cozy little bedroom. One summer she wrote a play, and forced her sisters and several neighborhood kids to perform it. (Some probably would remember her as a "control freak.")

In her teens, Carole continued writing novels in notebooks, and some were passed around her high school. Even then, she was eager to read the "reviews" on the blank pages left for that purpose—and luckily, most of them, if not all, were glowing. One of her favorite teachers, Mrs. Regina Scott, wrote a review that encouraged Carole to pursue writing as a career—something she wouldn't do for another couple of decades.

At 16, Carole wrote her best work yet—THE SWEDE, a romance inspired by growing up near the famous Indianapolis 500 race track. (At the time, she was madly in love with race car driver, Peter Revson.) Confident that it would be the next big best-seller, she packed it up and sent it off to **Doubleday.** It was promptly rejected with a form letter–and Carole officially became a professional writer—although she didn't know it yet. At the time, she was too naïve to realize that being rejected was a necessary, though unpleasant, aspect of a writer's life; she just assumed that New York knew what they were talking about, and apparently, she had no writing talent at all, so she gave up her dream. (And discovered boys, and ultimately, a husband.)

Fast-forward to the 1980's. Several momentous things happened that reminded Carole that she *did* have a talent for writing. She went back to college and did well in a creative writing course. This inspired her to start writing a romance novel about a race car driver (of course) and a news reporter. It never got published, but writing it did the job of getting her creative juices flowing again. And then...*drum roll*...something *really* exciting happened. Carole met Princess Di at Andrews Air Force Base. She hadn't wanted to get up early that morning to go to the flight line to see the royal couple arrive, but her friend, Diana, talked her into it. Who knew that meeting would be the start of a real writing career? Carole wrote about the encounter, and months later, the article appeared in the military magazine, **Family**, earning her $100. (And no, she didn't frame it; she spent it.)

Thus, ambition was born. Carole began to get published on a fairly regular basis—and began collecting *a lot* of rejections along the way. This time, though, she didn't let them deter her. Although she was doing well in publishing short fiction and articles, earning credits in magazines such as **Woman's World**, **Endless Vacation** and **The Washington Post**—(even publishing a story about how she met her husband in **Chicken Soup for the**

Couples' Soul), her dream to publish a novel remained elusive for 13 long years.

But finally, in February, 1998, she got the call she'd been fantasizing about from her agent, and a year later, her first novel, BORDER CROSSINGS, hit the shelves, earning glowing reviews and awards such as a 2000 RITA Award nominee for Best Romantic Suspense and Best First Book and a nominee for the 2000 Virginia Literary Award in Fiction. (This book will be reissued in January 2012; read the excerpt on page 451.) Six more novels followed, including the one you just read—LILY OF THE SPRINGS.

Carole is presently at work on a 7th novel, INCENSE & PEPPERMINTS, the story of a combat nurse in Vietnam, and hopes to have it out sometime in 2012.

She lives in Northern Virginia with the most wonderful man in the world, Frank, her husband of 38 years, and is blessed to be the mom of a talented daughter, Leah, also a writer, (www.mommiesneedsleeptoo.com) and a fantastic son, Stephen, and grandma to the two most beautiful boys in the world, Luke, 3, and Zealand, 2.

About LILY OF THE SPRINGS

A note from Carole Bellacera

I lost my mother to non-Hodgkin's Lymphoma in December 1998, just five months before my first novel was published. She'd been my cheerleader since those early days of writing novels in loose-leaf notebooks. In fact, she'd bought me my first typewriter, a Smith-Corona. Even now, I can close my eyes, and smell the ink from that typewriter—it brings back such vivid memories of creativity and hopes for realizing big dreams. But most of all, the remembered scent of that typewriter reminds me of Mommy.

She was too young to die. She'd been such a vibrant part of my life—always loving and vivacious. My friends in high school adored her because she always acted like one of the girls. Even when she became a grandma to my two kids, she'd take them to a water park and go down the slides with them, acting for all the world like she was 12 herself.

All through my years of being a struggling writer, she was there to give me encouragement, to bolster me up when I was down, to encourage me to keep trying and not let those rejections keep me from going after my dream. She was the first person I called when I got "the call" from my agent about BORDER CROSSINGS. It broke my heart that she never got to see that first published novel. She'd been diagnosed in 1993, and towards the end of 1998, the disease took a turn for the worst. But at least she knew I'd dedicated the book to her. I guess somewhere deep inside, I knew she might not make it to hold the book in her hands, so I told her. I'm glad I did.

Since she's been gone, I've done a lot of thinking about her and the 63 years she lived on this earth. I knew bits and pieces of her past—stories she'd told me from her high school days and what it was like growing up in rural Kentucky in the late 40's and early 50's. From looking at her high school yearbooks, I got the impression she'd been a popular girl. (Something I couldn't identify with because I was never popular in school.) Mommy could've had her pick of the boys, but somehow, she ended up with my father—a decent man now, of course—but as a teenager and young man, not exactly what you'd call the all-American, wholesome boy next door. Their marriage was rocky, to say the least, and yet, lasted a good 20 years before they finally divorced. Still, despite all the arguments, the tension-filled silences, the less than stellar behavior, I have no doubt that my father was the love of my mother's life. In one of our last conversations in the hospital, she pretty much admitted that.

Still...I wondered...what would her life had been like if she'd made different choices? Thus, LILY OF THE SPRINGS, was born. Through it, I wanted to give my mother the happy ending she never got in real life. I hope you've enjoyed reading it.

Questions for Reading Group Discussion

❖ When Lily found herself pregnant by Jake, and knowing he didn't want to marry her, were there any alternatives for her? What could she have done differently?

❖ How did having a friend like Betty help Lily to assert her independence?

❖ Some will criticize Lily for sticking out a bad marriage for so long. When would you have left Jake?

❖ Did you feel any sympathy for Jake at all? What about his dysfunctional family and abusive upbringing? Can that excuse or at least give insight into his horrible treatment of Lily?

❖ What did you think of the time period and setting? Was it a more "innocent time" or is that just our nostalgia talking?

❖ How did you feel about the historical events woven throughout the story ... Elvis, JFK, the moon landing?

❖ Do you think LILY OF THE SPRINGS would make a good movie? Who would you pick to play Lily? Jake?

❖ How soon did you start suspecting Jinx was having an affair with Jake?

❖ Did anyone guess that Debby Ann's character was autobiographical (inspired by stories the author heard from her mother, grandmothers and aunts about what a "challenging" child she was. And yes, Debby Ann Kitty really existed. Real name: Carol Ann Kitty.

❖ Discuss Lily's happy ending. Did she get everything she wanted and deserved?

❖ Did Jake get what he deserved in the end?

Coming in June 2012

An excerpt from the reissue of SPOTLIGHT, Carole's second award-winning novel.

Prologue

January 30, 1972
Derry, Northern Ireland

Rain misted the street as ten-year-old Devin O'Keefe pushed his way through the throng. In his right hand he carried an unwieldy sign that had been clumsily painted with five words: NO INTERNMENT. RELEASE CONOR O'KEEFE. It was a sentiment he believed with all his young heart, but he was tired and the sign had grown heavy since he'd joined the anti-internment march several kilometers out of town. They'd reached the middle of the Bogside, the Catholic ghetto where no sane Protestant dared venture for fear of becoming a target in the gunsights of the Provisional IRA.

As the marchers swept past the expressionless British soldiers dressed in battle fatigues and armed with Enfields, a new spirit of camaraderie seemed to pass through the crowd. Devin felt it. It was like an invisible current of electricity surging from one marcher to the next. *Oh, how proud Da would be if he could see me now!*

But his father wouldn't be seeing any of this. He'd been lifted by the Brits five months ago and locked up in the H-Blocks, the jail for political prisoners.

Along both sides of the road, Irish Catholics stood in the rain and cheered the crowd, some of them joining the march. Even priests and nuns were among the throng, many of them carrying banners like Devin's. A few faces along the roadside were implacable, some apprehensive, but most were jubilant. In America, Martin Luther King, Jr., had gathered blacks and whites alike to march upon Washington. Now, the Irish Catholics were doing the same, marching to Deny to win freedom for the oppressed.

Devin stood on tiptoe, searching the crowd for his brother, Glen, and his friend Pearse. His sign brushed a matronly woman's beehive.

She glowered at him. "Watch where you be goin', laddie." She smelled of cheap perfume and sour body odor.

"Sorry, mum. Excuse me, I must get through." He'd spied the black head of Glen up ahead. "Wait up, Glen!" Eagerly, he jostled his way through the crowd. His sixteen-year-old brother hadn't wanted him to tag along today, but Devin was determined to be a part of this historical march for freedom and justice. Stay home with his mum and sisters? No bloody way.

"Glen!"

At the sound of his name, the tall, slender teenager turned. A pained expression crossed his face when he saw Devin. "Jaysus, Devin. Now, didn't I tell you to stay home?"

Next to him, Pearse laughed. "Since when does Devy listen to you?"

Devin brushed past the last of the marchers to reach him. "Bugger you," he said, grinning up at him. "I came anyway."

Glen's brown eyes glimmered with worry. "You hardheaded little imp. Can you never do as I tell you? There could be trouble here today."

Devin shifted the heavy sign to his left hand and held it higher. "I have to do my part for Da. You know that. Sure, maybe this will make the Brits release him. And all the other prisoners as well."

Pearse nudged Glen. "Ah, give the little squirt a break, Glennie. Sure, his heart's in the right place."

Glen stared at his little brother for a moment, then his eyes softened. His hand fastened on the boy's arm. "All right. Stay with us, then. But don't be doin' anything foolish."

Devin grinned. He knew Glen didn't really mind that he'd come. After all, it was for Da.

Glen gave him a sidelong glance. "I thought by leaving you the guitar, it would keep you busy for a time."

"It did. I made up a new song." Devin threw him a teasing grin. "It's about Rosalie." He waited for the blush to spread over his brother's cheeks, and when it did, he laughed. "Ah, she is a nice piece of crumpet, isn't she, now?"

Pearse laughed, shooting a knowing look at Glen. "She is that!"

Glen glared at Devin. "Make up all the songs you'd like about Rosalie O'Connor. It's nothing to me. Anyway, what made you leave my guitar and come join the march?"

Just as Devin opened his mouth to answer, the peaceful Sunday afternoon exploded in chaos. Gunfire. Devin spun in the direction it came from, his eyes searching for the source. But before he could see anything, Glen—or someone—shoved him hard in the middle of his back. He fell to the ground, his face and hands grinding into the pavement. Terrified screams erupted around him. Devin tried to move, but his brother held him securely to the ground. Glen's savage, suddenly adult voice growled into his ear: "Bloody hell! Keep your head down, Devin."

Devin obeyed. Seconds later, he heard a dull thump and felt Glen flinch. A soft sigh whispered from his brother's lips, just inches from Devin's ear. Devin's bowels tightened as an ice-cold fear ate its way through his insides. He knew what this meant.

"No!" With renewed strength, he struggled up. Glen's limp body rolled away. His lifeless eyes stared at Devin, still showing the surprise he must've felt as the bullet entered his head just above the right temple. For a moment, Devin felt weightless, as if his body hovered above the still form of his brother, watching with a detached sort of curiosity. Then reaction set in. It was as if a leaden pipe had plowed a hole through his stomach. He gasped for breath, reaching a shaking hand toward the ominous trickle of blood oozing from Glen's wound.

"Glennie. Jaysus, Glen." Devin crouched on his knees, his hands touching Glen's face, brushing his black hair away from his forehead. His skin was still warm. He *was* still alive, wasn't he? Nothing could happen that fast, could it? "Blessed Mary, Mother of God . . ." Devin's voice broke. He couldn't go on. He bit his trembling bottom lip and leaned in to his brother. "I'll get help for ya. Just hang on, Glen. Ya got to."

Devin scrambled to his feet, eyes darting frantically. "Help me, Pearse! Glen's been hit!"

His voice was lost in a swirling vortex of activity. Desperately, he peered around. Where was Pearse? Wasn't there someone who could help him?

All around him, the marchers huddled on the ground, cowering from bullets still whizzing through

the air. He didn't see Pearse anywhere. Had he been
hit, too? Amid hysterical screams, Devin heard
someone murmuring the Lord's Prayer.

A hand reached out and grabbed his ankle.
"Help me ..."

Startled, Devin looked down. It was the woman
he'd bumped against only minutes before, her
beehive was now matted with blood. Everywhere he
looked, he saw blood. Even the air was rank with it.

"Devin! Get down!"

Blankly, he turned to look in the direction of
the panicked voice. Pearse was stumbling toward
him, motioning frantically, but Devin could only
stare at him in numbed confusion. Blood covered
the older boy's jeans and black shirt in paint-like
splotches.

Suddenly, a hot white fire speared Devin's
upper left arm. In slow motion, he could feel himself
falling. He could not protect himself from the
impact with the concrete; it scraped his cheek,
imbedding bits of dirt and gravel under his skin.
Another searing pain shot through his nose, driving
needlepoints into his skull. But it was nothing
compared to the agony in his arm. Groaning, he
lifted his head and saw blood from his smashed nose
dripping onto the street. He sat up, shaking his head
groggily. Almost immediately, everything dimmed;
he slumped to the ground. His hand moved to the
painful left arm and came back covered with blood.
In amazement, he gazed at the crimson liquid. So
much blood. Funny, Glen hadn't bled like this.
There had been only that one little round hole.

Devin's head swam. In the distance, he heard
the singsong whine of a siren growing closer. The
rain fell harder now, its cool wetness a balm against
his flushed face. His mind drifted as he stared up

into the scudding gray clouds. The dull throb in his arm faded.

Suddenly, Pearse appeared above him, peering down anxiously. Then he began to pull on his body, dragging him away. It hurt. Oh, Lord Jesus, it hurt. Finally, mercifully, Pearse stopped tugging on him and knelt down at his side. He ripped at his shirt and quickly tied a strip of cloth around Devin's bleeding wound. A *black armband*. Did Pearse know about Glen, then?

Tears welled in his eyes. "They killed him, Pearse. They killed Glen," he whispered. "Why are they shooting at us, Pearse?"

"Hush, now. Save your strength. You're still losing blood."

It was true. His vision blurred, and Pearse's voice faded in and out. Devin bit his lip so hard he tasted blood. He couldn't pass out now. He had to make his brother's friend understand.

"Pearse, please, I..." He grasped the older boy's hand, hot tears spilling down his face.

"What is it, Dev?" Pearse cradled him, bewildered tears in his blue eyes. His image wavered, growing close and then fading away.

Devin felt the curtain of darkness around him. No. He wouldn't give in. Not until he had the chance to make Pearse understand. Despite the pain that sliced through to his very fingertips, he struggled up onto his elbow so his weakened voice could be heard. "Pearse, I don't care if I burn in hell," he whispered. "I'm going to make those bastards pay for what they did to Glen!"

Available in print in May 2012

Now Available at Amazon Kindle

http://www.amazon.com/SPOTLIGHT
-ebook/dp/B0052ENA74/ref=sr_1_3?s=digital-
text&ie=UTF8&qid=1318344927&sr=1-3

Watch the Book Trailer

http://animoto.com/play/B1lUbKpQ6rGJlXk
P6bDqoA

ACKNOWLEDGMENTS

Thanks to all who helped bring LILY OF THE
SPRINGS to life.

Janice Robertson
Carlus Foley
Wilmoth Polston
Barbara Marshall
Christi Marshall
John Smallshaw
Tresa Underwood
Doris Lindblad
Helen Frenke & husband
Wes Spicher, Clear Channel Texarkana
Dave Weiss, DDS
Jim Ganley
Doug Wilson
Elvin Tiller
Jim Miller for the artwork on page 68